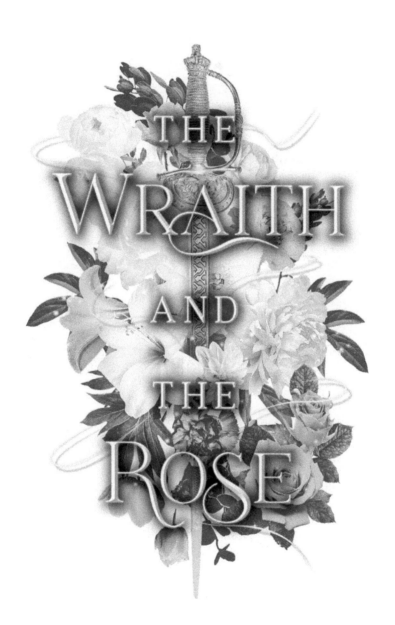

THE WRAITH AND THE ROSE

Also by C. J. Brightley

A Long-Forgotten Song:
Things Unseen
The Dragon's Tongue
The Beginning of Wisdom

Erdemen Honor:
The King's Sword
A Cold Wind
Honor's Heir

Fairy King:
A Fairy King
A Fairy Promise

Other Works:
The Lord of Dreams
Twelve Days of (Faerie) Christmas
Heroes and Other Stories

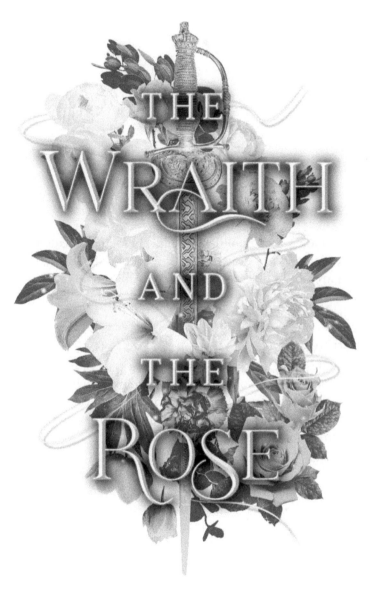

THE WRAITH AND THE ROSE

C. J. BRIGHTLEY

Paperback ISBN 978-1-954768-01-7
Hardback ISBN 978-1-954768-02-4
Ebook ISBN 978-1-005-14492-0

Published in the United States of America by Spring Song Press, LLC.

www.cjbrightley.com
www.springsongpress.com

Cover design by Kerry Jesberger of Aero Gallerie.

For my utterly delightful children, Natalie and Timothy – Thank you for your tender hearts, your clever, bright, curious minds, your sweet words of encouragement, and your love. You make the world a better place, and I am so very thankful that I get to be your mommy.

The Overton Manor

ACKNOWLEDGMENTS

Baroness Orczy wrote *The Scarlet Pimpernel* in 1905 and changed literature by inspiring the masked hero trope, from Zorro to Batman, Spiderman, and other heroes. I'm deeply grateful for the inspiration I found in her gallant hero, as well as the heroes and heroines of a thousand other books that fueled my imagination. Many thanks to those authors who fill their books with wonder, delight, and heroes worth believing in.

Several people have been particularly helpful in the completion of this book. My husband and children were sweetly patient with me as I flew through the first draft of the book in a flurry of excitement, and then settled into the editing process. Sarah W. read the book multiple times and offered insightful comments and encouragement. Constance L. cheered me on and helped tie up loose threads. Suebee R. was wonderfully encouraging and helpful. My parents both read the drafts and offered suggestions and encouragement.

I am so thankful to be surrounded by such kind, generous, wonderful friends. Thank you.

CHAPTER ONE

The Beginning of the Season

S pring warmth made the interior of the hired carriage a little stuffy, and Miss Lilybeth Rose Hathaway breathed a sigh of relief as it halted before the manor. She took her brother Oliver's arm as she alighted from the carriage. The two followed their father and mother up the broad marble steps to the door, where a footman dressed better than either of the two Hathaway men received them with an ill-concealed smirk.

They followed another footman down an expansive hall to the ballroom. A dozen lanterns along the way set the marble floor to gleaming and picked out the rich colors of the paintings along the walls.

The footman left them with the butler stationed at the open door of the ballroom.

"A moment, please." Sir Jacob Hathaway, her father, murmured. The butler nodded and stepped back. He was too well-trained to smirk noticeably, but Lily could feel the judgment in his gaze. The Hathaways were not accustomed to such exalted gatherings, and Sir Jacob wanted to observe before entering the ballroom.

Lily's eyes widened when the music rose from the small ensemble in the corner. The violinist set light, bright notes dancing over the murmur of the guests. Lily tried to see the musicians around her father's shoulder, but couldn't catch more than a glimpse of the plumes on their hats.

Sir Jacob finally nodded, and the butler read from the card the footman had given him.

"Sir Jacob Hathaway, Lady Hathaway, Mr. Oliver Hathaway, and Miss Lilybeth Hathaway." Only a few people looked up. Sir Jacob had been knighted several years before, but such a title was hardly remarkable among this assembly. Only Oliver's friendship with Sir Michael, one of Lord Radclyffe's sons, had gotten them the invitation at all.

Lanterns lined the walls and chandeliers dangled from the lofty ceiling, their mirrored sides casting dancing points of light over the walls and across the floor. A dozen footmen offered refreshments to the aristocrats gathered in tittering little groups around the dance floor. The one nearest them held a platter of tiny cakes with rose-lavender icing and cool slices of moon melon arranged in a scrumptious array. Another held a tray of cucumber swirls drizzled in some sort of fancy sauce, while yet another offered herbed, baked cheese and bold blackberry compote over the daintiest morsels of shortbread. Diminutive tables stood at intervals against the walls to hold overflowing vases of lilacs and early roses, along with sprays of tiny white flowers Lily could not identify. The scents of and took a half-step back, letting Lord Radclyffe decide whether he wished to turn back to his companion without seeming to snub him, or whether he wished to continue the conversation.

The lord smiled and turned away.

Lily leaned in to Oliver as they meandered toward the back of the room, having completed the first of the obligatory awkward greetings. "Are all the parties like this? What was that about Sir Michael?"

"Yes, and he was referring to a card game," Oliver murmured back. "Sir Michael is an honorable chap, though a bit flighty, and he got us this invitation because I asked him to."

Lily blinked at him, momentarily shocked. "I didn't know you were so well-connected."

Her brother looked down at her, dark eyes gleaming. "Well, you never got a proper coming out, did you? That's what we're here for. How are all these fops going to know how beautiful you are if we don't show them?"

Lily's mouth dropped open. "I didn't think it would be like this." She'd known that the purpose of the season in Ardmond was for her to be presented among the social elite in the hopes of catching the eye of a young nobleman. The concept was not new to her, but the experience of it was, and she found it significantly more uncomfortable than she'd expected.

Oliver chuckled and nodded her onward, so she turned to follow her mother. "Not *today*, Lily. In general. If they know you're as sweet and delightful as you are, you'll have no shortage of invitations. You'll have your pick of this lot. It's got to be better than the options you've had at home."

With a surge of relief, Lily saw her friend Lady Araminta Poole, daughter of Lord Poole, the Duke of Brickelwyte, and hurried to greet her. The rest of the Hathaways trailed behind her.

"You look lovely!" exclaimed Araminta. "The blue sets off your eyes especially well."

"Oh, I think you're the most beautiful flower tonight, Araminta." Lily smiled at her friend. "Sweet as honey, too. I'm so glad you're here," she added sincerely.

Araminta leaned closer and whispered, "I heard someone asking Lord Holmwood if Sir Theodore and Lady Overton and their son would be here. He said Sir Theodore had told him they would be!"

"Oh. Are you expecting them to be interesting, then?"

Araminta nearly gaped at her, but covered her shock with an elegant hand over her mouth. "Haven't you heard of them? I did not realize you were so far from all the gossip."

Lily's cheeks heated. "Well, our little town is hardly exciting, but it does have its charms. Why are they of such interest?"

"Well, first, Sir Theodore is only a baronet, but he is nearly as wealthy as the prince. Lady Overton is sublimely beautiful! And their son is the most ridiculous fop the court has ever seen, and despite how silly he is, you can't help but like him. He's funny in a self-deprecating sort of way, and he sets all the fashions. He has such beautiful manners." Araminta sighed dramatically in admiration.

"You've met them, then?"

"Once, at Lord Hastings's water party. He's a marvelous dancer."

Lily smiled, amused. "The father or the son?"

"Both, but I was speaking of the son!" Araminta giggled. "If this is your belated coming out season, you could do a lot worse, you know."

Lily frowned gently at her. "I don't like to think of devoting my energies so seriously to catching a husband, as if it ought to be my primary aim in life." Nevertheless, she had used her minor magical skill at glamour to hide a faded spot on her dress sleeve and conceal the worn hems of her father's sleeves.

Having the gift of glamour, she could see when others used the same gift, but she could not see through it. Few among the crowd had used any glamour at all, and those who did had used it sparingly; their attire was every bit as luxurious as it looked, even if they might have accented the lace of a cravat or changed the color of a gem. Even her gift of glamour seemed small and insignificant here in the wealth and privilege of Ardmond, the capital of Valestria and the center of culture and affluence. A fairy, of course, would be much stronger, and could see through any human-made glamour, but the reverse was not true; a fairy-made glamour would fool any human. A human particularly skilled with glamour might be able to see that a fairy wore a glamour, but they certainly would not be able to see through it to the true form.

Araminta returned Lily's frown more seriously. "Well, it ought to be a priority. How am I to spend my days doing good if I cannot afford to eat, and how can I afford to eat without a husband?"

Lily covered her chuckle. "I suppose that's true. I don't think you'll have to do much searching, though. Your future is not so far from home."

"Do you think so? I really am not sure how much more obvious I can be." Araminta's dark hair shone as she shook her head in mock despair. She had nursed a long-standing affection for Lily's brother for years, but Oliver had never noticed. Lily had offered to hint to him that her friend might be interested, but Araminta had not yet consented.

Lily turned to find her brother. He was a short distance away, just leading a lovely blonde back off the dance floor as they finished a reel. His dark hair gleamed, and his ready smile made him popular with both men and women. He was only two years older than she was, and they had spent happy years playing together after finishing their studies in the mornings. Lily had privately wished Araminta had had an elder brother of her own; it was good for a young woman to know that young men were not entirely mysterious and unfathomable, but rather humans much like themselves.

Oliver found her and smiled, then made his way over to her through the crush.

"His Royal Highness The Prince of Valestria. Sir Theodore Overton the Third, Baronet. Lady Overton." The butler's voice rang out over the dull roar of conversations and music. There was a shuffling and murmuring at the door, and a moment later, "Mr. Theodore Overton the Fourth."

She couldn't see the entrants, but the excitement was palpable in the air. Lord Radclyffe turned with the rest of the crowd, apparently eager to see the new arrivals. Surely wealth alone wouldn't justify this level of interest among so many rich aristocrats.

The music resumed and the Overtons made their way through the room toward the Radclyffes with some difficulty, accosted as they were by many well-wishers and interested parties.

"Theo! You owe me a game of whist!"

"Do I?"

"Theo, how delighted we are to see you again! You're resplendent as usual."

"Lady Ramsay." The voice was elegant and polite, nearly inaudible over the music.

Lily turned away and locked eyes with Oliver, whose mouth nearly dropped open at the simpering worship in the woman's voice. Oliver leaned close to murmur in her ear, "The Overtons must be even richer than the rest of these snobs."

Lily covered her chuckle with a graceful hand. "Apparently so."

Their father turned to them and said in a low voice, "The son is close friends with the prince."

Oliver's interest brightened, but he said confidently, "And they're also rich."

"Quite. They own half the shipping and most of the fabric industries, as well as several vineyards." Sir Jacob added, "I wish I could get you an introduction to the son, Lily. You could do a lot worse."

Lily blinked. "I don't need an introduction, at least not yet. What if he's a spoiled fop?"

Oliver snorted softly. "Well, nearly every man here is, but there are worse things in the world than men who like good food and nice clothes."

His father shot him a quelling look. "Do introduce us to those you can, Oliver."

Oliver dutifully introduced his family to the few young aristocrats he knew. Young Sir Michael Radclyffe smiled charmingly at Lily and asked for the next dance, which she accepted.

The young man bowed politely over her hand, though the kiss was so light it might as well have not happened at all. He led her through the steps skillfully and asked whether she had enjoyed herself so far, what she thought of the flowers, and whether she had promised dances to any other young men. She appreciated the gesture, but everything about the dance felt awkward to her. The steps of the dance were familiar, but the formalities felt more strict, and everything about it felt intimidating.

He handed her back to Oliver with a bow and a promise to introduce her to a friend once she'd danced with her brother.

"He was nice," Lily admitted.

"He's a good sort," Oliver agreed.

The dance with her brother was over too soon. This evening had seemed like a delightful idea when the invitation had arrived, but now, the glitter and sparkle seemed overwhelming.

Oliver led her to the side, where Sir Michael found them quickly. "Miss Hathaway, may I introduce my friend Lord Fenton Selby? Lord Selby, this is Miss Lilybeth Hathaway."

Lord Selby bowed politely over her hand, letting his eyes linger in a way that felt complimentary rather than disgusting. He was quite tall, with broad shoulders, a trim waist, and luxurious waves of hair that was a brown so rich it was almost black. His skin was a sun-kissed tan, and he had warm dark eyes.

He drew her into the next dance with a quick spin and a ready smile. There was little time for talking, but the cheerful music lifted her spirits. Perhaps this wasn't such a terrible idea after all. She would certainly try to make the best of it.

When the dance ended, she was nearly out of breath and her cheeks felt flushed. Lord Selby smiled down at her.

"You're especially lovely after a dance, Miss Hathaway," he said. "I'd ask for a second but it might be unfair before I've introduced you to a few more people. So consider this warning that I intend to ask you for another dance tonight."

"I will, my lord." She smiled up at him, charmed despite herself. He was quite attractive, if you liked that sort of dark elegant look. She decided that she did rather like it, when accompanied by a nice smile.

He hesitated, then added more softly, "Is there anyone to whom you would particularly appreciate being introduced?"

She glanced up in surprise, and he quirked his lips in a rueful smile. "I might regret it later, but perhaps the generosity of the impulse will stand in my favor."

"Thank you. It does." She couldn't help blushing at his regard, and she said, "I really don't know to whom I ought to be introduced. I would be much obliged to you for your wisdom in the matter."

Lord Selby was about to reply when he glanced over her shoulder and bowed to someone.

"Theo."

"Lord Selby! I'm delighted to see you here. Are you mono-polizing the lady's dances?"

Lord Selby winced. "Well, I was hoping to after introducing her to someone less suitable than I am, so that she might notice my charms all the better for the contrast." He sighed. "Miss Hathaway, Mr. Theodore Overton. Theo, Miss Lilybeth Hathaway."

Theo was a few years older than her twenty-three years, of an age with Lord Selby. He gave her a sparkling smile and bowed with a flourish. "I'm honored. Thank you, Lord Selby. May I have this dance, Miss Hathaway?"

Theo was as tall as Lord Selby, though a little leaner, with dark auburn waves a bit too unruly for the current fashion and bright hazel eyes. The lines of his face were delicately chiseled, and his straight nose and angular cheekbones had a light smattering of freckles. Everything about him spoke of privilege and elegance, and only the irrepressible friendliness in his face kept him tolerable at all.

Theo held out his hand gracefully. Lily smiled her thanks to Lord Selby and then put her hand in Theo's.

He led her out the dance floor, and Lily realized with a twinge of dismay that the musicians were beginning a slow waltz. This somehow seemed significantly more awkward than a faster dance like a reel, where she would be able to focus on the steps rather than the stranger before her.

"How are you enjoying the evening, Miss Hathaway?" He smiled down at her.

"It's a little overwhelming, to be honest. I am new to Ardmond." She winced and wished she could take back the words. "Everyone has been so kind, though."

"Better not to admit to any awe." His eyes gleamed with humor. "Are you not accustomed to being much pursued by excited young lords, then? "

"Not at all." She blushed. Was this the sort of conversation that happened at aristocratic parties? The conversations at home seemed infinitely safer and more predictable.

His smile widened.

She took the next few steps without speaking, and he murmured, "Where is home, Miss Hathaway?"

"A little town called Haven-by-the-Sea."

If possible, his eyes sparkled even brighter. "I know the place. There's a delightful orchard on the north side, owned by Mrs. Pattersley, I believe."

Lily blinked. "How did you know that?"

"I can't reveal all my secrets in one dance, or you'll never honor me with a second." He beamed at her.

The music shifted, and he whirled her into the next dance.

"Sir, this is a new dance." Didn't a second dance immediately after the first indicate that he intended to call upon her in the following weeks? Wasn't it intended as a signal of serious interest? Surely he wasn't interested so soon.

"Indeed." He glanced over her shoulder at someone, then met her gaze. "I'm sure you've been told a dozen times tonight how lovely you are, but when I say it, I mean it most sincerely."

She swallowed. "I didn't expect so many compliments, sir."

"Theo, please." His eyes were a quite unusual shade of green-brown which set off his fair skin and auburn hair. "Of the many who have complimented you tonight, who most pleased you?"

"That's a rather personal question." She blinked up at him in shock.

He smiled innocently. "Is it? I only wanted to know with whom I must vie for your affections. If it is Lord Selby, I'll have a great deal of trouble, for he's much too gallant and handsome for you to be swayed by the likes of me. But if it's one of the others, then maybe my good name, or some roses from my estate, will aid my suit."

He glanced over her shoulder again, and muttered, "Blast." Then in a sweeter tone, "Please save me another dance or three this evening, if you would be so kind, Miss Hathaway." As the music shifted again, he spun her to the side toward her startled brother, bowed over her hand, and strode off briskly.

She tried not to stare after him, but she couldn't help a surreptitious glance.

Theo had apparently abandoned her to head toward the prince, who stood near Lord Radclyffe not too far from the door to the ballroom.

A moment later, the butler intoned, "Lord Ash Willowvale, Special Envoy of the Fair Court."

The assembly music stuttered and then steadied, but the dancers stilled.

Framed in the spacious entry, the fairy was fully as tall as Theo, and as willowy as his name, with a shock of silvery white hair. His cold blue eyes were set deeply beneath his brows. His face was narrow and finely boned, and his mouth had a hard, uncompromising set that seemed as if he were poised to sneer at any moment. He was as pale as moonlight, so that the pink and blue undertones of his skin showed even in the golden light of the lanterns; even his lips were pale. If it were not for the coldness in his eyes, he might have been beautiful, in a strange, alien way, but the veneer of pleasantness was clearly thin.

Lily wasn't sure if Fair Folk fashion followed Valestrian, or the other way around, but in either case, Lord Willowvale was dressed appropriately for the party. His jacket was impeccably cut of a deep blue brocade that made his eyes glitter. His breeches were slim, well-fitting, and of a deep navy. His boots had the correct slightly squared toe shape for the season, and the cravat at his neck was tied with a precise knot.

He stalked toward Lord Radclyffe, apparently well aware of the convention of greeting the host first.

"Lord Willowvale," said Lord Radclyffe coldly, with the barest possible hint of a bow.

"Lord Radclyffe," returned the fairy with icy courtesy. "You know why I am here."

"I was informed that you had been sent to ferret out the identity of our revered national hero. You will find no assistance here. However, since we are not so discourteous as to send you back to the Fair Lands tonight, in your private person you are welcome." Lord Radclyffe said through gritted teeth.

The fairy was not *at all* welcome. Lord Radclyffe might be a bit pretentious for Lily's taste, but she couldn't fault his treatment of the fairy. If Lord Willowvale was intending to catch the Wraith, he would find no allies in the Valestrian court.

The mysterious Wraith had captivated the court for months, and all Valestrians, even the commoners, were proud that he was, apparently, one of their countrymen.

Three years ago, the neighboring country of Aricht and the Fair Folk had a brief, violent conflict. Officially it had never exactly been a war, but there had certainly been casualties. Valestria had sent several companies of soldiers in support of Aricht, for although Valestria and Aricht had never been particularly friendly, Arichtans were human.

The Fair Folk might have overrun Aricht completely, but for some internal conflict which had stolen the Fair king's attention and paved the way for a peace treaty. No one knew exactly what had happened, but it had followed not long after the Fair king's death and the coronation of the new king.

For two and a half years after the treaty, there was a tense, wary peace.

For the last six months, there had been rumors filtering out of Aricht of children stolen by the Fair Folk. One here, two there, another one again.

It was not clear to anyone exactly why the Fair Folk wanted children, though there were dozens upon dozens of theories. Some people thought the Fair Folk ate the flesh of children. Some speculated that human blood was necessary to strengthen fairy blood, and that their magic wouldn't breed true if not strengthened at intervals by marriage with humans. Some believed the humans were merely used as slaves or servants, perhaps because the Fair Folk looked down particularly useful in some way.

A mere month after the first children had been stolen from their homes in Aricht, three of the missing children turned up at the gate of the Valestrian king's palace in Ardmond. They were confused, pale, and exhausted, and the only thing they could say with any degree of certainty was that they had danced until they were insensible, night after night after night. When asked how they had escaped, they had agreed, after some argument, that a troll had pulled them from their beds, run through the woods, leapt in a hole, and tossed them out of the darkness at the gate.

A week later, two more children had similarly appeared, though they claimed their rescuer was an ogre, not a troll. They had given more detail about the darkness between the Fair Lands and the Valestrian palace gate. They said they walked for four hours in absolute darkness, and the ogre had carried the younger of the two children the entire way. The ogre had presented them each with an apple; he shoved the cores in his dirty pockets when they were done. The elder boy said he suspected the ogre was afraid of being followed, but the younger said he'd slept through that part and didn't remember it. The elder brother said he'd kept a tight grip on the ogre's rough jacket so as not to lose him in the darkness. At last they had emerged into the silvered brilliance of a full moon in front of the palace. The ogre had raised a fist and pounded on the door, then slunk away when the guard saw the children.

That had been nearly five months ago. Some hundred and fifty children had been rescued since then by the mysterious hero. Aricht, and then Valestria, had soon begun calling him the Wraith for his ghostlike ability to sneak in and out of the Fair Lands. He took on constantly varying disguises; quite often he appeared as one of the Fair Folk themselves. Several times he had been a troll or an ogre, once a kobold, and often as a man, though no one had ever recognized him later.

The children were of little help. Not only did the Wraith appear as all manner of creatures, but had apparently assumed different nationalities. He had used a native Arichtan accent at times, as well as Valestrian, Altavian, and Rulothian accents in different rescues.

In fact, the only thing to indicate that the hero was one person, or at least a team acting in concert, was the fury of the Fair Court, which had eventually revealed that after each rescue, there was some small piece of paper with a tiny rose inscribed upon it left in the place of the children. The Fair Folk had thus called the rescuer the Rose, after his insignia, but since this had not been revealed for some time, the Arichtan court had styled him the Wraith, and the Valestrian court had followed. The Wraith had remained the more popular name in Valestria and Aricht, but the rose symbol had immediately become wildly popular among both the nobility and common people.

The Fair Court had become increasingly angry. His Majesty Oak Silverthorn had never publicly admitted that the Fair Folk were stealing human children, but his envoy in Aricht, Lord Linden Brookbower, had made it clear to both the Arichtan king and the Valestrian ambassador that he intended to find and kill the Rose. Whatever the Fair Folk wanted the children for, it was important.

So far, only Arichtan children had been stolen. It had at first been speculated that the Wraith was Arichtan, which seemed logical since an Arichtan citizen would have more reason to risk himself for his countrymen than a Valestrian, Altavian, or Rulothian citizen would. But since the rescued children consistently reappeared just outside the Valestrian palace, the Fair Court now believed that the Wraith was Valestrian.

Lord Willowvale gave the slightest possible bow, his mouth twitching at the required civility when he apparently wished to more openly reveal his rage. "Your welcome is well understood. I do not require your assistance in my assignment."

"Very well." Lord Radclyffe raised his chin and turned away.

Lord Willowvale turned to the prince and bowed stiffly, his mouth tight. "Your Royal Highness."

"Lord Willowvale." The prince acknowledged the fairy and sketched a faint, mocking bow. "Welcome to Valestria."

Prince Selwyn smiled more warmly at Theo, who now stood at his shoulder. "I heard you bought another horse?"

"A very nice hunter. I took him out yesterday around the pond. I couldn't be more pleased." Theo turned to include the fairy in the conversation. "Do you ride, Lord Willowvale?"

"Yes."

Theo stared at the fairy expectantly, a pleasant smile on his face. Finally he prompted, "Do you have a favorite horse, then? Or a favored trail? Anything at all, really?"

The fairy stared at him, his narrow lips turning downward. "Yes. Why?"

"It is what we humans do at dances: we make pleasant conversation with fellow guests." Theo frowned faintly. "I haven't been introduced to you, though. I'm Theo Overton."

"What is your title, then?" The fairy's eyes flicked up and down, taking in Theo's immaculate lace cuffs, expensive shoes, and the fashionable cut and exquisite fabric of his jacket and breeches.

Theo smiled brightly. "I have no title at all, not even a courtesy title! My father is a baronet, so we're really not that important."

Lord Willowvale narrowed his eyes. "Why are you here, then?"

Theo's hazel eyes sparkled. "I like dancing, and the food is delicious."

The fairy's expression darkened. "I mean why did they let you in?"

"Oh, that's a puzzle, indeed. I think it's because I'm amusing." If there was mockery in Theo's smile, it was mostly hidden. "Also, His

Royal Highness Selwyn is too excellent of a whist player; if I don't agree to play on the other team, he'd have no opponents at all."

Lord Willowvale looked him up and down again. "Introduce me to the men of title here."

Theo blinked, then smiled kindly. "Lord Willowvale, it is not the custom in Valestria to order about free men, even when you are an honored guest." His smile brightened, and he added, "I would be delighted to do so, if you asked more courteously."

The fairy bared his teeth in a rictus of a smile, and Theo beamed at him.

"Please introduce me to the men of title, useless puppy," ground out the fairy.

Theo said with equanimity, "A puppy is charming and beloved by anyone of good character. Using the word as an insult is in poor taste, my lord. Come."

He led Lord Willowvale briskly across the room to the Duke and Duchess of Milburn, who exchanged icy pleasantries with the fairy. Then back across the room to the Duke and Duchess of Kaylin, Lord and Lady Pitts, then again across the room to the Marquess Lamplighter, and then crossed the room yet again to the Marquess and Marchioness of Wilhartney.

Lily watched with growing awe from where she stood beside her brother as Theo led the fairy back and forth across the room. With perfect courtesy, he introduced Lord Willowvale to everyone in attendance.

"What on earth is he doing?" she finally murmured to her brother. "He's dragging the poor man—fairy—across the room four dozen times rather than just turning to the person nearest."

"He's doing it in order of their rank," Oliver replied under his breath. "It's simultaneously polite and completely ridiculous."

Lord Willowvale's pale cheeks were slightly flushed with heat and anger as Theo finally led him to the Hathaways.

"Lord Willowvale, this is—" Theo hesitated, his eyes dancing, "—actually, I haven't been formally introduced either."

"Jacob Hathaway." Jacob bowed courteously to both of them. "This is my wife, Lady Imogen Hathaway, my son Oliver, and my daughter Lilybeth."

Theo beamed at them. "I'm honored to meet you. It's *Sir* Jacob, isn't it? You were knighted several years ago, I believe. I'm Theo

Overton, and this is Lord Ash Willowvale, Special Envoy of the Fair Court."

"Lord Willowvale." Sir Jacob bowed again, Lady Hathaway curtsied, and Oliver and Lily followed suit.

The fairy eyed them coldly, then abruptly said, "May I have this dance, Lilybeth?"

Theo cleared his throat. "*Miss Hathaway*, if you please."

Lord Willowvale shot him a murderous look. "I am well aware of your human conventions, puppy, but it is no insult to call a person by their name."

Theo smiled sweetly. "Yet is it not the height of discourtesy to address a lady with unwelcome familiarity? Miss Hathaway would be far too kind to hold it against you, I am sure, if you asked forgiveness."

The fairy glared at him wrathfully, then turned his cold gaze upon Lily. Through clenched teeth, he growled, "Forgive me, Miss Hathaway. Would you do me the honor of this dance?"

Lily bit her lip and glanced at her father, who gave her a slight, reassuring nod.

"Yes, Lord Willowvale," she managed.

Theo's eyes glinted, and he stepped back, letting Lord Willowvale bow politely over her hand.

The fairy's cold eyes met hers when he straightened. He led her to the dance floor with icy courtesy and placed his hand upon her waist. His eyes held hers for a moment, then he looked past her and around the room.

She didn't know whether he expected her to carry the conversation or if he preferred silence. The thought of making polite small talk with him was entirely too intimidating, so she kept her eyes upon his cravat and followed his lead without speaking. He was a skillful dancer, and she thought that if he would only smile, he might have many willing dance partners.

"What do you know of the Wraith?" he said.

"Nothing, Lord Willowvale."

"Nothing at all?" His interest sharpened. "That's interesting, as everyone seems to have heard of him."

She swallowed. "I know what the rumors say, that's all. I cannot know whether any of it is true."

He stepped away to let her follow the graceful turn of the dance, then stepped back closer. "What do you think of his actions?"

"He's a hero, of course." The answer was simple. She looked up at him. "If you think that because I am the very least of the guests here I will betray him to you, you are sadly mistaken, my lord."

He gave her a faint, amused smile. "Your loyalty is lovely. One can only wish it were directed at someone more worthy. The Rose has cost my people more than you know."

"How so?"

His smile turned cold again. "I am not at liberty to say. Suffice it to say that your national hero is an enemy of our people, and my cause is just."

She bit her lip. "Is it just to use human children for your own ends? How can you say that your cause is just, when the means are so abhorrent?"

Lord Willowvale's shoulders, if possible, grew even stiffer, and his eyes flashed dangerously. "When a human has the opportunity to be of service to a fairy, it should be grateful."

Lily raised her chin to meet his eyes. "Is that so?" Her voice shook a little. "Is that how you see us, as things to be used? I believe I've heard enough, Lord Willowvale."

The dance was nearly at an end. She began to pull away, but he held her a moment longer, his grip unyielding.

He bent over her hand, as proper and courteous as any Valestrian lord. "You have heard without understanding, and you know as little of your own hero as you do of us." He met her eyes as he straightened, and she trembled at his icy anger, but he said only, "Thank you for the dance, Miss Hathaway. I pray you enjoy your evening." He stalked away.

Before she had a chance to recover herself, Theo bowed before her.

"Would you honor me with the next dance, Miss Hathaway?"

She blinked at him, trying not to blush. "We've already danced twice, my lord. I think three would certainly be pushing the bounds of propriety."

His hazel eyes sparkled at her with irrepressible delight. "Indeed we have. I mean to have at least three more tonight, if you will so honor me."

Her mouth dropped open and she hurriedly covered the expression with one hand.

He spoke again before she could reply. "Also, I'm no lord. You must call me Theo."

She blinked. Was that proper? "But sir—"

"Just Theo!" His smile widened. "Please do say you will dance with me again." He held her eyes as he bent to kiss her fingers again with exaggerated courtesy.

She hesitated a moment more, and he stepped a little closer to murmur, "Yes, it is an expression of intent, and I mean it. You can always jilt me later. It won't reflect badly on you."

She swallowed, then gave a tiny nod.

He led her into the dance with a quick step, and they spun and turned and passed each other with little conversation. She knew the steps, though not as well as he did, and felt herself flushing with effort and embarrassment as she missed several steps. Then she was out of the rhythm and missed a turn.

Theo murmured, "One, two, three, step, turn," caught her hand and brought her back into the rhythm. Then he was away, turning with a new partner, and she stared at Lord Somebody for three steps, then Theo was back, beaming at her.

When the dance ended, she said breathlessly, "I'd like a rest, sir."

"Just Theo, Miss Hathaway," he murmured softly. "May I introduce you to my parents?"

She blinked up at him, feeling off-balance. The evening had quickly gone far beyond Oliver's promised night of sedate dancing and, apparently, a chance for eligible young lords to see the beauty of his beloved younger sister. The evening was meant to be safe and predictable, though more formal than she was accustomed to.

"If you wish," she said.

He led her to a couple who were conversing quietly near one corner.

"Mother, Father, this is Miss Lilybeth Hathaway, Sir Jacob Hathaway's daughter. Miss Hathaway, these are my parents, Sir Theodore Overton the Third, Baronet, and Lady Helena Overton."

Both of them smiled at her kindly, and she realized that Theo's sparkling friendliness was an entirely natural result of being born to these two people. Lady Overton had a warm smile and hazel eyes like Theo's. Her strawberry blonde hair was shot through with gray, and it was all caught up in the braids and curls so popular this season. Sir Theodore's face had the same delicately chiseled lines as his son's, and he had a few more freckles across his nose and cheeks than his son did. His hair was a similar auburn shade, and his eyes had a little more brown. Both of them had the lines of smiles around their eyes.

Lily curtsied as gracefully as she could, feeling far out of her depth.

"It is lovely to meet you, my dear." Sir Theodore bowed over her hand, and though she knew it was the proper courtesy, it seemed somehow even more absurd when the man bowing to her was her father's age.

Lady Overton inquired after her family, her home, and her interests. Sir Theodore listened in quiet approval. Theo disappeared for several minutes, but Sir Theodore and Lady Overton made her feel so comfortable that her momentary panic faded quickly.

When Theo reappeared at her side, his father asked, "May I have this dance?"

She blinked at him and glanced at Theo, then nodded.

The older man smiled kindly at her as the dance began, and she tried to relax. "Has my son completely overwhelmed you with his affection yet?" he said at last.

"It's a little startling," she admitted.

Sir Theodore chuckled under his breath but said nothing else.

When the dance finished, Theo bowed over her hand again.

"Would you honor me with this dance, Miss Hathaway?"

"Are you sure?"

"Please." His smile was warm and sweet, and she thought despairingly that he could have charmed anyone in the room. Maybe he had charmed everyone in the room already, and she was only the latest in a long list of conquests.

When the dance ended, Theo asked, "Would you care for some refreshment?"

"Yes, please. I'm a little thirsty."

He snagged a flute of sparkling wine from a passing footman and handed it to her. "What do you love about your home, Miss Hathaway?"

She glanced up at him, wondering if he was being condescending. There was nothing but innocent interest in his expression, so she said, "I love our garden. It was old before I was born, but it became overgrown while my father was away when I was young. Since he has been back, and I've been older, I have grown to enjoy working it."

"I imagine it's beautiful. Will you tell me more about it?" He drew her a little farther from the guests who had begun yet another quick dance.

"I planted a great number of roses a few years ago, so now there is a little rose garden. Jasper—he's my father's manservant, I suppose you could say—made several benches which now sit among the roses. He also helped me plant some delphiniums and hollyhocks and cottage pinks all along the south side, with lilies and primroses and ladies' mantle and lavender." She did love the garden, and she was proud of what she had done with it, though it was hardly a lady's work to get her hands dirty. Yet the expectant look in his eyes was disarming, and she found herself continuing, "Father has promised me three new peonies for my birthday. I have several varieties already, but they are such beauties I would love some more for the cutting garden."

Then her father was at her side, to Theo's apparent consternation.

"It's my turn, I believe," said Sir Jacob to Theo, politely but firmly.

"Of course," Theo murmured. He took her empty glass and bowed to them both.

Her father's presence was comforting, and for a moment, Lily just rested in his silence.

"Young Overton seems entranced," he said at last, with a hint of a smile.

Her cheeks heated, and she looked down at the toes of her slippers. "He does seem so," she murmured. "I'm a little afraid he's impulsive, and I'll only be interesting for one night."

Her father's arm tightened around her almost imperceptibly. "He does not have a history of pursuing young ladies and then losing interest."

She looked up at him. "You inquired?"

Her father chuckled softly. "A rich young lord dances with my daughter four times in one evening and introduces her to his parents? Of course I inquired about him. The worst thing anyone would say about him was that he's a bit of a simpleton. His friends are loyal. His elders find him charming and respectful. Eligible young ladies wish he'd flirt more."

Lily blinked. "Oh." She added, "He said he wanted at least two more dances tonight."

"Absolutely not."

Lily tried unsuccessfully not to giggle.

Her father muttered, "Shall I tell him no, or do you want to do it?"

"You are welcome to. I don't know that I could refuse him if he smiled at me."

Her father looked at her sharply. "It's that bad already? Heaven help us. It's not just the money, is it?"

Lily shook her head. "He asked about home and listened when I talked about the peonies."

He shook his head and sighed.

The hour was late, and even the most dedicated dancers among the guests had begun to slow. Somewhat to Lily's surprise, Theo was not waiting for them when the dance finished.

"He's with the prince," her father said. "Though I wonder that I am telling you at all. He's had more than enough of your attention tonight."

She glanced up at him quickly to see a rueful sort of humor in his eyes.

Theo had bent to listen to Prince Selwyn, who was murmuring seriously into his ear. The taller man nodded once, then continued to listen, looking over the room with a faint, thoughtful smile on his face. Finally he answered the prince and turned away.

Theo looked over the guests until he caught sight of them and approached them with an open, delighted smile.

Sir Jacob Hathaway's cautious expression softened. "No," he said preemptively. "It is late, and we're leaving."

Theo's smile faded. He caught Lily's hand and bowed over it, kissing her fingers lightly, then not quite letting go. "Must you depart so soon?"

"Yes," Sir Jacob said firmly.

Theo smiled again, warm and sweet and kind. He bowed deeply to her father. "Before you leave, may I introduce you to my parents?"

Sir Jacob blinked. "I... Yes, of course."

Theo led them first to where Lady Hathaway stood, and asked, "May I introduce you to my parents before you depart? It was a pleasure to meet you this evening, and I would hate to deprive my parents of the honor of your acquaintance."

Lily wondered whether he meant to be sarcastic, but there was nothing of impertinence in his expression. He looked open and sincere, all bright optimism and hope.

Lady Hathaway smiled and agreed. Theo led the whole group toward his parents, catching Oliver along the way.

He made the introductions with perfect courtesy, and while the elders made polite conversation, he caught Lily's eye and one corner of his mouth lifted in a conspiratorial smile.

He bowed over her hand again before saying, "Goodnight, Miss Hathaway," so softly that heat rose in her cheeks.

They departed for home in a haze of exhaustion, grateful for the brisk night air and sudden quiet, broken only by the sound of the horses' hooves on the road and the creak of the coach.

CHAPTER TWO
An Expression of Interest

W hen Lily wandered down to breakfast late the next morning, her mother said, "Young Mr. Overton has already left his card."

Lily blinked.

From his seat at the table, Sir Jacob said, "That seems precipitous."

Oliver had followed Lily down the stairs and put his hands on her shoulders to move her out of the doorway. "Maybe he's just decisive. Who *wouldn't* be entranced by Lily?" He smiled at her affectionately.

"Flatterer." She cut a thick piece of the bread her mother had baked the day before and spread honey butter over it generously. "I barely saw you last night. How was it for you, Oliver?"

Her brother shrugged. "All right. I danced with most of the girls once. Lord Selby was a little disappointed he didn't manage to claim a second dance with you." He eyed her curiously. "Did you really like Overton that much?"

She blushed and focused on her bread for a moment, hoping the heat would fade from her cheeks. "He has very nice manners," she said eventually.

Oliver studied her face and smiled when she blushed more deeply. But he said nothing else.

"What did you think of Lord Willowvale?" asked her mother.

Sir Jacob grimaced. "He's as sharp as they come. The Wraith had better watch his back."

"Who do you think it is, Father?" asked Oliver. "I had always assumed he must be some rich lord, but last night puts paid to that."

"I don't see why the Wraith must be rich," mused Lily. "There is nothing of heroism that requires wealth."

"No, but the disguises cost money. There's some minor magical talent running through many of the families we saw last night. Does the Wraith use magic?"

Sir Jacob said, "I haven't heard of it, but there's much we don't know. Surely he must know a little, or he wouldn't be able to traverse the Fair Lands at all."

"What if the Wraith isn't even human? What if he's one of the Fair Folk himself?" asked Lily.

Oliver blinked. "That's an interesting thought."

Sir Jacob said more seriously, "The Arichtan ambassador has grown more friendly since the Fair Folk seem to count the Wraith as one of us. Whether it's gratitude or self-interest, he's has been much more helpful lately."

"How?" Lily asked.

"He has been freely sharing how many children are missing with everyone he sees, in hopes that the Wraith will find out and help some of them. The gentlemen were all talking about it last night." Sir Jacob frowned at his coffee thoughtfully. "Apparently some of the victims' families are quite wealthy and have offered substantial rewards for their return. Others are penniless, farm children or orphans."

"Does the Wraith rescue them all, or only some of them?" asked Oliver.

Sir Jacob replied, "Any that he can, as far as we can tell." He looked up. "I wish I could help the man. He's doing God's work, and whoever he is, he's running grave risks."

Lily kept listening, but her thoughts whirled around her. The mysterious Wraith had caught her imagination, as he had that of everyone in Valestria. She was trying to imagine what he might be like when her father's next words caught her attention.

"There are twenty-three children missing now." The grief and sympathy in his voice brought tears to her eyes, and her sympathetic heart filled with compassion.

"What can we do for them?" she whispered.

Oliver said, "I heard the prince has established a home for the orphan children the Wraith has freed. Aricht doesn't want them, so we might as well keep them. He's going to educate them in trades or something."

Lily's heart caught at the plight of these poor children. Orphaned, unwanted, stolen, rescued, and abandoned by their own countrymen, they would find a home of sorts here in Valestria. "Maybe that is how we can help. May we visit the home?"

"I don't believe it's open to visitors; the children have been through so much. But it might be worth a try."

"I could teach them embroidery and gardening. We could start a garden there, if they have even a little plot of land." She smiled. "I wonder if we might even catch a glimpse of the Wraith."

Oliver scoffed. "I doubt it. I wouldn't imagine he's even involved. If I were him, I'd keep well clear of any ongoing connection to the poor children."

"We should not underestimate his heroism!" shot back Lily. "It is not unreasonable that he would want to help them even after they are back in the human realm. We should all be so ready to help our fellow men."

Oliver's eyes widened. "I'm not casting aspersions on the man! I'm as ready to help as anyone. I'll go with you, if you want to visit the home." He frowned thoughtfully. "Though what use we can be is a little beyond me."

The next morning a small wooden crate arrived addressed to Miss Lilybeth Hathaway.

Sir Jacob and Oliver brought it inside, and they opened it in the tiny dining room. A burlap sack sat inside, which they lifted out. Inside the burlap sack were two large, knobby roots.

"What are those?" Oliver asked wonderingly.

Pinned to the burlap sack was a note bearing a wax seal with the Overton family crest.

Lily broke the seal and read the note to herself.

Dear Miss Hathaway,

Enclosed please find two peony rhizomes. I have chosen two of my favorites, in hopes that you will enjoy them as well. The larger of the two is called Sunset Dream and blooms an incandescent coral, with bright yellow in the middle. The smaller is Sweet Surprise; its buds look nearly red, but when it blooms it softens to a bright, cheerful pink.

I do hope you like them. May the warmth of the colors remind you of my affection.

Yours most devotedly,

Theo Overton, IV

She handed the note to her father. Sir Jacob read it quickly and let out a soft breath. "Young Overton knows the way to your heart, apparently." He frowned at her. "What did you tell him?"

Lily blushed and smiled. "I told him about the garden and how much I enjoyed working in it, and that I was excited about the peonies you promised me."

Her father studied her. "Did you tell him I promised you three?"

"I did say you promised me some. I might have said three; I am not sure if I mentioned the number."

Sir Jacob said, "If so, this was nicely done, to not overshadow my gift. Where will you put them?"

"May I plant them here? I was thinking of home when I spoke of peonies, but the garden here would benefit from their color."

"Of course." Her father sat back on his heels. "This season in the city seems far too exciting already."

CHAPTER THREE
The Wraith

That same afternoon, the Wraith stepped out of the veil into the indigo forests of the Fair Lands. One of his Fair allies had left a note from another ally detailing His Majesty Silverthorn's planned schedule over the next week, and with it a dirty, tattered jacket with another note that said, "Kobold, 2 hrs."

The Wraith smiled as he pulled the jacket around his shoulders. Every time he wore a Fair glamour, he expected it to feel like something, but there was never any sensation other than wonder. His soft brown leather boots suddenly appeared larger and more worn. His tailored dove gray jacket and trousers appeared the dirty green and brown favored by kobolds resident in this part of the Fair Lands, and his hands appeared smaller and knobbier. He propped a tiny mirror against a tree trunk and examined the glamour for any flaws, unsurprised when he found none. Although he appeared slightly taller than most kobolds, the reflection indicated that he appeared considerably shorter than his true height, and nothing in his features or clothing was recognizable as human. His eyes sparkled a bright, malevolent yellow-green, and his smile revealed sharp, crooked teeth.

He studied the schedule, then folded it carefully and slipped it and the mirror into a jacket pocket.

He stepped back into the veil and set off into the lightless tunnel.

The veil had a strange, metallic scent for several minutes, and he hurried onward, not wanting to find out what that meant. Beneath his feet, the stone floor turned to loose, dry sand, and he slowed his pace, testing each step before putting his weight on the floor. When the ground changed again to a slippery damp substance that felt like decaying leaves beneath his boots, he stopped and put his hands against the wall. It felt like warm, polished wood, the faint grain barely perceptible beneath his fingertips. He pressed his magic into it and then continued a little farther.

He opened the door just a sliver, just enough to peek out to see that he was nearly within reach of the closest child, and not far from the others.

The children were dancing on a temporary wooden dance floor a few hundred feet from a Fair dwelling, something akin to a retreat at the foothills of the mountains just north of the Fair capital. The white spires and numerous windows sparkled in the clear Fair sunlight. A short distance to the Wraith's left, three bored Fair guards played a game of chance that involved several bones and an enormous violet crystal that glittered with something like sentience.

The Wraith studied the scene for several minutes, noting the positions of the guards and the pattern of the dance as the children circled the floor again.

He slipped through the door without being seen and left it just cracked behind him. Quicker than thought, he pulled the nearest two children off the dance floor and shoved them through the door.

The guards did not immediately notice.

The Wraith snatched up a rock and flung it at the purple crystal, which exploded in a blinding flash of violet light and an exuberant roll of thunder that made the ground shudder beneath their feet.

The Fair guards cried out in pain and dismay, covering their eyes even as they stood and drew their swords. Half-blinded, they managed a creditable formation with their backs to each other.

The Wraith had hoped something would happen when the crystal was broken, but did not expect the light to be so bright, and he, too, was half-blinded. He strained to see through the sparkling afterimage of Fair magic and grasped the hands of the last two children.

He pulled them off the dance floor and into the veil before the Fair guards had recovered.

In the utter darkness of the veil, the Wraith said quietly, "Don't be afraid, children. I'm taking you back to the human world. Can you be brave a little longer?"

Little whispers answered him, and one young voice said, "Are you the Rose?"

"The Fair Folk call me that, yes. Our own people call me the Wraith. I will answer to either." A smile made his voice warm and reassuring. "Are you able to walk?"

He clasped the hands of the two youngest children, and said, "Hold hands, please. Everyone stay together. The darkness is only a little dangerous, and we will be out of it soon. Tell me if anything frightens you."

They murmured agreement again.

He led them unerringly through the darkness to the door back to the human world. "Here we are. You'll be safe here."

CHAPTER FOUR
Fascination

T hree days after Lord Radclyffe's ball, Araminta visited Lily for morning tea. They hurried back to the little sitting room that looked over the tiny garden.

"How do you like life in the city, Lily?" Araminta inquired eagerly. "Your first ball was quite a success, I think."

"It's a little overwhelming, to be honest." Lily flushed. "You're used to this hustle and bustle, I think, but it all seems a bit much for me."

Araminta gazed at her compassionately. "You really do like the quiet life of Haven-by-the-Sea, don't you?"

"I do." Lily smiled. "I know it seems quaint to you, and I suppose it is, but I love the sound of the wind across the hills and robins every morning in the garden. Before we came here, I had started taking tea out in the garden most mornings, when it wasn't too cold or wet. The fresh air seemed like such a good way to start every day."

"But there was no dancing," Araminta lamented.

"Well, there were the little dances in the square."

Araminta gave her a serious look. "Yes, but those dances are not the sort of dances at which the daughter of a knight should be hoping to find a suitable husband."

Lily laughed. "I wasn't looking!"

"I know. Neither was I, back then." Araminta sighed. "It does seem so different here. That summer feels like a distant dream."

"It feels like home," Lily said firmly.

Araminta looked at her friend doubtfully. The two young ladies had met as children when the Hathaways had visited extended family in the Valestrian capital of Ardmond, where Araminta's family had lived next door to Lily's aunt and uncle. They had exchanged letters occasionally throughout the years. Last summer, Araminta had visited Haven-by-the-Sea and stayed with the Hathaways for a month.

Even after that time in the secluded little town, she did not seem to fully understand how different life was in a quiet backwater on the coast. Lily had thought before that maybe Araminta simply didn't want to think of it; she loved the busy social schedule of Ardmond, and she believed she was being kind to Lily by presuming she liked it as well. Thus pretending that Haven-by-the-Sea was more connected than it was seemed a benign social fiction.

Araminta was a sweet friend and had always been kind to Lily, despite her higher status in the intricate social hierarchy of Ardmond. Her father was the Duke of Brickelwyte, one of the smallest, least important duchies in the realm. Although the little duchy had not made her family rich, the title was notable, and Araminta had already courteously fended off several interested suitors.

She had quietly hoped for Oliver's interest to turn her way since that first summer, when she and Lily had been little girls and Oliver the dashing elder brother, a full thirteen to Lily's almost-eleven years.

The fact that Oliver was only a knight's son, and had not even been able to boast that status when they had first met, had not mattered then, and it didn't matter now, at least to Araminta. Perhaps it would have mattered to her parents, if they had perceived her interest, but only Lily had been let into her confidence. Araminta's interest in young men was lively, but Oliver had managed, without effort or even understanding, to keep her affection for years.

Lily had to allow that Oliver was a rather charming young man, for a brother. He was tall and handsome, with rich dark hair that naturally held the waves so currently fashionable. He had a lovely voice and pleasant manners with everyone, though of course he and Lily had squabbled at times when they were younger. The few times he had danced with Araminta, they looked perfect for each other; her dark hair was near the color of his, and her berry-red lips and vivacious manner were enviable. Her brother's magic was negligible, limited to beautiful hair that never seemed to be in disarray and an uncanny ability to keep white shirts crisp and unstained. Araminta's interest had not been sparked by his magic, but rather his sweet smiles and easy, friendly manner when they were young.

Lily could not imagine anyone she would rather have as a sister-by-marriage, and she had wished often that Araminta would let her nudge Oliver to consider her in that light.

This morning, while Araminta was recounting her experience of the ball and telling Lily of all the fascinating conversations she had missed, a letter arrived.

Lily accepted it herself, somewhat to the footman's horror. There really ought to be a servant to accept cards and notes. But they didn't have the money for that at the moment, and anyway it wasn't difficult. They did have Susie come five days a week to prepare lunch and dinner, and Lizbet to do the laundry once a week. But Susie hadn't arrived yet, and it would be silly to leave the letter waiting outside.

At home in Haven-by-the-Sea, Jasper maintained their house and garden. The expense of a second house in the city was substantial, even if only for a season; and Lily was only now becoming aware of how her family's circumstances were more precarious than she had previously understood. A series of unsuccessful investments and a disappointing harvest from the orchard on the estate had tipped them from frugal but comfortable to "rather concerned," as her father had explained it to them. Nevertheless, the season in Ardmond was considered a necessity for every well-bred young lady, and after delaying it for several years, her father had brooked no argument when he decided that this was the year Lily would be seen.

"Father, there's a letter for you," she called up the stairs, then ran up the stairs to her father's office.

He read it and handed it to her.

Sir Theodore Overton the Third, Bart., Lady Overton, and Theodore Overton the Fourth request the pleasure of the company of Sir Jacob Hathaway, Lady Hathaway, Mr. Oliver Hathaway, and Miss Hathaway at dinner at our estate Tuesday next at 5:00 pm. I look forward to your response.

Sir Jacob wrote a polite acceptance and gave it to Lily. "When Susie comes, ask her to have her brother deliver this tomorrow morning, if he can." He gave her a few coins for the young messenger.

"You seem to have bewitched him, Lily."

"I didn't mean to."

He smiled at her affectionately. "I am well aware of your innocence, sweet Lily. I think we'll know more about him after this dinner."

Lily returned to her guest. "I am sorry to keep you waiting, Minta. We've received an invitation to dinner, and Father wanted to write the acceptance before Susie arrives this afternoon."

Araminta asked, "I was enjoying the beauty of your garden. Although it is small, you've already made it more beautiful. Might I ask who the invitation is from?"

"The Overtons."

Araminta blinked in surprise, then smiled warmly. "You did make an impression!"

"I don't know how." Lily blushed.

"Well, it probably has something to do with how sweet you are." Araminta gave a soft chuckle. "Not to mention how lovely you look when you're slightly embarrassed about a compliment. I do think it likely you will receive more invitations, but perhaps not as many as you would otherwise. I think Theo Overton made his interest quite clear, and he is too popular for anyone to pique him intentionally. They'll wait to see whether you like him before pursuing you openly. Though honestly I'm not sure how you could refuse him."

Lily blinked. "He's not jealous or mean, is he?"

Araminta shook her head. "No, he's adored by both men and women. As silly and boyish as he seems, he's unaccountably kind to everyone. It would be low indeed to openly vie with him for a lady's affections, no matter how lovely you are."

"Then is it not surprising that he has not already married? How old is he?"

"Twenty-six? Twenty-seven? I don't know. Old enough that many ladies have set their sights on him and been disappointed." Araminta smiled to herself. "I've been saved only by virtue of already having my heart set on someone else. Perhaps not a particularly wise strategy, but I live in hope."

At breakfast the next morning, Lily pondered the question of the Fair Court's motives. "What do you think the Fair Folk want with the children?" she asked.

"I don't think they eat them," said Oliver. "That's just too horrible to imagine. I think it's more likely related to something else going on in the Fair Court. Maybe fairies thrive on human tears, and what produces more human angst than stolen children?"

"If that were true, they would have been stealing children for centuries then, and we have no reason to believe that has happened," Lily said thoughtfully.

"Don't we? The rumors have persisted for generations."

"Not in any numbers, then. What is different now?"

Oliver frowned. "And why are all the stolen children Arichtan? We have no reports of children missing from Valestria, Altavia, or Ruloth, as far as I know. I think it must have something to do with what happened between Aricht and the Fair Folk. Maybe the Arichtan government made a bad deal, and the children are paying the price for it. Or maybe the Fair Folk think Aricht has reneged on their agreement and this is the payment."

Lily said thoughtfully, "Lord Willowvale said that the Wraith had cost his people more than I knew. I wonder what he meant by that. It was as if he meant to justify the theft of the children, but he could not without giving away more than he intended to. He said that the Wraith is an enemy of his people, and that his—Lord Willowvale's—cause is just. I think he believed it wholly, too."

"He is a true believer, no doubt. I think he would kill the Wraith himself with his bare hands if he could."

"He also said that when a human has the opportunity to be of service to a fairy, *it* should be grateful." Lily grimaced. "He truly believes the children ought to be honored to be so tormented and used. How horrible!"

Her brother grimaced. "If there were a way to help the Wraith, I would do it."

"I don't know how we could. I will think on it, though." Lily frowned thoughtfully at her tea.

"So will I."

Only two days later, Lily cajoled Oliver into accompanying her to the palace to ask permission to visit the children's home. The location of the children's home had, of course, been kept in absolute secrecy, to keep the children safe from Lord Willowvale and any other Fair Folk who might bother them. Nevertheless, if the prince had established a home for them, he must know where it was.

Sir Jacob and Lady Hathaway, as well as Oliver, had told her that it was highly unlikely the prince would even see her, much less grant her request. What reason would the prince have to grant an audience to the daughter of a knight, one of the lowest of nobility, and not even a heredity title? Nevertheless, she felt bold, even a little courageous, when she and Oliver set off in a hired coach to the palace.

At the gate Oliver dutifully answered the guards' questions, and they were let through and directed to stop at the grand front entrance.

She kept her hand on Oliver's arm as they walked up the steps together. Already she was doubting the wisdom of this request, but she reminded herself of the children and what they had already suffered. If she and Oliver could be of service to them, they ought to be.

They knocked at the door and were greeted by a liveried servant.

"We are seeking an audience with His Royal Highness," said Oliver.

"Why?" The man did not blink.

"I'm Oliver Hathaway, and this is my sister Miss Lilybeth Hathaway. We've heard that the prince has established a children's home for the Arichtan children, and we were hoping we might be able to visit it to encourage and help them."

He looked at them evaluatingly, then said, "Come with me." They followed him through a marble-tiled hallway to a luxurious sitting room as large as their house. "Wait here, please."

They stood in the middle of the room, unsure whether they were actually meant to sit upon the silk-upholstered chairs. Oliver rubbed his hands upon his trousers nervously. Lily played with the handle of her reticule, trying to imagine what they might say and wondering how silly and strange he might think them both.

Several minutes later, a man about ten years older than Oliver strode into the room.

"Good morning," he said neutrally. "I am Robert Weldon, an assistant to His Royal Highness. Please sit down." He indicated two chairs and sat across from them. "His Royal Highness asked me to listen to your request."

He looked at them expectantly. His hair was a medium brown liberally sprinkled with silver, though his face was young.

Oliver repeated his introduction of himself and Lily and their request. Despite Oliver's apparent confidence, Lily nearly cringed at the awkwardness of the request. She suddenly realized that it sounded as if they meant to gawk at the poor children, as if they were mere spectacles for pity, not human beings.

She blurted, "I wish we could do more. Is there anything we can do?"

Mr. Weldon regarded them steadily. "The children are not available for visitors unless approved by His Royal Highness. Do you wish to apply for such approval?"

"Yes," said Oliver.

"What do you think you can offer the children?" The question was not accusatory or unkind, merely neutral, but it served to make Lily feel even sillier than before.

She swallowed. "I was hoping we might read to them, or I could teach the girls needlework. Perhaps deportment, or whatever else His Royal Highness would like taught."

Mr. Weldon's gaze softened almost imperceptibly, and he said, "What is your motive, then? Altruism?""

Oliver said, "I think it is shameful how the poor children have been treated by the Fair Folk, and especially so for the ones who have no home to return to in Aricht. It's nearly a patriotic duty to show them that Valestria is too honorable to abandon them to the streets, is it not?"

Lily added softly, "I feel so sorry for them. Maybe we can't offer much, but I would like to do what we can."

Her brother added, "Anyway, I would like to aid the Wraith, but since I don't know who he is or how to do so, the next best thing is to aid the children he risks himself for."

"What would you do for the Wraith?"

Oliver blinked. "I don't know. I have next to no magic of my own, but I should certainly like to be of service if I could. He's doing God's work, and making all of Valestria proud. I'd do whatever he asked, I should think."

Mr. Weldon asked them other questions, about their family, their home in Haven-by-the-Sea, their family finances, their friendships in the city, their opinion of Lord Willowvale, and their knowledge of the Fair Folk in general. At last, he stood and said, "I will make my report to His Royal Highness. You will receive a letter with his decision in a few days. Good day."

They departed, feeling both elated and oddly spent. They had asked the carriage to wait for them, so they clambered back into it and headed home.

As the gate was opened to let them out of the palace grounds, a horse and rider trotted in and passed them, heading toward the palace.

"That's Theo Overton!" said Oliver in surprise. "Father said he was close friends with His Royal Highness, but I did not think to see him today."

Lily shrugged. "I suppose it is like me visiting Araminta, although the palace is more impressive than the Poole estate."

"You're right." Oliver leaned back against the seat as the coach bumped into the street. "That was exhausting."

Lily could only agree. She found herself dozing over her embroidery that afternoon. The excitement of seeing the palace, and the anticipation of actually being able to help the children in some small way, dissipated into a drowsy contentment broken only by the delivery of a vase of white flowers and a little note.

Dear Miss Hathaway,

Please accept these as a token of my esteem and my eager anticipation of seeing your beauty next week.

Humbly yours,

Theo Overton, IV

She inspected the flowers with interest, then referenced the book Araminta had loaned her recently. White lily-of-the-valley indicted sweetness and humility; presumably at least the humility was a reference to his own attitude. Sweet woodruff also signified humility. A gorgeous white rose indicated innocence. Gardenia blossoms signified that he thought her lovely. The foliage, too, carried a message. Fern fronds told her he was fascinated, and ivy signified affection, friendship, and fidelity.

Lily blushed as she smelled the rose and gardenias again.

One morning not long afterward, a letter arrived as the Hathaways were finishing breakfast.

His Royal Highness the Prince of Valestria and its vassal states has approved the application of Mr. Oliver Hathaway and Miss Lilybeth Hathaway for admission into the Royal Children's Home. You are adjured to keep all conversations within the home, with the children, staff, and other visitors, in utter and complete confidence. No word shall be said of the children, the staff, activities at the home, or anything else, outside the home, and nothing relating to the children or the home or its activities shall be shared with anyone other than His Royal Highness under any circumstances.

The seal of the prince shone below in gold ink, and below that, there was a handwritten addendum that read:

In confidence, I entreat you to respect the privacy and safety of the children above all.

HRH Selwyn Alberdale

Below this was written the address of the children's home.

"Let's go!" Lily said in excitement. "I will pack some of my embroidery, and you must bring a story to read to the children."

Oliver acquiesced, and they were soon off.

The coach drew up in front of the house. "Please come back in three hours," said Oliver to the driver. He helped Lily down from the coach and gallantly offered his arm to her for the short walk down the path to the door.

The home was a spacious brick home at the end of a line of similar houses only one block from the palace wall. The entire adjoining block was bordered by high brick walls, and only the tops of a few trees could be seen waving above the uppermost bricks. A little garden surrounded by a white fence with a gate separated the rambling house from the street. The walls around the adjoining block bordered the garden and went right up to the house, so there was no way to see into the sheltered space. Climbing roses bloomed pink and yellow on white columns supporting a roof over the broad patio fronting the building, and more roses lined the edges of the yard. Delphiniums, lavender, and yellow irises bloomed in front of the patio, and two large planters flanked the door, overflowing with phlox, foxgloves, and hollyhocks.

The Wraith and the Rose

The effect was both welcoming and calming, and Lily's heart warmed toward the prince for providing such a lovely refuge for the poor children. The king, who allowed his son such autonomy in his charity, received a little of her gratitude too.

Oliver raised his hand to knock when the door opened and someone began to step out.

"Mr. and Miss Hathaway!" Theo Overton exclaimed in delight. "How unexpected!" His voice was light and friendly. For a moment, Lily thought there was an odd, wary look in his eyes, but then she was sure she had imagined it.

"Sir Theo?" Oliver blinked in surprise. "What are you doing here?"

"Just Theo, if you please." He beamed at them, as if nothing more lovely had ever been seen in all the world. "Your beauty has startled me, Miss Hathaway. I have such sweet memories of dancing with you at Lord Radclyffe's ball, but the light did not do you justice."

Her cheeks heated, and she tried to think of something clever to say. "Sir, you compliment me too generously. We are here to see the children, to see if we might cheer them with stories or embroidery. We want to help." She looked up at him inquisitively. "Why are *you* here, sir?"

He frowned at them both in mock anger. "*Please* just call me Theo. My father is the baronet, not me. Anyway, I was just leaving."

"If you're to be just Theo to us, you must call me Oliver as well," Oliver said.

"Were you here to see the children too?" Lily pressed curiously.

Theo scoffed gently. "His Royal Highness asked me to come to see if the accommodations were adequate. He knows how spoiled I am and wants to be sure the children are treated well by the crown. Who better to evaluate that than a pampered fop?"

Oliver stepped back and looked the other man up and down. His clothes were cut of the finest cloth and fitted by the best tailors to his lean, elegant figure, but they were not as extravagantly and frivolously overdone as might be expected. "Theo, I don't actually believe that excuse," Oliver said finally. "Why are you really here?"

Theo sighed softly and leaned in conspiratorially. Drawn in by his manner, they leaned close to hear him say, "All right. You've caught me. You must know my family is rather wealthy. We contribute a little to the expenses of the house. The children require good food to regain

39

their strength, and we've retained several tutors to teach them. There is also the housekeeper, who ought to be paid well for the good care she provides them. I cannot do much for the poor children, but if my money can provide anything to comfort the poor souls, I am happy to provide it. It is little enough sacrifice on my part, and it's patriotism besides." He raised a finger to his lips. "Don't tell anyone, though. It's much easier if everyone thinks I'm entirely selfish."

Oliver laughed quietly. "I don't think anyone believes you're selfish. You have quite a good reputation."

Theo straightened as if affronted. "I am so! I am utterly and completely self-absorbed." His eyes danced, as if he were playing a great trick on the world, and letting them in on it were infinitely amusing. "Besides, I don't want credit for sharing something I have more than enough of, anyway. There's nothing admirable in that."

Lily smiled kindly at him. "All the same, it is generous of you."

A faint flush crept over his cheeks, and he bowed. "Well, I cannot deny that I wish you to think well of me, but I entreat you to keep it to yourselves. I have a reputation to maintain, you know."

"As you wish," said Oliver reluctantly.

Theo held her gaze until she nodded, then bowed again, kissing the tips of her fingers with exquisite courtesy. "Thank you, Oliver, and thank you, Miss Hathaway. You have my deepest, humblest gratitude." Then he walked away as if he hadn't a care in the world. He stepped out of the garden and into a carriage that had drawn up and was apparently waiting for him.

"Was that odd?" Lily murmured to Oliver. "I think it was odd."

Oliver frowned thoughtfully. "He's an odd one, I think. Nice, though."

Lily smiled, thinking of Theo's dancing eyes and the warmth of his smile. "Yes, he is kind."

Her brother looked back at her. "You could do worse, actually. I do think he's serious about you."

Lily looked down, trying to hide the flush of her cheeks.

Oliver knocked on the door, and a woman about the age of their mother welcomed them into a spacious vestibule papered in cheerful white and gold. Oliver presented the letter from the prince.

"Yes, I was informed that you were to be admitted if you came. I'm Essie Porter." She smiled warmly. "Would you like a tour?"

"Yes, please," Lily replied. They followed Essie through the well-lit hall to an enclosed garden in the back of the house. Surrounded by high brick walls adorned by climbing roses, the expansive garden boasted a spreading oak near one corner and a broad, well-kept lawn. Flower beds lined each wall, filled with fading tulips, bright daisies, more delphiniums, and half a dozen other flowers. The whole space seemed designed to be both beautiful and engaging. A wooden swing hung from an oak bough, and a scuffed area beneath showed that the children enjoyed it often.

"This is the garden, as you can see. The children breakfast at seven every morning, for we believe a schedule is beneficial for them after their strange experiences. Then they come here to play for an hour before beginning their studies. They study arithmetic, literature, music, and practical skills. Both boys and girls are taught how to sew buttons, bake bread, clean and cook a chicken, wash clothes and dishes, and keep track of household expenses. The program is quite progressive, I believe." The pride in her voice was evident.

She led them inside and down another hall to a room where nine boys and girls sat at tables watching a middle-aged man read aloud from a thick book. The man's spectacles hung over his nose, and he made faces as he adjusted his voice for the different characters in the story.

"He seems to enjoy his work," Lily said.

Essie smiled. "He does." The warmth in her voice made Lily look at her more closely, and the other woman added, "John is my husband these thirty-four years."

"Is this all the children?" Oliver inquired.

"No, some of them are having a cooking lesson with Sadie, and some are sewing today. I'll show you." Essie led them to the detached kitchen, where a group of younger students crowded around a table.

A ruddy-faced young woman was watching each of her young charges pinch the edges of the pies in front of them. She looked up and grinned. "Mrs. Essie! We're almost done except for the baking. We have six chicken and vegetable and four raspberry pies."

Lily gaped. "Raspberry?"

The young woman gave her a thoughtful look, then turned her gaze toward Essie.

Essie nodded. "This is Miss Lilybeth Hathaway and her brother Mr. Oliver Hathaway. They came to spend time with the children, if there was any way to help."

The children in this group looked to be between the ages of six and nine, though Lily wasn't sure of that. She didn't have much experience guessing the ages of children. They stared at her and Oliver cautiously, then looked back at Essie.

Sadie nodded. "All right. You can come outside with us for their afternoon snack and play if you like. I'll just get these pies in the ovens."

Essie answered Lily's question Sadie had ignored. "We have a glass hothouse along the eastern wall. It isn't large, but we've been able to grow some delicious fruits in it to supplement the children's diets."

"Theo has been quite generous," Lily murmured.

Essie shot her a sidelong glance. "Indeed." She shooed them out after the children and pulled Sadie aside to speak into her ear for a moment. The younger woman nodded, then followed them out to the garden.

What followed was not only a light-hearted, enjoyable afternoon, but one that provoked much thought when Lily and Oliver departed.

Both were lost in contemplation on the drive back to their house in the city. It still didn't exactly feel like home, but it was familiar and comfortable, if not luxurious, and they were happy to return as daylight faded.

Over a simple dinner that evening, Oliver said thoughtfully to his father, "Does it profit a man to be generous if no one sees it?"

"It is beneficial for his character," Sir Jacob said promptly. "And for those who receive his generosity."

"Indeed." Oliver nodded. "What of his friends who do not know of it, and think the worse of him for it?"

Sir Jacob frowned. "What an odd question. I would speculate in that case that such a man likely has a reason, even if only humility. In any case, it speaks well of him that he doesn't want accolades for his good deeds."

The very next day Theo attended a garden party hosted by Lord and Lady Stewart and was disappointed to discover that the Hathaways had not been invited. He danced with the ladies once each, as was expected of all able-bodied men, and offered sunny smiles and compliments to everyone, as he usually did.

Lord Willowvale arrived not long after Theo did, though Theo doubted he had been invited at all, and greeted Lord Stewart with icy courtesy. Theo watched with interest as the Fair lord snarled at everyone in turn. The prince was not present, so Theo merely waited until Lord Willowvale had run out of more important people to insult and approached him.

"Good evening, Lord Willowvale," he said with a smile and a bow.

"Is it?" The fairy gave him the slightest possible bow and turned to survey the other guests.

Lady Stewart had clearly been disappointed by Theo's interest in Lily, and took the opportunity to encourage him to dance with her daughter Lady Sophia Stewart a second time. He demurred, pleading fatigue, and escaped to the side, where he listened to Lord Stewart telling an anecdote he thought amusing about some long-past hunting trip with far more delight than the story merited.

Dinner with the Hathaways would be infinitely more enjoyable.

CHAPTER FIVE
The Dinner Party

Two days later, Sir Jacob hired a carriage to take them to the Overton estate for the much anticipated dinner party. He had enquired how long it would take to reach the estate, and learned that the Overtons lived several miles outside the city in a spacious, luxurious manor and the surrounding acreage.

Lily wore her nicest dress that wasn't a ball gown. It was a demure blue, with delicate white lace around the modest neckline and wrists and white roses and lilies of the valley she had embroidered all around the hem the previous winter. Though it wasn't the height of fashion for dinner parties, the blue set off her grey-blue eyes and brown hair. The waistline nipped in flatteringly, and, most importantly, she felt pretty when she wore it.

Oliver and her father looked dashing in deep blue dinner coats that coordinated with her dress, and her mother had chosen a dress of a deeper blue. Lily thought the men looked dashing, and her mother beautiful.

"You look lovely, my darling," said her mother as she came down the stairs.

"Oh, dear," muttered her father.

She frowned up at him. "I thought I was supposed to be lovely, Father."

"You are lovely, and I could not be more proud of either of you." Sir Jacob smiled at them. "Poor Theo Overton is about to lose his heart. I hope he's prepared for that."

Lady Hathaway smiled. "He seems like a charming young man." She looked at her husband quellingly. "Jacob, we did come here primarily for Lily to have a season. This result is not entirely unexpected, you know. A beautiful daughter does attract the attention of admirers, and I see no reason at this point to be displeased that Theodore Overton is one of them."

Oliver smiled and looked down. "Poor Lord Selby. Never got a second chance."

Lily looked stricken. "Was I rude to him? I didn't mean to be! I was so overwhelmed by everything."

Her brother shook his head. "He'll survive. It's not as though he doesn't have options."

Lady Overton gave him a severe look. "That is quite enough of that sort of talk, Oliver."

Oliver shrugged obligingly. "Sorry, Mother," he murmured with a smile.

The drive was quiet, and Lily had all she could do not to twist her hands in nervous tension. Why she should be so nervous, she couldn't say.

When they turned off the road onto the long, winding driveway, everyone looked out the window with interest. Elegant birch trees lined the graveled drive, their silvery trunks bright. The carriage drew up in front of an enormous brick manor house.

The door opened as Sir Jacob was alighting from the carriage. A footman came out, and behind him Theo came and descended the stairs at little less than a run.

"It's an honor, Sir Jacob," he said earnestly. "Lady Hathaway, Oliver, Miss Hathaway." He offered a hand on one side of the steps as Sir Jacob assisted them from the other side.

He bowed most courteously to each of them in turn. "Thank you for coming. My parents are inside. May I escort you, Lady Hathaway?"

He offered his arm with the appropriate degree of respect, and Lily's mother smiled at him. Sir Jacob escorted his daughter, and Oliver brought up the rear.

The Hathaways tried not to gawk as they entered the beautiful mansion. The huge double doors opened into a spacious foyer with a wide staircase that arched upward toward an elegant balcony. Doors on either side led to the opposite wings of the house. The marble floors were inlaid in intricate interlocking patterns. The walls were papered in gold damask. Lanterns flooded the room with light, an extravagance at any time, but especially in such a large house.

Theo gave them a lively tour as he escorted them. "My parents occupy the east wing of the house, and they have given me the west wing. We eat together when we can. The kitchen is in the rear, and we share the staff of the house, although I do have my own assistant. It seems hardly fair to call him a footman, although I suppose he is. Anselm has been faithful for years, and I count him a good friend."

Lily glanced back at the footman trailing them just in time to see an affectionate smile cross his face before he resumed his studied air of controlled neutrality.

"The house is lovely," said Lady Hathaway.

"It has been in the family for generations. My great grandfather was born in one of the rooms in the east wing." Theo's friendly, easy hospitality seemed to make the great house seem cozier and more friendly than it had at first.

Sir Theodore and Lady Overton were gracious hosts, and before long they had drawn the Hathaways into pleasant conversation about the weather, the newest fashions in women's and men's evening attire, horseback riding, and other topics.

Lily said shyly to Theo, "You said at the ball that you knew of Haven-by-the-Sea. May I ask how?"

Theo's sparkling smile made her heart flutter with delight, and she resolutely told herself that she was being ridiculous. No one could possibly be so utterly charming; he must have some flaw.

"I got lost there as a child," he said confidingly. "I spent several hours roaming the cliffs until I found my way back to my parents."

Her eyes widened. "How old were you?"

"I was ten." He added with a mischievous smile, "My mother and father were not best pleased when I disappeared for six hours!"

Lily blinked. "There's not enough in Haven-by-the-Sea to be lost for that long."

He chuckled. "You might be surprised! On which end of the town is your family's estate?"

"You can hardly call it an estate, but it's on the southern end near the top of the hill. From my window, you could see north over the town, and from the upper sitting room, you could see out over the sea."

Theo listened with tender attention and offered every courtesy that a gentleman might offer to a lady at dinner. Lily, who had been concerned that the conversation would be terribly awkward, found herself feeling warmly delighted in his presence, as he appeared to be in hers.

The second course had just been laid when the footman who had welcomed them, Anselm, stepped into the room just after one of the servers. He handed a small, sealed note to Theo and murmured something in his ear.

Theo glanced at the seal, broke it, and read quickly. He stood and bowed. "Excuse me, Sir Jacob, Lady Hathaway, Oliver, Miss Hathaway. Father, Mother." He hesitated, then said, "A friend is in need. I doubt I'll be able to return before you must depart; if that is the case, please accept my humblest apologies."

His father stood, apparently intending on following his son into the hallway, and Theo stepped closer to murmur into his ear. Sir Overton nodded, his face grave, and then handed his son something hidden in his hand.

Sir Theodore turned back to his guests with a smile. Lady Overton gave her son her hand, almost as if she were passing him something as well.

Theo bowed deeply to the Hathaways. "Thank you for coming tonight. I hope I may see you again, Miss Hathaway." At her shy smile, he beamed. Then he hurried out, his steps quick and sharp down the hall.

Lily squashed her disappointment; she had dearly enjoyed Theo's friendly conversation, sparkling smiles, and attentive courtesy. But Sir Theodore and Lady Overton were delightful hosts and clearly intended to make their guests comfortable, so the odd tension eased almost immediately. Although they adhered to every nuance of the intricate rules of dinner parties, they made it seem easy and natural, and they didn't blink when the Hathaways inadvertently betrayed their small-town manners.

After dinner, Lady Overton, Lady Hathaway, and Lily retired to the drawing room, where they were served tea and tiny airy cakes adorned with crystalized rose petals. Lady Overton suggested a poetry reading and started them off with a sweet little love poem.

Lady Hathaway, only slightly familiar with this new fashion among the noble ladies of Ardmond, assented, and read the next poem in the volume Lady Overton had given her. It was also a love poem, and as she read, she glanced at her daughter. Lily blushed sweetly. When it was her turn to read, she felt awkward and strange, but as the evening went on, the pastime became more enjoyable. Lady Overton had a lively wit and a delightful sense of humor; she was unfailingly courteous, but not pretentious in the least.

Lily thought that she would be a wonderful second mother, then nearly shook herself for jumping ahead so precipitously. Theo had hardly proposed, and she barely knew him. Nevertheless, Lady Overton's company was thoroughly enjoyable.

When Lady Hathaway said reluctantly, "I believe we probably ought to be departing soon," Lily felt a real pang of regret.

The Overtons bid them goodnight with graciousness and warmth, and the Hathaways said their farewells with reciprocal warmth and affection.

In the coach, Sir Jacob said, "Well, that was unexpectedly pleasant."

Oliver said, "I really thought they'd be snobs, and I've never been so happy to be wrong. They're the nicest people I've ever met, I think."

Lady Hathaway said, "It's a pity Theo had to leave."

Lily caught sight of movement between the birch trees. The moon was full, and even among the trees there was a little light. She thought she saw a figure on horseback. She craned her neck to see better as the carriage followed a curve in the driveway.

The figure cantered up to the manor and dismounted, then handed the reins to the groom who had hurried to greet him. She thought she saw a second, smaller figure, too, and something about the second person seemed strange. His hair, if it was a boy, looked violet in the moonlight, but that was ridiculous.

She lost sight of them as the carriage turned.

"What did you think, Lily?" prompted her mother.

"What?"

"About this evening."

"Oh. It was delightful." Lily thought of Sir Theodore's kind face, with his smile lines and his warm eyes like his son's, and Lady Overton's sweet voice as she read poetry, and her delighted laugh when Lily had read the humorous poem she must have heard a hundred times. "It was reassuring, I think, because Theo seems so much like them. I thought it must be a façade at first, but I think he really is that friendly."

Oliver's white teeth glinted in the darkness as he smiled. "I actually like him, Lily."

CHAPTER SIX
A Little Magic

"I want to go to the Fair Lands and help the Wraith, and I want you to go with me." "That's absolutely mad." Oliver's eyes were wide.

"Why?" She met his gaze stubbornly. "He can't have *that* much more magic than you and I put together. He's human, isn't he?"

"Well, yes, but he knows what he's doing. He's brilliant, and he probably has a whole team helping him. I know nothing about the Fair Lands, except that they're perilous and unpredictable, and neither do you!"

"All we have to do now is find a way into the Fair Lands."

"No, Lily." Oliver looked panicked. "It's a terrible idea. What if the Fair Folk catch you?"

"What if they don't? I'll be careful. I won't go wandering around foolishly. I just want to see how it is there, and whether there is anything we might be able to do to help the Wraith."

The opportunities for a young lady to find passage through the veil to the Fair Lands without being discovered by her parents were few and far between. Lily didn't even know how to start looking, but decided that feeling around with her negligible magical senses was the most logical starting point.

She tried at various points around the city when she was out visiting Araminta or the dressmaker with her mother, but she had no success until one day when they passed near the children's home. She held her breath, trying to figure out from which direction the feeling came.

It was a fuzzy, indistinct sort of unsettledness, and the direction was difficult to pinpoint. The movement of the carriage made the exercise all the more challenging. The only thing she was sure of was that the feeling came from somewhere between the palace and the children's home, perhaps a bit to the south. It was a wide area.

Later that afternoon she asked Oliver to take her on a drive. Her mother looked a little confused by the request, but Oliver, seeing her expression, readily assented.

They hired a carriage and had the driver let them out as near to the feeling as Lily could determine. Once she and Oliver were alone, she murmured to him, "I felt an opening near here, I think. There was something strange."

Little groups of people strolled up the street, and Oliver and Lily turned to look around and wait for them to pass. When the people were out of earshot, Oliver said, "What does it feel like?"

"I'm not sure how to describe it. Like a hole, or a pluck in the fabric of the world. I wish my magic were stronger," she said in frustration.

"I can't sense it at all," Oliver said consolingly. "Where shall we go from here?"

He let her lead him down the street and into a disused alley. At the far end, there was another turn, and Oliver hesitated. "This really isn't a place for a lady."

Lily frowned. "We won't be here long. I just want to see." The little alley ended in a dirty little courtyard between several buildings. She drew him toward one corner. "Something here feels strange."

She put her hand against the wall, and it passed into the stone as if through water. She flinched in surprise, and Oliver jerked her away from it.

"Did it hurt you?"

"No, it was just strange." She looked up at him. "Let's go."

"Lily, please don't do this." He looked at her seriously. "I cannot keep you safe in the Fair Lands. I know nothing about them, and I have virtually no magic."

She trembled with the strength of longing within her. "We won't go far. I just want to see it, Oliver."

"This is a terrible idea. What will I tell Mother and Father if something happens?" He pleaded caution, but he wanted to go, to see the Fair Lands, to be part of the adventure.

"Come with me." She looked up at him. "You know I can always come back and go alone."

He met her gaze. "Don't, Lily. Please don't. I'll go with you now, if you promise me you won't go alone. Ever."

Lily bit her lip. "All right." A pang of guilt assailed her. She had manipulated him, although it had not been planned. The words had slipped out, a sudden 'what if I…' rather than an intentional threat. But he had agreed now, and she did not have it in her to stop now.

She stepped forward into the strange, transparent wall, gripping his hand tightly. Passing into the veil felt like a wash of cool water over her, and she sucked in a surprised breath at the chill.

Oliver stood close and edged slightly in front of her. "It's a tunnel."

Lily wasn't sure what she had expected, but a boring, dark, stone tunnel was not it. Something moved in the distance, and Oliver took a cautious step forward.

"What is that?" he whispered.

Lily shook her head wordlessly. The light from the courtyard behind them filtered in weakly and the shadows moved as if they were alive. The darkness in front of them shifted.

A short distance ahead, she saw a wooden door against the left wall of the tunnel. "Why don't we try that door?" she whispered.

"It's so close. Are the Fair Lands really that close to ours?" whispered Oliver in reply.

"I don't know." Lily strode forward with a sense of purpose, pulled Oliver after her. The door had a strange knob in the exact center, and she placed her hand on it with trepidation.

The knob turned easily without a sound, and she peered out cautiously before she stepped out. They appeared to be in a garden.

In the distance, there was strange, quick music made by unfamiliar instruments. A clear, high voice sang a wailing song above the musicians, and other voices sang and talked in lower tones. An unfamiliar rhythm tugged at Lily's feet, and she resolved not to dance.

Many of the plants in view were flowering, but none of them were familiar. There were tiny white star-shaped flowers in great low mounds lining paths of cobalt pebbles. Green flowers as large as her face drooped from fuchsia-trunked trees to her left. Before her were bushes with leaves that sparkled like gold in the silver light, which came from a moon far too large and close.

A rabbit-like creature with pointed ears like a fox and fur of a deep violet stared at her from beneath a bush, wiggling its nose. To her right, the cobalt path led beneath an arbor covered in deep blue roses.

Lily stepped out onto the path cautiously, and Oliver was only a step behind.

The little creature bared pointed teeth at them.

"Go away," Oliver whispered.

It hissed like a cat, then turned and flipped its long, fluffy tail at them in dismissal.

A deep voice from very close said, "Someone is here."

Oliver pulled Lily back with him into the tunnel and slammed the door shut just as another voice began to reply. The door handle jiggled, and Oliver pushed Lily ahead of him and ran.

The exit was not where they expected it to be, and they ran with panic in their veins before tumbling, with no warning, out into the same courtyard they had left.

Oliver steadied Lily. "That was awful and you're never going back," he said.

"It was beautiful!" At his flat look, she added, "And terrifying. You're right. I don't know what I could do there. But I wish I could... I don't know. Do something."

"You promised, Lily."

CHAPTER SEVEN
An Ally in Peril

T heo shoved the letter into an inner pocket of his jacket and hurried down the hall, though he didn't break into a run until he was out of earshot of the guests.

The letter that had so galvanized him read:

J. was discovered and fled into the tunnel four days ago. He has not returned. If you have not seen him, urgently request your help in the search. C.

Theo hurriedly belted on a sword, grabbed a canteen of water and an extra roll of bread. Then he saddled one of his horses and galloped away. The nearest easy entry to the tunnel was, at the moment, some three miles away, and it would take too long to open a closer door. He tied his horse to a tree with a quick apology, then stepped into the darkness.

The tunnels were Theo's magical gift.

The veil between the Fair Lands and the human world was always shifting and always dangerous, though marginally less perilous than the Fair Lands themselves. The veil itself was virtually impermeable to both Fair Folk and humans, but there were naturally occurring holes in the veil. To Theo, these holes seemed like tunnels which could be traversed in relative safety; his magic kept them solid around him and repelled most of the mind-bending dangers that resided within the veil itself. His magic was not, in itself, particularly strong, but he had honed it well. His quick intelligence and creative application of what magical talent he possessed had allowed him to travel without major incident for some time.

He was an accomplished swordsman, and a steel sword was particularly dangerous to Fair Folk. However, in most cases his disguise did not permit carrying a sword, and it was both easier and safer to rely on speed and unobtrusiveness than a blade.

This time he knew he might need it.

Young Juniper Morel had been one of his most faithful allies, and had been as courageous as any of Theo's older compatriots. If he had fled, the situation in the Fair Court must have been dire indeed.

Theo didn't risk a light in the tunnels; he had learned early on that many of the most dangerous predators that prowled the veil were drawn to light, and it was safer to navigate in darkness. He extended his senses, seeking any sort of Fair presence in the twisting, shifting passages.

It had surprised him that the Fair Folk could not sense presences in the tunnels as well as he could; he'd had several incredulous conversations with certain allies about it, unable to believe this piece of luck. At last he had attributed it to the one of the many idiosyncrasies of the veil itself, for the fact did not hold true in the Fair Lands.

There!

A faint Fair presence flickered a considerable distance away, and several more dangerous shadows lurked around it.

Theo ran. His steps were long and sure as he vaulted over gaping chasms of nothingness that yawned suddenly in his path and dodged down the shifting passages that reformed behind him in a different configuration.

He reached Juniper just as a serpent-like twist of darkness lunged at the fairy. Theo sliced off the tip of the protrusion, wincing at the icy chill that splattered across his face and arm. The chill left a tingly, numb sort of pain that would fade in an hour or so. The shred of darkness flipped and flailed in the darkness before reforming into part of the wall around them. Theo flicked a bit of magic into his fingertips for a moment of light.

Juniper stared up at him with wild eyes. "Theo?" he rasped.

"Yes, my friend. What has happened?" Theo knelt by the young fairy, taking in the stone that sheathed his lower body.

The young fairy shuddered, and Theo put a reassuring hand on his shoulder.

Juniper heaved a deep breath and, trembling, said, "I was attending Lord Nutsedge's ball. Lord Mosswing told me that he had heard His Majesty Silverthorn himself speaking to one of his retainers, saying I was a traitor to the Fair Court and should be detained. I fled immediately. Lord Mosswing gave me a token to open a door he had made for me; my magic is not sufficient on its own to even access the veil. He was able to get away and go with me to the doorway. He said he had prepared the way for me, and the passage should have been short. But once in, I could not find the way." He sagged, near fainting, and fell against Theo as the young man knelt beside him.

"It's all right. You've been very brave, my young friend." Theo examined the stone with misgiving. It seemed solid, and a quick pulse of his magic into it seemed to avail nothing. The stone was not entirely set; it seemed to flow very slowly around Juniper, and even in the short time Theo had been watching, it had crept an inch higher. In an hour or two, the young fairy would be entirely engulfed.

Theo frowned and tried a different sort of pressure on the stone, letting his magic spark and burn as it fought against the unforgiving stone.

"Have a drink." He handed the canteen to Juniper, then pulled out the bread. "You must be hungry. Do you know how long you've been in here?"

"Thank you." Juniper took the canteen and gulped desperately. Gasping, he forced himself to stop for a moment. "I can't tell. It's like eternal night. I've been parched." He rested his head against Theo's knee. "Thank you for coming."

His innocent trust only served to harden Theo's resolve.

Theo drew his sword and pressed the tip experimentally to the stone, which hissed as if it were water turning to steam. That sounded promising.

A dark shape flicked toward Juniper, and Theo caught it with one hand and ripped it from the wall. An eerie wail started by his ear, then stuttered into a disgruntled silence.

Theo flung the scaly thing in his hand into the darkness, then wiped his palm on his breeches.

Juniper shuddered beside him. "How do you do it?" he whispered. "The veil is horrifying to Fair and humans alike."

"I do what I must." Theo pressed his sword tip into the stone more firmly, and it sank in slowly, as if cutting through dense, tough leather. "If I cut straight down, will I injure your legs?"

Juniper shook his head. "Not that one. My left is out a bit behind me, though."

"All right. Let me know if it hurts." Breathing heavily with effort, Theo pushed the steel blade into the stone. Hissing and popping, the stone parted, and as Theo dragged the blade through the stone, it began to swell and pucker, like cut flesh.

When he had cut a semi-circle around the trapped young fairy, Juniper said, "Sir!"

A tendril of stone snaked up his torso and in a moment it had wrapped around Juniper's throat. The fairy began to wheeze, clawing at the stone.

Theo cut it at the base, and Juniper fell forward, gasping. The stone abruptly let go of his lower body, and he began to slide into the suddenly gaping hole.

Theo grabbed him under the shoulders and hauled him bodily out of the hole and some distance away.

Juniper wheezed and brushed terrified tears from his eyes. "Is it always like this?" he asked, his voice shaking. "I didn't give you enough credit."

"Not always." Theo eyed their surroundings cautiously. "I think it likes me, or at least has decided to ignore me most of the time."

"Most of the time."

Theo gave a low laugh. "Remind me to tell you about the time the ground disappeared under me and I fell into a great hall filled with a hundred thousand wasps and a hellhound furious that I'd woken them."

Juniper gave a startled laugh. "Somehow you survived."

Theo grinned at him and offered a hand. "Somehow. Come, you're always welcome at my house. We'll figure something out to get you home when His Majesty Silverthorn sees reason."

"Do you think he will?" Juniper accepted the hand up, then staggered into the wall, where he leaned dizzily. "I don't know that I'll be able to walk far, Theo."

"It's not far, but I can carry you if need be." Theo let the light fade.

Juniper flushed. "I'll make it."

"Just lean on me." Theo wrapped his arm around Juniper's slim shoulders and they started off.

CHAPTER EIGHT
An Invitation

Two days later a small crate was delivered to the Hathaway house in the city. The letter accompanying it read:

> Dear Sir Jacob,
>
> Please forgive me for my hurried departure at dinner two days ago. I deeply regret not being able to spend the evening with you and your family. If it isn't too forward, I would very much appreciate another opportunity to become better acquainted with your family.
>
> I had thought to suggest another dinner, but it occurred to me that spring is well underway and the gardens around our estate are already in full bloom. Next week I believe many of the roses will be blooming. Would you honor my parents and me with your attendance at a private garden party next Friday? We will begin with games on the lawn at 4:00, enjoy dinner, drinks, and dessert in the garden, and finish with more games or a stroll around the grounds.
>
> I look forward to your reply.
>
> Yours humbly,
>
> Theo Overton, IV

The crate contained a small burlap sack on which was pinned another letter addressed to Lily.

Dear Miss Hathaway,

Please forgive me for leaving so hurriedly. I had dearly hoped to spend the evening watching you smile, and had prepared several clever witticisms with that in mind. At least I had thought them clever at the time.

The plant which I have sent is a particularly beautiful rose which blooms the purest, palest pink I have ever seen. It is called Maiden's Blush. This specimen was propagated from one on our estate.

I do hope you like it.

Yours faithfully,

Theo Overton, IV

"He sent you a rose bush?" asked Oliver incredulously. "Is it an expensive one?"

"Undoubtedly." Sir Jacob looked into the burlap sack to see the root ball and the neatly trimmed canes of the bush. "The peonies certainly were. Where will you put it?" He addressed this to Lily.

"Perhaps by the south wall of the garden. It gets good sun." She looked up at him. "Will we keep this house after the season? If not, I should like to bring the plants with me when we return to Haven-by-the-Sea."

Sir Jacob hesitated, then said, "We will see. If we do not keep it, of course we will bring the plants with us. They are yours."

By that answer, Lily knew that he was concerned about the results of his investments.

Neither her father nor mother had ever hinted that she ought to marry for money. It was obvious they wanted her to marry well, of course, but that was for her own benefit, not theirs. They wanted her to be provided for and cherished, and they wanted her to be happy. They wanted her to be loved.

Sir Jacob wrote a polite acceptance and sent it with Susie's younger brother to the Overton estate. Lady Hathaway smiled encouragingly at Lily and said, "It will be a lovely afternoon, my dear."

The thought of the garden party made Lily's heart beat faster with excitement, though she was loath to admit it even to herself. She imagined Theo's sparkling smile and his exuberant enjoyment of life. Did he really love her already? Could love be that quick?

Surely not. She believed love developed slowly. Love ought to be entered into only after deliberation and careful exploration of each person's values and beliefs, their attitudes and little quirks. Surely, if Theo truly fancied her, it could only be infatuation.

She and Oliver visited the children's home again and spent a pleasant afternoon helping, or attempting to help, the caretakers with the children. Oliver read to the older children from a book of history which John selected for him, while Lily spent much of the time making mince pies with the younger children.

None of the children spoke of what they had experienced, and Essie had been quite emphatic that Lily and Oliver were not to question them. Lily's curiosity nearly got the best of her once. She had asked some of the children which activity they liked best at the house. It was intended to be well within the bounds of what Essie had said was permitted. One of the little girls said quietly, "Anything but dancing. I don't like dancing anymore."

Lily almost asked more, but bit her tongue. The poor child looked suddenly pale and tired, so rather than questioning her, Lily had merely knelt and asked if the girl would like a hug. Lily didn't have much experience with children, but it seemed the sort of expression that indicated a deep need for a mother's comforting embrace. The little girl stepped into her arms and rested her head on Lily's shoulder, shuddering, when Lily wrapped her arms around her.

Lily and Oliver returned home tired but elated. Perhaps they had not helped the Wraith himself, but they had provided some comfort to the children he had risked himself for.

Still, even with the visit to the children's home and several visits from Araminta, the garden party seemed to come too slowly. She wondered if she was infatuated with Theo, and decided that it was a distinct possibility. His gifts were both thoughtful and generous. His words were pretty and seemed sincere. Moreover, he was pleasing of face and figure, with beautiful manners and a delightful cheerfulness that made the world around him seem brighter.

It was logical that she was beginning to be a little infatuated. She cautioned herself that it was, it could only be, an infatuation. Love did not begin so quickly. Perhaps later she might love him, but this? This was merely excitement and pleasure at being so noticed by someone of undeniable charm.

She resolved to be logical and restrain her emotions. She did want to marry, of course, but she did not want to make a foolish decision because someone had lovely warm eyes.

Lily's resolve was tested three days later, when an extravagant bouquet of pink and coral roses was delivered by Theo's personal footman, Anselm.

He bowed and handed her the vase, which was unexpectedly heavy. "Would you like me to take it inside for you?" he offered.

"That's not necessary, but you're welcome to rest if you'd like before you go." The sun seemed especially hot this morning, and the footman was wearing a beautifully tailored coat that seemed too heavy for the increasing heat.

The footman gave her an astonished look, then smiled slightly. "I thank you, my lady, but my master has also given me another task with some urgency. I will let him know of your kindness."

"Thank you."

He bowed and strode back to the street, where his horse was tied. He mounted and trotted away.

Lily wondered what other task Theo had given him. What was involved in being the pampered son of a wealthy, aristocratic family?

She turned back to the vase of roses. The vase was heavy cut crystal, and the more she looked at it, the more grave her misgivings. It was a handsome gift, certainly, but it somehow seemed more serious than the wooden crates. His gifts had progressed from disconcertingly thoughtful and expensive to more openly romantic and possibly even more costly.

Dear Miss Hathaway,

May these roses convey the depth of my admiration and affection. I pray you find delight in them, as I find delight in your beauty.

Yours humbly,

Theo Overton, IV

She buried her nose in the roses and inhaled the sweet, fresh scent. It was heavenly.

CHAPTER NINE
The League

One afternoon Theo went riding in the countryside to meet several of his friends and allies. He brought Juniper along with him, and the young fairy had used a glamour to take the appearance of a blond, fair-skinned boy of about fourteen. His figure was the same, and Theo had acquired some clothes of the right size for him in unobtrusive colors and designs. Today he wore a white shirt, dove grey jacket and breeches, and unadorned, well-made riding boots. Theo had dressed in similar clothes, eschewing more ornate styles for this intimate group.

Just after lunch they rode out to the rendezvous point near the edge of the Overton estate on a little outcropping that gave them visibility over much of the nearby environs. They let the horses graze while they sat in the lush grass and Theo pointed out distant landmarks for his young friend.

Sir Michael Radclyffe arrived first, followed soon after by Lord Fenton Selby. Bernard Alexander, Sir Charles Bradbury, Sir Damien McNaught, Sir Andrew Whyte, and Lord Peter Roche followed in short order.

"All is well with you?" asked Theo, meeting each one's gaze in turn.

They nodded and murmured assent. Theo introduced them each to Juniper without mentioning the fairy's name.

"Who is your friend?"

"Before I answer, let me see if you can guess." Theo motioned Juniper forward to stand beside him. "Turn around, let them see all of you. Look closely, everyone. Who is this young man?"

They studied him.

"I don't know," said Lord Selby finally.

Theo smiled proudly. "Excellent. Juniper, please drop the glamour, if you don't mind."

Juniper appeared as himself. His clothes were unchanged, but his true face was thinner and sharper. His eyes were set a little farther apart and more slanted than in the human glamour, and they were a shade of teal blue not seen in humans. His skin was exceptionally pale, and his dark hair had distinctly purple tones in the sunlight.

He bowed to them politely and stood with his hands behind his back, trying to look unthreatening.

Theo put a reassuring hand on the young fairy's shoulder. "This, my friends, is Juniper Morel, one of our faithful allies in the Fair Lands. He was somehow discovered and the information passed from Lord Willowvale to His Majesty Silverthorn. Another of our allies was able to help him escape just in time. He had a rough time of it in the veil, too." Theo squeezed Juniper's shoulder and smiled. "So here he is. I wanted to test his glamour to see if it held up against scrutiny. I wouldn't trust it against Lord Willowvale, but against human eyes it is sufficiently convincing."

Lord Selby gave him a thoughtful look. "Would you put on the glamour again, please?" he asked.

Juniper obligingly did so, to the interest and further examination of the young gentlemen.

"That's fascinating," said Lord Selby finally. "I wish I had your talent. My gift is also glamour, and I've never been able to do anything more dramatic than make my boots look less scuffed than they are."

"It's because I'm a fairy, sir," said Juniper modestly. "The magic runs in our veins, and it's in the very air of the Fair Lands. We breathe it all our lives."

Lord Selby smiled kindly at him. "Yes, well, you use it well, and I am grateful for whatever services you have rendered to our leader."

Juniper said earnestly, "I owe him my very life! The veil almost ate me before he came to cut me out of the stone."

"Let's not tally favors among friends," said Theo hurriedly. "My point was to introduce him to you, and to see if you had any ideas on how we might use his talent here in the human world. I can't take him back to the Fair Lands until I sort out His Majesty Silverthorn. I need a lot more binding magic, and Juniper can help with that. What else might a young fairy's glamour be able to do for us?"

Lord Selby frowned thoughtfully. "I don't know. If Willowvale might see through it, or at least notice it, I doubt he could provide an alibi for you directly to Willowvale."

Juniper shook his head. "Nor would I be able to act the part, my lord. I do not know your world well at all, and although some of the conventions are similar, I would not like to inadvertently shame Theo by some misstep, after he has done so much for me."

Theo waved a hand dismissively. "Never mind that. Let me know if you think of anything, if you please. I was going to take him around the estate so that he may be a little more comfortable here. You're welcome to join us."

"I have a little magic for you," said Lord Roche. "I doubt it's much compared to what he can do, but I tried." He gave a crooked grin.

"Thank you," said Theo. "I'll take every scrap I can get."

All the men but Lord Selby shook his hand in turn, passing him what small bits of binding magic they had managed to produce since their last meeting. Lord Selby had no binding magic to speak of.

"What are you going to use it for?" asked Lord Selby.

Theo hesitated, then said, "I think you'd better just trust me on this for now, please."

Lord Selby gave him a flat look. "I'm not best pleased with that. How dangerous is it, then?"

With a cheerful smile, Theo replied, "That is a question I would prefer not to have to answer, my friend. The more magic I have, the better. My dear Juniper, I ought not be so pleased that you are here with us, but for entirely selfish reasons I am unspeakably grateful that you are."

Lord Selby's eyes widened. "I don't like the sound of that."

Theo clapped Juniper on the shoulder and said, "Come. Let us show you some of the most beautiful land in all of Valestria."

He whistled, and his two horses immediately began to amble back toward the little group.

"Up with you, now." He gave the fairy a boost into the saddle, then mounted his own horse. The others followed suit.

CHAPTER TEN
The Garden Party

A t last the day arrived.

Lily tried to ignore the flutters in her belly and the desire to try on six different dresses to see which one looked best. Instead, she held them up to look in the mirror and told herself that such a measure was less frivolous. She selected a lavender gown with a white satin sash. Indoors, she was afraid it was perhaps a little drab, but she thought it would show nicely against the green of the garden. She wove white and lavender ribbons into her braids before wrapping them about her head like a crown. The style made her neck seem slender and her shoulders elegant, though she was sure they were actually quite ordinary shoulders.

She told herself she didn't care whether Theo Overton the Fourth thought her elegant or lovely, but she knew it was a lie.

Her mother checked to see which dress she chose. When she descended the stairs, she was delighted and amused to find that her family had dressed to coordinate with her. Her father's jacket was a deep, dusky green, and his waistcoat was lavender. Her mother's dress was a deeper purple than Lily's, with cream lace and ribbons.

Oliver's jacket was a shade lighter than her father's, and his waistcoat a similar shade of pale purple.

"Was that entirely on purpose?" she asked with a smile.

Her father said, "Of course. We want to look good together."

"We look like we belong at a fancy garden party held at a beautiful estate outside the city," said Lady Overton seriously. "We do not want to look out of place. It's discourteous to the host and hostess."

Lily thought privately that the rules of courtesy in such high society seemed even more restrictive than she had imagined, but she couldn't fault her parents' logic. She certainly did not wish to be discourteous to the Overtons, regardless of whether anything serious resulted from Theo's interest.

Their hired carriage arrived, and they climbed in. Perhaps Lily was the only one who was nervous; certainly her parents and Oliver seemed relaxed. Why should they not be? They would not have to keep their wits when someone was smiling at them with effervescent delight.

Yet when they disembarked from the carriage, Theo did not meet them. Anselm opened the double doors and strode out to escort them up the steps.

Sir Theodore and Lady Overton met them at the top of the wide front steps and personally showed them through the foyer to the garden in the rear, pointing out the rooms where they might see to the necessaries and where the ladies might adjust their hair or attire if required.

"Theo was called away this morning on some business, but he should be back very soon," Sir Theodore explained regretfully.

"Is he called away often?" asked Sir Jacob. "I did not know he was so involved in your affairs."

"Oh yes, he's involved in many of my investments and the running of the estate. He was not best pleased to be called away this morning, but it couldn't be helped. All the same, he should have no trouble returning soon."

They began with croquet on the lawn. Oliver triumphed and was thoroughly congratulated by all.

After croquet they rested in the shade and enjoyed flavored ices while deciding on teams for lawn tennis. Just as they were about to begin, Theo strode across the grass to meet them.

"Forgive me for only just arriving. It is a pleasure to see you again, Sir Jacob, Lady Hathaway, Oliver, Miss Hathaway." He bowed to each in turn. His hair was damp, as though he'd just bathed and dried hurriedly, and his cheeks were slightly flushed. He bowed over Lily's hand and brushed a kiss as light as air against the tips of her fingers.

"Good afternoon, Theo," Lily murmured. She had not expected to feel so shy, but when he straightened and gave her that delighted smile, her insides felt fluttery.

"You've played croquet already, I see. I am sorry to have missed that. Have you had a chance to explore the garden yet?" He looked at the others, including them in the invitation.

"We have not."

"I would be most glad to give you a tour, if you would like."

As the ostensible host, it was appropriate for Theo to offer to escort Lady Hathaway, and he did so with perfect courtesy. She demurred politely, saying, "I thank you, but I am sure you would prefer to escort my daughter. My husband will escort me."

Theo then turned to Lily and offered her his arm.

Lily had all she could to contain her expressions of enthusiasm for the garden to a ladylike admiration rather than the unbridled delight she felt. White pebbled paths wound through banks of pink and white rose bushes in full bloom. Yellow, coral, burgundy, cream, and fuchsia roses filled the air with their sweet fresh scents, and the soft breeze carried the sound of birds singing.

Theo murmured to her, "Do you like it?"

"It's lovely," she breathed. "Do you come here often?"

"Not as often as I would like to." He smiled down at her. "Would you like to see my favorite nook?"

"Yes, please."

He said softly, for her ears alone, "You are so lovely when you smile, Miss Hathaway."

He led the group past a little pond where a mother duck shooed her six yellow ducklings farther away from the people. They turned down another graveled path past a weeping willow, and entered a hidden alcove surrounded by rhododendrons that were a riot of pink and purple blooms. A lilac at one end scented the air, and low-growing heather and dianthus fought for space beneath the taller bushes. A wooden bench sat between two peonies which were covered in a profusion of round buds.

"The peonies here are a pale pink; I've forgotten the name." He frowned in gentle frustration. "The rose there is Maiden's Blush, from which the one I gave you was propagated."

Lily covered her mouth, wishing she could hide her blush as well. She had assumed the gifts were merely exceptionally thoughtful, not personal as well. "Thank you," she murmured.

Sir Theodore said, "I believe the refreshments ought to be ready by now, if you would like to lead us back by way of the covered path, Theo?"

"Yes, Father." Theo assented readily and led them through a path covered by trees that trailed ten thousand purple blooms down through arched trellises over their heads. The light dappled their faces as the leaves above them moved in the breeze, and the effect as they walked was magical.

When they reached the tables set up near the tennis net, the refreshments were indeed ready. They spent almost an hour telling amusing anecdotes and enjoying cucumber sandwiches, salmon in green sauce, lobster salad, grilled chicken, grapes, melon, peaches from the south, lemonade, wine, and flavored ice. The interlude might have been awkward, but the Overtons were delightfully entertaining hosts.

When everyone was satisfied and ready to begin the long-awaited lawn tennis, Theo said, "Sir Jacob, may I speak with you privately for a moment?"

"Of course." Sir Jacob rose and followed Theo some distance away, where Lily lost sight of them behind a willow tree.

Some time later, Theo and Sir Jacob returned. Sir Jacob looked bemused but happy, and when he caught Lily's eye, he smiled proudly. What did that mean?

Theo asked, "Miss Hathaway, would you honor me with a short stroll? We will stay within sight of your parents." This assurance was unnecessary, for Lily trusted his sense of propriety absolutely.

She rose and put her hand upon his arm. He led her around the tennis court at a leisurely pace. Robins and other birds Lily did not know sang above them, and from a distant part of the garden she heard the distinctive call of a peacock.

They turned at the far corner of the tennis court and proceeded a little farther, until Theo drew her to a halt in front of an enormous purple rhododendron. He turned to face her and took her hands in his.

He took a deep breath. "Miss Hathaway, you must have perceived that I am entranced by you. Will you honor me with your hand in marriage?"

Lily blinked in wordless shock. He smiled at her, though his eyes were unwontedly serious. "Before you deny me, thinking me too impulsive or precipitous, I beg let me tell you a little more of my heart.

"My eyes perceive that you are beautiful, from your lustrous hair to your dainty feet. Your eyes sparkle and your smile is sweet and kind. Your family loves each other, and the lure of marrying into a family that is as loving as my own is powerful. Moreover, you are generous; I was informed that you and Oliver have visited the children's home more than once and were kind to the children.

"In short, my first impulsive feelings have been borne out by what I have learned of you. Please, Miss Hathaway, accept my adoration." He bowed over her right hand and kissed each fingertip, then repeated the gesture with the other hand.

Lily blushed furiously. Her hands were shaking, and she felt Theo's hands tighten ever so slightly upon hers, as if to steady them. He straightened.

"I... I... you hardly know me, though," she managed. "You are too kind, and you are overly generous in your estimation of me." Now why had she said that? She did not want to put him off; she wanted to understand.

He smiled a little, his eyes warm and bright. "I think not. I am delighted in your presence. I know there is much I have yet to learn of you, and much you have yet to learn of me. If you do agree to marry me, I pledge to spend my life learning how best to please you. I want to love you well."

She swallowed. "What did you tell my father to convince him to agree?"

Theo laughed low under his breath. "Only the truth, Miss Hathaway. That love is a choice, and I am determined to love you as well as any woman has ever been loved, in body and soul and spirit."

Lily was charmed, despite her best efforts. "I can find no objection, Theo, except to say that I don't want to disappoint you, after you have made such flattering assertions about my character and beauty. You are aware, I presume, that my family is not the equal of yours in society." The last statement was her last, futile effort to talk sense into him, because she realized, as she said it, that she didn't want him to change his mind.

He blinked. "Why on earth should I care about that?" He grinned, his eyes twinkling with irrepressible good humor. "Have you really no further objection?"

"None, sir." Her blush deepened further when he bent to kiss her fingertips again.

"Then you have made me the happiest man alive," he murmured.

CHAPTER ELEVEN
Planning Commences

T he wedding date was set for early fall three months hence, when the sun would still be warm but the breezes cool. Not only was it the first announced engagement of the season, but it would be the first wedding, and undoubtedly the most fashionable and extravagant celebration.

The wedding preparations took up much of Lily's time and attention over the following months and after the word of her engagement spread, she suddenly received dozens of invitations to tea, garden parties, dinner parties, and balls from families of high social standing.

While the son of a baronet was barely even considered hereditary nobility, the Overton family wealth had long kept them elevated in society and far more popular than their rank justified. Theo's father Sir Theodore had apparently been friends with the king for years, although Lily did not know the story behind that; that relatively recent connection to the throne also had given them more status than their rank would indicate. Theo's parents, and indeed the whole family, was considered not only likable but imminently respectable, and Theo's sparkling personality had only added to their popularity.

Oliver, too, became suddenly more popular, and was invited to go riding with various young men eager to show off the quality of their horses.

Oliver did not own a horse, and this might have been a social impediment among his new circle. The first note arrived from Lord Selby inviting him to go riding with Theo and several other young noblemen, and Oliver was about to write a polite, regretful refusal when another letter arrived from Theo.

Dear Oliver,

I was delighted to learn from Lord Selby that you would be joining us on our excursion next week. Allow me to offer you the use of one of my hunters. If you come to my family's estate an hour before the time noted in Lord Selby's invitation, I would be honored to have you meet them and select the one you prefer. Lord Selby's estate is a very short distance from mine, and we can ride there together.

Respectfully,

Theo Overton, IV

The following week, Oliver returned from the outing with wide eyes and a shocked expression.

"I take it you had a pleasant time," said Lady Hathaway.

Oliver seemed at a loss for words. "He gave me a horse."

"He did what?" said Sir Jacob in astonishment.

"I thought he meant to merely let me ride the horse for the afternoon, which was more than generous. His horses are beautiful, Father! They're all so well-trained and friendly. I selected a dark bay gelding named Dandelion, which he said was his newest hunter.

"I tried him out in the ring, then we trotted over to Lord Selby's estate, which is only three miles down the road. It is beautiful!" He smiled at the others. "There are rolling hills behind the two estates, so we took the horses on a long ride across the hills and back and forth over a little stream. Dandelion was a dream, nice and responsive, and eager to run.

"When we got back, we had ices on Lord Selby's lawn before Theo and I headed back to the Overton estate. We unsaddled and brushed down the horses, and while I was at Dandelion's head, Theo said, 'What did you think of him?' I said, 'I've never ridden better. He's beautiful.' Theo said, 'Would you like him?' And I said, 'Of course I would! Who wouldn't?' I thought it was just conversation, you know. Then Theo said, 'He's yours, then.' I tried to refuse, Father, I really did, but did you know that Theo can be quite stubborn?

I didn't. He's always been so agreeable, and yet he would not take it back.

"Of course I did say that we had no place here in the city to keep a horse; I didn't exactly say we couldn't board a horse somewhere, but he may have figured it out from my panic. He said he would be happy to keep Dandelion in his own stable until we had a place for him, but he's mine, and I should come and ride him whenever I wish. He told the groom to let me come and take him out at any time, because Dandelion is mine."

Poor Oliver looked as if his surprise still outweighed his glee, though the delight of riding such a lovely horse was sinking in.

"That horse must have cost a fortune," said Sir Jacob.

"Undoubtedly," Oliver agreed. "I asked him why he would do such a thing, and he said, 'Well, we are to be brothers, are we not?' What was I to say that? He'll be sorely disappointed if he expects an equivalent gift in return."

"I don't think he does," said Sir Jacob thoughtfully. "I really don't think he has any expectation of reciprocity, other than genuine friendship. I think that's just how he is."

Oliver looked at Lily across the table. "If it's a ploy to win my approval, so far it's working."

At a private ball a few days later, Lily heard a little more about the Wraith. Apparently, Lord Willowvale was beside himself with rage at the latest foray into the Fair Lands by the clever hero.

Araminta was not sure on the details, as the rumors had diverged into several versions, and Lord Willowvale had probably not provided much detail to begin with. What she had heard was that the children were dancing as usual, and a fairy they did not know came and waltzed them one by one off the dance floor under the noses of their overseers. Not all of them had disappeared, of course; even the most negligent fairy prison guard would notice if they had *all* disappeared. But eleven children out of some thirty had been slipped into the darkness.

No other details of the children's escape had made it to public knowledge. Lily happened to have visited the children's home that very morning, and although she had not seen the most recently rescued children, she had heard that the children had arrived the previous night.

Although she had visited the home several times by now, she was not entrusted with any information about the children, other than their names, or about their rescuer. Indeed, the very location of the children's home was meant to be a secret. However, this time she had heard Essie talking to John only by accident as she walked past a door with a little girl in her arms. The woman had said, "He takes too many risks."

"What would you have him do, then? Leave the poor souls to dance until they die?" John's low voice was nearly inaudible.

Essie's reply was lost among the clatter of children coming in from the garden.

Lily wondered what risks Essie meant. Did she know the specifics of what the Wraith did and how he did it?

When she was leaving that afternoon, she asked Essie, "May I ask how the Wraith gets the children from the Fair Lands to the human world? And how does he find them in the Fair Lands to rescue them?"

Essie gave her a flat look. "No, you may not ask."

"I…" Lily quailed at Essie's severe expression. "I'm sorry."

"Permission to visit here was given under the explicit understanding that you are to ask no questions and take no information out of this building or these grounds. Nothing. Will you abide by this?" Essie held Lily's gaze.

"Yes, I will." Lily's cheeks flushed. "I'm sorry."

Essie held her gaze a moment longer. "Be sure that you do," she said finally.

That evening, hearing the rumors of the children's rescue from what Lord Willowhaven had said earlier in the day, the audacity of the rescue took her breath away. The Wraith had masqueraded as a fairy himself and infiltrated the very dance floor of the Fair Court! He must be a formidable magical talent, as well as clever and capable in other ways. Yet he had carried out the brave plan unnoticed. How very fascinating!

Had a Fair ally been the one to infiltrate the dance floor, while the Wraith had merely been the children's escort through the veil? That would surely be more logical. Did he have Fair allies at all? Even if he did, such a rescue was daring beyond belief. He had been there, human in the middle of numerous Fair enemies, with children to protect.

How brave! How dashing! Lily's heart warmed toward the unknown hero, and she wished again that she might help him in some way.

Most people had some minor magical talent, but it wasn't much use. Some people were born lucky; they escaped childhood injuries with scratches and bruises rather than shattered limbs, and they won a few more rounds than was expected at card games or knucklebones. Some were fortunate when they farmed; their animals were fatter and healthier than their pastures would justify, and their harvests were rich. Some were gifted at their craft, and they made beautiful baskets, or swords, or baked delicious pastries.

No one, not even those of documented Fair Folk ancestry, could boast anything more than minor talent. It was enough to make life a little easier, but not enough to change the course of history. It wasn't even enough to change one's life, other than giving one reason to become a farmer rather than a milliner.

Did the Wraith have an unusually strong magical talent? Was that why he, or perhaps they, were able to navigate the Fair Lands? Was the Wraith even one person? Perhaps it was a team of people, a group of allies under one heroic leader.

Lily had such a minor talent she had never bothered to develop it much. Her talent seemed to be limited to minor changes in her appearance. She could make her eyes appear a little more gray or a little more blue, but they were still basically blue-gray. The effect wasn't much stronger than that achieved by wearing a different color dress, and faded within an hour or so if she didn't concentrate on it periodically.

She could make her hair stay in curls or elaborate hair styles without use of pins, but only for a short time before the magic faded. Pins were easier, because she didn't have to think about it. She could, if pressed, change the color of a fabric, and that effect lasted for an hour or two before fading. She had used this technique quite a few times when Father had been gone and they hadn't been able to afford new clothes. She couldn't fundamentally change the outfit, but changing the main colors and accents had given the illusion of a larger wardrobe than she possessed.

If she intended to go into the Fair Lands, she would need to develop her skill. What she would do there was a question for another day.

She experimented by changing the color of her eyes to a cold silvery blue, like that of Lord Willowvale. She did not like the effect; not only did she not look like herself, but the color seemed to wash out her face, making her look both unfriendly and slightly ill. Next she tried changing her skin tone, from a cool, pale tone through a warm mahogany. None of them seemed right, and what's more, none of the changes seemed remotely useful.

She didn't know how to seem like one of the Fair Folk in word or action, so making her appearance resemble one of them, however briefly, was probably of little use. Next she tried changing her skin to a rougher texture, like that of wood, then lichen. It was surprisingly difficult, but the effect seemed like it would be useful, if her imagined version of the Fair Lands were anything like the truth.

Her hair could be glamoured to look more like leaves, but she could not make the effect last more than a few minutes. With a week of practice, she could make her dress look like layers of leaves upon a forest floor for nearly half an hour.

Could she, perhaps, do the same with Oliver? Oliver was just as passionate to help as she was, but he had no gift of glamour. His gift was limited to the fact that his hair always held perfect waves, and his white shirts never stained, which, while both amusing and convenient, was hardly likely to be useful in this endeavor.

She had promised Oliver she wouldn't go back into the veil. How might she help the Wraith?

CHAPTER TWELVE
Lord Willowvale's Suspicions

T he Hathaways were invited to a ball hosted by Lord and Lady Pitts, the Duke and Duchess of Kaylin, which was most definitely a result of being gilded with the social popularity of the Overtons, especially Theo. It stretched the limits of their wardrobes to wear something that had not yet been seen at such an event, for doing so was not only gauche but bordering on disrespectful.

They arrived in a hired carriage; everyone else had their own coaches and drivers. Sir Jacob asked the coachman to return in four hours.

"Sir Jacob Hathaway, Lady Hathaway, Mr. Hathaway, and Miss Hathaway." The butler's voice carried over the music and sounds of merriment.

Sir Jacob led the way to Lord and Lady Pitts, where they paid their respects to the host and hostess. The prince was nearby, apparently listening to a quiet, funny anecdote told by Sir Theodore, with Theo, Lady Overton, Lord Selby, and Sir Michael in the same little knot of conversation. They paid their respects, and Theo immediately asked Lily for a dance.

He whirled her through the next reel, smiling at her the whole time, and directly into the next waltz, his eyes glowing. When the waltz ended, he swept her to the side of the dance floor to ask if she would like any refreshment before the next dance.

Theo leaned in a little closer to murmur in her ear, "You are so beautiful, Miss Hathaway. I do believe the room is brighter and the music sweeter now that you are here."

She blushed furiously, unable to think of a suitable rejoinder, and took a sip of the wine he had procured for her. Finally she managed, "Thank you," which seemed inadequate to her, but he seemed thoroughly gratified to see her smile and flushed cheeks.

Lord Willowvale accosted them at this moment. "Would you honor me with the next dance, Miss Hathaway?"

Having no excuse, since she had just danced with Theo twice, she assented.

The Fair lord took her hand with perfect courtesy and a cool look at Theo, who smiled warmly in response.

The dance was a slow one, with many formal turns and changes of partners. When he next strode beside her, he murmured, "You were in the Fair Lands, weren't you?"

Lily nearly froze with fear, but managed to keep her expression mostly unchanged. "Why would you say such a thing?" she asked. "How would I even get there?"

A cold, mirthless smile flickered over his face. "So it is true. Following your brother, I presume?"

She blinked. "Why would you think either one of us would go to the Fair Lands?" She realized belatedly that he had been guessing, and feared her weak denial had confirmed his suspicions.

They stepped away from each other for another turn, and she was faced with Lord Pitts for several moments.

"Your brother is a fine dancer," said the fairy when they met each other again, as if that fact were somehow relevant.

"Yes," agreed Lily.

"You have the gift of glamour, too. I see it on your dress." Lord Willowvale's icy eyes flicked up and down her dress.

He must see through the glamour she'd used to hide the fraying threads on her sleeves and mended tear near the edge of her skirt.

"Well, wouldn't you use a bit of glamour to look a little better dressed than you really are?" She felt strangely defensive. She wasn't ashamed of having little money; she was proud of her family and her father. Money didn't make a family or a man better, and indeed made some men worse.

The fairy smiled, startled, and said with a low laugh, "Fairies have no need of glamour to outshine any human. Pardon me, Miss Hathaway; I must go speak with your brother." He stepped out of the dance only a moment before it ended.

She followed at a cautious distance, both curious and concerned, though unsure what she could possibly do to help. Why did he want to speak to Oliver?

Oliver had been listening to Lord Radclyffe and several other lords discussing the merits of various fencing instructors when Lord Willowvale reached the little group.

"Oliver Hathaway," the fairy said coldly.

Oliver looked up. "Yes, my lord?"

"What business do you have in the Fair Lands?"

The little circle fell into a shocked silence.

Oliver paled. "None, my lord." His voice was steady, somewhat to Lily's surprise. He raised his chin. "Why?"

Lord Willowvale shifted, and Lily thought he looked like a snake about to strike. "I have reason to believe you were in the Fair Lands, and the only human adult who has ventured into the Fair Lands is the Wraith, and perhaps his sister."

Lord Radclyffe said stiffly, "I have no knowledge of the Wraith, but if young Hathaway were he, he would have allies here. Any man here would be honored to be so accused."

The fairy grinned, sharp and feral. "I have no doubt of that. Who here has the gift of glamour but for his little sister? I do wonder what gift you have, to be able to traverse the veil between our worlds."

Oliver glanced at Lily, then back at the fairy. "I am honored, my lord, that you think me so clever and courageous. If I were the hero, I would likely not admit it, but if I were not, I could hardly tell you about his methods."

Theo Overton appeared at Oliver's shoulder and said, as if he meant only for the fairy to hear, "My Lord Willowvale, it is unseemly to make such serious accusations at a ball. Pray contain yourself."

Lord Willowvale snarled at him, "Silence, you insolent puppy! I will conduct my investigation as I see fit!"

Theo blinked, as if innocently astonished at the fairy's anger. "Of course, my lord, but it may be to your advantage not to have *everyone* hate you."

"I care nothing for human regard." Lord Willowvale reached out and grabbed Oliver by the lower jaw, forcing the young man's face upward. Oliver was tall, but the fairy was taller, and his reed-thin body apparently held enormous strength, for Oliver tried in vain to pull away.

Lord Willowvale held Oliver's gaze, his lips curled in an expression of disgust.

Lord Radclyffe and the others were frozen in horror at the fairy's violence; two had reflexively reached for swords they were not wearing. Sir Jacob began pushing his way closer, but he was on the far side of the ballroom. He opened his mouth to shout, then apparently decided to hold his tongue.

Theo gently put a hand on Lord Willowvale's shoulder, ignoring the fairy's irritated twitch.

"My lord, contain your anger," he said, with a sharper edge of warning. "You will find yourself at a great disadvantage in your search for the Wraith if we are forced to perforate your insides with steel. I would much rather not, since you've been such a pleasant addition to our court, but I will if necessary."

The fairy held Oliver's gaze for another moment, then gave him a soft, contemptuous push away. "I don't think you're capable of what the Wraith has done," he murmured. "I could be wrong. He is apparently capable of appearing different than he is."

Oliver stood up straighter. "I am honored by the accusation, my lord, though I will confess that your assertion I am incapable of the Wraith's feats is a stinging insult. Out of the respect I hold for our host, I will overlook your ill manners and the insult."

The fairy laughed. "Indeed you will, for you do not wish to challenge me."

Theo said quietly, "Do not make yourself even more unwelcome than you already are, Lord Willowvale."

Lord Willowvale rounded on him with glittering eyes and bared teeth. "Silence, I said!"

"I am not *your* puppy, Lord Willowvale, and I do not answer to you." Theo smiled sweetly. "Just as you answer to your king, I answer to mine."

The fairy clenched his fists and glared, then looked around the ballroom, his eyes narrowing in thought. Lily sidled to Oliver's side and whispered, "Are you all right?"

"Fine." Oliver was trembling, though Lily thought it was more likely due to suppressed anger than fear.

Lord Willowvale said nothing when Theo gently shouldered himself between Oliver and the fairy, then edged Oliver and Lily further away.

"What a disagreeable guest," he murmured to them. "It really is most discourteous to attempt to provoke a fight at a social event. I commend you on your even temper, Oliver."

Oliver snorted and sent a glare over his shoulder at the fairy. "I wish I'd had your presence of mind."

Theo bowed gallantly. "I can be relied upon to have a ready store of pretty words for most occasions, and I am at your service." This theatrical behavior provoked the desired reaction—startled laughter from Oliver and a radiant smile from Lily.

Theo suggested to Lily, "Perhaps a dance might take your mind off the unpleasantness. Would you so honor me, Miss Hathaway?"

She smiled and put her hand in his.

"Oliver, I believe Lady Araminta does not yet have a partner for this dance," Theo said with a nod toward Araminta.

Oliver's expression brightened, then he shot a look at Theo. He leaned in closer to murmur, "Is it that obvious?"

Theo smiled conspiratorially. "No. I am a man deeply in love, and so I am exceptionally perceptive to signs of love when I see them. Go, then, and show your heart."

Oliver shook his head hurriedly. "How can I do that?"

"With courage!" Theo whisked Lily into the dance and gave Oliver an encouraging, "Go on, then!" before they moved across the floor.

When Lily and Theo were out of earshot, Lily murmured, "That was quite smoothly done. Whose interest did you notice first?"

Theo beamed at her. "His. I haven't had eyes for anyone but you since I first saw you, and when I had noticed her before, Oliver was not here to be pined over. I first saw him carefully avoiding any semblance of interest while sneaking surreptitious looks her direction at every opportunity. Then I saw she was doing the same thing, only with more batting of eyelashes and pretty little sighs. I take it this is a long-standing affection?"

Lily blushed. "Yes, although I confess I knew more of her side than his. I had not realized he was interested at all, much less that he was so smitten."

"Oliver and I are much alike," Theo said seriously. "I hid my affection for quite a long time before revealing it to you."

Lily giggled. "A matter of minutes, at most."

"It felt like ages." Theo spun her and brought her back to him. His murmured count helped her get back into the rhythm of the dance, and his hazel eyes danced in delight as she smiled her thanks.

The next morning, Theo spoke to his young guest over breakfast. "Juniper, would you mind very much letting me know what Miss Hathaway is using her glamour for? Lord Willowvale mentioned it last night and I can't see it myself."

"Do you think she is hiding some deformity?" the fairy asked.

"I shouldn't think her gift strong enough for that." Theo frowned.

"Would it matter if she was?" Juniper looked at Theo curiously.

Theo blinked. "No, I don't think so. I am just curious; I should hate to think that the kind look in her eyes or the sweetness of her smile are false, and she is actually sneering or mocking, thinking no one can see it."

Juniper nodded sagely. "You have not known her long?"

"No." Theo shook his head. "I was so sure, though. The hint, or potential, of being deceived is my only concern."

"When will I have opportunity to see her?" Juniper toyed with the last of the buttered toast on his plate. "I owe you so much, Theo. I really don't think you've any idea how terrifying His Majesty's magic is, or how cruel Lord Willowvale is when provoked."

Theo smiled at him serenely. "I am confident that I shall eventually find out. Until then, may I borrow as much binding magic as you can give me?"

Juniper's pale blue eyes widened. "I'd do nearly anything for you. You may have everything I can give."

"Thank you. I've been borrowing from the others, but you are quite a bit stronger, and I do believe I should like to bring this to an end within the next few months." Theo's smile wavered for a moment. "It's actually quite upsetting to see how terrified the children are, and I find no enjoyment in the rage that fills me when I think of the ones still waiting for rescue." He took a sip of hot tea and composed his face into his customary smile. "As for when you shall see her, I was hoping to call upon her this morning. I'll take a carriage, and you may accompany me. I'll deliver a vase of flowers and hope that she will come to the door to accept them. If she does, you will see her clearly. If she doesn't," Theo shrugged, "I will think of something else."

Theo strode quickly through the garden to the flowers he wanted for Lily's arrangement. Yarrow for everlasting love, in white because that was what the garden had and because it went best with the other flowers he wanted. Sweet woodruff for humility. Blue salvia, indicating that he thought of her. Lily-of-the-valley, for sweetness and purity. Blue asters, for patience and elegance. Finally, he tucked in several blue and white columbine flowers, indicating love and affection.

He stood back and looked at the arrangement, pleased with both the appearance and the layered meanings.

When he strode down to the front door, Juniper and Anselm were waiting for him.

"I can drive, if you think my glamour good enough to pass unnoticed as human," he said tentatively.

Theo shook his head. "I'd rather not risk it, at least not yet. Anselm, would you mind?" he asked the footman. "If you're busy, we can make other arrangements."

"I'll drive," said Anselm firmly. The servant's generous heart had already warmed to Theo's young guest. "It will be safer for you to stay inside the carriage, I believe."

When they drew up at the door of the house the Hathaways had rented for the season, Theo said, "Stay inside, if you please, Juniper. Just look out and see if you can identify what she's doing. If not, don't risk yourself by getting out. I don't want you seen yet."

"Yes, sir."

Theo frowned at him. "Don't *sir* me, Juniper. We're friends, not master and servant, and I'll thank you to remember it."

The young fairy nodded with a shy smile. "Yes, sir."

"It's bad enough when Anselm does it; I won't have it from you, too!"

Juniper gave a low chuckle. "Understood, sir." At Theo's scowl, he gave him a cheeky grin.

Theo hopped out of the carriage, straightened his jacket and collar, and then accepted the flower arrangement from Juniper. He strode up to the door and knocked.

Sir Jacob himself answered the door.

Theo blinked in surprise but kept his expression entirely composed. He bowed politely. "Good morning, sir! I was hoping I might be able to surprise Miss Hathaway with these flowers."

Sir Jacob's eyes widened, and he returned Theo's bow. "It's a pleasure to see you, Mr. Overton. My daughter and son went to visit the children this morning; they left less than an hour ago. Would you like to come in?"

"I don't mean to impose," said Theo. "But I would be grateful if you would deliver this to her, along with this letter."

Sir Jacob accepted the vase and letter and set them on the table inside. Theo tried to get a glimpse of the inside of the house without appearing rude. It was much smaller than he had expected; that was obvious even from the outside. The street was only separated from the house by a narrow garden, though the roses were blooming cheerfully. The front hall was narrow, almost cramped, papered in a slightly yellowed white on white damask. The parlor, partially visible through an open door, looked small but spotlessly clean. The dark green paper on the walls contributed to the close feeling. The end of a burgundy lounge chair was visible; the fabric was slightly worn but serviceable.

Sir Jacob turned back to Theo with a smile. "The flowers are beautiful. I thank you on my daughter's behalf. Would you like tea?"

"I thank you, Sir Jacob, but I have an errand I must run. Thank you for your kind invitation, and I do hope to see you again soon." Theo bowed deeply.

When he jumped back in the carriage, he glanced toward Juniper.

The young fairy shook his head. "I didn't see anything on the man."

Theo nodded thoughtfully.

The fairy ventured, "The house is smaller than yours. Which is more usual, for the human world?"

Theo glanced up to meet his eyes. "I should think something smaller and poorer than that, to be honest. Certainly my family is quite fortunate. My father has made a number of good investments, and he has taught me well. Such affluence comes with obligations, you know."

Juniper nodded seriously. "Of course."

CHAPTER THIRTEEN
Mundane Measures

T wo days later, Theo met Lord Cedar Mosswing at the appointed rendezvous location in the Fair Lands. They had known each other much longer than the conflict in Aricht and their alliance on behalf of the Arichtan children, and indeed had formed a deep loyalty when they were both mere boys. Before the war with Aricht, Lord Mosswing and Theo had held weekly fencing matches, and they traded victories as often as they had sparred. Most often Theo had met Cedar somewhere and they had traveled together to some remote location in the Fair Lands to practice, but they had also spent many happy hours on the Overton estate and on Lord Mosswing's estate not far from the Fair king's palace. Theo had become passingly familiar with much of the Fair capital and surrounding lands, though the Fair Lands were far too large for anyone to know well. Cedar's father, Lord Bitterberry Mosswing, had made it clear from the first days of their friendship that Theo was not entirely safe from other Fair Folk, and advised them to keep out of sight as much as possible. Lord Mosswing had died years before, leaving the title to his son Cedar, but by that time both Cedar and Theo had understood enough of the Fair Court to see wisdom in this discretion.

These meetings for fencing matches and exploration were when the two friends had honed their ability to traverse the veil and figured out how to send messages through the treacherous passages. The birds that carried their notes disappeared sometimes, lost in the veil or eaten by one of the many creatures that stalked the shadows of the veil. Even so, communication between the Fair Lands and the human world had never before been possible without actually crossing.

Moreover, Theo, and to a lesser extent Cedar, had honed his ability to pinpoint his friend's location. He could feel Cedar's location from within the veil, albeit with some concentration, and then open the door from the veil into the Fair Lands near his friend. However, he had not, as yet, been able to find anyone else in the Fair Lands from within the veil and open a door immediately beside that person. He also could not feel Cedar's location within the Fair Lands once he himself was in the Fair Lands. This baffled them both, but neither of them had been yet able to devise any sort of technique for greater precision from within the Fair Lands.

"You weren't followed?"

Cedar said, "No. Thank you for finding Juniper. Your honor grows by the day." He bowed his head briefly toward Theo. Cedar's eyes were a pale blue-green that shone against his walnut brown skin. His face was unlined, and his hair was an unexpected silver gray and stood out in ringlets around his face. His nose was strong and straight, and his mouth was grim. Theo had seldom seen him smile, but knew him to be both kind and honorable. They were opposites in nearly every way physically; Theo was fair, freckled, and buoyantly cheerful, while Cedar was dark and grave.

"Nonsense, my friend. I could not leave him in the veil! I am grateful for your assistance." Theo returned the brief bow.

"I had prepared the way for him. It should have been ten minutes' walk, at most. I expected a note from you the same night that you had received him safely."

"The way was long and circuitous, and the floor had begun to take hold of him by the time I reached him." Theo furrowed his brow. "Willowvale thinks someone else has been in the Fair Lands. He suspects Oliver Hathaway, and implied that he believed Lily is involved as well."

"Do they have any talent?"

Theo's doubtful frown deepened. "I had not thought so. Willowvale said Lily had a little talent at glamour, and I would not be able to see that if it were true, but I have heard nothing of Oliver's talent."

"Did one of them, or both, ruin the way I had made? If so, was it deliberate?"

"I cannot believe it of them. They have shown every evidence of being tender-hearted and compassionate. Although I suppose it could have been an accident."

"I heard someone there, just a moment before Juniper entered the path. But the door was closed when we reached it, and I saw no one."

"There was no way to identify them?"

"I could not feel any tug of magic. All I felt was that the doorway was still there, and I hurried Juniper into it. I had not thought to be able to accompany him that far. I did not think to recheck the way itself, and there would have been time if I had attempted it," Cedar said seriously. "There is another matter to consider. If the interloper was not one of them, and is not allied with you, could he be hunting you? Does the Wraith have enemies on the human side?"

"It is possible, but none have made themselves known. It is fashionable to be the Wraith's ally, as long as one assumes no risk in doing so. Lord Radclyffe, despite his flaws, nearly came to blows with Willowvale on the Wraith's behalf. It endeared him to me more than any of his lavish parties have."

"It would have gone poorly for Radclyffe," Cedar said grimly.

"Indeed. What manner of man can stand against a Fair Lord in combat?" Theo's eyes sparkled.

Cedar, startled, gave a low laugh. "Only a fool, Theo, too blindly focused on his goal to realize that he ought to lose."

Theo grinned at him. "I'll be a fool, then." More seriously, he said, "Have you been able to ascertain anything more about the magic they're using on the children?"

The fairy shook his head. "However, I did discover that His Majesty and his advisors have tried more avenues than I had previously given them credit for. This is a desperate ploy, not their first course of action. The land began fading when His Majesty Alder Silverthorn died just as the war with Aricht was beginning."

"Did Aricht do it?" asked Theo quietly. "They have never claimed it publicly, but everyone wondered."

"I don't believe so." Cedar's grave look grew even more serious. "I suspect it was one of the courtiers acting on His Majesty Oak

Silverthorn's behalf, but I cannot be sure. In any case, no one expected the fading of the land itself, and no one knew what to do about it. His Majesty does not seem to care for the land the way his father did, but he has tried nearly all manner of magic, with little success, to stabilize it. In desperation he turned to old legends of human captives. Our magic is often connected to dancing, and the legends often mention the captives dancing, so it seemed reasonable to him, or his advisors, to make the captives dance to strengthen the land."

Theo turned and peered over the wall, his eyes glittering with suppressed emotion. "Thank you, my friend. This is useful. I assume the focus on Arichtan children is punitive."

Cedar gave a slight, grieved shrug. "Perhaps. It also seems just to His Majesty to use the children of the nation he blames for the fading. If Aricht cost us something, Aricht should help make it right. But he does not have the same claim against Valestria or other nations."

"Was the murder on His Majesty's orders or only on his behalf?"

"I cannot say." Cedar hesitated, then added, "If I had to guess, I would say he was not aware of it until afterwards, if at all."

Theo nodded thoughtfully and looked over the garden wall again. "Ah, finally. Willowvale has just left. I'll bring the children out there." He pulled on his jacket and adjusted the collar.

The Fair lord looked where Theo pointed. "I see it."

"Take them to the tunnel. I'll go by a different way and meet you there. How do I look?" Theo glowered at Cedar and raised his chin.

"If I did not know your intentions, your facility as an actor would terrify me." Cedar's turquoise eyes flicked up and down Theo's form, noting every detail of his disguise. "All is as it should be."

Theo nodded. "Godspeed."

"Godspeed."

Theo slipped away through the garden to approach from another angle, while Cedar made his way toward the door Theo had indicated.

The Fair Folk had a good sense of the land, able to perceive the general outlines of the terrain and structures such as the palace without seeing them. According to Cedar and Juniper, Fair Folk could also sense the presence of the high entities, such as other Fair and humans, as distinct from animals such as the hart and ravusthin that wandered the hills, but they could not tell Fair Folk and human apart.

After much dedicated practice, Theo had just begun to be able to sense the presences of both human and Fair Folk, and the difference between them was discernible almost immediately. However, it took a great deal of concentration. Moreover, he could not identify any presence as a particular person. When Cedar asked about this sense, he could not explain how it worked, and they had concluded it was something like how the veil was more cooperative with Theo than with others. It was hardly reliable, but it was the best he could do at the moment, and the sense was especially helpful now that the Fair Folk had begun keeping the captive children in the palace itself. Theo could not, however, sense any of the lower entities, from the predators that ranged through the wilderness to the smaller creatures that frolicked around the royal grounds.

Fair Folk, of course, could do varying forms of magic, from commanding plants to do their bidding to taking the form of a stag, and could communicate more readily with dryads, naiads, and other sapient creatures. But without a demonstration of magic, or relative lack thereof, humans could look much like at least some of the Fair Folk. The Fair Folk had skin colors ranging from the pallor of Lord Ash Willowvale to deep ebony, with hair of any color of the rainbow, and eyes of many colors, in combinations not seen in the human world.

Theo, tall and lean, had perfected the haughty look in a mirror at home. Cedar had obtained Fair clothes for him and, cautiously, found a few Fair allies, including young Juniper. Theo had tested his Fair accent and carriage against Cedar before beginning the rescues.

The challenge, however, was that most of the Fair Folk, and all of His Majesty Silverthorn's soldiers guarding the children, were looking for a human. They did not know what he looked like, but any glamour Cedar might use to change Theo's appearance would attract their attention and invite suspicion.

Instead, Theo relied upon mundane measures. This time, he had dyed his auburn curls hair a deep purple with a mash of bitterblue blossoms and combed it into a ridiculous, gravity-defying fluff atop his head. He couldn't change the color of his eyes, but he rubbed dewberry leaf juice all over his face and the exposed skin of his neck, wrists, and hands, lending his fair skin a distinct greenish tint.

It didn't entirely hide the freckles across his cheekbones, but they were now a darker brownish green. He used a little more of the dewberry leaf juice mixed with a little charcoal to add more dark green freckles across his nose and cheeks and around his eyes. He rubbed the last of this under his eyes, along the sides of his nose, under his cheekbones, and under his jaw, making his eyes look hollow and accentuating the angular lines of his face and the length of his jaw.

The effect was, if not attractive, at least decidedly inhuman in a vaguely threatening sort of way. That was exactly the point.

Dressed in vibrant green and blue finery befitting a Fair noble, Theo sauntered through the garden and directly through the double doors of the palace. A servant bowed low to him, and he raised his chin with a haughty curl of his lips.

He continued on to the ballroom, where a small group of Fair nobles were gathered near one end. He surveyed the group, then sniffed and moved on to a sitting room. A Fair lady looked up at him from where she reclined on a window seat. Her hair was a soft turquoise, and her skin as pale as that of a naiad. Her cobalt eyes surveyed his elegant form with approval.

He strolled closer, looking around the room, then back at her.

"What purpose have you here, my lord?" she inquired.

Theo leaned over her to look out the window, then regarded her with his bright hazel eyes. "I have heard that His Majesty has human captives," he said coldly. "I want to see them."

She blinked in surprise. "They are not for the seeing, sir."

"You asked my purpose. I answered."

She laughed in a sound like crystal bells. "You are amusing, sir. His Majesty Silverthorn will enjoy arguing with you at least, though the conversation will be but short. I believe you may find him in the throne room, if you dare search."

Theo bowed to the Fair woman with icy courtesy. "I thank you." He turned on his heel and left the study, moving down the hall. Now, at least, he knew where the king was. Many of the other Fair Folk would be either attending him or seeking a boon from him.

When he passed a hallway to his left, he felt the faintest indefinable tug of humanity. He turned and followed the hall to another door to a stairwell, which he followed upward. He strode through a maze of corridors, following the vague sense he would have felt difficult to describe, if anyone had asked him.

He stalked down the upper hallway toward a large, ornate door, behind which he felt the small, frightened presences of the children. The door was guarded by two fairies with violet skin and golden hair that fell to their shoulders like molten sunlight. They wore the resplendent indigo and silver uniforms of His Majesty Silverthorn's royal guard, with the indigo-chased scabbards of swords at their hips.

"This way is not open," one of them said sternly.

"It is to me," Theo snarled. "Do you know who I am?"

"You are not His Majesty, so the way is not open." The guard placed a hand on his sword hilt.

Theo stopped and looked down his nose at the guard who had spoken, ignoring the other. "I am Lord Meadowhawk, and His Majesty himself told me—nay, he *begged* me—to see what the problem was with the human captives. They are not working as they should, you know."

"How so?" The guard did not remove his hand from his sword hilt.

"Have you not noticed the edges crumbling?" Theo scoffed. "Are you so blind to the effects on the land?" He turned to the guard who had not yet spoken. "You, remain at your post. You, what is your name?"

"Campion," the fairy answered reluctantly.

"Campion, come with me and I will show you." Theo reached past the fairy and opened the door, curling his lip in scorn at the other guard's move to stop him.

He pulled the door open and strode through first, as an arrogant Fair lord would. The room was blindingly bright; two walls were made of fairy glass and let in the brilliant sun, while the other two were gilded. The floor was polished white marble that reflected the light into their eyes. The only objects softening the harsh brilliance were three vines which climbed up the gilded walls and curled across the ceiling. Their leaves were as long as Theo's arm and gleamed deep green veined in luminous gold.

The children were clustered against the gilded wall as far as possible from the door. About half of them were asleep, and the other half looked up in apparent terror when the door opened.

Theo ignored them. He dragged the guard across the room, trying not to squint, and pointed out the window. "Look!" he barked.

Campion followed his pointing finger.

Far in the distance, the deep indigo forests were not as distinct as they ought to be.

"Do you see that? *That* is the magic fading, Campion. *That* is what the human children are not able to solve, dance though they may. Look there!" Theo whirled and pointed at the mountains to the south, which should have been pink-tinged but now seemed gray. "Does that look right to you?"

He turned back to the guard, his eyes wide and passionate. "That is what I'm trying to fix."

Campion stared at the window. "Why is it gray?" he murmured thoughtfully. "I had not noticed that."

"The very land beneath us is sick, Campion," said Theo, his voice shaking with controlled fury. "I need to examine the children to figure out why, and how to fix it."

Campion nodded once, his gaze still fixed on the mountains. "Do it."

Theo stalked over to the children and surveyed the little group. He glanced back over his shoulder to see that the guard was not yet looking, then raised a finger to his lips. He mouthed *Trust me.*

Two of the oldest, a boy and girl who looked to be about eleven or twelve, understood immediately. Their eyes brightened, but at Theo's stern look they controlled their expressions.

One of the youngest girls began to weep quietly, and turned to another child, perhaps a sister.

Theo said, "Wake them," and indicated the children still sleeping. The four who had not yet woken were difficult to rouse, and stared blearily at him even once they were sitting up. There were dark shadows beneath their eyes.

Theo snuck a quick glance over his shoulder again. The guard had ambled closer.

"This one," Theo nudged one of the closest boys with the toe of his boot, "is sick. I think that one and that one may be as well." His lips curled as if the children and their ailments disgusted him. "I am taking them to His Majesty. I will consult with him about my findings."

"You will not take them," said the guard in disbelief. "We have been charged to guard them."

"Not from His Majesty," countered Theo scornfully. "What could happen between here and the throne room?"

The fairy frowned.

"On my head be it if I let them out of my sight." Theo straightened.

Campion's mouth twisted doubtfully.

"Unless you'd rather watch the forests lose their color and crumble like the mountains," murmured Theo. "On your head be that."

Campion glanced out the window and let out a troubled breath. He nodded. "All right. Take them to His Majesty, then. I will escort you to the throne room."

Theo snarled, "I can control a few exhausted human children. I'd be happy to prove it with a blade if you like."

"On your head be it if they're stolen by the Wraith, then." Campion glared at him.

Theo glared back with all the arrogance of a Fair Lord for an underling, but did not deign to reply.

"Come, humans." He snapped his fingers and tapped his foot while the children scrambled to their feet. He didn't help them when another of the youngest began to cry quietly, though his heart twisted within him. One of the older children took the child's hand, and they set off down the hallway.

The guards watched him lead the children all the way down the corridor, so he snapped his finger again impatiently as he stood at the top of the stairs and shooed the children down ahead of him. They clustered like frightened ducklings around the oldest two.

When they were out of sight of the guards, Theo murmured, "Trust me, children. I'm here to help you."

"Are you the Wraith?"

"I am." He smiled warmly down at the little girl, his eyes dancing with mischief. "I am sorry I frightened you. Walk with me a little longer, and pretend to be afraid."

"My feet are tired," whispered one of the little ones, no more than six.

"I will carry you later," promised Theo. "For now, we must maintain the ruse, do you see? I am terrifying, and you are brave but despairing and alone."

The children nodded, trembling.

He led them through deserted hallways of gilt and sapphire, of fairy glass that showed scenes of fantastical monsters. The children gasped as a fanged, winged horse seemed to lunge at them from a mirror, and Theo covered a little girl's eyes and drew them onward.

At last, they reached the door where he was to meet Cedar. He had avoided all other Fair Folk to this point, but there was one outside with Cedar now, and he did not delay longer.

He opened the door and snapped his fingers at the children. "Out!" he barked, his voice all impatience and snide condescension.

Cedar gave him a surreptitious glance of warning, then said, "My lord, I am honored to introduce Lord Ash Willowvale, Special Envoy of the Fair Court to the Valestrian Court."

Theo wished desperately he had been able to discern the identity of the Fair lord before he had opened the door, but now there was nothing for it but to brazen his way through.

He gave a slight, arrogant bow, as if he outranked Lord Willowvale, and ignored the children, looking instead to Cedar.

The dark lord said, "Lord Willowvale, I am honored to introduce Lord Polyantha Meadowhawk."

Lord Willowvale gave a cursory bow, his eyes raking up and down Theo's clothes and back to his face.

"What are you doing with the captives, Meadowhawk?"

Theo narrowed his eyes. "They aren't working, Willowvale. The king's ploy is failing, and he asked me to find out why. Do you oppose His Majesty's efforts?"

Lord Willowvale blinked and studied Theo with suspicious eyes. "Where are you taking them?"

"What business is it of yours?" Theo snapped. "You have no authority over my assignment, which comes directly from His Majesty himself. Go ask His Majesty for an easier assignment if you cannot manage the one you have been given." He smiled coldly. "Go to the children's room and look at the mountains if you want to understand my urgency. Your task is trivial in comparison."

Willowvale hissed out a long breath. "Your arrogance will cost you, Meadowhawk," he murmured, still looking at Theo suspiciously. "You remind me of someone."

Theo snapped his fingers at the children and pointed at the path imperiously. Cedar took the hint and began to take the children down the path, though with a gentleness to his manner that struck terror into Theo's brave heart.

He stepped to the side, drawing Willowvale's attention back to himself and away from Cedar and the children. "Of the king, no doubt. I do hold his authority in this, and he will not be pleased to find that you have delayed my investigation. I bid you good day, Lord Willowvale." His icy bow was so slight as to be an insult, and the fairy took it as intended.

"I cannot say the same, Lord Meadowhawk," Lord Willowvale snarled. "However, I do look forward to the results of your efforts."

Theo turned his back on the fairy lord and walked away with his head high. When he was out of sight of Lord Willowvale, and sure that the fairy was not following him, he lengthened his strides. Only a little bit farther!

His Majesty Silverthorn's magic was so strong as to prevent anyone from opening a door to the veil close to the palace. Theo had conjectured once that it might be possible, but it would surely draw far too much attention, and he might be so exhausted after doing so that the escape would be of no use. Instead, after every rescue from the palace they were forced to flee some unknown distance away from the palace, until the feel of the king's magic had faded enough to allow the door to be opened quickly.

"That might have been it for you, my friend," he murmured as he caught up with Lord Mosswing.

The fairy gave him a sideways look of suppressed mirth. "We shall find out. I can plead innocence as well as anyone. If Willowvale himself did not recognize you, it will be difficult for him to accuse me with any credibility."

One of the little girls whimpered, and Theo swept her up in his arms. She shuddered against him, terrified of him, Cedar, Willowvale, the quivering golden flowers that brushed her shoulder as Theo carried her, and the sound of a hunting horn in the distance.

Theo stopped suddenly at an enormous tree with a sapphire blue trunk and fuchsia leaves that rustled and danced, though there was no wind.

"Here." It was closer than he would have liked to the palace, and the king would no doubt feel the door open, but if the hunt were already on, time was short.

He pressed his hand to the tree trunk and shoved with his magic, twisting it in between the fibers of living wood, pushing and pressing and pulling it open with a rush of effort that left him light-headed. He leaned his forehead against the blue bark and closed his eyes.

"Get them inside," he whispered.

Cedar ushered the children into the slender gap in the tree trunk. Theo let the little girl slide down, and Cedar gently pushed her into the veil. The king's magic battered at Theo's mind, and he blinked stars from his vision.

"Come." Cedar caught Theo's arm and tugged him to safety.

Theo let it close behind him only a moment before the hunt rushed through the clearing.

"Don't be afraid, children," he said. His voice was almost steady. "Tell me your names." He cared for them, certainly, but it was also a chance to let the dizziness fade and to get his bearings in the darkness.

Frightened voices answered him. Josie. Gertie. Beth. Tamsin. Violet. Julie. Tom. Alfie. Richard. Chloe. Loren. Grace.

"Who is too tired to walk?"

Three children shuffled their feet, but only one murmured something close to assent.

"I will carry you. Don't be afraid," Theo said. He knelt down. "Feel my shoulders here? Climb on my back, just like that." One of the little boys climbed on his back and wrapped thin arms around his neck. "There, see? I'm not frightening after all, am I?" He smiled into the darkness, knowing they would hear it in his voice. "Would you like me to carry you too?"

The little girl nodded, then whispered, "Yes, please."

Theo caught her up in his arms and stood with a huff of effort. The stars in his vision reappeared. Cedar put a hand against his shoulder for a moment to steady him.

"You're a good man," the fairy murmured into his ear. "I am glad to know you."

"Where shall we take you, my friend?" said Theo. "The other side of the garden?"

Cedar thought. "Yes."

Even Cedar did not have the facility with the paths through the veil that Theo did. It would be faster and safer for Theo to open the door for him to reappear some distance from the Wraith's path than for him to do it himself.

"Hold hands," said Theo. He waited until everyone had linked hands, then said, "Hold my jacket, please," to the nearest child. Cedar took the hand of the last child in line, and, so linked, they set off through the veil with Theo in the lead.

Ten minutes later, Lord Mosswing quietly joined a group of Fair Folk discussing the audacity of the Wraith, who had taken all twelve children out of the king's very palace. Theo had, as usual, left a slip of paper with a little drawing of the fairy rose on it, this time tucked in the sleeve of one of the guards in charge of the human captives. Campion, the guard, was pleading his innocence before the king.

The fairy rose was a hardy, unpretentious little flower that bloomed in many colors, though the most common was pink. It looked much like the wild roses of the human world, but Cedar was reasonably sure they were unrelated.

Months before, Theo had begun leaving these little slips of paper to pique the curiosity and anger of His Majesty Oak Silverthorn. Cedar wasn't entirely sure whether that was a valid purpose, but besides Theo's obvious delight in provoking the haughty Fair Folk, he had another purpose which he had not yet shared with Cedar.

"The mountains trembled," said one of the Fair ladies. "I could feel it through the ground. It must have happened as they left the Fair Lands."

The Fair Folk looked toward the distant peaks tinged a faint gray-green beneath the brilliant sky. Cedar thought, for a moment, that even the sky looked less vibrant in that direction, but told himself it was only his imagination.

Theo, his dearest friend, had promised he would figure out something to save the Fair Lands. The dark lord, full of misgiving, saw the grey shadows flickering across the mountains, and how the peaks had grown less distinct.

Time was indeed running out.

CHAPTER FOURTEEN
Family Concerns

L ady Hathaway said over breakfast one morning, "Lily, today I will begin practicing on your hair."

"Why?" Lily looked at her mother over the rim of her teacup as she took a sip.

"For the wedding." Her mother added carefully, "I do not think it necessary to hire a woman to do what I am perfectly capable of learning. We have nearly two months before the wedding to practice. I am sure we can agree on something lovely in that time."

Lily's confusion turned to pleasure. "I would love to have you do my hair, Mother." She added more softly, "Is Father well? Is something wrong?"

The men had already retreated to the study upstairs.

Her mother shook her head. "He is fine. Some of the ships he invested in have not yet arrived and it seemed wise to me to be frugal where we may. Do not be concerned, Lily; if I cannot do something satisfactory with your lovely hair, we will spend the money on a maidservant."

She flushed. "I'm not concerned about that, Mother; I am only concerned for Father, if there is anything to be concerned about."

"Your father will take care of his own concerns. He would not want you to worry." Her mother's smile was warm. "Your Theo will not be dissuaded no matter how simply I may do your hair. He is indeed quite smitten. Nevertheless, I do want you to be happy with your hair. It is an important day, and I want your memories to be entirely pleasant."

After breakfast, Lily visited the children's home with Oliver again and spent a pleasant morning with the children. Lily spent an hour teaching the oldest girls how to choose flowers from the gardens and then arrange them in vases. Oliver and John spent much of the time discussing the finer points of men's table etiquette in different social settings. None of these boys would need a nobleman's manners, but it would be beneficial for them to know how to comport themselves well enough to obtain positions in noble households. These were the orphans and street children, abandoned and alone before the Fair Folk had taken them from Aricht, and the thought of service in a noble household made some of them flush with hope.

There was a murmur of activity about the house even more pronounced than usual, and Lily wondered quietly if she would ever be entrusted with any more information. But she did not ask Essie anything.

Just before lunch, a few minutes before Lily and Oliver were to leave, Lily's charges had been given into the care of Sadie for washing up. Essie bustled into the kitchen and began slicing an enormous loaf of bread into thick slices. She got a block of butter from the cellar and a glass jar of honey, then poured a liberal amount of honey into a glass bowl. She cut chunks of soft butter into the bowl, then mashed the honey and butter together with quick sure strokes. The woman's brows were drawn together.

"Are you all right?" Lily asked gently.

"The poor dears," the woman muttered. "Some new ones came last night." She glanced up at Lily and added, "Don't say *anything*, you hear? The poor children have suffered enough."

Lily nodded. "The Wraith is very brave," she ventured.

Essie nodded, and Lily realized with shock that tears were sliding down the woman's cheeks. She silently proffered her spotless kerchief.

Essie huffed out a tearful chuckle. "I'm all right. Thank the good God above for the man."

"I do," murmured Lily. Without even noticing when she began doing so, she included the Wraith when she prayed at night for those she loved.

CHAPTER FIFTEEN
Smitten

"Would you come with me to the dance at Lord and Lady Hastings' manor?" Theo asked Juniper. The young man was already dressed in fashionable pale green silk that set off his bright copper hair and fair skin. His bright white lace cravat was tied in the newest style. "If we get there early, it is likely you will be able to see Miss Hathaway when she arrives."

"If you would like me to," Juniper said obligingly.

They set off in a carriage with Anselm as the driver, and spent the ride in companionable silence. Juniper said after some time, "Is glamour not a common gift among humans with magic?"

"Not at all, and when humans have it, it's never near as strong as that of any fairy." Theo glanced at him. "You've said before that no one will miss you while you're here, Juniper. I am sorry for that, but I wonder whether you might not be as happy here as in the Fair Lands, even once it's safe for you to return."

Juniper looked at him with wide eyes. "What do you mean?"

Theo smiled. "Only that you are welcome here for as long as you want to stay. Just keep it in mind."

"Thank you." The young fairy ducked his head and smiled.

When they arrived, Anselm positioned the carriage so they could see later arrivals as they stepped out of their various carriages and walked toward the door.

The Hathaways arrived in a hired carriage some time later. Sir Jacob jumped out, then Oliver, and the two men offered their hands to Lady Hathaway and Lily. All four of them were clearly visible in the graveled path before they reached the steps.

Theo looked toward Juniper.

The young fairy smiled, his bright eyes glowing with warmth. "The glamour is the most innocent thing you can imagine, sir. All I could see was that it hid the worn spots on her dress and a mended rip."

"That's all?"

Juniper nodded. "What I saw wasn't strong enough to do much more than that even if she'd wanted to. Perhaps she could do more, but I doubt she could make a stronger effect last long."

Theo made a thoughtful *hm*. "Thank you, Juniper. I hate to ask you to wait out here, but I believe Lord Willowvale was invited tonight."

"I don't mind at all, sir. I have—"

Theo sighed in mild exasperation. "Don't *sir* me, please, Juniper. Please."

The young fairy sighed as well. "I owe you a blood debt, Theo. You may discount that as an archaic Fair custom, but to me it is a weight and an honor. How can I treat you as an equal when you're my elder, my social superior, my leader, and my benefactor?"

Theo gave a soft groan. "Juniper, you're entirely too humble and kind for this world, much less the Fair lands. Let us put the argument aside for the moment. Would you prefer to wait or have Anselm take you home? There's dinner for you in the basket there, but I hate to think of you just sitting here bored."

"You said I could read your books earlier," Juniper said tentatively. "I took the liberty of borrowing one for the evening. I hope that was all right."

"Of course. Can you read it here?"

"Oh yes, I can see the words clearly. We have better night vision than you humans," Juniper replied cheerfully.

"All right." Theo stepped out of the carriage and turned back to his young friend. "If you get bored or Lord Willowvale seems to be paying too much attention or anything at all, please ask Anselm to take you home. He won't mind."

"Yes, sir." Juniper smiled at Theo's aggrieved expression.

Theo stopped to speak quietly to Anselm, who had already reclined cheerfully on the wide, padded driving seat. Then he strode up the wide steps and greeted the footman with a smile.

Several minutes later, the footman at the door of the ballroom boomed, "Theodore Overton the Fourth." The resulting buzz of excitement and conversation made it difficult to find Lily for a moment. He greeted Lord and Lady Hastings, the host and hostess, as well the prince and several others, all the while looking for his beloved.

At last! He saw her near her brother, who was speaking with Lady Araminta. Theo hid a smile at the faint flush in Oliver's cheeks. If Lady Araminta had noticed it, it might have encouraged her, but she seemed equally shy and flustered.

Theo greeted them with a bow. "Miss Hathaway. Lady Araminta. Mr. Hathaway."

"Mr. Overton." They bowed or curtsied in turn.

"Miss Hathaway, might I hope that you will honor me with this dance?"

"You might. I believe now that we are engaged, it is to be expected that I will honor you with several dances." She smiled and put her hand in his.

He beamed at her, then, as he drew her toward the dance floor, he lowered his voice and murmured, "Yet I do not take the honor for granted. I am more delighted every time."

"You must be positively enraptured."

"I am," he said, his voice warm and kind.

The footman intoned, "Lord Ash Willowvale, Special Envoy of the Fair Court."

A distinct chill greeted this announcement.

Theo ignored the new arrival as long as he could, but at the end of the dance, he said in a low voice, "Please excuse me, Miss Hathaway. His Royal Highness appreciates my support when dealing with Lord Willowvale."

He bowed deeply over her hand, and she watched him curiously as he strode toward the prince.

Lord Willowvale had, as was proper, first greeted the host and hostess with a bow, then greeted His Royal Highness. By the time he had finished bowing to the prince, Theo was at the prince's side and greeted the fairy with a courteous bow.

The fairy gave a stiff, unfriendly bow and turned to look across the room, his eyes flicking from face to face. His gaze lingered upon Oliver Hathaway, who was dancing with Lady Araminta, and he said to the prince, "Do you know the identity of the Wraith, Your Royal Highness?"

The prince blinked at such a direct question. "If I did, I would not tell you."

The fairy's lips twisted in something like a smile. "What do you do with the children who are stolen from us?"

"That is not any of your concern," said the prince more forcefully.

Theo said quietly, "It seems the Fair Court has more ability or more inclination to steal children from Aricht than from other nations. Why might that be?"

The fairy shot a sharp glance at him. "Why should you want to know that?"

Theo gave him a wide-eyed look of innocence. "How will we know how to avoid the same fate if we don't know what provoked it in the first place?"

Lord Willowvale's lips curled in scorn. "You cannot avoid it. The Fair Court will do what it must, where it must, when it must."

Theo straightened. "Here I thought *my* aristocratic pride was perhaps a bit unchivalrous." He looked at Lord Willowvale in awed admiration. "You, my lord, have humbled me."

Lord Willowvale muttered, "You halfwit!" He stalked away.

The prince leaned closer and murmured in Theo's ear. The taller man nodded, his attention never leaving the fairy.

Lord Willowvale appeared to be interested primarily in Lady Araminta, whom he accosted as young Sir Michael Radclyffe was about to dance with her.

"What do you know of the Fair Lands?" he said, shouldering Sir Michael neatly out of the way so that he faced Lady Araminta squarely.

She blinked at him. "Nothing, except that your people are prone to stealing defenseless children."

His eyes blazed with fury, and he said, "I did not ask what you know of *us*. I asked what you know of *the land*."

Oliver was suddenly at Lady Araminta's other side. "Why should she know anything of your land, other than that you have abominable manners? Leave her alone." He edged between them, though he offered no physical threat to the fairy.

Sir Michael took the opportunity to pull Araminta away, then stood at Oliver's shoulder.

Theo reached them just in time to say, "Lord Willowvale, I have no idea what argument you have with Lady Araminta, but it seems to me that you have decided to make yourself as offensive as possible to as many people as possible while you are in Valestria. Is there a reason for that, or is it merely your natural habit to court antipathy?"

This achieved its desired result of turning Willowvale's attention back to Theo.

The fairy rounded on him with hatred blazing in his eyes. "You utter nitwit. Silence your yapping before I silence you myself."

Theo took a half-step back and bowed politely. "How would you propose to do that, my lord? I would wager nearly everyone here would gladly join you in the attempt to get me to stop talking."

At this ridiculous rejoinder, Araminta's nervous fear overflowed into a giggle. Oliver snorted, trying not to laugh at his friend, and Sir Michael chuckled.

Theo gave Lord Willowvale a sparkling smile and turned away, shepherding Araminta and Oliver before him. "I do hope," he said over his shoulder, "that you choose to enjoy Lord Hastings' hospitality rather than harassing innocent maidens with unfounded accusations. It is most unseemly."

The titter of laughter that followed, emanating from Araminta, who was near tears with nerves, Oliver, who had decided to follow Theo's lead in brushing off the fairy's discourtesy, and spreading to everyone within earshot, made Lord Willowvale narrow his eyes in irritation.

His gaze followed them all the way through the next dance.

Oliver felt the fairy's shrewd attention as they exchanged places in the rows. "Please don't think of him more, Lady Araminta. He does not deserve your attention."

Araminta smiled tremulously up him. "I know. He has such a cruel air about him; I hate to think of the Wraith facing him."

"I'm sure the Wraith knows what he's doing," Oliver said confidently.

"I'm sure you're right," Araminta murmured.

Lord Willowvale smiled quietly to himself.

The Fair Court's Special Envoy to the kingdom of Valestria watched with interest as Oliver Hathaway called upon the Duke Brickelwyte, Lord Liam Poole.

The Poole family had a spacious house in the city not far from the Hathaway residence, which Lord Willowvale watched off and on for months. The Hathaways were of interest due to their sudden popularity in the Ardmond social scene, but that was clearly due only to their proximity to the Overton halfwit.

Lord Willowvale had probed every noble family multiple times over the previous months, both directly and indirectly, comparing their absences from parties and social events to the accounts His Majesty Silverthorn sent him of the Rose's known visits to the Fair Lands.

It could, of course, be assumed that the Rose had at least one, if not more, allies in the Valestrian court. If that ally were clever enough, there might effectively be two Roses, who split the duties and thereby avoided suspicion.

The sudden popularity of the Hathaway family had raised a new possibility. Lord Willowvale had previously assumed that the Rose must be a nobleman, for the manners of a Fair Lord were not so easy mimicked by a commoner, or one who had no experience in the rarified atmosphere of the human court, much less the Fair Court.

He had recently realized that this had led him to discount the possibility that someone of slightly lower status might be responsible. Someone like Oliver Hathaway, whose absence at most parties and social events would not even be noticed, much less remarked upon.

The boy was young and clever, and he certainly acted the part of an innocent well enough to put off suspicion. But through both his own meager connections and that of his father, he had somehow managed to befriend young Sir Michael Radclyffe, son of Duke Radclyffe, and thereby gain an invitation to a party that catapulted the entire family into prominence by way of Theo Overton's interest.

Oliver Hathaway could not have foreseen that his sister would have been so successful in her bid for a good match. It must have put him in quite a bind, as it now brought him also to prominence.

Lord Willowvale had set one of his servants to watching Oliver Hathaway for some time, just as they had watched the comings and goings of other families for periods of time. Of all the many men he had considered as the Rose, only Oliver Hathaway, and oddly enough his sister Lily with him, had been absent from the garden party that took place the day the traitor fairy disappeared.

The obvious conclusion was that the Rose had helped his Fair ally escape, and that Oliver was the Rose. The Rose would undoubtedly have prioritized the safety of his young ally over yet another social engagement.

Some pieces of information did not entirely fit; Oliver had an air of diffidence that did not lend itself to the belief that he was the bold and daring Rose, who had quite literally waltzed children out from under the noses of their Fair guardians.

Nevertheless, it was not impossible to imagine Oliver Hathaway assuming a more timid personality than he in fact possessed. It would certainly be a good cover. He had friends both noble and common, in his own little hometown and here in Ardmond, even before his rise in social status.

The wide streets and generous yards of this prosperous section of Ardmond did not lend themselves to easy surveillance, but Lord Willowvale was not above using a light glamour to avoid notice. He was much more talented at natural magic, with an affinity for plants, especially vines, but all fairies were easily capable of producing a glamour sufficient to fool human eyes.

Effecting another's manner was much more difficult, and Lord Willowvale, as all fairies, knew it was next to impossible to convincingly pretend to be someone known to the person with whom one was conversing, especially while avoiding outright lies. Instead, it was much easier and often more useful to pretend to be someone fictitious, and to avoid talking when possible.

Lord Willowvale had assumed the appearance of an utterly forgettable errand boy and thrown himself at the base of an enormous oak tree near the elegant entrance of the Poole estate. He lay back against the tree with his eyes half-closed in thought, with a satchel of excellent bread and cheese, a cold sausage, a canteen of water, a flask of brandy to take the edge off his boredom, and an as-yet unopened book near to hand.

Oliver Hathaway had arrived at the estate by way of a hired carriage. The Hathaways were apparently rather more poor than they wanted to appear; Lord Willowvale had immediately seen through Miss Lilybeth Hathaway's minor glamour upon her worn dresses. Lord

Willowvale had not previously considered how this affected Oliver's apparent interest in Lady Araminta; it was bold indeed for a son of a knight, of little means, to attempt to court the daughter of a duke, even one of only slightly greater means.

Oliver was welcomed in to the Poole house by a servant, who seemed familiar with him. Lord Willowvale had expected the visit to be relatively short, as human convention required at this point in a courtship, but he waited nearly two hours before Oliver exited the house.

The boy was smiling and slightly flushed, as if embarrassed but simultaneously delighted, and he bowed, still smiling, to the Duke, who had personally walked him to the door. When the door closed, he turned and began jauntily walking down the street.

Lord Willowvale threw the remains of his brunch and his book into his satchel and followed, intrigued.

The boy walked all the way home, a matter of only a mile and a half, but still it surprised Willowvale; humans who considered themselves part of the nobility did not often voluntarily walk through town, and certainly did not cheerfully whistle as they did so.

The boy was utterly and completely smitten.

CHAPTER SIXTEEN
An Invitation and a Letter

*D*ear Sir Jacob,
      I would be honored if you and your family would join my parents and me for a picnic luncheon next Thursday at 11:00 am. I eagerly await your reply.
      Respectfully,
      Theodore Overton, IV

The letter arrived with an extravagant arrangement of white calla lilies and chrysanthemums, deep purple heliotrope, green ivy and marjoram, and petite purple violets.

Lily regarded the arrangement with growing admiration. The letter for her that came with it read:

      My dearest Lilybeth,

      I hope it is not too presumptuous to call you that, since we shall be married in a few months. The time passes too slowly for me, and when I think of spending my days with you, my heart beats faster.

      If you were to receive one gift on your wedding day, what would you like it to be? How might I make that day pleasing for you?

      With utmost respect and tenderness,
      Theo

Lily covered her shy smile with a hand while looking back at the flowers. Theo was undoubtedly better versed in the language of flowers that had grown in popularity in recent years.

She ran upstairs and brought down the book Araminta had loaned her several weeks before. White chrysanthemums were truth, she knew that already, but what were the others? She flipped through the pages, feeling increasingly warm with embarrassed delight. Calla lilies were for beauty. Heliotrope was for eternal love and devotion. Ivy was for fidelity, marriage, and friendship. Marjoram signified joy and happiness. The little violets indicated loyalty, devotion, faithfulness, and modesty.

The arrangement was a gift and a promise, and the strength and beauty of the sentiment brought tears to Lily's eyes.

Shortly afterward, there was a knock on the door. A little boy presented a note to her that read:

Dear Lady Hathaway,

I am honored to produce your daughter Miss Lilybeth Hathaway's bridal dress. Please respond with a date and time for a first fitting at your estate.

Most humbly,

Mrs. Frances Collingwood, of Collingwood Apparel

Lily asked the boy to wait a moment and brought the note to her mother.

"I haven't contracted anyone for the dress yet," her mother said with concern. "I don't think Collingwood is within reach, either. You know that studio does the most extravagant of court apparel."

"I had heard," Lily said, frowning. "But I don't imagine they would resort to dishonesty to gain your business."

"I hadn't thought so either. Let me think."

Eventually her mother sent back a note that read:

Dear Mrs. Collingwood,

I am honored by the thought of having my daughter's dress made by your studio, but I must confess I had not thought it possible, given your busy schedule and the demands of those of more ready means. If you do have the time, my daughter and I will be free this Wednesday at 2:00 pm.

Sincerely,

Lady Hathaway

The note was meant to quietly note the Hathaway's limited budget, but Lily feared it was not clear enough. Lily gave it back to the boy, who was waiting, along with a few pennies for his trouble and to buy a snack on his way back to the clothier.

Nearly three hours later, the same boy was back, flushed and breathless at hurrying halfway across the city twice in one afternoon. He presented another note to Lily. She brought it to her mother, who read aloud:

Dear Lady Hathaway,

I will be honored to attend you and your daughter Wednesday at 2:00 pm. Please be assured that there is no one of higher importance in my schedule than your daughter, and my staff and I are delighted at the prospect of designing something to her, and your, satisfaction.

Most sincerely,

Mrs. Collingwood

"Well, that seems to brook no argument," her mother said with misgiving in her voice.

Lily said confidently, "We won't use them if it's too expensive. I'll tell them, if you don't want to."

"You shouldn't have to do that," said Lady Hathaway. "I suppose there's no harm in receiving them. Perhaps they are more reasonable than I fear."

Lily thought privately they were likely even more horrifyingly expensive than either she or her mother imagined, but did not say so. They could always refuse to continue with the arrangement after the consultation.

CHAPTER SEVENTEEN
Thrilling Heroics

T he message Theo received from Cedar the next morning indicated that the most recently stolen children were held in two different locations, both within Lord Willowvale's estate just east of the palace.

Theo examined the map he was making of the palace and its surrounding grounds, as well as the larger map of the Fair Lands. The palace itself was a rambling structure of at least one hundred rooms. Theo had not had opportunity to explore it thoroughly yet, but had come to the tentative conclusion that although the hallways sometimes shifted and rearranged themselves, the ground floor probably stayed upon the ground and the second floor stayed atop it; the east wing stayed generally to the east and the west wing generally stayed to the west.

Cedar had enclosed a sketched floor plan of Lord Willowvale's estate, caveated with a note saying that he had not been inside in several years and did not know how much the hallways might have moved, or if they did at all.

Theo blew out his breath and compared the map of the general area to Cedar's drawing of Lord Willowvale's estate and the tentatively sketched outlines of the edges of the king's magic that surrounded the palace.

He made his plan, then went to the east wing of the house to let Sir Theodore and Lady Overton know he was departing.

"Mother, Father, I'm leaving with Fen and Juniper for the Fair Lands. If you have any binding magic available, I would be most grateful if I might have it."

His mother looked at him doubtfully but handed over the little amount she had. Juniper would have been able to see it, but Theo couldn't. The young fairy had described it once as a sort of neatly folded crimson thread, although somehow it *felt* crimson rather than *appeared* crimson. "Is it always crimson?" Theo had asked with interest.

"I think so. I haven't felt any other sort of binding magic, anyway."

Now his mother said, "What are you doing with the magic, Theo?"

"I really don't think you will be happier knowing, Mother." He leaned down to where she sat with a book open in her lap and kissed her cheek. "Please trust me."

"Will you try to be at least a little bit safe, please?" She held his gaze.

"I will not do anything unnecessarily foolish," he promised with a smile.

"Be careful, son," said Sir Theodore, pressing his scrap of magic into his son's hand.

"Someday!" said Theo cheerfully.

"Godspeed."

Theo bowed to both his parents, watched them bid the young fairy farewell with admonitions to be safe, retrieved his sword and one for Juniper, and then strode quickly to the stable with Juniper following on his heels, already glamoured to appear human. He saddled his horse and helped Juniper saddle a well-behaved gray mare. Then they hurried to the Selby estate only a few miles away. A footman ushered him in to see his friend, who was in his personal study.

Lord Fenton Selby stood to greet him. "Good morning." He gave Juniper a half-bow, which the young fairy returned more deeply.

"Are you free for a trip?"

"Now?"

"Yes."

Lord Selby blinked. "All right."

"I suggest a sword this time," said Theo.

Lord Selby belted his sword on without a word and followed them out to the front door of his manor.

"I've gotten a better feel for the openings around our estate, and I can get us much closer to home now." Theo turned them back toward the Overton estate, striding across the hillside in a direct path rather than on the road. "In another week or so, I believe I should be able to pinpoint the location well enough to arrive back in my own garden. But for now, I think the closest easy opening I can find is about half a mile east of here. We might as well walk, if you don't mind."

As they walked, he explained the plan. "I'll open a doorway as close as I can to Lord Willowvale's front door. We should be so close to the palace that it would be much harder to open from the Fair side, so I'll leave you, Juniper, there, to keep it open so I don't have to open it again. Once it's open, you shouldn't have any trouble from the inhabitants of the veil. If you do, just let it close and I'll open it again if I must.

"Lord Selby, you and I will open a new door, where Lord Mosswing will meet us. He will have Fair attire for us, as well as some colored powders for our hair and skin. We will don our disguises, such as they are, and will approach the estate from this direction. You will be as close as possible to the door, so you might be visible. I will enter, find the children, and bring them to you. I expect there will be some difficulty, so after I have delivered the children to you, I will likely need to create a diversion. Take the children to Juniper and wait. I will join you. If the pursuit gets too close, retreat into the veil; Juniper knows how to close the doorway behind you. If you have to retreat into the veil, just stay where you are and I will find you."

A moment later, Theo stopped just before they reached a little copse of aspen and maples. "This is a good place. Are you ready?"

Juniper nodded.

"Before we set off, I do have one thing to say, Theo," said Lord Selby.

Theo smiled encouragingly. "Yes?"

"I really did not think you were this serious about Miss Hathaway." Lord Selby bowed.

Theo winced. "Thank you. I am sorry, my friend. I was a little abrupt that night."

Lord Selby smiled tolerantly. "I've never seen you so entranced. I couldn't be irritated because I was too amused."

"Truly?" Theo looked at his friend more seriously. "I do mean it when I say I'm sorry. It was rude of me. I meant to be charming and instead it was probably boorish."

"Well, I won't pretend I didn't envy you the admiring looks I saw her cast your direction. But please accept my sincere congratulations. You deserve the happiness I see in you, and I think she might actually be kind enough to deserve you, too." He looked down. "I do hope you will speak well of me to the next delightful young lady with kind eyes, though."

Theo said quietly, "I will not be able to prevent myself from the highest compliments. Thank you."

Lord Selby flushed. "Well, let's get on with the heroics, then. Is there really nothing else you want me to do other than wait outside?"

"Lord Mosswing believes the children are held in two different rooms within the estate. It will be challenging enough to find them. By the time I get to you, there may be more than enough opposition for the both of us to have the opportunity for heroics. I am glad to have you."

Theo led them unerringly through the veil, although they were plagued by a shadow that followed them at a distance for nearly ten minutes, growling at intervals.

"What is that?" asked Lord Selby eventually, with a hint of concern in his voice.

"Last time I heard a growl like that, it was... I'm not exactly sure. Something like a bear, perhaps, but not made of flesh and fur. The brief glimpse I got of it looked like thread or ropes knotted in interesting ways."

"Did you kill it?" Juniper asked in awe.

"No, I had children with me and didn't want to fight. I left the veil when it got too close. We explored some distant part of the Fair Lands for a while, until I hoped it had left or we were far enough from it for safety."

The growl sounded closer.

"Will we do the same this time?" Juniper asked.

Theo stopped to listen, pulling the others closer to him. It was challenging at the best of times to navigate in the veil, and the sound echoed and carried most strangely. Theo had privately suspected that not only did the tunnels themselves shift and turn when one wasn't looking, but that the inhabitants themselves were more nearly part of the veil itself than animals.

In a low voice, he said, "We're almost there. Keep hold of my jacket, if you please. Lord Selby, if you would be so kind as to take the rear position with drawn sword, we'll put Juniper between us."

Stout-hearted Lord Selby agreed. Careful with the swords in the darkness, they arranged themselves so that Juniper held their sleeve or coat tail with one hand and the two young human men brandished their swords.

The wall of the veil now felt like damp, crumbling bricks covered in an odd, trailing lichen. As Theo trailed his hand along it, waiting for the magic to feel just right, he wore an unconscious grimace at the clammy fibers that clung to his hand.

"Here," he said at last.

Just as he began to press his magic into the wall, Lord Selby let out a startled gasp and began to thrash.

Theo let go of the wall and brought a burst of light to his fingertips. Juniper cried out in fright when he saw the monster.

Lord Selby stabbed and thrashed with his sword but could not reach the body of the monster. The hulking figure remained out of reach but had sent rope-like tentacles forward from its mouth, or what Theo thought of as its mouth. The largest of these had wrapped around Lord Selby's throat.

"Watch your sword!" cried Theo. He lunged around Juniper and attacked the monster himself.

Lord Selby gave one last futile effort to cut the tentacle and then dropped the point of his sword. Juniper joined Theo as he stabbed at the base of the tentacle choking Lord Selby.

The monster abruptly dropped his victim and retreated into the darkness.

Theo hauled Lord Selby to his feet and opened the door, ushered Juniper out first, tumbled out with Lord Selby, and then whirled to stick the point of his sword into the gap as the door nearly closed with a snap. He pulled it back open and pressed a little of his magic into it, checking the corridor in the veil for threats before looking around.

Lord Selby put his hands on his knees and wheezed.

"Sit down, Fenton," Theo said. "You're all right." He kept a watchful eye on the bushes around them. They had emerged quite close to the east wall of Lord Willowvale's manor house, and though he did not hear any voices, there was no guarantee that they were alone.

Lord Selby shook his head, too proud and stubborn to fall to his knees, but still seeing far too many stars to risk standing upright yet.

Juniper said encouragingly, "That was horrifying. Have you been in the veil often, sir? That's courageous."

Lord Selby shook his head again and rasped, "Third time. Theo's barking mad if he does this every week."

The young fairy stifled a laugh. "Here is your sword, sir." Lord Selby had dropped it as Theo pulled him out of the veil, and the fairy carefully picked it up by the leather-wrapped hilt and handed it back to the young man.

Lord Selby managed, "You don't get enough credit, Theo."

Theo blew out his breath. "I'm sorry. It's always dangerous, but I hate that it seems to target you more than most. The veil has only tried to kill me two or three times."

Lord Selby gave an almost inaudible groan. "It's because I'm so lucky. You should bring me as a distraction more often and you'd get off without a scratch every time."

Theo frowned at him. "Don't say that, or I won't bring you back at all. You know it grieves me."

Lord Selby straightened slowly, rubbing at his throat and wincing. "It was a joke, albeit a bad one. Thank you from the bottom of my heart."

Theo looked at him doubtfully. "If you're not ready, we can wait a little longer. Lord Willowvale is supposed to be in the human world until at least tomorrow."

"I remember what air feels like now. Do we leave Juniper here?" Lord Selby rolled his neck, then his shoulders, adjusted his jacket, and took a deep breath. He smiled at the fairy. "You, my young friend, were wonderfully brave. I owe you a debt as well. Thank you."

"You're welcome, my lord." Juniper flushed and ducked his head.

The Wraith looked around and said, "Yes, we'll leave you here, Juniper. If anyone gets too close and you need to escape, go into the veil. I'll find you as soon as I can. Lord Selby and the children will attempt to meet you here." Theo looked toward Lord Selby. "If the door is closed, just keep going away from Willowvale's estate and any sound of pursuit. I believe I will be able to open a door near you once I'm in the veil myself. I'll make a distraction if necessary and follow you as I may."

Juniper and Lord Selby nodded.

Theo drew most of the borrowed binding magic from his fingertips and pressed it to the ground. It sank in without a sign, but Theo felt the vague tug and warmth somewhere near his heart before it faded. The remaining whisper twinged uncomfortably, then the sensation faded. "They won't pinpoint that, will they, Juniper?"

"No."

Theo led Lord Selby back into the veil. "Hold my jacket, if you please. I'll keep my sword ready. You may wish to do the same."

Only two minutes later, Theo opened another door to the Fair Lands and stepped out with Lord Selby on his heels.

"Good morning, Lord Mosswing," he greeted his Fair ally.

"Good morning, Theo, Lord Selby," Lord Cedar Mosswing replied. "It is good to see you again." The fairy bowed politely.

"Likewise." Lord Selby bowed in return. "Please call me Fenton. I think we're united in purpose enough to be called friends, even if it has been far too long since we've been on the same side of the veil."

Cedar nodded soberly. "Thank you. I am honored. Please do likewise."

"What do you have for us?" prompted Theo.

Cedar knelt and rummaged in a sack on the ground. He pulled out two jackets and two pairs of trousers. One set was a brilliant yellow and orange, while the other was a muted teal with magenta piping and golden embroidery across the shoulders.

Fenton looked at them with ill-concealed dismay. "How are we to remain unnoticed in those?"

Theo said confidently. "You will remain unnoticed in the teal. I will be bright as a beacon if I need to draw them away from you. The Fair Court adores color, and if we wore our fashionable human attire, we'd draw all the wrong sorts of attention, like a dead nettle in a bouquet of roses. We must be vivid to blend in."

The young men turned away from each other and pulled on the Fair trousers. There was a silky shirt with a green and blue pattern on it for Fenton and a fuchsia shirt with silver embroidery for Theo. They buttoned the Fair shirts on over their more subdued white human shirts. Theo transferred a steel key from his own trouser pocket to the orange ones he was now wearing.

Fenton pulled on his borrowed jacket and looked down at himself in horror, then covered his mouth to stop a burst of laughter at Theo's appearance.

"This is the most appalling thing I have ever seen in my entire life," he muttered. "Those colors with your red hair are a deeply lamentable combination, Theo."

Theo shrugged. "Indeed. However, I console myself with the knowledge that the one person whose opinion of my looks I truly crave is not here to laugh at me." He swept his gaze up and down his friend. "Your hair is dark enough it would be difficult to change, but we can make it harder for anyone to identify your face, if they see you again, with the aid of these colored powders."

With a clinical attention to detail, he instructed Fenton to put bright blue powder under his eyes in a dramatic sweep back to his temples.

"What is this for?" the young lord said with grave misgiving. "It won't hide my eyes or my face."

"No, but it draws attention away from what you really look like, and that's enough for now."

Theo applied a bright orange powder to his own face in a similar pattern. He rubbed a little yellow powder along his hairline and the hollows of his cheeks.

Cedar shot an amused glance at Fenton when the latter shook his head at Theo's expression of satisfaction.

"How do I look, Cedar?" Theo asked seriously.

"Not like yourself."

"That will do. Cedar, would it be possible to glamour some sort of distraction on the opposite side of the manor? I'd like to pass as few people as possible on the way in."

"Yes, but at least some of them will be able to identify it as my magic if it lasts more than a few seconds."

Theo blew out a thoughtful breath. "What about some sort of fascinating creature, a griffin or the white stag they so seek, flying through the garden in plain sight and disappearing just around the corner? The magic would disappear quickly but it would draw people to it, I should hope."

Cedar nodded. "All right. You shall have a white stag running from there toward the palace." He pointed.

"Excellent," Theo said to Fenton. "Come on."

They managed to avoid nearly everyone on their way to the wide door of the manor house. When they had almost reached the door, from the corner of his eye, Theo saw the white flash of the promised stag sail away over a hedge, and a burst of excited chatter arose behind them.

Fenton leaned against the wall and crossed his arms as if he were bored. Theo slipped inside the unlocked door and tried to get his bearings.

The hallway in which he found himself was empty, which was a welcome grace, but there were several Fair Folk in nearby rooms. The faint tug of humanity was difficult to identify among the myriad Fair presences throughout the building. He strode resolutely down the hall, glancing in rooms as he went.

At last he found a door guarded by a bored-looking fairy with golden skin and hair.

"What's behind the door?" said Theo conversationally.

The fairy gave him a narrow look. "None of your concern." His scarlet eyes flicked up and down Theo's brightly colored outfit and back to his face.

Theo laughed coldly. "Actually it is my concern. Lord Willowvale sent me to check on them and make sure they were ready for dancing when he returns."

"I don't know your face," said the fairy.

"I don't know yours either. What of it?" Theo raised his eyebrows. "You're welcome to watch if you like."

The fairy's eyes narrowed. "How do I know you aren't the Rose?"

Theo snarled, "How do I know *you're* not the Rose? Lord Willowvale will have both our heads adorning his garden gate if you don't let me carry out my assignment."

The fairy grimaced. "All right. Don't touch them. I'll stay with you at all times."

Theo watched with an expression of cold satisfaction as the fairy opened the door. The group was only five of the eight children Theo knew were currently held in the manor.

"Dance!" He snapped his fingers at one of the little girls.

She shot to her feet and took a few tentative steps.

"That's enough. Now you." Theo glared at another girl, who obeyed, trembling. "Enough." He turned to another.

He made each of the children take a few steps, and his tender heart twisted at his own cruelty. But now they were on their feet, and there was an alert wariness to them rather than that terrifying stupor he'd seen at first.

"Clasp hands, all together now. We're going upstairs."

"What?" exclaimed the fairy.

"You can come, watch dog," snapped Theo. "I need to see them together. There's an art to the dance, you know. It needs to have a rhythm to it."

The fairy blinked. "Oh." He followed them out warily, his hand never far from his sword.

Theo led the children and their captor up the nearest stairwell and down the hall. The room that held the remaining children was clearly identifiable in that it was guarded by another fairy.

"Well, open it up!" Theo barked.

"Why?"

"So Lord Willowvale doesn't put all our heads on his garden gate as decorations," he snarled. "He's coming back tonight and I need to be finished by then."

The fairy hesitated, glancing between Theo and the fairy beside him, then opened the door. "Go in."

Theo swept into the room with an imperious gesture to the children to follow him. The fairies watched cautiously from just inside the doorway. Theo had each of the children stand up, then had them all line up beside the door.

"Go stand there against the wall," he said coldly, indicating the corridor wall opposite the room. The children hurried to obey.

One of the fairies said, "You can't take them out there."

Theo drew his sword and indicated the fairy should step back into the room the children had just vacated. "I can and I will."

The two fairy guards drew their swords, and Theo, by dint of both surprise and superior skill, forced the fairy back a step.

He narrowly avoided being gutted by the other with a sidestep and a lightning-fast parry. He flicked the tip of his sword up to tap the fairy on the cheek with the flat side. For a split second, the fairy froze in shock, and Theo lunged forward to shove him hard, refraining from running him through. The fairy stumbled back two steps.

Theo pulled the door closed in their faces, dropped the sword, and held the handle while he dug in his pocket with his now-free right hand.

A scream of rage erupted from the other side of the door, and the handle jerked, nearly pulling the door back open. Theo huffed with effort as he kept it closed. He pulled a steel key from his pocket and jammed it in the lock, then shoved the last of the binding magic into the lock for good measure. The rattle abruptly ceased, though the sound of agitation and fury on the other side increased. Theo removed his hand from the handle and picked up his sword, keeping a cautious eye on the door for a moment in case the combination of steel and magic didn't hold.

The children had watched this play out without a sound, their eyes wide.

Theo turned to them with a smile. "Don't be afraid. We're going back to the human world, where you'll be safe."

One of the girls, who looked the most clear-headed of the group, said quietly, "Are you a fairy?"

Theo raised a finger to his lips and murmured, "I'm the Rose, or the Wraith, or whatever you want to call me. Come on, then. Let's get you home."

They met no other challenges before they emerged at the door where Fenton waited, trying to look inconspicuous. Just as the last child emerged from the hall, some sort of uproar began in the hall behind them. Theo closed the door and turned to the children with a smile.

"This is a friend. He'll take you safely to another friend, and they will take you into the veil and wait for me there. Go quickly, now. I'll wait here for a moment to be sure they see me, and then head that way," he said to Fenton, pointing in a different direction.

Fenton said, "Follow me, children." He led them away with his head held high, affecting as arrogant an attitude as he knew how. Theo waited at the door, listening to the growing commotion within as it approached the door.

At last Fenton and the children were out of sight around a bend in the garden path. Theo waited another few seconds, then pulled the door open just as someone was about to reach the other side.

"Hello!" He beamed at the startled fairy. "Are you looking for someone?"

CHAPTER EIGHTEEN
Gifts

L ily and her mother dressed nicely, then busied themselves with chores, embroidery, and reading for most of the morning. Lily practiced on the piano; it had been weeks since she had practiced any at all, so distracted had she been by the children and thoughts of the Wraith, not to mention the whirlwind romance with Theo. She warmed up her fingers and began to practice some of the more challenging pieces she knew.

A young lady was expected to be accomplished in many arts, and although she was not a talented painter or poet, she had acquired a little skill through practice. Music came more naturally to her, and she was quite a good pianist. She did not have the skill of a prodigy or an inclination to compose, but she enjoyed the practice. She had a good ear and a sweet, clear voice, though not particularly strong. It was reassuring to have met at least this qualification for a young aristocratic lady, and it would be wise not to let herself get too far out of practice.

She was still playing when Susie welcomed Mrs. Collingwood into the parlor. Lady Hathaway and Lily stood to welcome the dressmaker, who curtsied deeply.

"It is an honor," Mrs. Collingwood murmured. She presented a sealed envelope to Lady Hathaway. "I was asked to deliver this upon my first visit."

The seal was a simple rose, the next best thing to anonymity. Roses had been very much in fashion ever since the Fair ambassador in Aricht had revealed that the Wraith left a slip of paper with a fairy rose on it in the place of the children he rescued. Almost every Valestrian lord, and most of those of Aricht and Ruloth, had obtained a rose seal. Noble ladies wore roses in their hair, both real and made of jewels, and rose embroidery had become all the rage.

Lady Hathaway broke the seal and read. Then she pursed her lips and read again more slowly, debated with herself, then handed the letter to Lily, who had been trying exceptionally hard not to dance with impatience.

While Lily read, Lady Hathaway said, "Well, then, how do we begin? Do you take measurements first, or do we talk about the design first?"

Mrs. Collingwood suggested taking the measurements first and began to get out her tape measure and notebook, letting Lily read without being rushed.

Dear Sir Jacob and Lady Hathaway,

I beg your forgiveness for this little subterfuge. I have gathered that, due to no fault of your own, your family does not have extravagant means at the moment. I have taken the liberty of putting a deposit against an account in your name at my mother's favorite dressmaker and my favorite clothier. Mrs. Collingwood and her staff produce women's clothes of quality, and her brother Mr. Eccleston and his staff produce men's clothes of quality. Please do feel free to draw upon the accounts as you wish. I have deposited eight thousand pounds initially with Mrs. Collingwood, with an additional draw of four thousand pounds without any approval required. I believe this should allow for Miss Hathaway's wedding dress, as well as your attire for the wedding, and other dresses and items as you and Lily may desire. I have deposited the same amount with Mr. Eccleston, against which Sir Jacob and Oliver may charge their wedding and other attire. Mr. Eccleston will contact you about a week or so after this first meeting with Mrs. Collingwood.

I entreat you not to think this charity. It is a gift to those I admire and already love, and it is intended to lift a weight from your shoulders.

I would be much pleased if you did not tell Miss Hathaway about my involvement at all, only that she may choose the dresses she wishes, but I do understand if you choose not to engage in the morally suspect deception to which I have stooped. In either case, please do not reveal it to anyone outside your family.

Yours most humbly,

Theodore Overton, IV

Lily nearly choked when she reached the amount of the deposit. She read the entire letter a second time, and then carefully folded the paper and handed it back to her mother with wide eyes.

"Lily, why don't you and Mrs. Collingwood begin while I go speak to your father?" Lady Hathaway said with a smile.

It was quite a long time before Lady Hathaway returned. Lily and Mrs. Collingwood had finished the measurements and Mrs. Collingwood had begun to show Lily drawings of previous dress designs. They spent the rest of the afternoon deciding on designs for Lily's wedding dress and Lady Hathaway's mother of the bride dress. Mrs. Collingwood also suggested several other designs appropriate for dinner parties, and, at her mother's encouragement, Lily agreed to them.

Mrs. Collingwood had suggested a rose theme. "It is the height of fashion, you know."

"Roses are certainly beautiful, but I want to choose something Mr. Overton prefers." Lily smiled, unsure whether the dressmaker knew that Theo was the one paying for the dresses.

"Mr. Overton prefers to be at the height of fashion. My brother makes all his clothes and has assured me that Mr. Overton will be delighted to accommodate your preferences."

"Well, in that case, I suppose roses would be lovely."

The next morning Lily woke with a flutter of excitement. In only a few hours, they would leave for the Overton estate. She dressed and breakfasted early, then began to play the piano once she was sure everyone else awake. It was something of a miracle she hadn't been asked to demonstrate her competence yet, and she couldn't rely on that lasting much longer. It would be horrifying to be asked to play by Sir Theodore or Lady Overton and embarrass herself and her family by seeming unpracticed.

When everyone had dressed and breakfasted, her parents sat on the lounge chair and conversed quietly. Lily heard her name and Theo's several times, but tried not to eavesdrop too much. She continued her newest embroidery project, a lovely floral pattern on a handkerchief which she intended to give to Lady Overton. She already finished one for Theo.

The clock ticked away slowly on the mantel above the fireplace.

Oliver sat quietly turning the pages of a book, as if he were not nervous at all, and this, coupled with her own nervous excitement, made Lily say suddenly, "How can you read now, Oliver?"

He blinked at her in confusion. "Why should I not? The carriage isn't here yet."

Lily stabbed at the handkerchief fiercely. "Never mind."

A smile dawned on Oliver's face. "You're nervous, aren't you?" At Lily's blush, he said, "Theo adores you. There's no reason to be nervous."

Her mother said quietly, "I suppose it's getting close enough to the wedding that it seems more real now, doesn't it?"

"Yes, I think so." Lily's voice shook. "Sorry, Oliver."

At last the carriage arrived, and Lily felt her nerves increasing. Why should she be so nervous now? Was it merely the revelation of Theo's wealth that made her more shy than before? She certainly hoped not; she did not like to think that money was that important to her.

It was more that the extravagance of the gift made her uncomfortable. They didn't know each other well enough yet to justify that sort of lavish generosity. In their little parlor it had seemed abstract, but now she was to be face to face with him again.

When they arrived, Anselm was stationed to greet them, but Theo outpaced him to help them down from the carriage.

"Sir Jacob, Lady Hathaway, Oliver, Lilybeth." He helped the two ladies down from the carriage and bowed to them each in turn.

Theo showed them through the house again and out to the garden, where his parents stood to greet them.

"I will go prepare the refreshments," said Anselm with a slight bow to Theo.

"Thank you, Anselm." Theo smiled brightly at the footman before turning to the guests. "Would you like to begin with a game of croquet? I missed it last time, but I was informed Oliver was a formidable opponent." This was said with another sparkling smile, and Lily felt herself silly for being nervous at all. He was determined to make everyone feel comfortable.

Lily was enjoined to go first, and so she obligingly hit the purple ball toward the first wicket. To her surprise, it passed through the wicket and ended in a good position for the second some distance to the left. What followed was a hard-fought game filled with much laughter. Lady Hathaway was the surprise winner, and Theo presented her with a magnificent bouquet of peach roses.

Theo must have selected the color specifically to be applicable to anyone who might win the game; peach roses signified sweet friendship, sincerity, and gratitude, which were all perfectly acceptable sentiments regardless of the identity of the victor. Lily gave him a sidelong look. He was more observant and thoughtful than she had thought at first, and the thought cheered her.

"I believe the refreshments have been made ready, if you would like to walk to the pavilion," Sir Theodore said. He offered his arm to his wife, and everyone followed him to the white tent that had been set up on a spacious brick patio.

They enjoyed chicken salad on flakey twisted pastries, tangy cucumber salad, spicy peach jam on homemade flatbread, some sort of delicate pasta dish that tasted of lemons and herbs that Lily had never heard of, roasted asparagus with curls of expensive cheese melting over it, melons, grapes, strawberries, and blackberries. Then there were flavored ices and chilled wine, blackberry pie and whipped cream, and chocolate mousse and a sweet dessert wine. The extravagance of the menu made Lily's heart turn over with something that felt almost like guilt. She looked at Sir Theodore, Lady Overton, and Theo and thought that perhaps it wasn't so much guilt as being entirely out of her element.

During dessert, Lady Overton asked to switch seats with her son. She slid gracefully into the wicker chair beside Lily and said, "Now that the wedding is drawing near, I wanted to see if you had a maidservant to bring with you, or if you would prefer that we hire someone for you." She smiled warmly.

Lily swallowed, feeling a little embarrassed. "I've never had a maidservant before, Lady Overton. I don't know what to do with one."

Lady Overton's smile softened. "The house staff already handle the cleaning, laundry, and meals, so really your maidservant would only have to help you dress, style your hair, and other personal tasks."

"I've always done those things myself," she said tentatively. "Perhaps I could wait a little before I decide?"

"Of course, my dear."

After everyone was entirely satisfied with the refreshments, Theo suggested a stroll through the gardens before more ices and a game of darts. He offered his arm to Lily and said to Lady Hathaway, "Shall we stay within sight, or would you like to join us?"

Lady Hathaway answered with a smile, "Please lead on. I would very much like to see more of the beautiful garden, as well as speak with your mother."

So Theo escorted Lily through a section of the garden which she had not yet seen. Some distance behind them, Lady Overton and Lady Hathaway walked together, chatting in low voices. Together, they provided more than enough supervision to satisfy the most zealous sense of propriety.

"What color will you be wearing for the wedding, Lilybeth?" asked Theo.

"Green." She glanced up at him. "Shall I send you a fabric sample?"

"Yes, please." He smiled. "I will coordinate with your dress."

She bit her lip, then said, "My mother showed me your letter."

A pink flush lit his cheeks, and he looked down.

"Thank you," she said quietly.

"You're welcome," he murmured. "I pray it did not make your parents uncomfortable. Or you."

His embarrassment seemed as genuine as his kindness always did, and Lily's tender heart warmed to him.

"There was a brief moment of discomfort," she admitted, almost under her breath. "Then I decided that, if you were really as generous as you seemed, you wouldn't want that. You have been so generous to me and to my family, Theo. What sort of gift would you like to receive?"

He was silent for a moment, and she looked up to see him regarding her with those bright hazel eyes. The corners of his mouth turned up in a surprised smile, and he murmured, "Lilybeth, you have startled me. I did not think to be asked such a question."

She laughed softly. "Did you not? You asked *me* the very same one!"

"But is it not my privilege to shower you with gifts? That privilege *is* a gift, for I doubt you bestow it lightly."

Her right hand was nestled in the crook of his left arm, where she could feel the lithe muscles of his side against the back of her hand

and the swell of his biceps beneath her fingers. He rested his right hand on her left for a moment, then turned to face her. He took both her hands in his and smiled at her, his cheeks still slightly pink.

"Your acceptance of my suit is a gift, Lilybeth. Please do not ever feel that you need to give me anything other than your heart. I do hope to earn that, even if it takes some time." He bowed over her hands and kissed them one at a time.

Their two mothers discreetly changed their path to give them a semblance of privacy without actually being out of sight.

"You are well on your way to owning that entirely," she whispered, her cheeks heating.

He straightened, delight dancing in his eyes, and murmured, "You give me great hope. How might I continue to make progress toward this worthy goal?"

Lily looked down at his hands still holding hers. His fingers were long and narrow, almost delicate, but had a masculine strength to them entirely different than her own. They were as pale as alabaster, lighter even than her own, and dusted with a few stray freckles.

"I think you should tell me about yourself," she said thoughtfully. "I know you are generous, cheerful, and kind. But I don't know whether you are musical, whether you enjoy reading and what sorts of stories you enjoy, or whether you speak Arichtan or Rulothian or even some more exotic language. I don't even know your favorite color."

He beamed at her, as bright and warm as the sunshine on her shoulders. "I am not particularly musical, but I do like dancing. I love reading, and the more swashbuckling the stories, the better. I speak both Arichtan and Rulothian quite badly. And my favorite color is the blue-grey of your eyes."

She couldn't help chuckling. "Surely you had a favorite color before seeing my eyes, though. What was it?"

He laughed. "Both blue and green. Green for growth and springtime and the richness of the created world, and blue for honor and for the immensity of the sky. It always seemed to me to be singing of possibilities."

When she still looked interested, he added, "When I was a boy, I used to go to the rose garden, lie on my back on the ground, and look at the sky. Every time I went, I saw a new shade of blue. The deep gray before dawn that's hardly even blue at all, the cerulean of midmorning, the deep navy of twilight, and a thousand shades in between."

Lily's eyes met his, and she smiled in delight. This was what she had hoped to learn about him, those quiet little memories that made a person unique and shaped their lives.

"Are you laughing at me?" he murmured. He didn't sound angry, but Lily hastened to explain.

"No, not at all." She shook her head. "I had hoped to learn what experiences have shaped you, what taught you to be generous, what made you who you are."

Theo's eyes danced, and he said, "Your concern for my tender ego is commendable. But I confess I would not mind so much if you laughed at me, so long as it amused you. I love to see you laugh. I am pleased to find, though, that you are much too kind to mock me."

"How could I?" Lily bit her lip. "I would like to laugh *with* you, but I could never laugh at you. That would be cruel."

"Once again I am proven wise in my affection," Theo said.

Lily added, "I confess your ego does not seem so tender to me. You seem to be utterly impervious to Lord Willowvale's insults."

Theo laughed softly. "It is easy to ignore an insult when you have no respect for the one who utters it. It is much harder when it comes from one you revere and love."

"Whom do you revere and love?" she asked impulsively.

He raised an eyebrow at her. "Well…"

She laughed. "I wasn't fishing for compliments! I want to know who shaped you."

"My parents," he said quietly. "My father has a fascinating story, but it is his to tell when he is ready. It is one of steadfast courage and faith in a profoundly alien land. My mother's story is one of creative application of one's gifts on behalf of another, with selfless motives. It brought them together and provided a truly unique example for me, both as a child and now."

Lily looked up at him curiously, seeing the warmth and affection in his eyes. "May I ask them about it?"

"Not yet." His answer was soft. "Wait until after the wedding."

She wondered why he asked that, but did not ask.

"Whom do you revere and love?" He returned the question.

"My parents." She smiled. "My father was knighted four years ago, for courage on the field when Aricht was at war. He was in one of the companies we sent in support against the Fair Folk. His commanding officer fell, and not only did he take up the banner, but he led the rest of the company to victory. He has always been brave, of course; certainly as a child I admired him. But I saw how difficult the transition was back to our quiet life in Haven-by-the-Sea, and how he fought his own memories to be able to smile at us again. My mother loved him so generously through the worst of his dreams and reminded him who he really was. He is a hero, but he is also a beloved father who taught his son how to be a good man and me what to look for when I was ready to think of young men."

She had not looked at him while she said this; it had the feel of a confidence that was not entirely meant to be shared. Her father's nightmares were not truly hers to reveal to anyone. She carried on quickly, "So you see, I didn't grow up in the privilege that you did. This life as a knight's daughter, right at the edge of nobility, is new to me. We were merely landholders in a tiny town on the coast. We had enough to understand that we had an obligation to be generous to those less fortunate, but not enough for a few failed investments not to threaten the entire estate." She flushed. "I'm sorry, I didn't mean to dwell on that. I only intended to let you know that my upbringing was not like yours in privilege and manners, and although I have tried to learn what a knight's daughter ought to, I fear I will disappoint you in some way."

Theo's answering smile assuaged any lingering doubts. "Difficult as it might be to believe, I have had opportunity to pursue young ladies before and have refrained. I was waiting for someone irresistible. What I saw of your character was more attractive than any pretty manners or expensive clothing."

Lily's cheeks heated. "That's a high compliment. I will endeavor to deserve it."

"Father, what shall I give Theo as a wedding gift?" Lily asked desperately.

Her father looked at her over the rim of his tea cup. They were sitting at the breakfast table, and Lily had asked the same question at least once a week for the last five weeks.

"I thought you were embroidering a handkerchief," he said mildly.

"I did. But it's not remotely enough." She didn't voice what they all knew about the Overton wealth and Theo's generosity, but the fact hung in the air all the same. One hand-embroidered handkerchief did indeed seem rather pathetic in comparison.

Lily said, "He likes riding. He and Lord Selby, and several others, go out frequently. Maybe something related to that? But what?"

Oliver frowned. "He's particular about his tack. I wouldn't dare choose something as a gift without knowing exactly what he wanted."

Lady Hathaway said, "Something personal would be preferable, I would think. Perhaps a cravat?"

"What about a nice pen set? He said he is involved in his father's business. I am sure he would like to be reminded of you as he does the accounts," said her father.

Oliver nodded. "That is a good idea."

Accordingly, Oliver escorted Lily out to the nicest pen and stationery shop in Ardmond. Lily's eyes widened at the prices neatly noted beneath each beautiful pen and pen stand. The display was overwhelming, with hundreds of pens of many different types of wood and barrel shapes, several hundred varieties of nibs, and an equal number of inks.

After a moment, a thin, serious man emerged from the back of the shop. "May I help you?"

"I'm looking for a gift," Lily said with a nervous smile.

"For whom?"

"My husband-to-be."

The man's gaze raked her up and down. "And what is his name, Miss?"

"Theo Overton."

The man's eyes lit up. "Miss Hathaway? Is this a wedding gift, I presume?"

She blinked. He knew her name? "Yes," she said.

"I'm Reginald Mather, and I will be delighted to help you choose something for Mr. Overton." The man's thin, cool face was transformed by his smile. It seemed everyone loved Theo, although in this case Lily imagined his wealth was a contributing factor, in addition to his charm.

"He prefers a slimmer barrel, like these." Mr. Mather indicated one to her left. "And he prefers medium to thin nibs. He considered this one when he was here last."

"What wood does he like?" Lily asked.

"If I were choosing a gift for him myself, I would probably choose a rosewood. It has risen in popularity in recent months, you understand, and he has not purchased a rosewood barrel from me, at least. It is likely he does not have one yet."

After some discussion, Lily selected a dark rosewood and a deep burgundy ink. Oliver suggested a pen stand of rosewood inlaid with maple, holly, cherry, and other woods in a floral motif that included a spray of the now popular roses, along with a lily. "It really is perfect, considering your middle name," he murmured into her ear.

Mr. Mather seemed deeply satisfied by their selections, and Lily understood why when he totaled the purchase. The amount made her flinch. The proprietor said gently, "I am happy to extend credit, if you would prefer."

Lily shook her head, internally wincing at the awkwardness. "No, thank you." She glanced Oliver, who had been carrying the money from their father for the gift. Oliver paid with a smile, thanking Mr. Mather for his assistance.

On the way home, Oliver said, "It was a good choice, Lily."

"I hope he likes it."

"He is so delighted to be marrying you that I really don't think the gift matters much. It is a good gift, though." Her brother smiled at her affectionately as the carriage rolled to a stop in front of their house. When they entered, they found a vase of white lilies and snowy jasmine, with a deep blue and white iris, and blue and white hyacinths.

Oliver asked her about the different meanings and she had to look up the flowers, not yet having memorized them all.

"The white lilies are for purity and virginity, the white jasmine is for sweet love and amiability, the iris is for faith, trust, wisdom, hope, or valor, the white hyacinths are for loveliness, and the blue ones are for constancy." Lily blushed pink as she closed the book.

"Do you think he knows all the meanings by heart, or does he look them up?" Oliver asked with interest.

"I imagine he knows them." Lady Hathaway spoke with confidence. "That young man knows exactly what he's doing and what message he's conveying. He's as bright as anyone I've ever met. We're lucky he's devoted his intellect to being charming, I think."

Lily gazed at her mother in surprise but said nothing.

CHAPTER NINETEEN
The Most Beautiful Wedding of the Season

T he morning of the wedding dawned clear and bright, as beautiful an early autumn day as any bride could have wished. The ceremony was scheduled for early afternoon. Lily and her family ate a quick, early lunch before heading to the chapel with plenty of time. The Overtons were already there, but Theo stayed properly in his room while Lily was ushered in so that he would not see her.

The chapel was exquisite, and there had been little additional decoration required. Lily stood at the back and looked forward to where she would stand in a few hours and pledge her life to Theo. The light through the stained glass above her gilded the pews and the edges of the altar.

She and her mother found the room where she would dress. Mrs. Collingwood had delivered her dress and the matching slippers earlier that morning, and they were neatly hanging as promised.

A vase of orange blossoms, white and pink roses, and ivy stood on a table near the window, along with a letter and a little wooden box.

My dearest,

I pray that you are as filled with joy this morning as I am. I hope you like the necklace. Don't feel obligated to wear it today if you have already chosen something else.

Yours always,

Theo

Lily set the letter aside and picked up the box. The top was carved in a finely detailed rose pattern.

"It's beautiful," her mother said softly. "From young Mr. Overton, I presume."

Lily nodded. She opened the box and gasped. She carefully lifted the necklace out and set the box on the table.

A delicate trio of diamonds nestled like roses between marquise cut emeralds and gold leaves. The gold chain was so delicate as to nearly disappear.

Lily placed it back in the box. "I'll put it on after my hair is done."

She took a deep breath and looked at her mother, feeling suddenly nervous. The wedding was really here. She was getting married in an hour.

"Sit down," her mother said.

Lady Hathaway brushed Lily's hair gently, watching her daughter smile to herself in the mirror.

"You look lovely, my sweet daughter," she said softly.

Lily's gaze met her mother's. "I didn't expect this when we came to Ardmond for the season, Mother."

Lady Hathaway chuckled softly. "Neither did any of us. We certainly hoped you would find someone you liked, but this was a surprise."

"Is it proper for me to be so excited, Mother?" Lily flushed. "I mean, in the most ladylike way, of course."

Her mother laughed aloud. "Darling, it is not only proper but right. You are meant to find delight in your beloved. It is only before marriage that these ideas of propriety ought to stand between a man and a woman. Afterwards, you belong to each other in every way, and that should give you both joy."

Lily's blush deepened as she thought of Theo's tall, elegant form. She imagined how he would smile at her with his warm eyes full of sparkling delight. For an instant, she imagined the touch of his hands, then put the thought away to savor later, when it would be right and proper.

Her mother braided her hair in the new style, then artfully arranged the braids at the nape of her neck, pulling out strands to frame her face. She tucked a petite violet into the arrangement as Lily had requested, indicating modesty, faithfulness, and devotion, and a white rose bud beside it, indicating virtue and chastity.

She helped Lily change into her dress. The soft green set off Lily's rich brown hair, and she hoped Theo liked the style she had chosen. Mrs. Collingwood's design was both the height of current fashion, setting off her waist, and unique in its intricate embroidery. Roses picked out in silver and white thread cascaded from her waist to tumble in beautiful symmetry around her feet. More petite roses lined the elegant neckline and followed the line of her sleeves.

"Turn around." Her mother stepped behind her to lace up the back. The boning pressed tight, and she sucked in a breath. Her mother slipped the necklace around her neck and clasped it in the back.

"You are so beautiful, Lily." Lady Hathaway kissed Lily's cheek and brushed at her own eyes.

"Don't cry, Mother!" Lily spun to wrap her arms around her mother.

"They're happy tears," sniffed Lady Hathaway. "I am so proud of you, of your heart. I have prayed for so long that you would find not only happiness but true, enduring love with a good man, and I think my prayers have been answered."

Lily brushed dampness across her own cheeks. "Thank you, Mother."

Her mother's dress was a similar but darker green, with less extravagant embroidery. Roses of golden thread lined the hem, neckline, and sleeves.

The guests had begun to arrive, and Lady Hathaway stepped out to ensure that everything was properly ready. Lily applied powder to her cheeks and then stood barefoot, rereading Theo's short letter. She looked up to admire the flowers. Orange flowers for bridal festivities, purity, and chastity, pink and white roses for grace, perfect happiness, and charm, and ivy for fidelity, love in marriage, affection, and friendship.

Lady Hathaway said from the doorway, "It's time."

Lily slipped on her shoes, took a deep breath, and stepped out.

Her family waited beside the open double doors at the back of the chapel. The organist began a quiet, happy tune, and Oliver escorted Lady Hathaway to the front row, where they sat. Some of the hired attendants closed the doors again to allow Lily and her father to get into position.

Lily's heart thudded raggedly. She wondered wildly whether he would smile, whether he would like her dress, whether he would have second thoughts.

Her father offered her his arm, and she placed her hand upon it. His solid strength beside her steadied her heart.

He looked down at her and said, "You're so beautiful, Lily. You've made your mother and me proud in so many ways."

"Thank you, Father." She leaned her head against his shoulder. "I love you."

"I love you more."

She smiled at his warmth and the unshed tears in his voice.

He added, "Theo adores you. But if ever he doesn't, I'll straighten him out for you."

"Thank you, Father."

When the music changed, she raised her head. The next breath she took trembled with anticipation and hope.

The attendants opened the doors, and she looked up the aisle to meet Theo's gaze.

The smile that lit his face was bright with transcendent joy. His eyes held hers, and his hands trembled at his sides, as if he ached to hold her in his arms already.

Sir Jacob took a step, and she followed his lead step by step between the rows of guests. In the back of her mind, she felt the hundreds of admiring gazes upon her and heard the quiet whispers of approval. But she was only aware of her father's steady steps and Theo's smile.

His eyes were damp when he met her at the end of the aisle.

"I give you my daughter," said Sir Jacob formally. He enfolded Lily's right hand in both of his own before gently placing her hand in Theo's.

"I will cherish her," replied Theo. He bowed deeply to Sir Jacob.

Sir Jacob gave them each a slight bow and sat beside Lady Hathaway in the front row.

Theo's hand was warm on hers. He turned toward the priest, and she followed his lead.

The priest spoke about the sacred bond of marriage, of what it meant to love sacrificially, and of how delighted he was to join the scion of an illustrious and beloved family to his betrothed in holy matrimony.

Lily's heart fluttered with joy. The light glinted on Theo's copper eyelashes, on tears of joy not yet fallen, and she trembled in wonder and awe.

They faced each other, and his hands trembled nearly as much as hers did.

Theo's gaze did not leave Lily's face as he repeated the words of his vow after the priest. His warm hazel eyes met hers, and he smiled, shy and delighted and overwhelmed.

Her voice shook as she vowed before God and king to honor, serve, and love Theo until her last breath. The vow had weight, and she welcomed it, for it would be a delight to love him always.

It was impossible to be nervous now, despite how many people watched. His hands were strong and gentle on hers, and his eyes danced with solemn delight. She could not look away from him, and she did not want to.

For a moment, the priest had them face the congregation again.

"Honored guests, I present to you Mr. and Mrs. Theodore Overton, IV. You may kiss your bride."

Theo turned to Lily and squeezed her hands. His eyes held hers, and he leaned down to kiss her on the lips ever so gently.

The tender touch sent a spark through her whole body. She trembled, and he did too, then he kissed her more hungrily.

Nearly incandescent with joy, he looked out at the crowd, and then looked back at her, unable to focus on anything else. His eyes remained on her as they descended the steps.

At the bottom of the steps, he kissed her again, one hand still holding hers, and the other arm wrapped around her waist. He murmured, "Thank you, Lily, for you have made me the happiest man in the world."

Her cheeks were glowing when he pulled away. The two of them were so full of love and joy they nearly floated down the aisle.

Theo helped her into the waiting phaeton, then climbed up beside her. The phaeton was a light, open carriage, and Theo had chosen this one to best show off the joy of the newlyweds. Many were made for only two people, but this one included a driver's seat. Anselm beamed with pride as he clucked to the horses.

Theo and Lily waved to their guests as they set off. They headed directly to the Overton estate, where Sir Theodore and Lady Overton and, nominally, Sir Jacob and Lady Hathaway would host an exquisite outdoor reception.

Theo couldn't keep his eyes off Lily for the drive. He turned to her and said quietly, "I do hope you are as happy as I am, my love." He brought her hand to his lips and kissed it, holding her gaze. His eyes danced at her blush, and he kissed her again. And again, with great fervor.

Lily felt that the phaeton was quite unnecessary, for she could have floated all the way to the Overton estate in a cloud of joy. She discovered that, when Theo kissed her, she did not want to keep her hands demurely folded. She wanted… well, what she wanted was not fit to be carried out in an open phaeton, that was sure.

At the Overton estate, they stationed themselves at the entrance to the gardens and received well-wishes from hundreds of noble and wealthy families. The bank of pink roses behind them was in riotous bloom. The Hathaways greeted the guests first, then the Overtons, and finally Theo and Lily, before the guests moved off toward a spacious patio prepared for dancing.

The crown prince was one of the first guests to arrive in a gold-trimmed carriage drawn by two white horses. He bowed before Theo and Lily, murmuring polite greetings and congratulations. He leaned closer to murmur something in Theo's ear.

"Really." Theo blinked. "My joy today is utterly unassailable, even by him."

"As it should be," agreed the prince. "Nevertheless, I thought you should know."

Theo bowed his thanks and turned to kiss Lily again before accepting the congratulations of Lord and Lady Hastings.

While the newlyweds and their parents greeted the guests, the musicians played quietly. Once all the guests had been welcomed, Theo said, "Would you honor me with the first dance, my love?"

"I would be delighted." She smiled up at him, admiring the elegance of his cheekbones, the quick intelligence in his eyes, and the kindness of his smile.

He escorted her to the patio with exquisite courtesy. His eyes never left hers, and he smiled with perfect happiness that matched her own joy. She barely heard the music swelling around them, lost as she was in the joy of this beautiful moment.

As the song ended, Theo pulled her scandalously close. Her cheeks flushed, and he murmured, "Do let me demonstrate how ardently I love you, dearest Lily," before kissing her again.

Breathless with the kiss and the desire that had arisen within her, Lily could only nod helplessly and kiss him back, in full view of several hundred people.

It really was quite shocking, she thought distantly, but she couldn't bring herself to regret any of it, because Theo was sparkling at her with such transcendent joy, as if she were the cause of that brightness in his eyes.

CHAPTER TWENTY
The Reception

L ord Willowvale arrived in a graceful black carriage drawn by two bay horses, which he drove himself. He jumped out and strode toward the garden with all the confidence of a Fair lord on his own estate.

Theo noticed his arrival, but ignoring the Fair lord took little effort, for he was entirely focused on Lily's beautiful eyes and her gentle smile, which filled him with an all-consuming joy.

Out of the corner of his eye, Theo saw Lord Willowvale make the bare minimum of socially acceptable pleasantries to his parents and the elder Hathaways, as the joint hosts of the event. Then he turned to Oliver and Theo lost sight of him, focused for a moment more on his new wife, who looked at him with adoring eyes.

Lord Willowvale then made a beeline for the prince, and Theo said reluctantly, "My love, I hate to say it, but I must excuse myself for a moment. Lord Willowvale has invited himself to the celebration and is attempting to tease some information from His Royal Highness. Duty calls."

Lily said, "May I come with you? What is to be done?"

Theo smiled down at her in surprised pleasure. "Merely to distract him. His Royal Highness is both kind and good, but not always adept at seeing the implications of the questions he answers, and it inclines him to more openness than His Majesty prefers."

A moment later they reached the prince and Lord Willowvale. Theo bowed to each of them, and Lily curtsyed beside him.

"Congratulations," Lord Willowvale said to Theo. "It seems at least one person believes you have at least one redeeming quality. I assume it is your money."

Theo blinked and laughed lightly. "Well, I certainly hope she likes more than my money, but I will allow that it might have given me an early edge in the competition. What prospects do you have, my lord? You are, I understand, rather fetching by Fair standards, and with both wealth and a noble title besides. Are those qualities not enough to entice even a desperate Fair maiden to overlook your personality?"

Lord Willowvale snarled, "I would that I could wish your new wife well, but I fear there is no happiness to be had in the company of such a simpleton." He looked toward Lily and said, "Instead, I offer my most sincere condolences, Mrs. Overton."

Lily curtsied again. "I am grieved by your misjudgment of my situation, my lord. I am quite sincerely joyful, and I wish you such joy in the future. Perhaps if you understood a little of joy, you would be able to see it when it is before you."

Lord Willowvale curled his lip and began to turn away, then looked back at her. "Mrs. Overton, I would be honored if you might save me a dance later." His voice was low and cold.

"Yes, my lord," she said reluctantly.

The prince shuddered as the fairy stepped back and bowed stiffly to the little group.

"Thank you, Theo," the prince murmured.

Lily looked at him and realized he was even younger than she'd thought upon their first meeting. His extravagant clothing, resplendent with jewels and lavish silk embroidery at the cuffs and down the front of his jacket, had lent him an air of sophistication that had overawed Lily at first. Now she saw the youthful curve of his cheek and the way he tried not to wring his hands nervously as the fairy moved away. He could not have been more than eighteen, at most.

She murmured to Theo, "How did you and His Royal Highness become friends?"

He smiled down at her and answered in a way that included the prince. "My father and the king became friends, so I was fortunate to be invited along on several hunting trips when His Royal Highness was a child and I was only a youth. As the second youngest of the party, it fell to me to entertain His Royal Highness while we waited for things to get interesting."

The prince said seriously, "Theo offered me honesty when everyone else flattered me. It was a gift, and I have always been grateful."

"What did he tell you?" asked Lily, interested.

"That I was spoiled. Not in so many words, of course."

Theo said with a laugh, "It wasn't quite like that."

Oliver hovered at Lily's shoulder, and when she turned to him, he said, "May I have this dance, little sister?"

She curtsied to the prince and her husband, who took the opportunity to bow over her hand and kiss it with most surprising fervor.

Oliver whirled her onto the portion of the patio which was currently being used as a dance floor.

"Yet another person telling you how lucky you are?" Oliver said with a smile.

"I shall never grow tired of hearing of my husband's many charming qualities."

"You're glowing with happiness, Lily. It's beautiful to see." Oliver grinned at her.

"Thank you." She beamed at him. "I hope you find a similar love, Oliver. I don't think you'll have to look far."

His cheeks flushed. "Did you know, Lily, that it is quite a bit more frightening for a gentleman to ask a beautiful girl to dance than it is for said girl to accept or refuse?"

"I can only imagine," she said gently. "Yet how are you to dance with her if you do not ask? She certainly cannot ask you."

He groaned. "I know. And if I do not ask, she will dance with some other man who is more courageous than I, and that is intolerable."

"You've already called upon her, and you've known her for years. You've danced with her before!" Lily smiled up at her brother. "You know she will be delighted to dance with you."

"I shall have to be courageous, I suppose."

The song came to an end, and he began to lead her back toward Theo.

Lord Willowvale suddenly appeared before them. "I would like to claim my promised dance now."

Oliver glanced at Lily, who said, "As you wish, my lord." She smiled reassuringly at her brother.

Lord Willowvale smiled coolly and took her hand, every motion proper and courteous. He led her back out to the dance floor.

"You do seem happy," he said. His voice was not filled with snide disdain, but rather a sort of surprised confusion.

She glanced up at him. "I am."

"I did not think you were the type to marry for money, no matter how convenient. How did he convince you?"

She licked her lips. The fairy's expression looked as though he felt bereft, but did not want to admit it, and her tender heart went out to him.

"He was kind to me," she said, "when there was no particular reason to be so. Also, it is difficult indeed to resist a man who is utterly delighted to be in your presence and makes himself delightful to be around."

Lord Willowvale did not seem entirely satisfied by this answer. "Does it not bother you that there is so little logic in that? What motive would he have for such behavior?"

"I'm sure I don't know what you mean by that." She frowned at him.

The fairy frowned back, silvery blue eyes searching her face with an unusually earnest expression. "Do you not fear that you will be pulled into something you were not prepared for?"

"Like what?" She didn't try to keep her irritation out of her voice. "I think your accusations rather beyond the pale, and I wonder that you dare make them at our very wedding reception!"

Lord Willowvale said coolly, "Then I am to understand that you are aware of the Fair magic woven through this garden?"

Lily blinked.

"Your new husband has secrets, Mrs. Overton. Deception is not a promising start to a marriage," Lord Willowvale said.

"I'm sure he has reasons," Lily said carefully.

"Oh, I'm sure. I just wonder what they are." Lord Willowvale smiled. "It's probably nothing; he's too stupid to be up to anything nefarious. I wonder if it is Sir Theodore's doing, rather than your idiot husband's. Perhaps you should ask him."

Lily forced a smile. "I will. Perhaps it is one of your people. Are you the only envoy your king sent to Valestria?"

Lord Willowvale stopped dead in the middle of the dance, his gaze locked on something over her shoulder. He dropped her hand.

"Who is that?" He pointed.

She turned and looked.

"Where?"

"There," he insisted, and finally she saw a youth standing on the far side of the pond, nearly hidden behind a bank of purple rhododendrons. His clothes were green and almost disappeared behind the leaves. His hair and skin were fair, and he seemed to be smiling, though it was difficult to discern any nuance in his expression at this distance. Behind him was another man, both older and taller, with dark hair.

"I don't know," she said. Neither of them had greeted her and Theo when they arrived, and in fact she was reasonably confident she had never seen them before.

"Excuse me," Lord Willowvale murmured, and set off with purpose in his steps.

The young man and his companion did not notice immediately, but when they did, they disappeared into the garden. Lord Willowvale broke into a sprint. He hurdled a rose bush without slowing and careened around a hedge, lost from sight.

"What is going on?"

Theo's question startled Lily. She answered, "He saw someone. Two someones, I suppose."

Theo said, "What did you tell him?"

"He asked who they were, and I said I didn't know." Lily hesitated, looking up at Theo. Her new husband, always so bright and carefree, looked a little strained. "He also said there was Fair magic woven through the whole garden." She swallowed, watching Theo's expression.

Everyone knew fairies couldn't exactly lie. They could twist words into knots, but they could not flat out lie. If Lord Willowvale had said there was Fair magic in the garden, then there must be Fair magic in the garden.

When Theo glanced down at her, his eyes had the faintest hint of guardedness, and her heart twisted inside her. Why would he be guarded? What was he hiding?

"Excuse me," Theo murmured. "I'll be back in a few moments."

He strode off in the direction Lord Willowvale had taken, though at a slightly more sedate pace.

It was more than a few moments before he and Lord Willowvale returned together, the tension palpable between them. The mysterious youth and his companion were nowhere to be seen, and Lord Willowvale had the air of a wolf that had missed its intended kill.

Theo smiled cheerily at Lily and whirled her into the next dance, while Lord Willowvale stood with his arms crossed looking out into the garden, as if he expected to see his quarry again at any moment.

"What happened?" Lily murmured to Theo when they were out of earshot.

"Nothing whatsoever." Theo smiled, and Lily knew that he knew exactly what had happened. Or perhaps he was just delighted at the prospect of Lord Willowvale being thwarted, regardless of the Fair lord's purpose.

Lily felt a twinge of dismay, not at Lord Willowvale's angry presence, but at the distinct feeling that she did not know what was going on. "What about the Fair magic in the garden?" she asked cautiously.

Theo glanced over her shoulder, then focused on her again. "Pray let us not discuss this now, my love."

She nodded, quashing the sense of injustice for the moment. The day was too beautiful and full of joy to let one little niggling worry steal a moment of happiness.

Theo leaned closer to murmur in her ear, "What might I do to see your smile again, dear Lily?"

She looked up at him, at the warmth in his eyes, and smiled. "I am only worried, Theo, for I feel that there is something I ought to understand and I do not."

He pressed a kiss to the tender skin just beside her ear and breathed, "Please trust me."

Then the song was done, and although it would have been entirely proper for her to dance with her husband again, for it was her wedding day, the prince asked so courteously for the next dance that Theo smiled his assent, and she accepted.

The young prince was as chivalrous as all of Theo's friends, and he complimented both her dancing and her husband several times before the song ended.

Then Lord Selby asked her to dance, and she accepted with a smile.

"You are quite lovely, Mrs. Overton. Theo has been even more fortunate than usual."

Lily blushed, and said, "I feel the fortunate one. I do believe I owe you thanks for your kind introduction."

Lord Selby's eyebrows rose, and he smiled wryly. "I cannot say I was entirely glad to do it at the time, but I am glad to have seen my ill-tempered service to my friend result in such a happy union. I am delighted for you both."

"Thank you, Lord Selby."

When the music ended, Lord Selby looked around. "I do not see your husband, my lady. I should be honored to escort you for another dance, if it please you, but perhaps you would prefer a little refreshment?" He cast his gaze over the scattered crowd again.

Was it her imagination, or did he look concerned?

"I would like to sit down a moment, I think," she said.

He escorted her to one of many chairs set around in little groups and stood at her side, still looking for Theo.

Where was he?

"Have you by any chance seen Lord Willowvale, Mrs. Overton?" he said at last.

"Not in some time," she replied.

His lips pressed together.

"Ah, there is Oliver. Just one moment, my lady." He stepped forward to get Oliver's attention. "I should like to bring Mrs. Overton a glass of wine. Would you attend her until I return?"

Lily smiled at Lord Selby's overly proper courtesy. It was hardly upsetting to be left to sit alone for a few moments in a chair in the Overtons' garden, but it was not entirely polite to leave a lady unattended at any time during a party, much less a bride sitting alone on her wedding day.

Where was Theo?

She looked around but did not see him.

Oliver said, "Lord Selby asked me to attend you, little sister." A hint of suppressed laughter made his voice warm. "I believe he's off in search of wine for you. Where is Theo? He's normally so attentive. I can't think what he would be doing now."

"Neither can I," murmured Lily. She wasn't upset, exactly. Certainly she wasn't angry or insulted. It was more a growing sense of concern that Lord Willowvale had not been entirely wrong when he said Theo was hiding something.

If he were right about Theo, what was her husband hiding? Who was the young man who had so intrigued Lord Willowvale?

As if her thoughts had drawn him, the fairy approached her. With a nod to Oliver, he addressed her directly. "Did you see that young man clearly?" he said without preamble. He did not mention the other gentleman.

"Not really." She stood, feeling that replying to him from a seated position while he stood over her, tall and imposing, was both intimidating and discourteous.

He gazed at her, his expression thoughtful. For a moment, there was no bitterness or anger in his face, just a sense of quick, dangerous intelligence, and she thought how handsome he might be if he added kindness to the mix.

At last, he said, "Did you see that he wore a glamour?" His eyes were fixed on her face.

She blinked. "Maybe," she said slowly. "There was perhaps a hint of a glamour, but I cannot be sure. If there was one, it was very strong."

"It was fairy-made. Why would your husband have a fairy on the grounds of his estate?" said Lord Willowvale softly.

"I have no idea," said Lily honestly. "Why do you think it has anything to do with Theo?"

Lord Willowvale smiled. "I have no reason to yet. I doubt your idiot husband has any idea that the boy is a fairy at all, or even that he exists."

"Are you sure he wasn't sent by your king?" said Lily.

"My king has entrusted the mission to me." Lord Willowvale smiled coolly. "I realize you do not like me, and I don't care. Nevertheless, my king knows me to be competent. Rather frustratingly, he required that I swear to cause no unnecessary harm in your court and among human kind as I pursue my mission."

"I didn't know that." Lily gazed at him, feeling as though this news shed new light on the Fair Court in general and on Lord Willowvale in particular. "You can still cause necessary harm, though," she said with a question in her voice.

"Indeed." He smiled icily. "Judgment of what is necessary has been left to me." He looked across the crowd, then back at her. "I wonder if the Rose would bother to rescue an adult human."

She swallowed. "Is that a threat?" she said quietly.

Oliver spoke for the first time. "I really don't see what you hope to gain by trying to ruin my sister's wedding reception."

The fairy glanced at him. "How amusing, that you think this has anything to do with your sister at all." He raked his eyes up and down Oliver. "I wonder what the Valestrian throne wants with Arichtan children," he mused.

"What?" said Lily.

"Well, the children stolen from the Fair Lands must go somewhere." Lord Willowvale sat in the nearest chair and leaned forward confidentially. "The Fair ambassador in Idosa has informed me that scarcely a third of them are ever returned to Aricht."

"I'm sure they're well-treated," said Lily.

"Do you know that? How?" Lord Willowvale smiled.

"I… I mean, I'm sure the Valestrian throne would not mistreat innocent victims of fairy mischief." Lily felt herself fumbling.

"Have you seen them? What if the king, or the prince, uses them for their own nefarious purposes?" Lord Willowvale pressed. "How can you know they are well-treated, when they are never seen again?"

"I have seen them! They're… well, they're healthy, and…" Lily stumbled over her words, suddenly aware of all the things she ought not say.

"They're…" Oliver's words were cut off by the return of Lord Selby.

"Lord Willowvale, I am surprised at you," said Lord Selby mildly. "It is monstrously bad form to try to pump a newly married lady for information on your own failed task while her beloved is busy ensuring that his guests are lavishly wined and dined. At her wedding reception, no less!"

Lord Selby handed Lily a glass of sparkling wine and handed Lord Willowvale the other. He added confidentially, "Mr. Overton has been kind enough to provide the musicians with the music for a Fair song, in an effort to lighten your customarily sour mood. Pray don't repay him by using this lovely occasion for your own unconscionable ends."

Lord Willowvale accepted the glass of wine with a bemused air. For a moment, Lily almost thought he might soften enough to let a genuine smile light his face, but instead he said quietly, "It is difficult indeed to let even the best of human hospitality bring joy to a heart burning with terror for one's own much superior people."

Lily began to say, "What do you——" when Theo swept into their midst, eyes shining, with the sunlight gleaming on his bright auburn hair.

"My beloved, come away with me and dance. I would be grieved indeed if your memories of our wedding day were to consist more of Lord Willowvale than of my devotion." In a moment he had whisked her onto the dance floor and into the next dance.

He beamed at her, all delighted adoration. How handsome he was, with the light of love in his warm eyes!

So why did she feel that sense of betrayal?

She pushed it aside for the moment and enjoyed the feel of Theo's hand on her waist.

He leaned down to murmur in her ear, "My love for you grows by the moment, dear Lily. How may I best please you the rest of the afternoon?"

"I should very much like to spend every moment in your arms," she said almost inaudibly, her cheeks heating.

His answering smile made her knees suddenly weak. "I cannot think of anything that would delight me more."

When the dance ended, her father requested a dance, and of course she had to accept. Then she danced with Sir Theodore, then Sir Michael Radclyffe, then Lord Radclyffe. Once she saw Lord Selby speaking in Theo's ear, and her husband nodding, his eyes on her, full of love and warmth.

All the time, in the back of her mind, she wondered whether Lord Willowvale was not entirely wrong after all. He had made himself detestable, and she could not excuse any cruelty to children, no matter how justifiable the Fair cause.

Yet, her tender heart had responded to that one moment when it seemed that he had shown vulnerability. If he truly cared about his people and his land, of course he would be tempted to ignore the social niceties of a foreign land while striving to save his own.

At last, the guests began to depart. The musicians continued playing even after the last of the guests left. Anselm let them know they could rest and begin packing their instruments.

Sir Jacob and Lady Hathaway bid their generous hosts goodbye, then found Lily and Theo sitting in contented exhaustion near the dance floor. Theo had cajoled Lily into sitting by his side on a chaise lounge and had wrapped his arm around her. She leaned back against him, relaxed and suddenly sleepy in the aftermath of so much excitement. The thrill of that chaste touch, the length of her back against his well-knit side, fought for primacy over the lassitude that had seized her mind. She could feel him breathing, feel the warmth of his body against hers. She leaned her head back against his shoulder; he sighed happily and relaxed further.

Sir Jacob said, "My most sincere congratulations, Theo. I am proud to have you as a son."

Theo began to carefully extricate himself from Lily to bid his father-in-law farewell, but Lily stood with him.

"Thank you, Sir Jacob. I am most honored by your regard and your trust." Theo bowed with exquisite courtesy, and his eyes shone with delight.

"Thank you, Father." Lily threw her arms around her father, who patted her on the back.

"I love you, Lilybeth Rose, heart of my heart," he murmured into her hair.

"I love you, Father." She gave him a last squeeze and turned to her mother.

"I love you, Mother." Her mother's embrace brought tears to her eyes, and she wrapped her arms around her mother's waist. "Thank you for everything." Her mother murmured her love into Lily's ear, and Lily tightened her embrace.

Oliver bowed to Theo and said, "Congratulations."

Theo returned the courtesy, murmuring his thanks.

Oliver hugged his little sister. Then the Hathaways departed back through the garden.

The birds sang over the leaves rustling in the warm breeze. Both elder and younger Overtons relaxed in the long-awaited tranquility.

Theo said softly, "How can I best please you now, my love?" He took both her hands in his.

Lily smiled up at him, drinking in the warmth of his eyes and the light of love in his smile.

Then Anselm came at run. "Theo!"

Theo turned, his shoulders stiff.

The servant shot a cautious look at Lily, then whispered into Theo's ear.

Theo's jaw tensed. He bowed over her hand and kissed it, then pulled her into his arms. "I must go, Lily. I will tell you everything when I return." He kissed her cheek, her lips, and her hand again, then tore himself away and sprinted toward the stable.

Lady Overton watched him go, her mouth twisted in an anguished frown.

"What's going on?" Lily asked Lady Overton in a shaking voice.

"It is not my right to say," the lady answered quietly.

Theo, mounted on his favorite hunter, thundered out of the stable and up the drive at a dead run.

Anselm looked after him with grave eyes, then bowed deeply to Lily. "Mrs. Overton, I would be delighted to show you to the suite Mr. Overton had prepared for you. A rest may be just the thing after such an exciting day."

Lily heard the compassion in the servant's voice, and it almost brought her to tears.

"I think I'd like to wait out here for a while, if you don't mind," she whispered. She had hoped, had expected, that Theo would show her to her personal suite and his own.

"As you wish," he said quietly.

Lady Overton said, "I would be happy to sit with you, if you would like. But I understand if you would find solitude more restful."

"Thank you, Lady Overton. I think I would prefer to be alone. I am a little fatigued." Lily's voice betrayed the tears she hadn't yet shed.

Lady Overton stepped closer and wrapped her arms around the younger woman. "Please believe me when I say Theo has a good reason for what he does. He adores you, and nothing but the most serious crisis could tear him away from you, especially now." She put her hands gently on Lily's shoulders and met her gaze. "He has scarcely slept in weeks for thinking of the joy of this very day with you."

Lily licked her lips and nodded, trembling.

CHAPTER TWENTY-ONE
The Wedding Night

L ily sat in the garden alone. The birdsong changed around her from afternoon to evening sounds, and the buzz of the insects singing in the trees around the garden grew louder.

The shadows grew longer.

Anselm brought her a lavish tray of pheasant breast stuffed with cheese and herbs, a rich roll, roasted carrots topped with sugar-crusted walnuts, a little salad of delicate greens she did not recognize and a tangy dressing, fat green and red grapes, and a glass of wine beside a tumbler of cool water.

"Sir Theodore and Lady Overton asked if you would allow them to join you out here for dinner," he said.

She swallowed. She did not feel up to pretending to be optimistic at the moment, but she could not bear the thought of telling them they could not eat with her in their very own garden after such consistent generosity. "If they wish to, I would be glad to see them."

The dinner was quiet and fully as awkward as Lily had feared. Lady Overton's refusal to answer her question earlier had told her that she could expect no answers now. The lady made a valiant effort to lighten the mood by telling a humorous story from Theo's childhood.

"He climbed that tree when he was only four years old. Can you imagine? I came outside to see his nurse weeping in fear at the foot of the tree, and him unable to hear he was so high!" Lady Overton pointed at the tree in question, an enormous oak on the other side of the pond. "It was terrifying! My husband and Anselm both ended up in the tree trying to convince him to come down."

"Was he hurt?" Lily asked obligingly.

"Not him!" Lady Overton smiled fondly. "We always said he had the luck of—" she stopped. "Well, he had God's own hand upon him, keeping him from harm."

"What else did he do?"

"Well, he once tried to save a foal from drowning in the pond in the pasture," Sir Theodore remarked. "He was only six, and the foal could swim better than he could, so that was a bit of an adventure. I consider it quite an accomplishment on our parts, and that of Anselm, that he made it to adulthood at all." His kind hazel eyes were so like Theo's that Lily was reassured, for a moment; how could someone with eyes like that leave her on her very wedding night? Theo must have had a very good reason indeed.

"Thank you. I feel a little better," she said truthfully.

"Good." Lady Overton smiled at her across the table. "I do hope you will sleep well tonight. I am sure that Theo would not want you to worry. Would you like me to show you your suite?"

Lily felt a twinge of panic. If she waited a little longer, surely Theo would come, and she could pretend that these hours since he had left had not even happened. If she went to her suite, then she accepted that the evening was nearly over.

"I… I would like to wait out here a little longer," she whispered. "Please. I wanted Theo to show me." She wiped at her eyes.

Sir Theodore stood, pretending that he did not realize she was weeping. Lady Overton murmured, "Oh, Lily, I do not know when he will be back, only that it will be as soon as he can be. Will you not let me make you comfortable?"

"I don't think I want to be comfortable yet." She wiped at her eyes more fiercely and forced a tremulous smile. The light from the windows fell across her hands, highlighting the streaks of tears.

Sir Theodore said, without looking at her, "Please know that should you need anything, now or later in the night, we are here for you."

"Thank you," she whispered.

Lady Overton stood. "When you are ready, you may reach your suite by going through those doors, up the main stairs, and to the left. That wing belongs to you and Theo. Follow that corridor to the end. There is a door to your private chambers at the end. When you go through it, you will be in your shared private sitting room. Theo's suite is to the right, and yours is on the left. You will find all your effects there. You may also summon a maidservant with a pull of any of the ribbons, and a manservant, usually Anselm, with a pull of any of the chains. Ask for whatever you need. This is your home, and we want you to be comfortable."

"Thank you," Lily whispered again. "You've been very kind."

They left then, holding hands, which ought to have been encouraging to Lily. It was an unusual display of affection for such a prominent family; by allowing her to see them doing so, they were showing that she was truly one of their family.

As much as she appreciated the thought, she felt bereft.

She sat alone in the dark. Tears trickled quietly down her cheeks, and still she sat, trying to imagine what might be important enough to justify Theo's departure.

The tears dried. She listened to the birds quiet and the bugs change their tune as the moon rose and the night drew on. The lights from the house darkened one by one, but the lamp nearest the windows remained lit.

The air grew cool and damp, and she shivered.

It must have been past midnight when she finally rose, stiff and chilled. She stood at the table and looked into the shadows that filled the garden.

Had she really gotten married that very afternoon? The innocent hope and confidence of those moments in the chapel seemed to belong to someone else, years ago.

She walked slowly to the door, which opened easily.

She jumped when she saw a shadow rise from where it had been sprawled in a chair in the corner.

"Mrs. Overton," Anselm said quietly. "I didn't mean to scare you."

"You waited up for me?"

"Yes. Shall I show you upstairs?" He looked rumpled and half-asleep, but his voice was kind.

"Lady Overton told me how to find it. You can go to bed."

He gave a low chuckle. "I think you misjudge all of us, if you think you'll be left to find your way to your room alone in the dark on your wedding night. Theo may have been called away, but you're hardly abandoned, Mrs. Overton."

She smiled her thanks, and he took up the lantern and led the way up the stairs, holding the lantern to the side so that it lit the steps for her.

The corridor was papered in a beautiful white on white damask, which caught the lantern light with an elegant glow. Anselm opened the door for her and stepped aside, proffering the lantern.

"Here you are, Mrs. Overton." He bowed formally to her.

"Don't you want the lantern?" she asked. "I can see by the moonlight through the windows." The silvery light spilled through the windows which filled the far wall of the spacious sitting room.

"I know my way around the place by now," Anselm said with a smile. "Good night to you."

He set off back down the hall.

Lily held the lantern up into the darkened corners of the room. There were two generously sized couches of velvet, though the competing silver moonlight and warm yellow lantern light made it hard to judge the color. There was a fireplace on each side wall, and beside the fireplace were shelves of books and art objects made indistinct by shadow.

She turned to the left and entered her suite. She lit another lantern from the first, which she left on the low table before the fireplace, which obviously was the other side of the one in their shared sitting room. A vase of roses stood on the table, and the fresh scent in the air told her they had been cut that morning.

Through another door she found her bedroom. The room itself was spacious and bright, with white paper on the walls and a rich blue rug on the floor. Another vase of roses stood beside the bed.

A tall wardrobe stood against the opposite wall, along with a beautiful bureau, and a cedar chest sat at the foot of the bed. There was a lovely blue spread upon the bed, intricately embroidered with roses in white and silver thread. She found her belongings, including the filmy white nightgown she had planned to wear this first night, hanging in the wardrobe. There was another door, which led to a small room whose purpose she did not know.

Lily dressed silently and carefully hung her wedding dress in the wardrobe. She washed her face in the basin and patted it dry with the soft cotton towel, then held up the lantern to examine herself in the full-length mirror on a stand beside the wardrobe. Her eyes were wide and slightly red. She looked tired. Her nightgown was nearly sheer, and she had not yet dared imagine Theo's expression when he saw it.

She smiled sadly and saw that the sadness was even more obvious than she had hoped.

She looked at the bed.

A spirit of boldness overtook her. Despite his absence, Theo had given every indication that he adored her.

They were married.

She found a thick dressing gown of rich brocade and pulled it on. Then she went back to her sitting room, blew out the second lamp, and crossed into the shared sitting room. She hesitated at the door to Theo's room. This was bold, indeed, and her courage nearly failed.

With a deep breath, she turned the knob to enter Theo's suite.

The sitting room was arranged much like hers, though the couch was a different color and the walls were darker. There was a general air of masculinity about it, though in the shadows she couldn't identify what gave her that impression. Perhaps it was merely that there were no roses on the table.

With more trepidation, she went through the open door to his bedroom.

Again, the room was much like hers, though the colors were different. Along the near wall was a rack of elegant swords; their blades gleamed bright in the dancing light. The spread on the bed was burgundy and embroidered roses gleamed in gold and silver. There were two doors on the opposite wall, corresponding to the one in her room.She peeked through one to see that the little room was used as an enormous wardrobe. Neat rows of exquisite jackets and trousers hung ready for use, with their matching slippers and boots lined up on the floor. The other was a darkened room lined with bookshelves, with a desk and chair in the middle and a window on the opposite wall which looked out to the distant hills.

She turned back to the bed.

She was not, in actuality, bold enough to climb into his bed. The very thought made her queasy with both the audacity of the idea and mortification at the thought of what might follow. He should be there to consent to such intimacy. Invading his private sanctum like this was already beyond reasonable.

Instead, she found a light coverlet on a nearby chair and curled up on top of the bedspread.

She did not expect to sleep quickly, but her thoughts had been whirling for so long, and she was so exhausted, that it was only moments before dreams claimed her.

Lily jerked awake as someone stomped into the room, snarling almost inaudibly.

She gasped, suddenly aware that this little romantic endeavor had been an absolutely terrible idea.

"Who's there?" snapped Theo's voice from the darkness.

"I... I'm sorry," Lily whispered. "I was..."

Theo said blankly, "Lily?"

"I'm sorry," she said again, trembling. "I thought... I don't know what I thought. I'm sorry."

"What did you tell Willowvale?" His voice shook.

"What?"

"Yesterday at the reception! Every time I turned around, you were talking to Lord Willowvale! What did you tell him?" He fumbled for something, muttered under his breath, and then a match flared to life. It caught his face for a moment, then he held the match to the lantern wick.

The wick caught, and he turned the lamp up as far as it would go. They stared at each other.

Theo had already shed his beautiful jacket; it was tossed over the chair near the door. The vest beneath it was missing a button, and his exquisite silk shirt was darkened with sweat. His cravat was half-untied, though she was not sure whether that had been done purposefully or not. His eyes were wild and red-rimmed.

She licked her lips. "Nothing, I think."

His gaze grew hard. "Nothing," he said flatly. A muscle in his jaw worked. He held the lantern up and looked her over more closely.

She clutched the dressing gown close at her neck, unwilling to feel entirely vulnerable before this new, frightening person. Theo had never been angry. She had not known he even could be angry.

"Where have you been?" She bit her lip and stared at him with wide eyes.

His mouth twitched, and he looked her up and down again. He stepped closer. "What did you tell Willowvale, Lily? *Please* tell me."

His eyelashes were damp, as if he had been weeping, and the shock of that observation dried her mouth. "I don't... nothing, I think." It was difficult to even cast her mind back that far; she had thought so much of Theo's absence, of her own disappointment, that Lord Willowvale seemed a distant and inconsequential memory. "I... he asked why I seemed happy," she whispered.

Theo let out a short, hard breath, and said, "I adore you, Lily, but I think tonight I am far too angry to appreciate your"—he waved a hand, encompassing everything from her state of scandalous undress to her very existence—"romantic efforts."

She clutched the dressing gown with both hands, as if it would shield her from the ice in his words. "I'm sorry. I won't trouble you again." Her voice shook.

"What did you tell him?" Theo's voice cracked.

"Nothing!" Lily whispered. "I'll... I'll leave you now." She tried to lift her chin, but a dry, painful sob caught in her throat.

Theo did not move, only watched her. The light danced on the walls as his hand holding the lantern shook.

She fled to her room and closed the door behind her, then curled on the bed and wept.

Lily finally fell asleep from sheer exhaustion some time before dawn. She dozed fitfully, but woke again when golden light spilled across the bed. She gave up on sleep and dressed, trying to focus on the simple actions of hanging her nightgown and dressing gown and putting on matching slippers. If she thought about the night before, tears sprang to her eyes, and she didn't want to weep again.

She washed her face and looked in the mirror. Her grey eyes looked haunted, and she swallowed, trying on different smiles to see which ones looked the most convincing. None of them were particularly good.

She took a deep breath and let it out slowly, then opened the door to the shared space.

Theo's door was half-open, and it was apparent he was already gone. She stepped quietly to the door and peeked in. The bedspread was hardly disturbed; it looked like he had not slept in his bed at all.

Lily gathered her courage and opened the door to the corridor. The house was quiet, and she made her way down the main stairs before she heard any hint of voices. She followed the sound to a small dining room flooded with morning light. When she peeked around the corner, she saw Theo eating with his parents.

He saw her, too. He stood and bowed formally. "Lily," he said. "I would be honored if you would join us for breakfast." His tone was cool and perfectly controlled.

She stared at him. "Are you angry at me?" she whispered, not caring whether his parents heard either the question or the answer.

Theo said quietly, "You have assured me that there is no cause to be angry, so I must not be." He bowed again and indicated the seat nearest him, which was set with bright white china.

She crept to the seat, feeling suddenly mouselike and more unsure of herself than she had ever been.

Lady Overton glanced between them, her eyes anguished, then looked down. "Perhaps there has been some misunderstanding," she murmured.

"I certainly hope so," said Sir Theodore. His gaze on Lily was cool and unreadable, but not exactly hostile.

Theo served her eggs and sausage from the platters in the middle of the table, then poured tea for her from the pitcher. He offered her the platter of fluffy biscuits and then the little pots of butter and berry preserves in succession.

Lily had never felt under such intense scrutiny in her entire life, and she felt herself cracking into a thousand weeping pieces. Theo's gaze was steadily upon her, as if he would see into her soul.

She could not force any of the smiles she had practiced, and instead it was all she could to do say, "Thank you," when he had finished serving her.

The weight of his regard made her want to keep looking down, but in a moment of courage she looked up to meet his eyes squarely.

The shadows under his eyes stood out because he was so pale; he must not have slept at all. Nevertheless, his shirt was fresh and crisp, and his hair damp, as if he'd bathed already.

And his eyes! He looked as though everything he'd ever hoped for had been stripped from him and left him utterly desolate.

"What happened?" she whispered. "What's wrong?"

He swallowed and smiled, but it didn't reach his eyes. "Nothing."

CHAPTER TWENTY-TWO
The Other Side

T heo ran from the reception toward the stable, where Juniper met him, as Anselm had said he would. The young fairy formed the glamour as quick as thought. "You want it to wait until you're out of sight?"

"Yes, please. One for the horse as well. People know this one." Theo saddled the gray gelding faster than he had ever saddled a horse before. He grunted with effort as he pulled the girth tight, then put on the horse's bridle. He jumped into the saddle.

"Here." The young fairy passed him his sword, which he buckled on, and then the glamour. "Godspeed. Wait! Here's the binding magic, if you can use it." He pressed the magic into Theo's hand, and it was so strong that Theo gasped, feeling that his heart was being tugged out through his fingertips for a moment.

"Thank you. Stay out of sight."

"Yes, sir." Juniper's words were lost in hoofbeats as Theo departed at a run.

It was nearly four miles to the children's home, and Theo nearly wept with frustration when he had to let the horse slow. He did not yet have the control of the veil to ensure that if he went into it, he would be able to come out close enough to the children's home to save time.

So he let the horse trot, then canter, then trot a little more, pushing it harder than he ever had.

The children's home looked almost serene when he finally reached it. He rode the horse directly into the garden and jumped off, leaving it lathered and blowing hard. Both the front and back garden were empty.

Theo sprinted inside.

There was a sound from the stairwell, and he headed for it at a run.

Essie screamed, and children were crying.

Lord Willowvale stood halfway up the stairwell, sword in hand. "Come now, you cannot believe there is any use in this resistance. Give me the children and keep your lives."

Theo said from the bottom of the stairs, "Leave now and keep your own, fairy."

Lord Willowvale turned his head in surprise, and John, holding the top of the stairs with a sword in hand, nearly skewered him. Lord Willowvale batted the sword away, then took several steps down toward Theo.

"Who are you?" growled the fairy. "You wear a glamour, far too strong for human making, but I do not think you a fairy."

"I believe you call me the Rose. I do carry a thorn." Theo brandished his sword, intentionally leaving a vulnerability to tempt Lord Willowvale to strike.

The fairy did so, lunging down the stairs with startling speed, leaving John panting at the top.

Theo narrowly missed being run through, and he stumbled backward, exaggerating how off-balance he was.

"Who are you?" snarled Lord Willowvale again, following up with a flurry of lightning-fast attacks.

Theo said nothing. Like all fairies, Lord Willowvale was faster, stronger, and more coordinated than most humans. Only Theo's long training with Cedar enabled him to parry and riposte quickly enough to avoid being gutted.

By retreating, he managed to draw the fairy a little farther into the living room.

"Leave off your foolish attempt to distract me," snapped Lord Willowvale.

"Leave off your depraved attempt to punish children for your own land's malaise," retorted Theo.

The glamour he wore was that of a broad-shouldered middle-aged man, with dark hair and the shadow of a beard. His clothes were dark and well-made, though hardly as exquisite as Theo's wedding attire.

"Are you a soldier?" Lord Willowvale mused as he drove Theo around the chaise lounge in the sitting room and out toward the lobby. With a flick of his wrist, he managed to open an ugly gash on the outside of Theo's shoulder.

Theo hissed in pain and drove in with a lunge that surprised Lord Willowvale, who stumbled backward. Theo drew the tip of his sword across the fairy's throat lightly, letting the iron burn a bright red streak without drawing blood.

The fairy's eyes darkened in fury, and he redoubled the speed of his attacks.

"You shall not have the children," said Theo, breathless and steadfast.

"If I kill you, I will."

Theo laughed aloud, and the sound, changed as it was by the glamour, sounded wild and haughty. "If I kill you, you won't," he retorted. "Is that what we're to do now? Kill each other here? How did you find this place?"

The fairy snarled, "Mrs. Overton gave the last clue I needed. Now I know what to look for. If you hide them again, I'll only find them more quickly." He stepped back, his chest heaving, and eyed Theo warily. "I've had enough for now. Take your little temporary triumph and enjoy it, for it will not last long." He bared his teeth in a cruel smile and bowed.

Theo returned the bow, and his gaze did not leave the fairy until Lord Willowvale strode easily out of the house. He watched as the fairy studied his mount, then departed, without having given any sign of having seen through the glamour and recognizing the animal.

Only then did Theo walk back to the bottom of the stairs. "He's gone," he said. His voice sounded strange in his own ears, breathless and cold and a little too deep.

John descended first, his sword still in hand. "It is you, isn't it?" he asked cautiously.

"Yes," said Theo. "Are you hurt?"

"No." The older man's voice shook. "I was inside and Essie was outside with the older girls. They were picking tomatoes and peppers." He swallowed, trying to steady his voice. "He came around the corner of the house, from the front, and caught two of them with his hands. He ripped a hole in the world and disappeared with them. He had just come back for more when you arrived."

The man sat down heavily on the chaise lounge so recently the scene of a fight.

Essie came down the stairs next, looking around cautiously before calling up to the remaining children, "You can come down."

They came down hurriedly and clustered around Essie and John, eying the unfamiliar glamoured Theo with unease.

Theo stood and pressed a hand to his mouth, his mind racing.

Lord Selby, generous of heart and never one to speak ill of anyone, had told him he had overheard Lord Willowvale and Lily speaking of the children. He had not heard much, and had not wanted to misinterpret what Lily had said. Perhaps it had been nothing.

Yet here was Lord Willowvale, at the house Theo had tried so hard to protect, and two children, already traumatized and exhausted, had been stolen back to the Fair Lands. Theo had promised them they would never have to endure that dancing again, never have to fuel a dying land's survival with their tears and terror.

And somehow, Lily had been responsible.

A dry sob caught in his throat, and he turned away to look through the window at the street.

Essie came to stand at his shoulder. "You're bleeding," she said quietly.

He swallowed. "Will you bind it before I go to find them?"

The woman nodded. "It was Elizabeth and Miriam." She swallowed. "I cannot say there is anything good in this, but if there is a blessing, I suppose it is that they are some of the strongest girls here. They had recovered more than most of the others."

Theo looked down at her. "Thank you. Nevertheless…"

"Nevertheless." Essie nodded. "Come to the kitchen."

He followed her to the kitchen and took off his jacket. When he had put it on that morning, his heart had been so full of hope and joy. He unbuttoned his vest and shirt, exposing the gash on his upper arm.

Essie squinted. "It's quite hard to see. Do you have any control over the glamour at all?"

Theo shook his head. "No. I'm sorry."

The woman made a pfft of dismay. "Don't apologize to me, after you've just saved us from that horrible fairy. I'll do the best I can with what I see, and you tell me what I'm missing."

Juniper had focused his efforts on Theo's skin tone, facial features, clothes, and general build, but had not changed much that would be covered by his clothes. To Essie, the gash was more or less in the right spot, but it was indistinct. Though it was not as deep as she had feared at first, the edges were torn; the tip of Lord Willowvale's rapier had entered cleanly before he had flicked the sword sideways.

Essie washed the wound, and Theo watched with clinical interest, trying with everything in him not to think of Lord Willowvale's words.

Essie patted him on the shoulder when she was done. "It will be all right," she said quietly. "You're not alone in this, you know."

He nodded once, because it would reassure her. "Let me take you someplace safe. If he knows you're here, it's only a matter of time before he comes back."

"Where?"

John and the children stood nearby in a tense little group. Theo swallowed, debating internally, and finally said, "The palace has the best security, and even Lord Willowvale will find it challenging to get in and out."

The veil was harder to access near the palace; neither His Majesty nor anyone else knew whether that was the reason or the result of the fact that the palace had been built in that location. In any case, it was one of the most difficult places in the country to access from the veil. It was not quite as strong an effect as that surrounding the Fair palace, but it was still generally effective to prevent doors from being opened into the palace itself. Theo had practiced, several years before, with the permission of the king, but to his knowledge, no one else either Fair or human had ever entered the palace or the grounds from the veil. Moreover, the palace had a great many guards stationed at the perimeter, and Theo was confident His Majesty would assign more to guard the children once he was aware of the necessity.

The two caretakers blinked. "How will we get in?"

Theo smiled bleakly. "That I can manage, though not with enough precision to minimize explanations. You'll have to brave the veil, though." He looked at the children, who stared at him in wide-eyed apprehension. "Can you be brave?"

He glanced up at Essie, who nodded sharply.

"I'll do it for the children," she said.

Theo's shattered heart warmed a little at this. "You are truly an inspiration," he said sincerely, glancing between Essie and John. "I suppose you ought to gather what you want to take with you. I don't know when we'll be back again, or how safe it will be to send someone for your effects. So pack quickly."

He washed the blood from the slit in his shirt, not because he would wear it another day but because it gave his hands something to do. Then he put it back on and put his vest back on over it. He tugged the vest down and straightened his shirt. The jacket was ruined too; only a little blood had seeped through the layers of fabric, but the cut in the sleeve could not be repaired without the mending being obvious. Nevertheless, he washed it and put it back on too.

He stood at the window in the sitting room while John and Essie helped the children pack one small bag each, full of clothes and a few books. He felt cold and hot in succession, and he told himself it was the burning of the wound, but he knew it was a lie.

He went outside and took off his horse's tack, gave it the best rubdown he could with a few handfuls of grass, and gave it water from the well. He closed the garden gate.

By the time he finished, the children and their guardians had gathered in the room.

"Stay close to me," he said. "Hold hands, because it's dark in the veil. I could make a light, but it's safer in the dark. John, please take the rear position with your sword drawn. Everyone else, line up in pairs. Hold the shirt of the person ahead of you, and the hand of the person beside you. Essie, please take the middle position. We want to be close together, so please don't lag behind."

This was more children than he had ever taken through the veil at once.

"You were attacked by the floor before, weren't you?" he asked one boy standing near John. The boy nodded, pale and frightened, but determined not to cry. "Then you should be here in the front, nearest me." Theo gave the boy what he hoped was a reassuring smile, though he could not be sure how it looked with his glamoured features.

"If anything bothers you, tell me immediately. Don't wait until you can't speak. We'll be as quick as we can." He looked at their terrified expressions, and his tender heart twisted inside him. "Thank you for your courage, dear children," he whispered. "I'm sorry it has come to this, but I promise you, I will end this, no matter what it costs."

Then he opened the door and led them into the veil.

The palace was not far away through the veil, but it seemed longer to those frightened children and their protectors. Theo kept up a quiet, one-sided conversation as they walked, both to distract the children from their fears and himself from his grief.

"If you go down that path to the left, you'll find the west country, all bright green hillsides and craggy cliffs by the sea. But yesterday that path probably led someplace entirely different. Where do you think it might have gone?"

The children murmured half-hearted, mostly inaudible responses, and he carried on.

"Maybe it went to the southern coast. Maybe if I had followed it yesterday, I might have found myself at the seashore, playing in the waves. Have you seen the ocean? Have you ever made a sandcastle? If you haven't, maybe I'll take you sometime."

One of the children whimpered behind him, and he said, "Is something wrong?"

"No, I'm just scared." The little whisper tore at his heart.

"We're almost there. Think of the sunlight on the waves, and the freshness of the salt breeze in your face. Just a moment more, and here we are." He opened the doorway with a grunt of effort, and braced himself against the slimy, shivering wall of the veil while he ushered everyone through.

"Where are we?" asked John with misgiving.

Theo looked around, pushing aside the vague fuzziness of fatigue. They were in a study that seemed familiar, though he could not remember having been there before. There was a table in the center, and he had an uncanny sense that there ought to be a desk instead, with a different sort of chair. The window was a little too tall. He stepped toward it and looked out, seeing the palace garden from an unfamiliar angle.

"I'm not exactly sure," he said at last. "Follow me."

This must be one of the rooms he had never before seen, similar to but yet not identical to the study he remembered. He led them into the hallway, and everyone clustered behind him.

The red-carpeted corridor was empty, and he strode down it confidently, knowing that eventually he would find a room or hallway he recognized.

At the next corridor he continued toward the sound of voices.

He rounded the corner to see His Majesty Lance Alberdale conversing with his son, His Royal Highness Selwyn Alberdale, surrounded by six of the royal guard.

Theo sighed in relief. He dropped to one knee and said, "Your Majesty, please forgive me for this interruption, but I have great need of your generosity."

He blinked when six swords were at his throat.

One of the guards growled, "Who are you, and how did you get here?" His eyes flicked to the children behind Theo.

Essie and John had curtsied and bowed deeply, but the children were staring in trembling confusion.

Theo heard one of the children begin to weep quietly, and said with a little heat, "Edouard! You know me."

"I do not." The guard pressed the sword closer to his throat.

Belatedly, Theo realized why the guard was so tense. "I'm wearing a glamour. Let me take off my jacket and His Royal Highness can vouch for who I am. I don't want to say my name in front of the children." Still on one knee, he removed his jacket, wincing as the movement pulled at his wounded arm.

The jacket maintained its glamoured appearance until Theo dropped it on the floor. At the sight of the exquisite embroidery on Theo's wedding attire which he had seen that very afternoon, Prince Selwyn sucked in a breath. "He's a friend. Let him speak with us privately, if you please."

The guard looked up in surprise, then sheathed his sword.

His Majesty glanced at his son. "You're sure?"

"Yes."

Theo picked up his jacket again, and the king led them to the nearest room, which happened to be a spacious sitting room. The guards stationed themselves at the door, which John closed behind them. Essie and John shepherded the children to the far side of the room, giving Theo as much privacy as possible.

Theo dropped to one knee again and bowed his head. "I'm Theo Overton, Your Majesty. Lord Willowvale attacked the children's home, and I didn't know where else to take them." He looked up, searching the king's face.

"Theo?" the king said. "Stand up, my boy. What sort of glamour is this?"

"A Fair friend made it, so Willowvale wouldn't be able to identify me yet. I'm sorry." Theo stood.

"Did I see blood on the sleeve of your jacket?" said the prince.

"It's fine." Theo let out an anguished breath. "May I leave them here with you, Your Majesty? I know it is much to ask, but he took two girls back to the Fair Lands." He clenched his hands and steadied his voice. "I do not want to leave them there any longer than I must."

His Majesty Lance Alberdale nodded. "Yes. If we can keep them safe, we will."

"Thank you, Your Majesty. Your Royal Highness." Theo bowed deeply.

"On your very wedding day," the king murmured under his breath. "I am sorry, my boy." He reached out to squeeze Theo's shoulder.

"What else can we do?" said the prince quietly.

Theo sighed. "I don't... I don't know. If you have any binding magic, I'll take everything you can give me."

"Binding magic?" said the king. "What will you do with it?"

"I would rather not say, Your Majesty, but I promise you it will bring no harm to Valestria."

The king shot him a shrewd look. "I know you well enough to know that already. All right, I can give you this." He pressed a little magic into Theo's hand, and it felt like a flutter of butterfly wings, light and ephemeral, in comparison to Juniper's fierce strength.

The prince merely shook his head; he had no binding magic to speak of.

"Thank you," said Theo. "If I may, I will bid my friends farewell and leave them here."

"Go on then," said the king. He strode to the door and spoke quietly to one of the guards, who jogged off to fetch a servant.

A moment later, Theo stepped back into the veil.

Theo ran headlong through the veil, letting the pounding of the blood in his veins distract him from the pain in his heart. There was little chance of rescuing the girls Lord Willowvale had stolen, but he could not give up without at least investigating.

When he was too exhausted to run any farther, he slowed to a brisk walk. He trailed his left hand on the wall beside him at times, feeling the different textures of the veil itself. There was little to be learned from the textures themselves, though; he knew where he was, and where he should go, by the feel of the magic beneath the texture.

Cedar had asked him about it before, and he had tried to teach his Fair friend, but it seemed the understanding could not be easily taught. Today the slick feel of damp, polished stone indicated that he was near the indigo forests to the northwest of the Fair palace. Tomorrow the same sensation would indicate that he was approaching the roaring valleys of the west. He asked the veil through his fingertips how to get where he wanted to go, and it was more or less obliging. It had been more cooperative of late, and he imagined the binding magic had been a factor. That did not mean various hostile inhabitants of the veil, or manifestations of the veil itself, would not seek to eat him or otherwise hinder his progress, but those incidents too had seemed to decrease in recent months.

When he had caught his breath, he ran again until his legs and lungs burned. At last, he stepped out of the veil into the indigo forest and collapsed at the base of the nearest tree.

He pressed half of the magic from Juniper into the ground beneath him, wincing at the burn of the magic. Juniper had said it was like a crimson thread, but Theo had always felt it as a warmth that threaded through his heart and down through the veins in his arm into the ground. Juniper's magic was so much stronger than any he had felt before, that rather than warmth, it felt like the white heat of the sun. Yet it was not painful, exactly; it was a burn like love, a longing so deep it shook him to his bones.

He sat for a moment afterward to catch his breath. It was too dark to see the indigo trunks and sapphire leaves above him that rustled in the gentle breeze. He let his head fall back against the trunk behind him. Here, alone in the indigo forest, with nothing but a few silent birds for company, he let himself think.

Lord Selby had carefully, quietly, warned Theo that he had heard Lily and Lord Willowvale speaking of the children. He had heard Lily say that she had seen the children, but he had only just come up, and did not know if that was all she had said, or only all that he had heard.

Lord Willowvale had certainly made himself as agreeable as possible to Lily. Theo did not think of himself as particularly jealous; he knew that a lady would be obligated to speak courteously to a gentleman, whether she particularly wanted to or not. Yet the tenderness in her expression when she had been sitting, and Lord Willowvale had said something Theo had not quite heard, rankled. Why should Willowvale be deserving of that tender, compassionate look? Any other fairy, but not Willowvale!

Theo shoved himself to his feet, clumsy with exhaustion, and opened another door into the veil. He jogged for nearly an hour, until he could go no further, and stepped out onto a mountainside dusted in white snow and pink flowers unlike anything in the human world. He fell to his knees and pressed the binding magic deep into the ground. The burn was deeper this time, and he let out a soft, pained breath before the sensation faded. He kept his hands pressed to the ground, coaxing the magic deeper.

He looked south toward the capital and caught his breath. In the Fair night, lit by a hundred thousand alien stars and a bright blue sliver of moon, the Fair city was so far distant it could barely be identified as a warm glow half-hidden behind a hill.

He opened another door into the veil. This time he walked, and at last, he let the tears fill his eyes. Still holding his sword, he used the back of his right arm to brush at the tears; his left hand felt the quivering warmth of the wall, like the exposed muscle of some great animal, and he grimaced. The silk of his sleeve and the texture of the embroidery rasped at the tender skin around his eyes, and he blinked angrily.

He stepped into the Fair Lands again only a short distance from Lord Willowvale's manor.

This stretch of the garden was not one Theo knew particularly well, but he could imagine the general shape of the land. Behind him was a gentle hill covered in a labyrinth of fairy roses. Their blooms were faded and the petals were drying on their stems and upon the ground, but the faint scent of remembered sweetness filled the air.

To his left was a large, mossy clearing which contained a number of stone benches around a central ring of stones. Theo had never seen this area in use; he had speculated that it was the site of either bonfires, or some sort of ceremony relating to the ring of stones.

He had emerged from the veil by stepping out of the trunk of an enormous tree, and although he could feel that Lord Willowvale's manor was near, he did not see it until he looked to his right through the thick hedge of some variety which name he did not know.

Theo began to cautiously approach the house, though he had no plan to enter it yet. When the nearest door opened in a splash of golden light, Theo was momentarily blinded by the brilliance that surrounded the silhouettes. He squeezed his eyes shut, trying to avoid being entirely night-blind, and pressed himself to the nearest tree and hunkered down in the shadow.

The door closed, and the three fairies trooped gaily to the open area, passing by him without noticing. Theo lowered himself still further, feeling on the ground for any sticks or dry leaves that might betray his presence with a sound.

The fairies flung themselves on the stone benches nearest the ring of stones.

One of them spoke, and Theo realized with surprise that it was Lord Willowvale.

"The Rose was there," he said thoughtfully. In the blue moonlight, Theo could barely see him raise a glass of golden wine high. The fairy was sprawled bonelessly on the bench, his head resting against the back and his glass lifted up above his head, as if he were looking through the liquid at the brilliant stars above. Theo could not see his face clearly, for he was facing away from Theo's hiding spot at an angle, but his posture looked nearly as tired as Theo himself felt. The thought gave him a perverse sense of satisfaction, which he immediately squashed. It felt ungentlemanly, if not outright unkind, to be so satisfied by the fatigue of his opponent, however detestable he might be.

One of the other fairies tossed a burst of magic at the ring of stones, and the air blazed into flames which danced in fantastical shades of violet and cerulean.

"How did you find the children?" said one of the fairies. "I thought you were at a wedding."

Lord Willowvale gave a low, scornful chuckle. "I was. Lilybeth Hathaway, now Mrs. Overton, was a wealth of information."

Theo's heart broke a little more.

"Did you learn anything else useful?" the fairy continued.

Theo could not see the faces of the other fairies clearly, but this one seemed vaguely familiar. Perhaps they had passed in a corridor once.

Lord Willowvale tipped back his glass and drank half of it. He muttered something indistinct, then said more audibly, "His swordsmanship tells me he's trained with a Fair noble. No human is that fast without Fair training, and he used that defense Barberry introduced ten years ago."

A sick sense of dread came over Theo.

The third fairy, whose voice Theo recognized with a shock as that of His Majesty Oak Silverthorn himself, said, "That is indeed useful. Lord Larch, you will undertake that side of the investigation."

"I am honored, Your Majesty," the other fairy said.

"What else, Lord Willowvale?" said the Fair king.

The fairy drained his glass and tossed it into the fire, where it shattered, producing scarlet sparks that danced among the flames for a moment before disappearing. "He has at least one Fair ally in the human world. It might be that young one you discovered. I saw two guests wearing Fair-made glamours at the wedding, but I couldn't see through the glamour, and I wouldn't have recognized that one if I had seen him. One of them is likely to be the Rose's Fair ally; the other could have been a human wearing a glamour, or another one of our kind. I don't know if that's the one who taught him the Barberry defense or not; if so, you may not find your quarry here, Lord Larch." He rearranged himself on the stone bench, and his profile, hard and tight, was visible to Theo as a silhouette against the fire. "I wish you all the best in the search. We shall put the Rose to the flame and see how he burns."

Theo had never exactly met the king, but he had heard him speak once several months before, and on two occasions before the war with Aricht. To hear Lord Willowvale now speaking to him with such familiarity made Theo lament again the changes in the Fair Court in recent years.

His Majesty Silverthorn leaned forward, and the light caught his dark hair for a moment, though Theo could not see his expression around Lord Willowvale's shoulder. "Your service to the crown will be rewarded in due time, Lord Willowvale. Your zeal has not gone unnoticed."

All the while this conversation had gone on, Theo had carefully felt for the human presences within the manor and palace and surrounding grounds.

The children were so distant, and so surrounded by Fair presences, that there was no hope of rescuing the poor children tonight. Not without a disguise and a plan.

Theo slid silently back behind the tree and into the veil.

For a moment Theo only stood there, letting the successive waves of misery shake him, before he began to walk back toward the human world.

Time was much shorter than he had hoped if Lord Larch was now seeking out a Fair collaborator. Cedar had been discreet, of course, but eventually he would be discovered.

Juniper, too, had been sighted, although not yet identified. Lord Willowvale would undoubtedly continue the hunt for Theo's young Fair friend, and the search would likely center upon the Overton estate.

And Lily.

His mind shied away from the agony of her betrayal. What had she told Lord Willowvale that led him to discover the children? At the very least, she had been careless, after countless admonitions and pleas to not speak of them at all. Certainly not to Willowvale, of all people!

At worst, she had deliberately betrayed them.

When a stone serpent snapped at his face in the dark, he barely caught it before it buried its fangs in his cheek. He wrenched it from the wall and threw it to the ground, then stabbed it through the head with his sword. It made a high-pitched shriek as it died, then sank into the lichen-covered floor of the veil as if it had turned to water. The shriek echoed down the tunnels and back, gaining new depths, and something else roared in reply. A strange clicking reached Theo's ears, like the sound of rat claws, if the rat were the size of a dog and galloped like a horse.

Theo ran, his chest heaving, and finally stumbled out of the veil about half a mile from the children's home, when the creature was far too close for comfort.

It was long after midnight, and the air was cool and damp. He walked through the deserted streets toward the home. The familiar buildings now seemed strange and bleak in the silvery light, so different than the blue moon and pink streaks in the Fair sky.

His horse had remained in the garden, eating much of the grass and half the vegetable garden. Now it was asleep in the rear corner.

"Oh," Theo sighed. "You poor animal. I'm so sorry." He cajoled it into waking up and put the saddle blanket and saddle on, cinched just tightly enough that it wouldn't slide off. Then he led the horse out of the garden.

He walked home, leading the horse the whole way. After such a fast ride, with no warmup, earlier in the day, he didn't want to strain it further.

An hour later, he reached the barn. He threw his beautiful jacket, now much abused, over the stall wall and picked up a brush.

He leaned his head against the animal's side for a moment before he began.

"Theo?" came a whisper from the darkness.

"Yes?" He turned.

"Did you get there in time?" asked Juniper.

Theo swallowed. "Not entirely. Some of the children were taken back to the Fair Lands. I went after them, and—" His throat closed, and he swallowed. "I could not get to them, not without a disguise and a plan. I heard Willowvale and Silverthorn talking, with Larch, if you know him. Cedar's position has become much more risky, and yours is becoming more so, too."

Juniper nodded wordlessly. He took the brush from Theo's hand. "I'll brush him," he said quietly. "May I take off the glamours?"

"Yes, please."

Juniper began brushing down the horse with long, sure strokes. "If I may say so, sir, I think you would benefit from sitting down now."

Theo made a choked sound halfway between a laugh and a sob. He leaned against the stall wall and slid down to sit in the straw. "I am a little tired, I suppose. But I cannot sleep for what I have learned."

"What is that?" Juniper spoke softly, as if Theo were a skittish horse.

Theo swallowed hard. "I do not want to believe it. But Lord Willowvale implicated Lily in his discovery of the children's home."

Juniper looked at him sharply. "Surely it was unintentional."

"I should like to think so." Theo's voice cracked. "But Willowvale did not give that impression in the least."

"He is not above deceiving you for his own ends."

"He didn't know I was there."

Juniper's hand trembled, and he said nothing else for several moments. "Be that as it may, you won't be able to think of anything brilliant if you don't rest at least a little. I'll finish with Milo. Sleep, eat a little, and I'll be ready to do your bidding when you wake."

Theo let his head fall against the wood. "Juniper, you are a gem among both fairies and men. I am glad to know you." He shoved himself to his feet and rubbed the horse's nose, then patted the young fairy on the shoulder as he squeezed past him out of the stall.

He retrieved his jacket and headed for the house.

CHAPTER TWENTY-THREE
The First Days of Wedded Bliss

B reakfast ended in a painful silence.
Sir Theodore stood. "You ought to talk about it," he said quietly.

Theo looked Lily square in the eyes. "What is there to say?" he murmured.

Lily put down her fork. She could not bear his icy facade any more. To go from his kindness and warmth of the previous months to *this* was not something she could comprehend, much less endure.

"I think I will go for a walk in the garden," she whispered.

"Do you not want to finish your breakfast?" asked Lady Overton.

Lily said tremulously, "I am no longer hungry." She stood and curtsied to Theo. If he were to be excruciatingly formal, she would return the courtesy.

What did he think she had done?

The question ate at her, but she was not ready to face it. He had asked her about Lord Willowvale the previous night.

She fled into the rose garden. The sun was warm on her face, and the morning birdsong was as soothing as anything could be.

Surely Theo did not think she favored Lord Willowvale? At their very wedding? She had been polite to the fairy, nothing more. Anyway, such an accusation did not make sense; Theo had seen her, danced with her, after Lord Willowvale had been gone, and he had not seemed upset then.

Something else had happened.

She continued walking, finding new vignettes of cultured beauty at every turn. There was a white alcove, full of white Iceberg roses, baby's breath, white camellias, snowy anemones, and a fragrant gardenia. There was a little fountain surrounded by purple and blue flowers, and a pair of white iron chairs and a petite matching table surrounded by a profusion of pink and coral roses.

Lily focused on the exploration; the overwhelming beauty of the garden helped push her emotions back a little so that she could think.

Had Lord Selby said something to him? What could it be? But Theo had seemed perfectly happy after Lord Selby had departed.

Theo had received a message which had come through Anselm, and that had prompted his departure. But even then, he had not seemed as angry, only hurried and concerned. Only when he returned had he been... angry.

She sat on a hidden bench surrounded by banks of rambunctious purple rhododendrons and let the tears she had been holding in begin to slide down her cheeks.

A shadow fell over her and she looked up.

She gave a startled little shriek, and the fairy did likewise.

The fairy's appearance changed faster than thought, and she was left blinking at him, half-risen from her seat.

Without a word, he fled down a path in the garden.

"Wait!" she called after him.

There was no reply, and he did not return.

Lily sat down slowly, trying to replay the moment in her mind. The fairy had seen her, cried out, and disappeared.

Why would a fairy be afraid of her?

She had barely gotten a split-second glimpse of him, more an impression than an actual image. A narrow face, wide eyes of a bright blue more teal or turquoise than any human could boast, and wild curls of deep violet.

Maybe that was the glamour, and the human face was his true face. She blinked, trying to remember him clearly. A slight build no taller than herself, and quite young. Hair of golden blond, and fair skin. Blue eyes, a human blue, not the improbable gem-like turquoise.

She sat with her hands in her lap, listening to the birds sing over the hum of insects and rippling murmur of the fountain.

Lily collected herself at last, prodded into action by the edges of hunger in her belly and the growing warmth of the day. She stepped quietly out of the little alcove and tried to get her bearings. The garden was vast, and this section was unfamiliar to her. She could not see the manor house, surrounded as she was by enormous bushes, so she began walking back the direction she had come.

Several minutes later she had figured out where she was and headed toward the great house that she had imagined would someday feel like home.

She found the patio empty and turned toward her suite without meeting anyone until nearly running into Anselm at the top of the stairs.

"Mrs. Overton," he said with a bow. "Mr. Overton asked me to send a tray up to your room."

She swallowed. "Thank you," she said. "I… what message did you bring to him yesterday?"

The man blinked, and his expression grew more carefully neutral. "I am not at liberty to say, my lady."

"Mr. Overton was happy before it, though, I think."

The servant bowed, hiding his face. "Begging your leave, my lady, it is not my place to speculate or tell tales."

Lily bit her lip. "That's true. I'm sorry. I only wanted to know what had happened. He seemed angry at me when he returned." The statement was her gentle attempt to probe for any information, but Anselm was entirely too savvy for it to be effective.

He said only, "Mr. Overton's business is his to share, if he chooses to. Not mine."

She nodded, and he bowed again, then strode away.

Lily found the promised tray in the shared sitting room. Theo was nowhere to be found, which gave her a twinge of intense relief and, simultaneously, a deep sense of desolation.

She ate on the couch. Perhaps she might invite her mother for tea, and her mother might have good advice. Lady Hathaway was wise and kind, and Lily felt she needed more wisdom than she possessed at this moment.

When she finished eating, she went to the window and looked out at the garden.

The elevated viewpoint helped her get a better sense of the paths in the garden, and she realized that much of what she had walked that morning was part of a larger, symmetrical area of plantings nearest the house. To the left she could see the stable, and beyond that a training ring, with white-painted wooden jumps set up for horses. The large paddocks extended beyond that, rising to a distant hill; beyond that hill, though she did not know it, was Lord Selby's ancestral manor.

A movement caught her eye, and she looked back toward the stable to see Theo emerge. He strolled into the garden with his hands shoved deeply in his pockets and his shoulders slumped.

Lily's heart went out to him, even as her own wounded spirit protested that she had also been wronged. He looked so miserable, and that was so un-Theo-like, that it struck her as deeply wrong.

Then another movement caught her eye, and she sucked in a surprised breath. The young man—fairy—who had surprised her earlier slipped out of the bushes and approached Theo.

How very odd! Did Theo know he was a fairy, or was he deceived by the glamour? The glamour would have fooled Lily, if she had not seen him for half a second without it. Was it the same fairy, or the same glamoured appearance, she had seen from a distance at the wedding, the one that had so perturbed Lord Willowvale?

She had just resolved to go tell Theo that this young man was a fairy, when Theo looked directly up at the window.

Their gazes caught.

Theo bowed in acknowledgement of her attention, and then glanced up at her again. The youth beside him bowed to her as well. Theo held her gaze for one more moment, then nodded and continued walking, his attention on the young man, or fairy.

Lily's mind raced. Were all fairies as horrible as Lord Willowvale? The youth she had seen, with his eyes wide in surprise and perhaps fear, did not seem particularly fearsome.

But he was not honest, either, if he were pretending to be human to Theo.

She resolved that, no matter what Theo held against her, he needed to know that he was in danger.

She hurried down the stairs and out into the garden again.

They had walked quite some distance by the time she reached the location where she had seen them, and it took her nearly fifteen minutes of hurried walking in the late morning heat before she managed to find Theo.

The youth was nowhere to be seen, but Theo must have heard her coming, for he turned to face her. He bowed formally.

"Mrs. Overton," he murmured, and the name, though she loved it, felt like a slap in the face.

Lily was quite hot by now, and the exertion and heat and fear had made her cross as well.

"Mr. Overton," she said grumpily, with a curtsy, then immediately repented of her irritability. "I am sorry to disturb you, since I am sure you must be busy. But I saw something that I thought you should know."

"What is that?" He swallowed and smiled, and although it didn't reach his eyes, she saw that it cost him, and that grieved her anew.

"This morning, when I was sitting in the garden alone, the young man you were just speaking with surprised me."

"Yes?"

"I think he's a fairy," she said, her throat feeling tight. "I don't know what he means here, but for just an instant, I saw him without his glamour, and I think he's a fairy."

Theo said, "Why would a fairy be here?"

She blinked at him. "I am sure I don't know, but I thought you ought to be aware of it. He cannot be honest, if he's wearing a glamour before you and pretending to be human."

Theo's gaze flickered, and he murmured, "Would you walk with me in the garden for a moment, my love?"

She swallowed and stepped forward to tuck her hand in his arm, which he had offered to her with perfect courtesy.

"Were you frightened?" he asked quietly, without looking at her.

She took a deep, tremulous breath and let it out. "Only a little. He seemed frightened of me, and it is hard to be frightened of someone when they flee so quickly. But..." She glanced up at him. "I know not what I have done to make you so cold to me. I wish you would let me know so that I might repent of it." She trembled, not daring to look up again. "Although you seem to hate me so suddenly, I do not wish you to be deceived by someone you trust. I believe he is a fairy; if he is not, he presented me with the glamour of a fairy, and I cannot understand why he would have done that and then given me his true face and then fled. Might he be the same person Lord Willowvale chased at the reception?"

Theo was silent for so long that she did, at last, dare to glance up at him. His face was stony, as if any crack in the facade would lead to its utter dissolution.

He opened his mouth, then pressed his lips together. She waited, feeling that patience was her best course of action.

Finally, he said, "Thank you for telling me. Please do not tell anyone else, I beg you." There was an odd roughness to his voice.

"Are you in trouble?" she whispered, as if anyone were around to hear them.

He gave a short huff of startled laughter and looked down at her with a strange warmth in his eyes, as if seeing her anew. When he smiled this time, it did reach his eyes, just a little. "The situation is under control," he said. "I *beg* you, my love, do not speak of it to anyone."

She bit her lip. "If that is what you wish."

He swallowed, then nodded. "I thank you."

Lily said impulsively, "I do love the name Mrs. Overton, and I am proud of it, because I was delighted to marry you, but I do so like it when you call me Lily."

Theo nodded sharply. "It is neither the first nor the last of many mistakes you will have to forgive me for, I am sure," he said, with a catch in his voice.

"My mother told me, several years ago, that marriage is a long commitment to forgive each other out of love."

Theo said nothing, only ducked his head in another bow.

They walked in silence for quite some time, until they reached, quite to Lily's surprise, the expansive patio on which they had danced only the day before, to the accompaniment of music and cheerful congratulations.

She looked up at Theo.

He bowed to her, still terribly formal, his face pale and strained, and he held out one hand to her. "Would you honor me with a dance, Lily?"

She could hear how her name almost stuck in his throat, the rough edges of emotion she could not identify.

Lily curtsied to him, but it was not meant to be cold this time. "I would be delighted to," she murmured.

They danced with no music. His hand trembled in hers, and she bit her lip and tried to hold back tears. She could not ask why he looked at her as if he were drowning; she knew he would not say. She caught her breath and bit back a sob.

They danced for much longer than one song, slow and melancholy and silent, and at last they stood facing each other.

"Thank you, Lily," Theo said.

"Thank you, Theo." Lily wanted to throw her arms around him, wanted him to kiss her until she could not breathe, but instead she waited for him to show her what he wanted.

He shuddered again, then bowed, deep and long, and kissed her hand with trembling lips.

The second morning after the wedding, Lily woke when the sunlight brightened her room to a white and gold glow. She dressed in one of her new dresses Mrs. Collingwood had made and went out to the shared sitting area. Theo was waiting, dressed in immaculate pale blue trousers and a matching vest over a crisp white shirt, with a tray of tea, fruit, and light pastries.

"Good morning, my love." Theo stood to greet her and bowed over her hand.

"Are we to be this formal forever?" Lily's voice was only a whisper.

"I am sorry." Theo invited her to sit beside him. He poured hot tea from the pot into their two delicate tea cups, painted with pink roses and accented with shining gold on the rim. "How might I please you, Lily?"

Her lips trembled, and she wanted to weep. Why was he not delighted, as he always had been?

"I just want you to be happy." She looked at him with tears in her eyes. "I don't know what happened, or what I did, to make you so... so unlike yourself."

His eyes flickered, and she thought for a moment he might weep himself. Then he smiled, and though it wasn't quite like before, there was warmth in it too. "I... shall do my best to be so, my love." He looked down at the tray. "I asked for a light breakfast this morning. Then, if it would please you, I thought we might go for a drive around the grounds, then return for a mid-morning tea."

Lily swallowed. "I would like that."

He clasped both her hands in his and bowed his head over them, as if he were praying, though he said nothing aloud.

The meal was quiet, but perhaps a little less tense than before.

When they had finished the last of their tea, she said, "I did have a gift for you."

He blinked at her, and said, "You didn't…"

"I wanted to," she whispered. She stood and hurried to her room. From the trunk which still contained most of her belongings, she pulled the pen stand and pen that she had chosen for him, as well as the handkerchief she had embroidered.

Her cheeks flushed pink when he accepted the gifts.

"Thank you, Lily," he said quietly. "These are lovely."

He offered her his arm; they descended the stairs and he took her to the front steps, where a bright little two-seat phaeton was ready for them. The horses were beautifully matched bays, and Theo stopped to stroke their noses and introduce Lily to them. He helped her up, then jumped in himself.

The drive was quiet; Lily admired the extensive grounds, and admired Theo's skillful hands as he drove. By the time they returned, she was getting a little hungry, and Theo had apparently planned for this too, for tea and cold meats and fruit and fancy cheeses she had never before tasted were waiting in a nearby alcove in the garden. Theo's eyes scarcely left her, and whenever she looked at him, he smiled a little. It was not the effervescent joy she had always seen in him, but there was something familiar in it, and it reassured her.

That morning set a routine for the next two weeks. She would wake to the sunlight, dress, and have breakfast with Theo. He invited her to enjoy the library, and she spent many afternoons in it, reading by the windows that looked out upon the formal garden to the north of the manor.

He asked if there was anything she might like to do, and she answered that she enjoyed playing the piano. He immediately led her to the music room and let her know that she was welcome to play the beautiful piano therein.

"Shall I play something for you now?" she asked with a smile.

"If you wish."

Lily chose the most romantic music she knew, a delicate, sweet little portion of a larger movement in a concerto. She had never played it so well.

When she looked up, Theo said quietly, "Thank you, my love. That was beautiful."

In the evening, they would eat either in a pretty little dining room on the west wing of the house, just the two of them, or in a larger dining room with Sir Theodore and Lady Overton. The meals were quiet and a little melancholy, marred as they were by the great, unknown hurt between them, but after that first breakfast, they were also careful and kind. Lily, though she felt wronged, appreciated the Overtons' kindness all the more, for all of them, herself included, made an effort to speak of pleasant things.

The third day after the wedding, Lady Overton asked her at dinner, "Theo told me you had been reading. Have you found a book you particularly enjoy?"

Lily told them that Theo had invited her to read anything she liked, and she had found a history of Valestria that was educational, though rather dry. Theo was quiet, as he had been since the wedding, but he managed a wistful smile at this.

The next morning, she found a well-worn book entitled *The Pirate King of Wakelin* on the low table in the shared space beside a fresh bunch of pink roses from pale shell-pink for innocent first love to a deep reddish-purple for passionate adoration. A few white sprigs of honeysuckle peeked out, signifying sweetness and the bond of love.

That gesture, only four days after the wedding and the subsequent hurt, was immensely reassuring to Lily. She spent much of the day devouring the book, which was not only immensely entertaining, but shed new light on Theo's character. She wasn't entirely sure how to interpret what she'd learned, but it was decidedly different than the history book she had been attempting to slog through. There was a great deal of sword-fighting and several grand speeches, and a triumphant victory of the most heroic sort at the end. The most delightful part of the whole book was imagining Theo as a bright-eyed child, devouring this story, and others, full of gallantry and derring-do.

"May I ask my family to tea soon?" Lily asked one morning about a week after the wedding.

Theo blinked. "Of course. Please invite them whenever you wish. This is your home."

She swallowed, then nodded. "Thank you."

That very afternoon she sent a note to her family by way of Anselm, who gave it to one of the stable boys, inviting them to tea the following day, if they were free. Only a few hours later she received the reply stating that Oliver was committed to an afternoon lawn tennis tournament with several new friends, but her parents would be delighted to see her.

The next morning she had breakfast with Theo again. He said, "Please convey my regrets to your parents; I have a commitment this afternoon that I must honor."

"I will, though I am sure they would have been delighted to see you."

"I am sorry I cannot be there." He gave her a sweet, though slightly melancholy smile. "I do hope you have a lovely time."

"May I ask what your commitment is?" Lily ventured tentatively.

He swallowed and looked down at the tea pot. "It is a private matter, my love. I will be honored to tell you, if it is ever possible."

She reached out to touch his hand, wanting to comfort him, though she didn't understand why he might need to be comforted. "I understand."

He glanced up at her through his coppery lashes, then down at her hand. He bent to kiss her fingers and murmured, "Thank you, my love."

Shortly afterward he departed on his horse, looking tall and elegant and entirely untroubled by the distance between them.

Her parents arrived not long after by way of a hired carriage. Anselm met Lily at the door as she hurried to greet them. As he opened the door for her, he said, "I will be delighted to take them home when your visit is completed, Mrs. Overton."

"Thank you, Anselm," she replied.

When her father helped her mother down from the carriage, Anselm repeated this offer to her father, who accepted and sent the driver back to town.

"Anselm, would you mind showing us where we might have tea together?"

"Not at all, Mrs. Overton." He showed them to a sunny little sitting room that looked over a sheltered little patio and a bank of pink roses. "I will return with tea in a moment." He let the door close quietly behind him.

Lady Hathaway had already perceived that Lily was not quite as deliriously happy as everyone had expected her to be after such a beautiful wedding to a man obviously madly in love with her.

"How are you, my darling?" she asked quietly. "You seem troubled."

Lily hesitated, then said, "I am not entirely sure, Mother."

At this moment Anselm returned with tea. He set out the tray and poured everyone's first cup of a sweet-scented jasmine tea which paired perfectly with the accompanying petite flaky pastries topped with whipped cream and raspberries. Lily waited until Anselm bowed and departed, giving them a little privacy.

"Did something happen?" asked her mother when they were alone.

Lily took a sip of tea, considering her words. "Theo is desperately unhappy about something, and I think he believes it was my fault. But I do not know what it was, and he will not tell me."

Sir Jacob asked, "Has he been unkind to you?"

"No, Father." Lily blinked back unexpected tears, thinking of that first night, when they ought to have been so happy, and then putting the memory aside. "But it is so unlike him to be melancholy, and I do not know how to help him, or myself, find the happiness we both expected."

Sir Jacob gazed at her, and she knew he saw the tears in her eyes and the trembling of her lip. He put his hand over hers reassuringly.

She brushed at her eyes and said, "I don't even want to speak of it now. I'm sorry. I oughtn't to have said anything."

Her father said quietly, "You don't owe us an explanation, Lily. But we love you, and we want you to be happy."

"I am. I ought to be. He's been so kind to me, even after... whatever happened." She brushed tears from her eyes. "He sent his regrets, by the way. He was disappointed that he could not be here to see you."

She showed them around the gardens and to the library, then, after more tea and talk of the garden, they allowed themselves to be taken back to the city by Anselm. Lily wondered what Sir Theodore and Lady Overton would think she had told them, but at dinner that evening, both they and Theo merely asked if she had had a pleasant visit.

CHAPTER TWENTY-FOUR
The Children's Home

E very day, Theo met her for breakfast in their shared sitting room. He was always up before Lily, beautifully dressed and elegant, though several times he eschewed the formality of jacket and cravat.

The shadow of grief over him seemed to fade. Lily was not sure whether it was truly receding, or whether he was becoming more able to feign something like his customary cheerfulness. The act was not entirely convincing; he was still quieter and more melancholy than she had imagined possible before the wedding, but he smiled sweetly at her and asked about her family, what books she was reading, and when he might take her on another carriage ride.

One afternoon, Theo was returning from an errand in Ardmond on Pepper, a dapple gray mare with a nice smooth gait and a proud head. When he turned from the main road onto the long curving driveway to the Overton manor, he felt a faint unease in the magic of the land, and slowed. It was nearly impossible to sense the presence of human or Fair Folk in the human world; even in the Fair

Lands it was challenging. So Theo slowed Pepper to a sedate walk and looked around as he passed between the birch trees.

There, coming from the rear of the house around the western side, was Lord Ash Willowvale.

Theo narrowed his eyes. What was the fairy doing at his house? In his garden?

The fairy strode to the edge of the lawn, where he had left a horse tied to a maple tree. He untied it and mounted with admirable grace, then trotted up the drive.

The moment he spotted Theo was clear; his sharp expression tightened, and his lips twisted in disdain.

Theo bowed with exaggerated courtesy when Lord Willowvale was nearly past him. The fairy returned the faintest sketch of a bow but said nothing. Theo walked the grounds, trying to feel if the magic was different, but he could discern nothing.

He spoke to Anselm later and asked how long Lily had spoken with Lord Willowvale.

"I was not aware that she had," said Anselm. "When do you mean?"

"I saw him this afternoon in the garden. Did he not come to the house?"

"He did not. I did not know he came, nor did your parents, as far as I am aware. Mrs. Overton spent much of the afternoon in the garden, but I did not see them together. I believed her to be reading."

Theo grew a little more pale, but said nothing.

He asked Juniper whether he had seen Lord Willowvale, and the young fairy said that he had not. He had spent the afternoon in his suite engrossed in a book. His window had been open to let in the breeze, but Juniper himself had been out of sight on a low window seat.

The very next morning Theo took Lily on a stroll through the garden. He offered his arm with his usual devoted courtesy and smiled when she accepted it. He matched his stride to hers and led her through the last of the late-blooming roses, where he pointed out lush blooms for her to smell.

"What do you do, when you leave for the day?" she asked. She closed her eyes and smelled the white rose he had indicated.

"I have business for my father, as well as my own pursuits," he said. "Most of it is quite boring."

Lily glanced at him. He wore a faint, pensive smile that seemed so unlike the effervescent joy she had thought an essential part of him.

She said tentatively, "I was wondering if I might be able to go back to the children's home. It has been over a month since I was there, and I did so enjoy my time there."

Some odd tension passed over his face so quickly she wondered later whether she had imagined it. Then he said, "I would be honored to take you myself, if you would like me to. My obligations today do not require me until late this afternoon."

"I would like that very much." She smiled sweetly at him, hoping he would smile, which he did.

They walked back to the manor, and at the door Theo said, "Please excuse me a moment. I will have the phaeton readied."

Soon they were on their way. Theo, now dressed for going out with jacket and cravat, was as elegant as usual. Lily had chosen a new green dress that coordinated nicely with his attire, yet she felt somehow shabby in comparison. He wore sophistication so naturally, as if it were part of him, and she was not yet entirely accustomed to it.

Nonetheless, she felt a swell of delight as the phaeton set off. Theo drove them himself, and she admired his skillful, easy control of the horses and the strength and elegance of his hands. She snuck a furtive, admiring glance at his profile. Everything she saw pleased her: his straight, narrow nose, his refined jaw, the elegant angles of his cheekbones, and his delicate lips always ready to smile. Always, until now.

"What are you thinking, my love?" he asked, glancing at her in turn.

Heat rushed to her cheeks and she murmured, "I was… well, I was thinking how much I like sitting next to you."

He shifted the reins to one hand and took her hand in his to kiss it. "There is no place I would rather be than beside you, my love," he murmured. There was the faintest catch in his voice.

"What is wrong?" she whispered. "Why are you not happy with me? I thought… I thought you would be."

His jaw which she had so admired tensed almost imperceptibly; if she had not been looking so closely, she would have missed it.

He said lightly, "I *am* happy with you, my love." He caught up her hand again and kissed it, as if to prove his words true.

Lily said nothing else, for she was afraid that if she did, she would weep in earnest. She did not want his false happiness; she wanted his trust and his delight, or if not his genuine delight, at least honest grief and the opportunity to repent of what she had done. She almost tried to carefully extract her hand from his, unable to bear the thought of pretend affection, but she could not quite convince herself to pull away from him first.

She waited for him to withdraw.

He never did.

Instead, his eyes still on the road, he pressed another kiss to the back of her hand, then on each knuckle in turn, then another into her palm, and another on the tender skin on the inside of her wrist. He did not look at her.

Her hand trembled in his.

His lips brushed her skin as carefully and tenderly as if he expected her to pull away.

The affection was as intimate as anything since the wedding, as anything she might have imagined, and yet he did it on the open road. To be fair, no one was on the road with them, but it still seemed scandalous. Yet he kissed her almost meditatively, as if each kiss were a deliberate decision. These kisses were not delighted, but neither were they light or false.

When a carriage came into view going the opposite direction, he shifted her hand to rest upon his forearm, and glanced at her with the hint of a melancholy smile before looking ahead again. He sketched a polite bow to the other driver as they passed.

Neither of them said anything else until they reached the children's home. The yard looked different to Lily, but she could not say exactly why. Theo stepped down from the phaeton and offered her his hand. When she stood beside him, he offered his arm and escorted her to the door. She glanced at him again before knocking.

There was no answer.

She knocked again, then said, "It is strange to get no answer." She strained her ears, but heard no sound of children's voices or footsteps.

"They are not here, Lily," he said quietly.

She looked up at him again in surprise. "Why not? Where are they?"

He produced a key and unlocked the door. Lily felt a distant sense of surprise at this, but of course it was not entirely beyond belief that he would have a key to the door if his money helped pay for the house and staff. He offered her his hand as she stepped over the threshold, then closed the door behind them.

Lily walked with quickening steps through the house, looking in the living room and kitchen, then the three classrooms with increasing alarm. The children were all gone, and there was a sense of desolation about the house that gave her the impression they had been for some time. She opened the door to the garden and ran out, taking in the overgrown grass and faded delphiniums, then closed the door in a daze. The kitchen was empty; a sharp knife and two spoons sat by the basin, as if they had been washed and left to dry, and the inhabitants of the house had disappeared before putting them away. She ran back to where Theo still stood in the vestibule, lean and elegant and apparently unconcerned with the children's or the staff's whereabouts.

"Where are they?" she asked, near tears.

"I cannot say," he replied.

"You knew they weren't here!" she said, feeling the sharp accusation in her voice. "How did you know? Why didn't you tell me this morning?"

He swallowed, and for an instant his eyes met hers, and she knew that his apparent indifference was only a facade. "I am sorry, my love." He clasped his hands behind his back, and swallowed again, as if his words nearly choked him. Then he said quietly, "I must ask again, what did you tell Lord Willowvale?"

She covered her mouth. "I don't understand." She blinked back tears. "Why are you asking me that? Are you jealous?" Her voice rose in incredulity. She could not imagine it, but men were strange creatures.

He gave a choked little laugh. "Should I be?" His gaze held hers. "When did you last see him?"

"At the wedding." She stared at him, her cheeks flushed and her eyes welling with tears.

He pressed his lips together, then murmured, "Did you not speak with him yesterday?"

"Of course not! Why would I?" Her lip trembled.

Theo swallowed again. It was not impossible that Lord Willowvale had evaded her notice, as he had that of Anselm. "I cannot imagine why you should want to speak with him. I am glad to know you agree." If the words tasted like ash in his mouth, Lily didn't know it, because his voice was steady.

"Where are the children?" Lily whispered.

"I cannot say." He shrugged and turned away, as if he did not care. "It is really none of my concern, anyway. I am sure the prince has found some other location for them."

Lily stared at him, trying to reconcile the tenderness of his kisses in the phaeton with his strange accusations and now his detached unconcern. He no longer seemed interested in the conversation at all, and the taut emotion of only a moment ago had disappeared like smoke.

"I think I should like to go home now," she said at last.

He offered her his arm without a word.

Neither Lily nor Theo said anything unnecessary on the way home, but the silence was not exactly icy. If anything, Theo seemed thoughtful and melancholy, but not angry.

When he helped her down from the phaeton at the front door of the manner, she said quietly, "There is no reason for you to be jealous, Theo."

He blinked at her, as if baffled by the statement. "I'm not." He said it simply, his voice soft and full of sincerity, but that answer only confused her all the more. He bowed, beautifully proper as always, then said, "If you will excuse me, my love, I will see to the horses."

He met her at dinner and said nothing more of the children, their disappearance, or that fraught conversation, either that day or later. In fact, he seemed to have entirely forgotten it by the next morning.

As usual, he met her for breakfast, already exquisitely dressed. She had worn one of her older dresses; he had seen every dress she owned by now, and it wasn't an appropriate occasion for one of her newer, more elaborate dresses. She had put a little glamour upon it to hide the frayed edge of the hem and the worn areas at her elbows.

She had gathered by now that Theo had no gift of glamour, for he did not seem to notice it at all, much less remark upon it. Instead, he asked if he might give her a ride around the estate, for there was a beautiful view across the pond at the rear of Lord Selby's garden from a certain hill.

As he drove, he pointed out sights she had not noticed on their previous ride, which had followed a slightly different route. There was a tree he had loved climbing as a child, and there was the stream that fed Lord Selby's pond. He and Lord Selby had once found a nest of turtle eggs near a fallen tree at the far end of the pond.

When Lily glanced at him surreptitiously, she could not read his expression. She sighed softly, aching for the joy she had expected with him.

"Are you tired, my love?" he asked solicitously. He looked at her, his eyes warm and kind.

"I'm fine," she said.

"I had a picnic prepared, if you would so honor me." He said it almost tentatively, as if she would refuse.

"I would be delighted." She smiled up at him, and the smile was not as forced as it might have been.

Theo stopped the phaeton upon a grassy knoll and helped her down. He spread a blanket upon the lush grass and lifted a large picnic basket from the back of the phaeton; Lily wondered that she had not noticed it earlier. The basket folded out to form a little table, and from the interior Theo pulled slices of thick bread still warm from the oven, a little pot of honeyed butter, slices of ham and turkey, grapes, sugared nuts, wine glasses wrapped in thick cloth, and a bottle of light wine. He smiled sweetly at her, then focused on the food for a moment. He prepared a plate for her and poured her wine before fixing his own.

"Why are you doing this?" she asked suddenly.

"Doing what?" He blinked.

The question welled up within her, too large and fraught to speak aloud. Her eyes filled with tears, and she brushed at them. "All of this," she whispered.

He inclined his head toward her in a simple, sincere bow. "I love you, Lily," he murmured.

She stared at his copper waves, then met his warm hazel eyes as he straightened. There was a guardedness there that seemed deeply, horribly wrong, hidden behind the warmth and kindness she had always known to define him. She bit her lip and looked down, wiping the tears from her eyes with one hand while the other clenched the fabric of her skirt.

Theo gently took her right hand between his and bowed over it, then pressed a kiss, light as a summer breeze, to each finger in turn. His lips were warm and soft, and his exquisite green jacket pulled over his shoulders as he bowed, showing his lean, athletic figure to perfect advantage. She wished desperately he would kiss her properly, but she did not say it.

The distance between them seemed to be growing, and she was too afraid, too grief-stricken, to know what to do. Theo's devoted courtesy seemed to simultaneously offer hope for some resolution and increase her distress.

One evening she ate dinner with Sir Theodore and Lady Overton in the garden. Theo was away on business, and though Lily appreciated the Overtons' kindness in including her at dinner, she also felt the strange awkwardness between them. Clearly they knew something of what had come between Theo and Lily, but they avoided the topic entirely, treating her with their customary warmth.

During the second course, Lily ventured, "Before the wedding, I asked Theo who had shaped him, and he said you both had been an inspiration to him. He said I might ask you about it after our wedding."

Sir Theodore said gently, "That was kind of him. However, I believe it is not yet time to share that story with you."

Lily felt a sinking feeling of rejection, and it must have shown on her face.

Lady Overton said kindly, "I would like to know whom you admire, Lily. It is a lovely way to get to know someone better, and I look forward to the opportunity to share our story with you."

Some two weeks after their visit to the children's home, Theo said during their quiet breakfast together, "There is the garden party at Lord Holmwood's estate tomorrow. I ought to have told you before. I was planning to attend, if you wouldn't mind. Then two days later there is Lord Hasting's ball."

Lily swallowed. "Do I have anything fancy enough to wear?"

He raised one eyebrow. "I should think so. Has Mrs. Collingwood not adequately supplied you?"

She looked down. "I... don't know how much is left on the account. I didn't want to presume."

"It was a gift." Theo stared at her, slightly pale. "Did you think I would retract it?"

"No, of course not." She bit her lip. "I just didn't want to presume, especially after..." She could not look at him.

He stood. "I may be a clod, but I don't think I am a miserly clod. Let us see what you have and then we will decide." He swept her up with him through her private sitting room, through her bedroom, and into the empty closet, where he stopped suddenly.

"Where are your clothes?" he said blankly.

"In the wardrobe."

He turned to her, looking confused. She showed him the wardrobe and winced when he opened it, feeling somehow embarrassed to have him see her dresses hanging up. It seemed intimate somehow, and they were not yet that intimate. Her idea of meeting him on their wedding night in his room, dressed only in her sheer nightgown, seemed not only alien in its boldness, but mortifying now, a month later.

Theo selected a dress. "This one looks lovely on you, and I don't believe you've worn it at a party yet, only at the private party with our parents and Oliver. Then for Lord Hasting's ball... this one. I'll ask Mrs. Collingwood to devise a wrap for you to coordinate with one of my jackets."

"Thank you."

He hesitated, then said quietly, "You should have her make you some more dresses, if you like."

"Thank you." Heat suffused her cheeks.

He was gone much of the rest of the day, only returning that evening, with Lord Selby in tow. Interestingly, Theo had the vague edge of glamour about him, but Lily couldn't see anything that looked unusual.

Why would Theo be wearing a glamour? Where had he gotten it? From his young fairy friend? Lily had not seen the young fairy after that one strange day in the garden.

Lord Selby stayed for dinner, and that was informative too. Lord Selby had, of course, excellent manners, and made himself pleasant to all. Afterwards, he retired with Theo and Sir Theodore to the study, while Lady Overton and Lily went to the parlor for dessert and to read a little before retiring for the night.

"How long have Lord Selby and Theo been friends?" she asked her mother-in-law.

"It must be nearly fifteen years by now." The older lady smiled at her. "Lord Selby is a year younger than Theo, but it has never stood between them. Lord Selby's father passed away unexpectedly a few years ago."

"How sad!" Lily exclaimed.

"Yes. We have been quite honored to be able to spend time with him. My Theodore had been able to offer advice and fatherly wisdom at times. I believe he may be here now for something similar."

Lily frowned. "Oh. That is very kind of you."

Lady Overton nodded with a faint smile. "He's quite a wonderful young man, and we are glad to have him in our lives."

At this moment, Theo left the study and strode down the hall toward his wing of the house, and Lily said, "Thank you. I should probably follow him."

"Goodnight, my dear." Lady Overton's gaze followed Lily all the way to the door.

CHAPTER TWENTY-FIVE
A Stolen Beauty

Theo drove the little black two seater phaeton to Lord Holmwood's estate the next day. Lily sat beside him, quietly admiring his skillful driving and enjoying the soft breeze that blew over the hills carrying the sweet scents of hay and heather.

"Is everything all right with Lord Selby?" she asked impulsively.

Theo glanced at her. "Yes. Why should it not be?"

"I just wondered. Your mother said he sometimes comes to your father for advice."

Theo gave a quiet huff that was almost an affectionate chuckle. "He does, yes. He is no longer able to help a certain friend, and my father has been in the same situation. He wanted to speak to my father about how difficult he feels that position to be, and what he might do about it."

"Is there anything to be done?" Lily asked with interest.

"No." Theo smiled at her, his hazel eyes warm. "Anyway, the friend can manage without Lord Selby's assistance."

"Does that hurt his feelings?"

"He's far too selfless for that. No, he's genuinely grieved, and the feeling does him much credit." Theo turned his attention back to the road. "Please don't speak of it at the party, my love. A man's private concerns brought to a close friend do not bear repeating in public."

Lily swallowed. "Of course not."

Because Theo had driven them himself, he took the phaeton around to the side, where one of the grooms took the horses, and helped Lily down onto the brick path beside the driveway.

The garden party was ostensibly to celebrate the first day of fall, but really to show off the expensive new fountain Lord Holmwood had recently had installed. The spread was not half as luxurious as that at Theo and Lily's wedding reception, but it compared well with nearly every other garden party hosted that summer. The garden was bright with brown-eyed Susans, goldenrod, stonecrop, heleniums, and chrysanthemums.

As Theo led her toward the gathered nobility, his customary cheerfulness and sparkling wit descended upon him as if by magic. Lily had all she could do not to stare at him in awe; for a month he had been shadowed by some secret grief, and now, before all these people, he was as carefree and sunny as a beloved puppy.

Was the grief not real, or did it only trouble him in her presence? Lily could not help feeling a little hurt. Perhaps instead he was merely a talented actor, able to hide his true emotions. She did not want to doubt his love, but the ease with which he assumed this façade brought a tiny, terrified little undercurrent of doubt that nothing had been genuine at all. She squashed it. Whatever was going on, this was only an act. It must be!

At the party they greeted Lord and Lady Holmwood, then were free to greet other friends and acquaintances. Theo was, of course, always terribly popular, and as newlyweds they were greeted and congratulated by everyone. He complimented everyone with practiced ease, leaving ripples of laughter in his wake.

"Will you honor me with this dance, Lily?" He turned to her.

The dance almost felt like nothing had ever happened between them, and Lily had a strange moment in which she felt utterly disoriented. She smiled up at him and saw only the familiar, beloved warmth in his eyes, the slight crinkles beside his eyes as he smiled back, the scattered freckles across his nose and cheeks. His hair shone like copper in the brilliant sunlight. Her left hand felt the strength of his shoulder, and the other the gentleness of his hand as he guided her into the next turn.

After three dances, for he did not even pause between them, Theo guided her to the side, where he procured a glass of wine and a tiny plate of some sort of cheese drizzled with a fruit sauce.

"How do I eat this?" She glanced up at him.

"With your fingers." He picked it up and presented it to her, so that she might eat it from his hand. It seemed ridiculously, scandalously intimate behavior for a party, but when she met his gaze, he quirked one eyebrow at her and smiled a little, as if daring her to accept it.

She did, carefully, quickly, and as discreetly as possible, and he leaned forward to murmur, "We *are* married. If they want to talk, let them talk. I certainly don't mind everyone knowing that I adore you."

But when he withdrew so that she could see his face, there was that faint uncertainty in his eyes. She took his hand in hers and smiled.

From his position near the much-vaunted fountain Lord Willowvale watched with interest as Oliver Hathaway danced with Lady Araminta Poole a third time. His Majesty Silverthorn had sent an alarming message to Lord Willowvale that very morning, noting that the mountains were quite lost in the mist and that the indigo forests were only pale gray. There were other concerning symptoms of the Fair Lands' malaise, but those two had been the ones that could be most clearly appraised from the palace itself.

Time had nearly run out.

Lord Willowvale stepped forward and asked, "Lady Araminta, would you honor me with this dance?"

The young lady swallowed and said, "Yes, my lord."

He danced with her, noting the paleness of her cheeks and the tremor in her hand. She was frightened, but she did not want to show it. He was quite a good dancer, and it was as easy as thought to put a faint glamour over them both and whisk her right off the dance floor and into the garden. She danced all the while with him, her eyes locked on his; he smiled at how easily manipulated humans were. She only heard the music, and felt the rhythm of his movements, and saw his steady silver gaze on hers. She did not notice that the stone beneath her feet had turned to grass, or that they were surrounded by rose bushes no longer blooming rather than other dancers.

He opened the door to the veil with a gasp of effort and jerked her into the darkness before she had a chance to cry out. The door to the human world snapped shut, and Araminta stood in a stunned silence beside him.

"Where are we?" she said in blank incomprehension.

Lord Willowvale said roughly, to cover his breathlessness, "The veil between worlds. Come along." He caught her wrist and began to tug her along.

He hated the veil. He hated the squishy damp lichen beneath their feet now and the broken bricks that followed. He hated the sudden buzzing of hornets from a distant cavern. He especially hated the things that lived in the veil, or were of the veil, the silver bull he'd once barely escaped, the tentacled thing that lived down that corridor, and the kelp-like plants that sometimes clung to his feet.

The darkness only made it more frightening. He could easily conjure a light, but it would only draw the predators more quickly.

"Where are we going?" Araminta asked tremulously.

Lord Willowvale did not answer for a moment as his heart thudded raggedly at the effort of keeping the veil open around them. The stone walls had an unnerving tendency to want to close in around him, and he had long suspected it would crush him if given half a chance. All Fair Folk knew the veil was treacherous at best; by its very nature it was changeable, and it often appeared to have something of a personality, if not sentience. It had taken a disliking to Lord Willowvale almost immediately, but it bore no such antipathy for the Marquess Camphor or his brother Aspen, who had been tasked with the actual procurement of the children from Aricht. Lord Willowvale had, as indeed had many others, been forced to conclude that the dangers were simply to be avoided if possible, and opposed if necessary.

"The Fair Lands," he said quietly. "It will be safer for us both if you don't speak."

"Why?" Araminta whispered.

He pulled her forward, his grip bruising her wrist.

"Ouch!" She yanked her arm futilely.

"Quiet, human, before something decides to eat us both," he snarled.

At that she quieted, partly because of his words, and partly because she heard something large padding quietly behind them.

"There's something back there," she murmured after several minutes.

"I know. We'll be out before it reaches us."

True to his word, Lord Willowvale opened a door only a few minutes later, while the unknown thing stalking them was quite a bit closer but had not yet reached them.

He stepped out into his own garden and breathed a surreptitious sigh of relief. Araminta shuddered beside him, then looked around. It was twilight in the Fair Lands, and the garden itself was mostly dark. Only the luminescent fronds of moon grass glowed at ground level. A few bright spark bugs danced among the drooping limbs of a willow. Above them, the pink and turquoise streaks in the sky were faded and dim; Lord Willowvale doubted whether human eyes could even perceive them now, especially if they were not looking for the beautiful colors.

"Come." He pulled her forward, still gripping her wrist.

"Where are we?"

"My garden."

"Why did you bring me here?" She attempted to pull away again, but the strength of a pampered human lady was nothing compared to that of a Fair Lord, superior by nature and refined by training in both the sword and other arts.

He did not answer. Instead, he tugged her, resisting all the while, to a room on the third floor. Here he pushed her into the middle of the room, closed the door behind himself, and stood against it. He waved a hand and the chandelier high above them brightened.

Araminta looked around, then stepped to the window to look out over the darkened gardens. There was a bed against one wall and a little water closet visible through an open door on the opposite wall.

"This shall be your room while we wait for the Wraith." Lord Willowvale smiled, not entirely cruelly. "You are merely bait. I have no love of humans, but I also have no particular grievance against you personally. The bed is comfortable enough, and you shall have adequate meals three times a day. There is a space for personal needs through that door."

Araminta blinked at him, too confused to be angry. "Why should you think the Wraith would come for me?"

The fairy's smile grew wider. "Why should he not? If he will come for children he has never met, he should certainly come for his beloved."

She stared at him. "What?"

"We shall see." Lord Willowvale added, "you may turn the light on and off by touching this section of wall." With that, he turned and strode out, closing the door behind himself.

With a growing sense of impending disaster, Araminta tried to open the door, but she was not surprised when it was impossible. She tried turning the light off and back on, and was relieved to note that the chandelier cooperated as promised. She turned the light off and let her eyes adjust to the darkness, then looked out at the garden. What she could see of the landscape was just alien enough to be disconcerting.

The concept of a garden was there, but the look of it, even in the darkness, was more frightening than any she had seen before. There were several trees in a bunch that clustered together, their long, drooping fronds like those of a willow, but they seemed to be dancing together, though no other plants seemed to be affected by any wind. Another area had a group of long, spindly trees with spiky needles for leaves, and one of them, quite unexpectedly, exploded silently, sending needles out in all directions. The resulting bare trunk and branches crawled with lights so tiny she almost thought she was imagining it.

Araminta had infinite faith in Oliver; she had admired his quick mind, handsome visage, and kind heart since she was ten years old. However, she did not believe him to be the Wraith. It had never really crossed her mind, and she wondered that Lord Willowvale had come to that conclusion.

He was brave, of course; her loyal heart was sure of that. But the Wraith? Surely not.

Nothing else happened that night from Araminta's perspective. She was left in solitude, and eventually lay down on the bed. After a while she undressed and slid under the covers.

Once she was safely and securely imprisoned in one of Lord Willowvale's more modest guest rooms, the Fair lord made his way back through the veil to Lord Holmwood's party. He returned scarcely an hour from the time he had left; the hurried passage through the veil left him winded and even more bad-tempered than usual, because the fear that threaded his veins was allowed no other outlet.

He threw himself morosely into a stone bench near the dance floor with a glass of wine and watched the gathered crowd for fifteen minutes. The Overton idiot and his new wife were dancing again, their eyes locked on each other in adoration. It made him vaguely ill; how could a pretty woman, who appeared reasonably intelligent for a human, tolerate such an empty-headed, frivolous fool?

He pushed the irritation aside and focused on Oliver Hathaway, who had begun to circle around the dance floor with more purpose in his steps. The youth had apparently realized that he had not seen Lady Araminta for quite some time, and had begun looking for her. Lord Willowvale let him look for a few more minutes, then stood and stalked over to where he had positioned himself near the edge of the dance floor.

"You're looking for Lady Araminta, aren't you?" he said quietly.

Oliver glanced at him. "Yes. I haven't seen her recently, and was hoping to dance with her again."

Lord Willowvale smiled. "Your little admirer is currently my guest in the Fair Lands."

"What do you want with Lady Araminta?" Oliver said in shock.

"You, of course." Lord Willowvale's white teeth glinted as his smile widened. "When the Wraith took children from us, we did not know what to look for, and the necessity of the children's work dictated that they be held in certain locations. Lady Araminta is necessary only as bait. We can hold her in a more secure location."

"I'm not the Wraith! I'm not who you want and he has no reason to rescue her."

The fairy shrugged. "Be that as it may, the trap will spring at the appropriate time." His thin lips curled in a small, mirth-filled smile. "I will wait to see what we catch."

Oliver gaped at him.

Lord Willowvale gave him a slight, mocking bow, and stepped back, letting a faint glamour fall over himself. No one would accost him now, with an air of unimportance layered over a general impression of a footman's garb.

Oliver stood in shock for a moment, his gaze focused somewhere in the middle distance, before he shook himself and looked back toward Lord Holmwood's merry guests.

He went first to his father and pulled the older man aside, whereupon they engaged in an intense, murmured conversation.

Interesting. Was Sir Jacob involved in the Rose's work?

Then Oliver and Sir Jacob together approached Araminta's father, the Duke Brickelwyte. Lord Poole listened to them without speaking, though his gaze roved over the crowd, looking for the offending fairy.

Lord Willowvale watched, unnoticed, while Oliver, Sir Jacob, and Lord Poole continued their quiet conversation. He stepped close enough to hear Oliver's quiet, passionate plea for Lord Poole's forgiveness, and his assertion that although he had no idea why Lord Willowvale seemed to think he was the Wraith, he would gladly go rescue Araminta, if he could find his way to the Fair Lands.

Lord Willowvale was not discouraged by this. Humans lied with great regularity, and he did not expect the Rose to announce it, even privately, to reassure someone he did not yet know well. Some time later, Oliver and his parents departed for home. About half the guests had taken their leave by then. Lord Willowvale retrieved his black phaeton and followed them home, staying far enough back that they apparently had no idea anyone was there, much less that it was he.

He retrieved his satchel from beneath the seat and sent the horses with the phaeton back to his house with a will-o-the-wisp for a guide. The grooms would handle the horses. Lord Willowvale stationed himself near the front door of Hathaway residence beneath an overgrown hedge.

No one left the house that night, and indeed there was no sign of magic at all. Lord Willowvale ate one of his two pears and half his sausage, and enjoyed a few sips of exquisite Fair brandy as a nightcap near midnight, but otherwise nothing but the birds broke the monotony until morning.

When the sky began to turn from grey to blue, Lord Willowvale rubbed his eyes tiredly. Still, nothing happened.

At last, near noon, Oliver emerged from the house. He began walking toward the road where he would be able to hire a carriage. Lord Willowvale jumped up and followed with his satchel over his shoulder.

Oliver hailed a little phaeton for hire, a worn-out little vehicle driven by a worn-out little man. Lord Willowvale hopped on the back as it drove away, unnoticed.

The phaeton drove Oliver to the Overton estate. Apparently the boy felt the need to tell his sister of his predicament as well. Lord Willowvale's scornful assumption of Oliver's purpose was proven correct, as only a few minutes after Oliver's arrival, he and Lily were walking in the garden.

Lord Willowvale followed at a distance. The grounds intrigued him more than Oliver's conversation with his sister, although he did listen enough to understand that Oliver was telling his sister that he was not the Rose. There was a great deal of fairy magic throughout the grounds; there had been a passage made into the veil, and presumably all the way to the Fair Lands, only a few days before, somewhere nearby.

His attention snapped back to the conversation when Oliver said, "Please help me, Lily. I need to get there."

"What will you do?" Lily's voice was anguished.

"I don't know! Skewer that Lord Willowvale through, I should hope." Oliver lowered his voice.

"How will you even find her?"

"I have no idea. But somehow it's my fault that he targeted her, and I cannot let that stand."

"No, of course not." Lily sighed. "What of the Wraith? Can we ask him for help?"

"How can I? I have no idea who it is."

Lord Willowvale narrowed his eyes and turned half his attention back to the magic beneath the garden. It threaded through the roses, making them bloom more exuberantly than any others he had seen in the human world. That proved nothing, of course, about Lily, her brother, or the Overtons; there were places with a greater concentration of Fair magic innate in the very soil.

If Oliver were the Rose, though, why would he be asking his sister for help to get into the veil? The Rose, whatever other qualities or abilities he might have, clearly had an unnaturally strong ability to enter, navigate, and leave the veil. He would not be asking for help from his confused and frightened younger sister.

Oliver and Lily eventually made their way back toward the house, but not before Lily had entreated Oliver to devise at least an outline of a plan before he ventured into the Fair Lands.

CHAPTER TWENTY-SIX
A Growing Distance

Oliver said to Lily as the door closed behind them, "I should probably speak with Theo about it. There's a distinct chance that when I enter the veil, it will be the last I see any of you. I should tell him thanks for everything."

Lily nodded, then said carefully, "You might find him a little less cheerful than you expect."

At Oliver's surprised look, she added, "I don't really want to talk about it. Things have been... different... than I expected."

"How so?" he said with sudden concern. "He hasn't been cruel, has he?"

"No." Lily shook her head. "I think something happened, something he thinks I was responsible for, but he will not, or cannot, tell me what it was. But it must have been horrible, for the look in his eyes, Oliver." Her voice shook.

"I wonder what it was?" Oliver studied her face. "Are you all right, Lily?"

"I shall have to be, I suppose." She forced a smile. "As terrible as it is, it does not compare to Araminta's plight. Let's not speak of it more now, please."

Oliver nodded, then looked around. "I am in awe of this manor, Lily. How do you find your way around?" He glanced at her, apparently unsure how she would receive this attempt to lighten the mood.

"I have gotten lost at least four times," she said with a smile. "I just keep wandering about until I find a room I recognize, or Anselm finds me."

"Anselm?"

"Theo's manservant. He has been quite kind to me, too." Lily led Oliver toward the patio where she had last seen Theo at lunch, but he was not there. Anselm was disappearing down the hall, and Lily called out, "Anselm, wait, please!"

He immediately turned and bowed. "Yes, my lady?"

"My brother would like to speak with Mr. Overton, if he is available."

"I am sure he will make himself available. Please wait in the little parlor across the hall and I will let him know you would like to see him." Anselm bowed again.

The parlor across the hall was dark and ornate, apparently devoted to displaying a collection of exquisite silk paintings depicting exotic animals. The framed images lined the walls nearly from the floor to the high ceiling. A desk in one corner was inlaid with light mother of pearl that shone against the dark wood in designs that echoed the pattern in the deep green rug on the floor.

A few moments later, Anselm appeared. "He is delighted to see you, Mr. Hathaway, and he will be here in a few moments. In the meantime, I will be glad to bring you some tea. Excuse me."

He disappeared and returned with a tray bearing a pot of tea, three delicate porcelain cups on matching saucers, and a tray of tiny lavender pastries. The pot emitted the soothing scent of a light mint tea.

Theo stood in the doorway a moment later. "Oliver! What an unexpected pleasure!"

Oliver returned Theo's bow with a wan smile. "It is always a pleasure to see you, but the reason is hardly pleasant."

"Sit down and tell me." Theo allowed Anselm to finish pouring the tea and devoted his full attention to Oliver. His hazel eyes were as warm and kind as always, and he looked away from Oliver only to glance at Lily with a smile.

Oliver poured out the story, with all the horror of Lord Willowvale's accusation and his own helpless despair. Theo's sympathetic murmurs, and Lily's anguished silence, gave Oliver time anew to consider his plan as he spoke.

"So, I will try to find a way into the Fair Lands, find Lady Araminta, and bring her out. Anyway, if Lord Willowvale thinks he has caught the Rose, he will probably let her go. Wouldn't he? He would have no use for her if he believes the Rose captured." Oliver gave a rueful half-smile. "When I think about it that way, it is nearly a patriotic duty to go and let him capture me, so that the Rose may continue his work."

Theo turned to Lily. "My love, would you excuse us a moment, please?"

Lily blinked. "I... I suppose." She stood reluctantly, feeling Theo's eyes on her as she stepped out of the room. She tried to squash a vague sense of being insulted, but the effort was not entirely successful.

She wandered to the larger sitting room nearest the front door and sat in the velvet couch, feeling suddenly irritable and more worried than before. The only reason Theo would want to exclude her was because he did not trust her.

Theo rose and shut the door behind Lily, resolutely suppressing guilt at excluding her. It was not for his own sake that he guarded his words, but Juniper's and the children's.

He sat back down at the table and took a sip of tea, considering his words. "I entreat you in the strongest possible terms not to go into the veil," he said at last. "Lady Araminta will not be harmed. Let the Wraith handle her situation."

Oliver frowned. "How will the Wraith even know of it? There are rumors that His Royal Highness knows who it is, but I have no claim upon His Royal Highness, that I might beg his help."

Theo looked down at his tea. "What would you tell him if you could?"

"I would beg his help! Lily and I went to the children's home for months, hoping to help somehow, but I always wanted to do something more. Yet now I find it is I who must beg, and I have nothing to offer in return. I should hope the man's heroism extends to chivalry for an innocent young lady as well as children."

Theo smiled again, and because Oliver did not know him as well as Lily did, he found it convincingly sunny. "I will be sure to convey the message."

Oliver froze. "You know him?"

"I do."

Oliver stared at him wide eyes, bright and hope-filled. "Please, Theo, I implore you! Tell me how I might beg his help, what assistance I can be, anything! I just want to help Lady Araminta." His voice shook, and he looked away, hiding the tears in his eyes.

"Trust me, Oliver." Theo smiled reassuringly. "He will be glad to help." He frowned faintly. "However, it may be another day or so before he is able to retrieve Lady Araminta."

"What? Why? How can you know that?"

"Please trust me. There are plans already in motion on behalf of children, who are not treated nearly as well as Lady Araminta will be."

"I do, but... how can you possibly ask me to do nothing, while she's trapped there?" Oliver cried.

Theo said quietly, "I will get her as soon as I can. I promise on my life, I will." He held the other man's gaze steadily. "She will be fine. She's useful to Willowvale now. He's cruel, but he's entirely focused on his goal. He will not divert from that in order to cause unnecessary distress to Lady Araminta."

A taut silence followed, broken only when Oliver said, "Are you quite out of your mind? Are you saying you're the Wraith?"

"I am."

"Does Lily know?"

"Absolutely not, and she will not, either. I had not intended to tell you, only I don't want you to do anything reckless."

Oliver stared at him. "You're serious."

"As death." Theo smiled as reassuringly as he could. "She will be fine, Oliver. She's probably in Lord Willowvale's own manor, in a little guest room. She'll be tightly guarded but unharmed. He'll feed her at the usual intervals and everything. Don't worry."

Oliver sat back, pale and stunned. "All this time," he murmured, looking at Theo with wondering eyes. "All right. What can I do to help you, then?"

Theo chuckled quietly. "I don't suppose you have any binding magic, do you? I need every scrap I can get."

"Not a bit of it. My magic is rather trivial." At Theo's inquisitive look, he said glumly, "My hair is never mussed and my shirts don't stain."

"Ah, well," said Theo philosophically. "It was worth asking." He stood and faced Oliver squarely. "If you value the Wraith's work at all, don't tell Lily."

Oliver's eyes widened. "Why not? She wouldn't betray you for anything."

"I am sure you are quite right. Nevertheless, do as I say." Theo held Oliver's gaze until the other man nodded reluctantly.

"If that is your wish."

"It is."

"Then I shall return home. Thank you, Theo."

Oliver bowed and Theo returned the courtesy.

Theo walked with them to the door, where he bid Oliver farewell and offered him a ride back home. "I have been meaning to go see Sir Michael. I'll take you home in the phaeton, if you like, and go by his estate on the way back. Do you mind, Lily?"

Lily shook her head, wondering if she ought to feel left out by the obvious lack of invitation. But a man certainly had the right to visit his own friend without his new wife in tow. "That's fine."

Theo bowed to kiss her hand. "Thank you, my love. I'll be back soon." He swept out the door, taking Oliver with him.

Theo returned two hours later, after delivering Oliver to Sir Jacob's house in the city and a quick visit to Sir Michael and his father Lord Radclyffe to ask for binding magic. Sir Michael asked his father for the magic on behalf of the Wraith; even Lord Radclyffe did not know that Theo was the elusive hero. After asking the stablemen to unharness and rub down the horses, he went to his parents' wing of the house, where he found his father deeply engrossed in his investment accounts and his mother equally engaged in a book.

"Mother, Father, I shall be in the Fair Lands tonight. I'll tell Lily that I've been called away on business. Would you please invite her for dinner? I shall likely return late."

His father looked up at him. "Will you be taking Juniper?"

"Not this time." Theo sighed. "There is a complication." He told his parents about Lord Willowvale's misapprehensions about Oliver and Lord Willowvale's resulting abduction of Lady Araminta Poole.

"What a horrid fairy." Lady Overton frowned. "That poor girl."

"I agree. All the same, Lord Willowvale is unlikely to treat her as badly as the children are treated. I shall, of course, do my best to extract her tonight, but I doubt it will be possible. She is likely held in one of Willowvale's guest rooms, and accessing those will be difficult. The residential areas have magical barriers that I haven't figured out yet. I will try to do some reconnaissance and at least assure myself that she is safe for the moment."

Lady Overton stood. "Will you be careful?"

He grinned. "As ever."

"How can we help?" asked Sir Theodore.

Theo sighed. "I doubt there is anything you can do from here. Lord Radclyffe and Sir Michael gave me a little binding magic, but Juniper is so much stronger, I doubt it will make much difference. I'm most concerned about Oliver and Lily. I told Oliver I would handle it, and I think he trusts me at least a little, but I cannot tell her."

"I really think you ought to talk to her. There must be a misunderstanding," said Sir Theodore quietly.

Theo ran a hand over his face, covering his anguished expression, then looked up at them again. "I know. But I also know what I heard. I cannot risk it, not while there are children still there, and Juniper in hiding. Once it is all over, maybe." He clasped his hands behind his back to hide their trembling.

"Oh, Theo." His mother was not fooled, and she put her arms around him.

He shuddered and said quietly, "Thank you, Mother. Father." After bidding them farewell, he went to Juniper's suite, where the young fairy answered the door with a book in hand.

"Good afternoon, sir."

Theo gave him a flat look. "Good evening, Juniper." He closed the door and said, "I'm going to the Fair Lands tonight, and I was hoping you might have some binding magic for me."

"Of course!" Juniper said. "How much do you want?"

"I have the feeling we are running out of time. I hate to ask it, but I would like everything you can muster."

Juniper swallowed. "Yes, sir. Just a moment."

Theo was not able to see the binding magic itself, only feel it when it was given to him and when he pushed it into the ground in the Fair Lands. So to him, Juniper's effort appeared oddly anti-climactic.

The fairy, already fair-skinned, slowly became deathly pale and began to sway on his feet. Still he continued doing whatever he was doing, until suddenly he gasped, "Here." He grasped Theo's outstretched hand.

Theo nearly cried out at the white-hot magic that lanced up his arm and into his heart. He caught Juniper as the fairy sagged and would have fallen to his knees, and pulled him to the chaise lounge only a few feet away.

"That was quite a valiant effort," he said quietly. "Thank you, Juniper."

The fairy's eyelids fluttered closed for a moment, then he mumbled, "You said you needed everything I could give."

Theo sighed. "I did, and I do. If this works, it will be as much your doing as mine, I think."

"What are you doing with it?" Juniper took several deep breaths and sat up unsteadily.

"I don't think you will be happier knowing, my friend. But trust me that I do it with great love for the Fair Lands." Theo poured a cup of tea from the nearly cold pot and handed it to Juniper. "I'll send Anselm with dinner for you as soon as it's ready. Sleep well tonight, and recover your strength. I think I may have need of more as soon as you're able."

Juniper frowned. "I fear for you, Theo."

Theo smiled reassuringly. "Don't worry. Thank you, with all my heart."

A few minutes later, Theo faced the most difficult farewell.

He found Lily in their shared sitting room with a book, as if she had hoped to be found.

"My love, I have been called away on business. Forgive me for missing dinner tonight."

She looked up at him, surprised. "Tonight?"

"Yes. I'm sorry."

She placed her book down. "Could it not wait?"

Theo shook his head. "Unfortunately not. My parents will be delighted to have you to dinner, if you would like to eat with them."

"When will you return?"

"Likely not long after dinner, but it could be later. It depends on what must be done."

Lily stood and twisted her hands together. "Will you kiss me goodbye?" she asked tentatively. "You don't have to. I just... thought..."

Theo stepped forward and bowed over her hand, then kissed her cheek as lightly as a breeze. "I'll be back soon, my love."

Then he swept out of the room, as if his heart did not ache at the distance between them.

Lily sighed and looked out the window at the garden. The fall-blooming goldenrod, chrysanthemums, and stonecrop had begun to take precedence over the last of the roses and rhododendrons. What had happened the night after the wedding? Was there any way to heal the rift that had suddenly appeared between them? For days, she had thought he cared as deeply about it as she did, but she had begun to doubt. As troubled as she was by Araminta's abduction, he had offered her little reassurance, and now he was off on business.

He would not even kiss her properly, on the lips. How much could he care, if he would not even kiss his own wife when invited to do so?

CHAPTER TWENTY-SEVEN
The Ogre

Theo stepped out of the manor on the opposite side, where he knew Lily would not be able to see him. He strode toward the garden, feeling the edges of magic tickling his mind.

There! With a sense of long-overdue triumph, he opened the door to the veil just at the edge of the lawn, only fifty paces or so from the manor itself.

The walls slid around him, and there was a distant rumbling as if some stone tunnel were caving in. He pressed a hand to the wall, and the floor thrashed beneath him, nearly sending him into a suddenly open abyss just a few feet away. Then it quieted, and he stood still for a moment, letting the veil settle.

He strode quickly through the darkness, letting his left hand trail lightly along the wall. Once, the texture was that of grass, and he stopped, surprised. He touched it with the other hand, wondering at the fresh smell and lively health of a plant which needed sunlight in the perpetually dark tunnels. Something slithered over his hand and he grimaced and continued on. Only a few minutes later, he exited the veil, stepping into a tiny grotto lined with amethyst crystals. Cedar sat in the fading light in front of the grotto, with his back to Theo.

"Good evening." He stepped out and spoke quietly. "What do you have for me tonight?"

Cedar looked at him thoughtfully. "The children have been split up until time for them to dance, and there's a human woman in Lord Willowvale's manor."

"I know of her. How is she?"

The fairy smiled faintly. "Fine, as far as I know. I saw her in her window two hours ago, and she seemed healthy and as calm as one might expect a human lady abducted by Lord Willowvale to be."

Theo looked around. "Where are we? I was aiming for you when I opened the door. This doesn't look like the royal grounds or Lord Willowvale's garden."

"We're south of the palace. I doubt you've been here before."

Theo knelt and pressed the borrowed binding magic to the ground. He squeezed his eyes shut against the flash of pain and heat as the magic left him. He would have little time later to disburse the magic, so he pressed it all into the ground, coaxing it deeper until it connected with the magic he'd left in previous months with a surge of strength. Then he said, a little shakily, "Where are the children?"

"Four of them are here, dancing now. The other twelve are in the palace. There is a weak spot here, where the ground has begun to flit away when you're not looking directly at it. They brought the children to dance in hopes that it will work."

"It won't, or at least not quickly enough." He stood. "All right. I take it you judged the others impossible to reach at the moment."

Cedar frowned. "I think we will need a better plan than I could devise last night. The poor children here are the ones most desperately in need of rescue. They've been dancing for nearly twenty-four hours already. I don't think it has made a bit of difference; at least I have not seen anything. Two of them are the girls you already rescued; they're the most fatigued, I think."

Theo nodded, his jaw tight.

"I thought it had been quite some time since you had been an ogre, and it might work well here. The fairies here are known to each other, but an ogre will have the gleam of magic all over it anyway. A glamour will hardly be noticeable upon an ogre's form."

Theo nodded again. "Will you be able to change my voice? Last time I only talked to the children, so it didn't matter, but if I am to intimidate the fairies, I cannot sound like this."

The fairy hid a smile. "Agreed. Also, since you are covered in magic anyway, might it be useful to have some sort of protection? I was thinking a sort of shell. The guards here particularly like throwing lightning and these concussive magic balls into the trees. If they give chase, you'll want a brief moment of protection, especially for the children."

"Yes, please."

With a moment of concentration, Cedar had given Theo's tall, lean form the appearance of a wonderfully intimidating ogre. His eyes gleamed a feral green in a pasty white, misshapen face; his lower jaw protruded so that his canine teeth were visible. He appeared to wear a much-soiled tunic the same color as the dirt ground into his skin.

"The glamour will last about two hours. That should be plenty of time for you to get safely away." The fairy looked him over and smiled a little more when Theo bared his teeth menacingly. "Try the shell to make sure you can do it."

The magic was a prickle in Theo's shoulders, and he didn't know how to use it at all, but when he thought of the protective shield around himself, the magic snapped silently into place. It felt like a soap bubble in his mind. Cedar tossed a handful of leaves at it and watched with satisfaction as the leaves hit the invisible barrier and slid down it to the forest floor.

"The protective magic won't last forever against direct hits of their concussive magic, but it should hold a little while. If I fill you with too much magic, you won't be able to think clearly enough to get away. If it breaks, which I hope it doesn't, it will scatter magic all over, which will give you a little edge of concealment if they try to sense your presence. What else can I do before we go?"

Theo murmured, wincing at the volume of his altered voice, "Don't you need to be at the palace?"

Cedar frowned. "I do not like to leave you here, knowing what you walk into."

"I shall be glad indeed of your safety and reconnaissance work when I return," the ogre said as softly as he could. "There is very little time left, I think, and I shall need you in place for the end. Please, Cedar."

With a sigh, the fairy assented. "Godspeed, Theo."

"To you as well." The ogre bowed courteously to the fairy, then started off through the woods in the direction his friend indicated.

The rescue itself was relatively uncomplicated, all things considered. The poor children were staggering with weariness, half-starved and dehydrated, and the fairies watching them had long since ceased paying any attention to them. The children danced upon a wooden floor made for the purpose and surrounded by something that appeared at first glance like a low picket fenced painted a cheery yellow. When Theo looked at it from the corner of his eye, the binding magic still in his heart combined with Cedar's protection spell let him see some additional magic, like a faint golden netting that bound the children to each other, to the dance floor, and to the strangely indistinct area nearby.

The forest floor seemed to be covered in slowly churning grey mist, although Theo knew that the forest had actually begun to turn into the mist. He knelt and pressed the rest of his binding magic into the ground, clenching his jaw as the burning thread lanced down his arm and into the ground. The mist seethed suddenly, then subsided a little.

It began to melt slowly back into the ground, or the ground began to reform slowly beneath the visible mist.

Theo ran silently toward the captive children. At the edge of the dance floor, he beckoned to the nearest one, a boy of about ten with haunted eyes.

The boy looked at the fairies, then at the ogre. Apparently deciding that the ogre was less terrifying, he stepped out of the dance.

In an instant the attention of all ten fairies snapped toward the dance floor.

Theo bared his teeth and roared, startling himself with the volume of his glamoured voice. Cedar had outdone himself with the authenticity of this glamour.

One of the fairies began to scream in a high-pitched wail. Another one gave it a vicious shove, and he, along with the eight more courageous fairies, began to take defensive positions against the other side of the dance floor. They apparently intended to use the magic of the structure, along with the prisoners, as shelter while they encircled the attacking ogre.

Lightning blasted past his ear, and he flinched.

Then he roared again and charged toward the dance floor, as if he meant to run right through the middle of the children toward the fairies.

A fairy with fair skin and brilliant green hair reflexively shot a fiery blast of magic at him. Theo threw himself to the ground just in time to avoid being incinerated, then shot back to his feet. The magic, as he had hoped, had blasted a hole clean through both sides of the magical barrier around the dance floor. He threw himself through the gap into the floor and put up the defensive magical shell. He bodily picked up two children and shoved them into the relative freedom of the forest, then hauled the other two children out. He roared at the fairies again.

All this time he had kept the defensive shell up, though he could feel it beginning to weaken. Cedar's magic was strong, but it had not been intended for this direct assault. But in the moment, seeing the poor boy's exhausted, hopeless face, he could not think of anything more effective.

Now, he pointed them through the woods and roared, "RUN!" The children pelted off in one direction, while he raised his arms and lunged at the fairies, provoking one last bit of panic that he hoped would slow them. He didn't know much about the ogres of the Fair Lands, but he knew that they were credible threats to even the strongest fairies.

He sprinted after the tired children, who had not made it very far, and gathered them into a little knot. It was harder than he'd hoped, since they were, somewhat understandably, terrified of him, but they were slow with fatigue and he was at his quickest and most alert.

"Stay together," he said as kindly as he could, in his gravely ogre voice. "You'll be safe with me." He pulled them quickly through the forest.

A blast of fiery magic splashed against his shield, and he felt it failing.

The boy in the lead stumbled and fell into a hollow large enough to hide all of them, formed by the tangled roots of an enormous tree that had fallen and ripped the ground up with it.

"Hide here!"

Theo turned to look at their pursuit as he pulled the children into the sheltered nook behind the fallen trunk. A tangle of buckthorn hid them from view momentarily, and he crouched beneath a sheltering bough as he pulled the last girl into the hidden space. He turned to hold a finger to his lips.

"Be silent," he said, as quietly as he could.

A bright flash of lightning ripped through the air to his left, and a fireball passed over his head. The fairies had lost sight of them, still confused after the ogre's terrifying attack.

Through the leaves, he could see that the fairies had split up in pursuit. He prayed they would not be able to sense the human presences, much less identify them as human.

Another fairy threw a fireball in his general direction, which he ducked.

A blast of lightning came from another direction, and he saw it only from the corner of his eye.

The ogre flung itself in front of the children just as the protective magic snapped. The sheltering bough above the little hollow crashed down upon its head, and dirt and rocks from the tangled roots above and the hillside pelted both ogre and children, covering most of the bough, much of the ogre, and nearly all of the entrance to the tiny shelter.

The children were stunned into terrified silence. The ogre was knocked insensible. It lay facedown in the dirt and broken tree limbs and roots, one arm flung toward them.

A sound above them made the children freeze.

For long minutes they crouched, terrified and mute, listening to the sound of pursuit above. There were several more crackles of lightning, and twice the ululating call of a hound, but higher pitched and wilder, from far away.

A distant horn sounded, and they waited, scarcely daring to breathe.

The ogre twitched one long hand, then gave an almost inaudible groan as it woke.

The children pressed themselves against the far wall, as if they could burrow into it to escape the terror before them. Yet the ogre before them was less frightening than the fairies hunting them, so they kept silent.

The ogre clutched its head in its hands and breathed out a low, agonized breath. It curled into itself, then seemed to gain a little more awareness. It tried to press itself up from the dirt before realizing it was half buried. Then it stopped and looked around, finally seeing the children in the shadows barely out of arms reach.

"Don't be afraid," it rasped. "I'm here to help you."

The eldest of the boys whispered, "You're an ogre."

The ogre gave them a wan smile. "Only for today." They had hidden so long in the little hole that the glamour had begun to fade. When he smiled, they saw his white, straight teeth, not at all ogre-like, inside the beast's great mouth.

"Are you human, then?" the boy asked. "Do you want help?"

"Yes, and yes, please."

Maybe it was the 'please' that finally convinced them that he wasn't an ogre after all.

"Who are you?"

Their rescuer swallowed and put his head in his hands, taking slow breaths. "It's a secret," he said finally. He twisted with a hiss of pain to shove some of the dirt and rocks off his back.

It took several minutes to remove enough debris so that Theo could slither free. He peered out the tiny opening to the outside, then listened for long minutes. At last, he said, "Right then. We're actually quite close to the way home. Stay with me."

He squeezed out the hole and crouched dizzily at the top. The darkness was nearly absolute, and they could see him only as a vague outline against the unfamiliar stars. The Fair Lands had ever-shifting streaks of pink and cerulean across the sky, brightly visible at night and lighter during the day. Against the pink hue, they saw his double profile, both human and ogre, for a moment as he looked around, listening, then motioned them to come out.

"Hold my hands." He gave them a reassuring squeeze. "We're almost there."

He led them quickly through the trees. The children were terrified, but the human ogre did not seem frightened at all, and that reassured them. At last he led them around a tree twice, then stepped into utter darkness.

"What is this, sir?" gasped one of the younger children.

"Just a little shadow to keep us hidden. Don't be afraid." Theo kept his voice light and reassuring. He led them through the darkness for what felt like hours, keeping his steps steady as long as he could. At least there was no sound of pursuit. The inky black spun around him.

"We'll have to stop for a moment." He stumbled to his knees and retched. The motion only made the pain and nausea worse, and he heaved again. He bent double, resting his head on the cool, smooth stone floor.

The murmurs of the children brought him back from the haze of throbbing agony in his head and weakness that made him tremble. He struggled to his feet and groped for them in the darkness, finding first their shoulders, then their small hands.

"We're nearly there. You've been very brave. Just a little farther."

It was not only a little farther; it was at least another hour. He staggered drunkenly toward the door he could not see, murmuring reassurances to the frightened children clinging to him.

Finally, he said, "I need my hand. Here, hold my jacket." He guided the child's hand to the cloth, then let go. He opened the door with his free hand, and they stepped out of the darkness into the shadows beside the guardhouse outside the palace. He stared at the guardhouse for a moment in confusion. It would have been better to take them to the palace, where Essie and John would care for them, but he must have become disoriented in the darkness and taken one too many lefts. Or was it rights?

Theo raised a fist and pounded on the guardhouse door. At an answering sound from inside, he stepped back into the shadows. He waited until the guardsman opened the door and brought the children in, then slipped away.

He didn't make it far. Dizzy, aching, and nauseated, he leaned against a wall, thinking muzzily of his options. Finally he stepped back into the veil and collapsed just inside the entrance. He didn't even notice when the darkness took him.

CHAPTER TWENTY-EIGHT
A Lonely Morning

T heo groaned and blinked into the shadows, then struggled to his feet. He braced himself against the damp stone and took deep, slow breaths to quell the nausea while he tried to get his bearings. The way home was not far distant, and he staggered toward it, bracing himself against the dripping wall.

The door, or what he thought of as a door, to the human world opened readily to him, and in the right location. He closed it carefully behind him.

The lawn was silvered by moonlight, already damp with dew. It must have been an hour or two after midnight. He stumbled across the grass toward the west wing of the house and let himself in.

He leaned against the wall at intervals as he made his way through the corridor. The wide, sweeping stairway loomed above him, and he paused at the bottom, gathering his strength.

"Thank God." The whisper came from his left. Anselm raised a candle and took in Theo's appearance. "You're dead on your feet, sir." He pulled Theo's arm over his shoulders and began to haul him upstairs.

"Gently, my friend," Theo groaned.

"Where are you injured?"

"I'm all right. Just need a bit of sleep." Theo stumbled on the next step and would have fallen but for Anselm's solid strength beside him.

"You don't look it. Shall I call the physician? Your dinner's long cold but I can warm you something. Beef broth to start with?"

"Just sleep, Anselm. I need to look cheerful for the ball tonight."

Anselm huffed in disbelief. "Cheerful isn't the problem, sir. You need to look alive, and that's more of a stretch."

Theo laughed under his breath. "You know me too well." Then he grew silent, because the steps were swimming before his eyes in a most alarming manner, and he did not want to heave up whatever little remained in his stomach onto the loyal servant's slippers.

"Here we are, sir," said Anselm. "Let me get you undressed."

"I'm fine. Go to bed, Anselm."

"Just cooperate before I wake your mother and tell her the state you're in." Anselm did not mention Lily. He did not know exactly what had passed between them, but he knew that it was not the time to prod the wound.

Theo blinked dizzily at the pattern on the rug. "That's blackmail," he muttered. "You should be ashamed of yourself."

"Yet I am not." Anselm pushed Theo's hands aside and began to work on the buttons of his shirt.

Theo closed his eyes.

Distantly he heard Anselm's hiss of dismay at the bruises across his back, the ugly scrape from the broken end of a branch, the dirt that had slithered down his collar and gathered at the small of his back beneath his shirt, and the knot on the back of his head that Anselm found with careful fingers.

Then there was only darkness.

Breakfast was a lonely affair. Lily had hoped Theo would come to breakfast, and if they could not entirely trust each other, these quiet mornings were at least the beginning of reconciliation. But he did not appear. She did not dare venture into his private suite, so finally she wandered down to the dining room, which was empty.

She asked Anselm, "Will Mr. Overton be coming down for breakfast?" She hated that her voice sounded so forlorn.

"No. He will take breakfast in his suite this morning."

"Oh."

The servant kept his eyes straight ahead and his face carefully schooled into a neutral expression. He did, however, say blandly, "If I may, my lady, I would venture to guess that his absence this morning has little to do with you. I believe he has a headache."

Lily nodded, not believing a word of it. Anselm had been troubled by the rift between them, and he would try to mend it at every opportunity.

"Thank you, Anselm," she murmured.

CHAPTER TWENTY-NINE
Disappointment

L ord Willowvale had conscripted two of his servants to continue his surveillance of Oliver that night while he snatched a few hours' sleep on the wide seat of a nearby carriage. The servants were sworn to wake him if Oliver did anything at all.

He woke to the grey light of dawn, having slept nearly the whole night through, and stormed up the oak tree from whose branches his lackey had been watching the Hathaway front entrance.

"You didn't wake me? Why not? Has he done nothing at all?"

"No, my lord. Nothing." The fairy gestured at the door. "I've heard nothing from Hemlock, either."

Lord Willowvale, fuming, walked around the block to find the other fairy perched comfortably in an old maple tree with a view of the rear of the house and the small, enclosed garden.

"Nothing?" he asked in disbelief.

"Nothing, my lord."

At that moment, Oliver emerged from the rear door. He proceeded to spend the next two hours pacing the garden.

Lord Willowvale climbed the tree and settled in to the crook of a branch. Over the following hours, he became increasingly frustrated and irritable at the young man's apparently impotent distress.

In recent months, Lord Willowvale had accused nearly everyone in the Valestrian court of being in league with the Rose, albeit always in the form of a question to skirt that pesky inability to lie. He had spent a great deal of time studying human facial expressions and trying to understand those alien creatures. Miss Hathaway's reaction to his accusation had been the most interesting, indicating not only fear but some level of shocked, unhappy assent, though she had not exactly said as much. This had supported Lord Willowvale's vague but growing suspicion of her brother Oliver.

The fairy who had been surveilling the front of the house came to the bottom of the tree in which they sat. When Lord Willowvale jumped down to meet him, he informed the Special Envoy that there had been a confirmed Rose incident the night before in the Fair Lands some distance from the palace. Four children had been taken by the Rose to the new, unknown refuge.

Lord Willowvale sighed, frustrated to the depths of his soul, and growled to himself.

"Keep following him, in case anything interesting happens," he said finally. "I'm going to the Fair Lands to investigate."

Lord Willowvale's clever theory that Oliver Hathaway was the Rose was unraveling before his eyes. The Fair lord was entirely focused on his goal of catching the Rose and not unwilling to reconsider his conclusion based on new information. But he had precious little other information to work with. Perhaps the interrogations of the fairies tasked with guarding the children would yield something useful.

CHAPTER THIRTY
A Troubled Afternoon

A nselm entered Theo's suite not long before noon, having already ascertained that Lily was not in the shared space and thus would be unlikely to overhear anything. He was alarmed to see that the young man was still asleep and had apparently not shifted since Anselm had helped him into bed in the early hours of the morning.

"Theo," he said quietly. "Wake up. You need a bath."

To Anselm's immense relief, Theo groaned and turned his head, but that was the extent of his response.

"Wake up, Theo," Anselm said more firmly. He strode to the window and flung the curtains open, letting the golden late morning light flood the room.

Theo groaned again and covered his face, then mumbled, "Anselm, if you don't close the shades I'll vomit on your shoes, and you'll deserve it."

Anselm pulled them halfway closed. "What happened last night?"

"I think a tree fell on me." Eyes shut tight against the light, Theo tried to sit up and nearly fell out of the bed.

"You're bleeding," Anselm said in surprise. "I didn't see that last night. I should have looked closer."

Theo grunted, his head buried in his hands.

Anselm drew closer and gently pushed the young man's hands aside. "From your ears, sir." The servant looked at each ear and determined that the bleeding had stopped. The right ear was the worst, and there was a dark spot on the pillow where Theo had laid. Anselm pulled the pillowcase off to wash.

"Shouldn't wonder. My brain was nearly turned to jelly," Theo muttered. "I'll be all right."

"I'll heat bath water. I don't think attending the ball tonight is wise."

Theo sat with his eyes closed, picking at the blood crusted around his right ear. "I'll be all right," he repeated.

"I'll bring up some beef broth while the water is heating." Anselm looked at Theo doubtfully. "I'll help you downstairs. Don't go gallivanting about yet; you look a bit wobbly."

Theo mumbled something like agreement, and the servant hurried off.

When Anselm returned with a cup of steaming beef broth, Theo still sat slumped on the edge of the bed.

"Here's a bit of broth, Theo. Drink it, please."

Theo took the cup mechanically and stared at it. "Were you here a few minutes ago, Anselm?"

"Yes, sir." The servant looked at him in concern. "Don't you remember?"

Theo swallowed. "Yes, I do. I just… wasn't sure." He drank a little from the cup, then lowered it and stared at the broth again. "What time is it?"

"Almost noon."

Theo looked up, surprised. "Have any messages come?"

Anselm regarded him with misgiving. "No, sir. Please drink your broth."

Theo rubbed a hand over his face, then drained the cup. "No messages," he murmured. His hand shook when he handed the cup back to Anselm, who set it on a nearby table.

"You're sure there were no messages?" he asked again. "Cedar was going to check on Lady Araminta again to be sure she was safe."

"It has been an hour since I checked. I can go look again." Anselm frowned. "Let me get you to the bath first."

"I'm fine," said Theo in vague irritation. He rose, then staggered and would have lost his balance except that Anselm caught him by the upper arms and steadied him.

"Sure you are, sir, and I'll just have you put your arm around my shoulders while we go downstairs to the bath for my own amusement," said Anselm grimly.

"All right." Theo made no more protest, and said only, "Anyway, I'm going to be dancing tonight, so I'd better save my strength. It's embarrassing, Anselm."

The servant huffed a laugh under his breath. "Why? I won't tell anyone you leaned on me."

Theo steadied as they walked, but Anselm didn't trust him on the stairs.

Anselm added, "Anyone else would be dead, you know. You have the hardest head of anyone I've ever met."

Theo grinned. "I am truly superlative."

This good-natured jibe reassured Anselm, as Theo had intended. He was thinking more clearly, though the pounding in his head had not abated and the ground seemed to shift beneath his feet with every step.

He managed to climb into the bath without losing his scant broth lunch or falling in headfirst. He soaked in the warmth until the water grew cold, scrubbed in the chill, and rinsed with water nearly hot enough to scald him. By the time he finally dressed, he felt almost functional, despite the ever-present throb in his head.

"How is Lily?" he asked in a low voice.

"Quiet and troubled." Anselm added, "I'll bring you lunch in your room, if you aren't up to seeing anyone yet."

Theo sighed and closed his eyes. "I feel like a coward."

Anselm's lips twisted in dismay, but he said nothing.

"I think I'll eat on the private patio, if you don't mind bringing lunch out. Would you let her know she is welcome to join me?" Theo consoled himself with the thought that the decision was now hers, but the guilt remained. She wanted to be pursued, and he was withdrawing.

Anselm walked with him out to the patio, ready to lend a steadying hand, if necessary, but Theo didn't need it. He let himself gently down into one of the padded chairs and nodded when Anselm quietly excused himself.

Anselm walked first to the sunroom where Lily was sure to be found reading. "Mrs. Overton, Mr. Overton has elected to take lunch on the private patio. He invited you to join him, if you'd like."

Lily looked up at him and bit her lip. "Would he like me to, or was he just being kind?" she asked quietly.

"I'm sure he would be delighted to see you," Anselm lied without a twinge of guilt.

Lily rose and brushed a hand over her skirt. Why should she be shy about seeing her own husband? It was ridiculous. But the tension of the past few days, coupled with Anselm's obvious unhappiness, played upon her nerves. She clasped her hands together, trying to steady them, but they kept shaking. Her stomach turned over.

It wasn't as if Theo would be cruel to her. Even in his disappointment he had not said anything outright unkind. It was that deep, soul-crushing grief and regret in his eyes that had wrung her soul. Yet did she not have just as much reason to be disappointed?

She followed Anselm into the hallway, then turned toward the patio while Anselm hurried to the kitchen.

She looked out the window, hoping to catch a glimpse of Theo before seeing him face to face. She told herself it would calm her nerves.

He was sprawled in one of the chairs, which was turned to overlook the garden. He was slouched so far down that his auburn curls barely peeked over the back of the chair, and his long legs were stretched out in the sun.

Anselm emerged from another door and approached with a tray, which he put on the table near Theo's right hand. Lily couldn't hear what they were saying, but she was surprised to see Anselm kneel at Theo's side, listening with a concerned expression on his face.

She shifted, wishing she had the courage to go outside, and the movement must have caught the servant's attention, for he suddenly glanced her direction. His eyebrows lowered, and he gave the slightest beckoning motion, as if he wanted to command her but knew it would be inappropriate.

Theo must have said something, for Anselm looked back at him, then shook his head. He did not look at her again.

Lily stepped back from the window.

Maybe she would have gathered her courage by evening.

CHAPTER THIRTY-ONE
A Brave Farewell

Oliver arrived in a hired carriage just after lunch. He greeted Lily with badly concealed impatience, asking for Theo. There were dark shadows under his eyes.

"I haven't spoken with him today. He's probably still out on the patio. Have you slept at all, Oliver?"

"Not really. I must speak with Theo, Lily. Please."

With a pang, she recalled Theo's oddly slouched posture and wondered whether he still had a headache. Still, Oliver seemed to think it was important, so she led him toward the patio.

They met Anselm in the hallway. "Is Theo still outside?" Lily asked tentatively.

"Yes. Does Mr. Hathaway wish to speak to him?" Anselm looked between them.

"Yes, please." Oliver answered hurriedly.

Anselm hesitated, then said, "Please wait in the study. I will let him know you are here."

Oliver said, "I can come to him!"

Anselm shook his head. "Please wait in the study, Mr. Hathaway." His voice had assumed the calm air of competency that encouraged even the highest-ranking noblemen to cooperate.

Oliver hurried away, and Lily followed in his wake. "Lily, I actually need to speak to Theo privately. I'm sorry."

She blinked at him. "All right." With a frown, she walked to the front parlor with her head held high. Yet another layer of disillusionment settled like gauze over her heart.

Why should Oliver be more interested in talking to Theo than to her, and indeed wish to leave her out completely? She would not have minded had it been a jaunty afternoon ride over the hills or a hunting trip with other young gentlemen. But to so blatantly ask her to leave, when she already felt so ill at ease!

Lily did not mean to be angry. She did not want to be angry. She stuffed down the feeling and focused on Araminta's plight. Was there a way to help her from here?

Oliver paced anxiously in the study. It seemed to him to be suddenly small and close, the air stifling.

Theo entered with a murmured thanks to Anselm, who had apparently walked him to the very door of the room. The servant bowed and shut the door.

Oliver stared at Theo with wide, anguished eyes. "Did you see her?"

"No." Theo crossed his arms and leaned against the door-frame, as lean and elegant as ever. "However, a trusted friend and ally saw her from a distance earlier in the day, and said she appeared to be fine. There were complications, and I was unable to reach her last night."

"Complications?"

Theo nodded once, then decided it would be wiser to sit down on the chaise lounge before he fell over. He sat half turned so that he could see Oliver. He gestured toward the chair across from him, and Oliver sat, one leg bouncing a nervous rhythm.

"Are you all right? You look rather pale." Oliver looked more closely at Theo.

"I have a bit of a headache," Theo admitted quietly. "Don't worry, Oliver. My friend will let me know if Lady Araminta's situation becomes dire. In the meantime, please trust me."

Oliver buried his face in his hands. "I am trying to, but I cannot think of anything but how frightened she must be, and how horrible Lord Willowvale is, and how I *must* do something immediately." His voice cracked.

Theo sighed softly. His head ached dreadfully, and the pounding made it difficult to think. "I swore to you I would bring her back, and I will."

"Can I help?" Oliver asked in a low voice. "Please tell me what to do. I'll do anything."

Theo said, more sharply than he intended, "Don't *ever* say those words, Oliver! Not to me, not to anyone, and especially not when a fairy might hear you." Sudden nausea rose, and he closed his eyes and swallowed. "Go get some sleep, Oliver, if you can."

Oliver shuddered and stared at him. "I can't sleep, knowing she's a prisoner of that horrible Willowvale."

"Nevertheless, please try to trust me." Theo held Oliver's gaze until the other man nodded. Theo stood then. "I am sorry to be so rude, but my headache is actually rather vicious. I think I would like to lie down before the party tonight. Please do make yourself at home here, if you like. Just don't tell Lily what we discussed."

Recognizing the obvious dismissal, Oliver stood as well. "Thank you, Theo," he said dully.

Anselm was waiting at the door and, after having been volunteered by Theo to provide Oliver a ride back to the Hathaway residence whenever he was ready to leave, followed Oliver and Theo back to where Lily was waiting.

"I thought we might walk in the garden a little," said Lily hopefully.

"All right." Oliver's shoulders slumped.

Theo bowed solemnly to her and turned away without another word. She watched him go, trying not to feel hurt.

Oliver and Lily walked through the garden for some time without saying anything. The sun was still high overhead. After the darkness of the study, the brilliance was almost disorienting.

Lily finally said, "How did your talk with Theo go?"

"I... it doesn't matter." Oliver ran his hands through his already thoroughly disheveled hair. "I can't stand it, Lily!" His voice broke. "I have to go to her."

She brushed tears from her eyes. "What if Lord Willowvale catches you? Or someone worse?"

Oliver firmed his jaw and turned to her. "Then I will be brave. If the Wraith cannot save her, I must at least try. I would rather die trying to do what I know is right then stay here in safety, waiting for someone else to save the woman I love."

He pleaded, "Please, Lily. Please help me get into the veil. I'll do the rest."

"What if you don't come back?" she whispered, anguished.

"Then at least I *tried*!"

Lily was unable, despite her best efforts, to refuse her brother's heart-rending plea. She trembled and shook her head, but it was futile.

"Please, Lily."

"There's magic here in the gardens, though I don't understand it all." She swallowed hard. "There's probably an opening just over there, I think. It's not open, though."

Oliver pulled her in the direction she had indicated, and she followed reluctantly.

She stopped at the hedge, feeling the tingling edges of magic. The door was not open, but it was waiting for her, as if it knew she wanted it. She put her hand up to the leaves nervously, and the door opened as if eager to oblige her.

"I don't like this," she whispered. "I don't like that it was so easy. I don't like you going."

Oliver nearly crushed her in a quick embrace. "Thank you, little sister. I'll be back as soon as I can."

"What if you're not?" Her voice cracked.

Oliver said firmly, "Tell your husband. He might have a good idea or two. But don't worry. I'll back in a few hours, I hope. If not, well, I'll face whatever comes bravely. Don't tell Mother and Father until tomorrow, if I'm not back before then."

"Do you have a weapon or anything?"

He indicated a dagger hidden in his jacket. "Don't worry." He leaned forward to kiss her on the forehead, then stepped into the veil.

The door closed behind him before Lily was ready.

The afternoon grew warmer. Thin white clouds skidded by high above without providing much shade at all. At last a cool breeze danced through the leaves of the camellias and gardenias nearby, bringing sweet scents and a promise of rain that night.

Lily waited by the hedge, sitting on a bench just opposite the vanished door for hours. She lay on her back and looked at the sky, admiring the shades of blue as Theo had once described.

As he had told her in happier times.

Anselm eventually found her and said, "My lady, Mr. Overton asked if you would like to refresh yourself and have dinner before departing for the ball tonight." He looked at her with concern, but did not inquire as to why she had been sitting, or lying, on the same stone bench for five hours now.

"Thank you." She walked beside him back to the house.

"My lady, I never did take Mr. Hathaway back to his residence in the city. Where is he? I will have one of the stablemen take him."

"That won't be necessary." Lily swallowed. "He left already."

"Oh." Anselm pondered this.

Lily bathed and dressed simply, then went upstairs to prepare for the ball. There was a tray with a lavish dinner waiting for her in the little sitting room, along with a vase of goldenrod, orange ranunculus, amaranthus, dark hellebore, and ivy. Before she ate or dressed, Lily got out her little book of flower meanings to try to interpret Theo's message. Goldenrod was encouragement and healing. Ranunculus told her that she was charming and attractive. Amaranthus signified unfading love. Hellebore either referenced a scandal, or meant that Theo still held hope despite darkness. And ivy meant marriage, fidelity, friendship, or affection. Or all of them together.

This was the first bouquet that had, however indirectly, referenced what had happened between them. She almost found it encouraging, but for the firmly closed door to Theo's side of the apartment.

Anselm entered with a bow, then let himself in to Theo's side without knocking.

She ate alone, staring at the hellebores and wondering if their darker meaning was the only true message. Eleven times in that hour she got up to look out the window, hoping to see Oliver in the garden. She couldn't quite see the right hedge from where she stood, but if he headed toward the manor he would be visible.

Her grief and disappointment rose in waves.

At last she left the tray and went to her room, where she sat at the lovely vanity and stared at herself in the mirror. She tried to apply the minimal makeup she wore, a little powder for her nose and rouge for her cheeks and lips, but the motions felt alien.

She felt tingly and sick with fear for Oliver, while grief for herself surged more deeply within her.

Through her closed sitting room door she heard the muffled sound of Anselm leaving Theo's room and walking out to the shared space. Theo said something to him about the phaeton, and he replied, then his steps receded down the hall.

There was a knock on her sitting room door.

CHAPTER THIRTY-TWO
An Offer of Help

"**C**ome in." Lily marveled that her voice sounded so serene, so peaceful. Nothing felt peaceful.

Theo opened the door quietly. He was already dressed for the party, resplendent in green and pale gold that set off his auburn hair.

Lily suddenly felt so very angry that for a moment she could not breathe. Why was he so ridiculously pretty, so beautifully attired, so carefree, when her brother and Araminta were lost in the Fair Lands?

"Did you have a good afternoon?" she managed. She did not know what sort of answer she expected, or even desired, from him. Maybe she only wanted reassurance.

He smiled brightly. "Indeed! I selected a new cut of jacket which Mr. Eccleston will make for me. I think it will be quite popular."

Lily swallowed and looked back at the mirror, as if seeing him in the glass would give her some new insight.

A jacket! The emptiness of it took her breath away, and her voice shook when she said, "I wish you were the kind of man a woman could come to if she were in trouble."

In the brittle silence that followed, Theo caught her eye in the mirror. The intensity of his look startled her, and he said, with infinite care, "Are you in trouble?"

His eyes were so tender, so kind, that she almost, *almost*, confided in him. She wanted to trust him. Oliver had said to tell Theo if he didn't come back.

But the man who spoke of a jacket, as if she cared about fashion now, while her friend was captive, could not be expected to understand or take seriously Oliver's plight either.

She let out a tremulous breath. "I... no. No, everything is fine."

Her voice betrayed her, full of desperate fear and self-loathing. Why had she let Oliver go into the veil at all? How could she have refused him, when Araminta was in danger? Every swirling thought brought more self-condemnation.

"I would serve you, if I could," he murmured. His hand hovered just above her shoulder, as if he wanted to touch her but was too shy, or too unsure of her, to risk it. His gaze held hers in the mirror.

She caught her breath on a sob and looked down. Those eyes could charm a stone, she thought furiously, and yet he *would* disappoint her. Her brother would die, and Araminta with him. Maybe even the Wraith as well.

"There is nothing you can do." She put all the coldness of her anger, all the hatred for her own helplessness, into her voice.

The silence that followed grew chill, and she looked up to the mirror to see his eyes shuttered.

He gave her a slight bow that felt as distant and cold as that of a stranger. "I am ever at your service," he murmured.

Then he turned away.

She kept her eyes down, then glanced up to peek at him as he stepped out of the room. He stopped in the doorway and turned, as if to look back at her, and she looked down, playing with the necklace in her hands as if it consumed her attention. She looked up cautiously as he turned away again, and there was a strange weariness in his shoulders that caught at her heart. She had wounded him, and the guilt layered atop the other heart pain so for a moment she could scarcely breathe.

He didn't deserve her coldness. He was foolish and shallow, and he cared too much for trivial things, but he was not unkind. He would at least have comforted her with pretty words, even if he would have been as helpless as she was.

Theo met her at the bottom of the stairs. "You are beautiful as always," he murmured. He smiled at her, and it was cool and distant.

"Thank you." Her voice shook. Did he know how frightened she was?

He slipped her hand into the crook of his elbow as he led her to the coach.

"You're trembling, my love." The words were nearly inaudible.

"I'm just cold," she whispered. He made a soft, unconvinced sound and helped her up the steps.

Anselm burst from the door and hurried toward them. Theo waited until the servant drew close enough to speak into his ear. After a moment, Theo nodded gravely and stepped into the coach with her.

His fair skin looked wan in the dim light, and for a moment the shadows seemed deeper beneath his brows.

The coach started briskly, and he switched seats to squeeze beside her. He lifted the opposite seat and pulled out a soft blanket.

"If you lean against me, I will warm you." The simple, kind words brought tears to her eyes. She leaned forward, and he wrapped the fabric around her, careful not to disturb her hair. Almost tentatively, he let his arm settle around her, drawing her gently against the warmth of his body.

She rested her head on his shoulder.

Into the rattling darkness, she said, "Are you ever afraid, Theo?"

He drew in a quiet breath, then let it out without speaking.

She shifted, wishing he would answer, wishing he would say something.

Finally, he murmured, "It would not be gentlemanly to admit to it. If you are troubled, I pray you confide in me."

Tears sprung to her eyes, and she wiped them away surreptitiously.

"I would be of service, if you would let me." The words hung in the air, soft and gentle and kind.

She took a shuddering breath. "I don't think you can help. I don't think anyone can help." Only the Wraith could, and who knew if he would? No, of course he would, because he was heroic and courageous enough to face the Fair Folk. But for a man, not a child? It was much to ask.

She wiped tears from her eyes again and settled into her despair. There was no way to tell the Wraith of her brother's plight, no way to beg the hero for succor, even if he would give it.

Yet her mind worked furiously, unwilling to completely give up hope, no matter how hopeless the situation.

Theo said nothing else. His arm was warm around her, but he was distant. His heart must be a thousand miles away, and it grieved her, but there was no use asking such a simple mind, however kind, to undertake such an overwhelming threat. Even to think of it would be too much for him; it was certainly too much for her, and she had had two days to ponder the problem.

When the coach stopped at the palace, Theo rose and stepped out first, then helped her down with excruciatingly correct gallantry. Despite his courtliness, she felt his withdrawal, his cool distance, and it grieved her. But there was no time for grief over her marriage. Theo's chivalry was limited to manners and beautiful clothes, and his refinement was not what she needed. She needed courage and action.

She needed the Wraith. She would throw himself at his feet and beg for help. Surely someone at the ball would know how to contact him. He had allies in the court; she was sure of it. There must be a way to speak with him tonight, if only she were clever enough to find it.

CHAPTER THIRTY-THREE
A Desperate Plea

S he placed her hand on Theo's arm and walked up the long steps at his side. Everything about him was perfectly, lavishly elegant. His jacket was cut in the newest, most extravagant style, and his trousers showed off his trim, athletic frame. It really was remarkable that a man of such leisure should so effortlessly maintain such an enviable figure. She *ought* to be grateful, she told herself fiercely. He was unstintingly generous with her; she wore the diamond and emerald necklace he had given her, and more diamonds sparkled in her ears. Her dress was made of the finest silk, cut and sewn by the most popular dressmaker, with a new wrap of lace that cost more than she wanted to imagine.

The footman welcomed them and escorted them to the ballroom. She glanced up at Theo's face surreptitiously as they walked. His jaw was tight, and his mouth was set in a hard expression she had never seen before. Then he must have perceived her attention, because he glanced down at her and his expression softened.

But he said nothing, only looked ahead again and raised his chin. He greeted the next footman with his habitual smile, and his cheerfulness seemed, even to her eyes, to be entirely unfeigned. Either he could not hold a thought in his head long enough to be serious even now, or he did not care as much as his sympathetic words earlier had implied.

She forced a smile, and they entered the ballroom together, heads held high.

He danced with her, and his smile was as kind and loving as always, his arm around her as strong, though his eyes were shuttered and distant. He looked at her as if he had lost her and were grieving the loss, but she felt it was he who had left her. Or perhaps it was merely that she had grown out of the first love, when his pretty words and generous gifts and cheerful equanimity were enough.

She needed what he could not be.

Maybe the distance between them was her fault after all; she needed him to be greater than he was, and her disappointment was inevitable. Was it not her own fault for expecting something of him so beyond reason?

Desperate for the Wraith's aid, she felt herself drawn to him as if in love, though she knew that was ridiculous. She loved his tender heart for children, she loved his intrepid heroism, and she loved his brilliant mind that conceived all the many disguises and plans he used. She could not lament valuing these things, but guilt twisted within her that she suddenly desired them so desperately, as if Theo were not enough for her. If she ever did manage to find the Wraith, she owed it to Theo to keep this hint of unrequited love to herself.

Foolish he might be, but Theo did not deserve that betrayal.

Lily resolutely focused on the warmth of Theo's eyes, the elegant, masculine beauty of his cheekbones and jaw, and the sweetness of his faint smile. Despite the distance between them, he was unfailingly kind to her. He loved her generously and well, despite whatever troubled him. There was character in it, a determination to love without counting the cost, and she clung to that.

When the dance ended, he held her for a moment, his eyes still on hers with an odd intensity. Then he turned to greet Lord Selby.

"Good evening, Lord Selby. I trust your mother is well?" Theo's smile seemed as cheerful and carefree as always.

Lord Selby met Theo's smile with an answering warmth. "Indeed. Are you free for a private luncheon next week?" His look made it clear that he included Lily in this invitation.

Theo beamed. "Of course! We are delighted to accept."

Lord Selby continued, "I must prevail upon your good nature and ask for the next dance with your wife. Mrs. Overton, would you so honor me?"

"Yes, my lord."

As Lord Selby took her hand, Theo leaned in to murmur something into his friend's ear.

Lord Selby nodded.

He led her to the dance floor as the music began.

The music was slow and the dance might have been intimate, if she had been paired with Theo, and if things had been well between them, but with Lord Selby it felt like an excruciating reminder of what she had lost.

Neither of them spoke for the first two passes. Finally, during the third pass, Lord Selby murmured almost inaudibly, "You are troubled, Mrs. Overton."

"I am," she admitted.

"What troubles you?"

She should *not* have admitted it to a man who was not her husband. It was folly, and she knew it was folly, but her nerves were wrung out and raw, and for an instant all good sense fled. "I have need of the Wraith, and no way to contact him." The words were nearly a gasp, pure emotion wrought into words, so quiet she marveled later that he had heard her at all over the music.

Only the rigidity of his hand when he took hers for the next graceful turn betrayed his surprise and dismay.

"Why?" he said under his breath.

"I cannot admit it. It is too terrible!" Tears swam in her eyes, and she blinked them away.

"Go to the library after the next dance. If he is to be found, it is likely to be there." Lord Selby's voice was dismissive, as if he had no idea whether such a miracle were likely at all, but she grasped desperately at the thin thread of hope.

"Thank you."

He bowed over her hand, all proper respect and courtesy.

She watched him walk away, wondering if she would see him speak to the elusive Wraith. Who would he speak to next? Would that person be the Wraith, or another go-between? Would the Wraith already be at the library, or would Lord Selby ask him to meet her? Did Lord Selby know the Wraith himself? Was Lord Selby himself the Wraith? Would Lord Selby betray them?

Her heart pounded, and she grew faint with the sudden terror that she had somehow betrayed the Wraith already, and both he and Oliver were lost. No! She would not believe it; she would not despair yet. Lord Selby had always been kind to her, and he was friends with Theo. Whatever other faults Theo had, he did seem to have good taste in friends. Lord Selby would not betray them to Lord Willowvale.

Where was Lord Willowvale?

The Fair envoy had cornered Theo and seemed furious, snarling like some sort of pale wolf. Lord Selby stood at Theo's shoulder, and young Radclyffe was just a step behind, with several others she knew close by. Everyone seemed frozen in the unbearable discomfort of watching someone else violate all rules of good breeding and manners.

Lord Willowvale growled something Lily could not hear, but she could tell it must have been horrible, for Lord Selby flinched, his hands clenching at his sides.

Theo laughed, clear and careless and light. "Surely you do not mean to so violate the treaty between our peoples, Lord Willowvale! I know you to be a patriot above all, and I would hate to sully your good name by accepting. Let us go in peace, my friend."

"You are a coward and an imbecile, Overton. Prove your worth with your sword, and I'll retract the first insult, at least." Willowvale straightened.

Theo smiled with gentle humor and ducked his head. "As you say, my Lord Willowvale. Nevertheless," he stepped forward and straightened the fairy's cravat with both hands, "I do know how to tie a cravat." His smiled widened and gave the fairy an elaborate, mocking bow. "Good evening, my lord."

Lord Selby gave Lord Willowvale a flat, unfriendly look as he, too, bowed, and followed Theo through the crowd.

The fairy stood in trembling fury, hands clenching spasmodically at his sides, before he stalked toward the prince, apparently intent on provoking another fight.

The library! Lily remembered and hurried away. The short hall between the ballroom and the darkened library was empty but for the exquisite furniture, and she slipped into the library carefully, closing the door behind her.

The room was shadowed, lit only by the moonlight streaming in the row of windows. To her left and right tall bookshelves loomed; a couch stood to one side, while several chairs and a low table clustered near the fireplace to her left. There were several other doors to the spacious room; she presumed they opened to hallways or a study or sitting room.

She was alone, and she caught her breath in fear and hope. Maybe he would come.

She pressed her hand to her heart, feeling it beat desperately, and closed her eyes, willing herself to be calm. She strode to the window and looked out upon the moonlight-silvered garden. The rose bushes were carefully trimmed and dark, and the tall spiraled topiaries seemed alien in the strange light.

"Do not turn around," said a rough voice behind her.

Lily gasped. The voice was unfamiliar, though there was something in it that seemed not entirely unknown.

"You came!" She put every desperate hope into those words, every prayer she had breathed in recent days.

"What do you ask of me?"

"My brother!" She caught her breath on a sob. "He was caught in the Fair Lands. It's my fault! Oh, I wish I could take his place! Lord Willowvale probably thinks he's the Wraith and will kill him! Or maybe he never even made it through the veil!"

There was only silence, and she shuddered. She almost turned and threw himself at his feet, but she imagined he would not want that.

"How did he get into the veil?" he said at last.

"I helped him open a door." The immensity of what she asked pressed upon her, and she buried her face in her hands. "Forgive me. I... I shouldn't have..."

She felt the movement of air as he took a step closer.

"Are you real?" she whispered. "I've prayed for you so long, wished so desperately that you would come tonight, and now I fear it's only a dream."

He put a hand on her shoulder, and she trembled. The hand was gloved, and even through the fabric, she felt she ought to recognize him. He was a man of flesh and blood, and she had danced with nearly every man at court more than once over the last months. But only Theo had touched her shoulder, and never with gloves. She put her hand over his, and for an instant she imagined he trembled as well. Then he drew back, and the chill air on her skin gave her a sense of desolation and inevitable tragedy.

"I will bring him back to you. I swear on my life."

The relief and terror welled up in a rush too great for tears, and her convulsive sob was dry and broken.

She heard his sharp intake of breath and felt his tension in the air behind her, but she did not look, though everything in her wished to see the face of the hero.

"Thank you," she whispered.

There was the soft, almost inaudible rustle of fabric, and she imagined him bowing to her. Then the door clicked quietly, and she was alone.

For several minutes she stared blindly out at the gardens. Was the light more beautiful now that she had hope?

At last she gathered the tatters of her courage and straightened. She patted at her eyes, drying the last of the tears, and pulled the wrap around her shoulders.

She entered the ballroom again and looked for Theo. She felt wrung out and exhausted, and she wondered if it were too soon to depart. It was Lord Hastings' ball, after all, and it would not do to be discourteous.

For several minutes she could not find Theo among the many dancers; only when she looked again along the wall to her left did she finally see him. He was apparently deep in conversation with Lord Selby.

He looked up, apparently noticing her gaze upon him, and smiled at her across the room. Then he turned back to Lord Selby for a moment more. The young lord nodded several times.

Then Theo began to make his way toward her, exchanging cheerful pleasantries with several people along the way.

"You seem less troubled, my love. Have tonight's festivities lifted your spirits?" His hazel eyes on her face were unexpectedly serious.

She took a tremulous breath. "Yes, thank you."

Theo hesitated, then said quietly, "If you wouldn't mind, I would prefer to leave soon."

Lily looked up at him surprise. He never wanted to leave early from a ball; he enjoyed dancing and music, and the card games that would follow.

"Is something wrong?" Now that she actually looked at him, he was more pale than usual, and he looked tired. Perhaps he was ill. "Are you quite well?"

He smiled with something like his usual warmth, but there was something in it that worried her. Distance, or fatigue, or something she had not seen before. "To tell you the truth, I have had a touch of headache today, and the music seems to be decidedly unhelpful." He bowed over her hand, an unnecessary courtesy, but it always seemed to please him to do so. There were shadows under his eyes, she was sure of it, though it was easy to miss in the shifting light of the chandeliers and lanterns.

"I wouldn't mind leaving," she said.

He offered his arm, which seemed another unnecessary courtesy, and she felt a rush of shame that she wanted him to be different when he was already so kind and gallant.

Since no one realized they were leaving, no one stopped them to exchange pleasantries as they departed.

Theo helped her into the carriage, then climbed in after her. He opened the blanket and wrapped it around her shoulders, then settled against the back of the seat, gently pulling her to sit resting against him.

The simple comfort of his warmth and kindness was enough to bring tears to her eyes again.

He bid her goodnight at the door to her suite; he kissed her fingertips, and, in what seemed an impulsive move, stepped closer to press a kiss to her forehead.

She looked up at him, startled, and he looked down.

"Forgive me," he murmured. "Your beauty overcame me."

She took in a tremulous breath and let it out.

The distance between them seemed infinite; she stared at the rich crimson rug, at the tips of her shoes, at his shoes, but she could not look at his face.

"Goodnight, Theo," she whispered.

"Goodnight, Lily." He bowed to her, and the formality felt like a dash of icy water on her already frayed nerves.

CHAPTER THIRTY-FOUR
Realization

L ily lay in her bed staring at the ceiling, then the wall, then the ceiling again.

She finally gave up on sleep. Her eyes were gritty and her emotions worn. She pulled on her brocade dressing gown and stepped out into the shared space.

Theo's suite was closed.

She knocked tentatively. There was no answer, and she imagined him sleeping the sleep of the innocent.

Her hand trembling, she knocked again, and still there was no answer.

She was his wife, after all. She tentatively turned the door handle, which opened without a sound. The sitting room was empty, and she knocked again at the door to his bedroom. There was no answer, and she turned the door handle even more cautiously than before.

The shades were closed against the moonlight, and she could see nothing at first. The room had the sense of emptiness, though, and that gave her a frisson of fear, which she resolutely ignored. He had been tired; she was sure of it. He must be deeply asleep. The emptiness must be merely her imagination.

As she drew closer to the bed, the fear rose, and when she lit the candle, she knew she would see the bed empty and unrumpled.

A distant sound caught her ear, and she froze, listening.

She heard Theo and someone else speaking in low tones, then another voice joined them, perhaps Anselm. The door closed again, and there was silence.

She hurried downstairs, candle held high, to see Anselm retreating to the servants' quarters.

"What has happened? Where is Mr. Overton?" she asked.

He turned to her, startled, and said, "Business, my lady. Business has called him away."

"In the middle of the night? What business?"

Anselm bowed politely. "I am not privy to all my master's business, but I would wager my master thought it urgent. I am sure he will return as soon as he is able." He hesitated, then added, "He left you a note at the breakfast table."

She whispered her thanks and nearly ran to the breakfast room. A folded piece of paper was propped against the vase in the middle of the table.

Lilybeth was written in Theo's neat, elegant hand across the front, and when she turned it over, the wax seal bore the Overton family crest.

It was so formal.

She put the candle down on the table, and the flame wavered as her hand shook. She broke the seal and unfolded the paper, pressing it flat against the table so the candlelight danced across it.

Dearest Lily,

Urgent business has called me north. I beg your forgiveness for my absence; I had hoped to bid you farewell in the morning, but duty calls. I shall return as soon as I may. While you wait my return, if you do at all, please know that I long for you with every fiber of my being.

Yours faithfully,

Theo

The 'if you do at all' caught at her heart, and she gave a broken little sob, then pressed the letter to her breast. She had been too cold to him. She had not meant to be cold!

What business could be so urgent as to call him away in the middle of the night? She strode to the window and looked out upon the garden, at the black velvet sky growing grey to the east.

She walked slowly back up the stairs.

Without any particular plan, she stepped into Theo's private office. For all these weeks they had been married, she had never actually stepped foot into the room, and had only looked in once through a crack as he closed the door behind himself.

A heavy, ornate desk stood in the center of the room, and a well-worn leather chair sat behind it. On the right side of the desk was a neat stack of letters, all sealed and ready to be sent.

An account book lay closed. She hesitated, feeling as if she were intruding into something private. Theo had never invited her to look into his finances, but he had not withheld anything from her, either, so she mentally apologized as she opened the book and flipped through the pages. Page after page showed neat notations of expenses and income from a variety of sources. After some thought, Lily realized that most of them were from shipping investments.

A quill pen lay neatly beside an inkwell. The rear wall of the study was lined with bookshelves laden with hundreds of books. Lily turned to study the titles, raising the candle so the light would fall on them more clearly.

A Brief Historie of Faery Mischief. Snares and Traps of the Fair Folk. The Silverthorn Dynasty: An Incomplete History. Tambling. The Fair Folk. The Tale of Martellus and Avenian. Myths and Legends of the Fair Lands. Lily surveyed the titles with astonishment. Theo had never evidenced any particular interest in the Fair Folk, other than taking a lively and enduring delight in provoking Lord Willowvale.

The extensive library on the first floor contained nothing pertaining to the Fair Folk.

What possible reason would Theo have to read this many books about the Fair Lands?

A sick sense of dread began to unfurl within her, and she covered her mouth.

For several minutes she simply stood at Theo's desk, thinking, with tears trickling down her cheeks. She stepped to the window and looked toward the garden again.

CHAPTER THIRTY-FIVE
A Clever Plan

T heo spent three hours opening and closing doors into Lord Willowvale's manor, slowly working his way closer to the rooms in which Araminta and Oliver were now imprisoned. He opened the veil the tiniest crack, so he could see the room. If the room was empty, he could step through and try to sense Oliver or Araminta. If the room was not empty, he would merely glance through the crack without being noticed. The manor was vast, and the layout of the veil did not correspond to the layout of the manor in the least.

The two human captives were separated by two rooms and on opposite sides of a hall. The magical barriers had been an obstacle at first, but Theo had figured out that if he opened the door just this way, he was able to slip past the obstruction. Cedar was not able to edge his magic past this obstruction, and so was unable to help with opening the doors, though he steadfastly remained by Theo's side.

Nevertheless, it took hours to pinpoint the locations. Accuracy became more difficult as Theo grew increasingly fatigued. Opening the doors from the veil into either human or Fair worlds had always been easier than opening doors into the veil, but after well over a hundred such openings, he was bone tired.

Finally he had both locations in mind. Oliver was sitting in a comfortable chair in the corner of a room, bound hand and foot by vines that looked like honeysuckle, though their white flowers were edged in gleaming silver. Araminta was locked in her room but not otherwise restrained.

Once he had determined their exact locations and was sure he could reach them, he said to Cedar, "Now we will make the decoy. We'll go to the roaring valley for this, I think."

They walked through the veil for an hour and stepped out into the blue moonlight. Cedar and Theo gathered sticks and vines which they wove into a human-sized figure.

The cool, dewy early morning of the forest felt wonderfully fresh, but Theo's head throbbed mercilessly, and he leaned against tree trunks at intervals.

"Are you well, Theo?" Cedar asked.

"Yes." Theo slid down the tree trunk and let his head rest against it for a moment. He pressed his fingers to the loam beneath him, pushing the last of the binding magic deep into the ground. He pushed it deeper until he felt it connect with the binding magic he had left there before.

Juniper had nearly killed himself generating this much binding magic so soon after his last great effort. Theo's tender heart grieved the cost to the young fairy, but Juniper was both strong and brave. He'd given Theo all the binding magic he could muster and collapsed before Theo could catch him. When he'd regained consciousness, he'd given Theo yet another breath of magic, another little snippet of hope.

At last the stick and vine simulacrum was the right size and shape. Theo carried it back through the veil to just outside Araminta's room in Lord Willowvale's manor.

"I'll step out here and retrieve Lady Araminta. While I'm doing that, please make this as human as possible. Then we'll go to Mr. Hathaway's room, I'll open the door, you'll put the finishing touches on the glamour so that Lord Willowvale's magic is confused, and I'll get Mr. Hathaway into the veil."

"Are you sure, Theo?" Cedar suppressed a shudder. "Lord Willowvale is powerful."

"I promised, Cedar." In the darkness, Theo could not meet Cedar's gaze, but he found Cedar's solid shoulder and squeezed it reassuringly.

The fairy shook his head doubtfully. "I fear for you."

Theo smiled. "I promised to save the Fair Lands as well, and I have not forgotten. I will endeavor not to let him kill me yet."

"Be careful."

Theo laughed, light and careless, but said nothing more.

He opened the door.

Theo stepped out of the veil, took Araminta by the hand, and pulled her into the veil before she managed a single word of surprise.

"Don't be frightened, Lady Araminta. It's me, Theo Overton, and this is a dear friend of mine. In just a moment, we will take you back home."

To her credit, Araminta reacted to this extraordinary news and turn of events with a moment of silence to think rather than hysterical tears. Then she said, "Are you the Wraith, then?"

"I am, but it's a secret," Theo said with a smile in his voice. "Although I doubt it will matter much in a day or two. All the same, I entreat you not to tell anyone."

"If I must stay quiet, I will, but I do thank you quite sincerely. I should like to be able to tell people who rescued me, if I may. What do you need to do before you take me home?"

"Please do not tell anyone. It would be terribly inconvenient, among other things. Oliver Hathaway came to rescue you as well, quite courageously, and has gotten into a bit of a situation."

Araminta might have reacted to this news, but Theo turned his attention to Cedar and continued, "In a moment, I will step out into his room. As quickly as you can, put the finishing touches on our decoy here, and I will induce the vines to change their focus. As soon as Mr. Hathaway is free, take him and Lady Araminta home. There is something else I must do, and if I have the opportunity to do it tonight, I will take it. Don't wait for me."

Cedar's discomfort with this plan was clear, but Theo led them a few feet down the corridor and asked, "Are you ready?"

"I suppose."

Theo opened the door and peeked out, then stepped out with the simulacrum in his arms.

Oliver, half-asleep, with his head turned sideways against the back of the chair, reacted with belated surprise. He whispered harshly, "Run!"

"Just a moment," said Theo, glancing quickly between the decoy, which had taken on Oliver's appearance almost immediately, and Oliver himself.

"Not yet," said Cedar from the door.

Theo said, quite calmly, "He's almost here."

Cedar said, "Now."

Quick as thought, Theo shoved the simulacrum into the chair, half-atop Oliver and half beside him. The vines loosened in response, momentarily confused as to which was the real person, and Theo yanked the largest coil off Oliver.

Oliver scrambled from beneath the writhing vines while Theo alternately hauled him out and directed the loose tips of the agitated vines back toward the decoy.

The vines wrapped around Oliver's ankle, and he sucked in a breath as it tightened painfully.

Theo said, "Take her and go! I'll get Oliver into the veil for you when he's free."

Cedar snapped the door shut and took off through the veil with Araminta.

Theo yanked one loop of the vine over Oliver's foot and put it around the simulacrum's foot. The vines switched their attention to the decoy for a moment and relaxed their hold upon Oliver, who immediately clambered free.

Theo opened a door to the veil with a grunt of effort and shoved Oliver through it just as the vines abruptly transferred their attention to Theo. Within a moment, he was immobilized from the waist down.

"Stay where you are," Theo said to Oliver. "He'll be back for you in a moment." Then he closed the door in Oliver's startled face.

CHAPTER THIRTY-SIX
An Encouraging Revelation

V ines wrapped more tightly about Theo's legs and chest, and they now bore vicious, needle-sharp thorns which slid easily through the cloth of his shirt, jacket, and trousers into his flesh. Turned toward the door of the room as he was, he could no longer see the simulacrum now trapped in Oliver's place.

For a moment, both hands were still free, and he fought to liberate one leg. The thorns lengthened, and he hissed in pain. Blood flowed freely from the punctures, leaving gruesome streaks down his formerly white shirt. Abandoning the attempt to free his leg, he cupped his hands and caught some of the blood that dripped from a wound in his side, then breathed the last of his borrowed binding magic into the crimson liquid. Then he flung both hands out wide to spray the blood in tiny droplets across the room, where they splattered across the floor and opposite wall.

Lord Ash Willowvale strolled into the room just as the vines caught Theo's wrists. Thorns stabbed through the cuffs of his shirt and into the thin skin of his wrists. They slid between the fine bones to hold him with arms outstretched.

The fairy lord stepped closer and tilted his head. "I did not expect to see you here, puppy."

Theo smiled. "I cannot say the same, unfortunately."

"I'm impressed that your effort to free Oliver Hathaway was successful," Lord Willowvale said.

Theo nodded, hiding a wince as a particularly cruel thorn dug deeper into his side.

The fairy continued, "However, you must be disappointed that he was recaptured so quickly."

Theo nodded again. "I did expect you to be prompt, but I admit I am impressed. You're quite thorough, considering."

Lord Willowvale took a few steps toward the young man, studying him with cold eyes. "Considering what?"

"How arrogant you are." Theo met the fairy's icy gaze unflinchingly. "Hubris, my dear Lord Willowvale, has been the downfall of many greater than either of us. It would be wise to avoid it."

The fairy glanced over Theo's shoulder and apparently recognized the simulacrum for what it was. Theo felt his shock more than he saw it. It was a ripple of dismay that came through Willowvale's vines, a tremor in the air that smelled of roses and blood, a flicker of the golden light that flooded the room. His eyes narrowed, and he looked back at Theo, who smiled radiantly.

The fairy clenched one hand, and the vines complied, piercing Theo ever more deeply. The pointed thorn ends grated against bone, then found new angles and slid farther in.

"You are ruled by your hatred," Theo whispered. The fairy's clenched hand made the vines so tight they creaked. "You should try love. When you love more deeply than you fear, you can do nearly anything."

"I do hate you," Lord Willowvale said. He surveyed the thorns and noted the one just touching the right side of Theo's throat close to the vein. The young man had grown increasingly pale as the wounds continued to bleed.

The fairy made a little motion with one hand, and the thorn at Theo's throat grew longer. Theo could not shift away; a hundred other thorns pinned him in place.

"Yet I think it would be to my advantage to show the king what insolent human has dared infiltrate his court. He will be intrigued to learn how you did it."

"Do you think I would tell you?" Theo whispered.

The thorn slid through his skin and pierced the vein so that a slow, steady pulse of blood welled up on the skin. It dripped down the vine to the ground.

Theo held his chin high, though his eyes had become slightly glassy. "How entertaining should I be when His Majesty Silverthorn arrives?"

"As much as possible." Lord Willowvale smiled. "It won't be long."

"I will be delighted to surprise him, then."

Lord Willowvale stood with his hands behind his back, studying Theo's bloody form with distaste. "You have been a great deal of trouble to us," he murmured, as if to himself.

Theo tried to keep his breaths steady, but his heart seemed to be racing inconveniently. "That was not my goal, if you can believe it," he said at last.

"Was it not?" Lord Willowvale said conversationally. "What was your goal, then?"

"The children." Theo smiled with all the cheerfulness he could muster. "Piquing your pride was only a pleasant side effect."

The fairy made a careless motion with his hand, and the thorns dug deeper. Theo closed his eyes and thought of Lily.

Eyes still closed, he murmured, "How did you find the children's home, Lord Willowvale?"

The fairy gave a startled huff. "Your wife was unwise enough to admit that she had seen the children and that they were well-cared for. I reviewed my surveillance of her brother's movements over the last months and realized where it must be." He gave a low, malicious chuckle. "That must rankle you, I wager, that your wife and her brother were so instrumental in your downfall."

Theo smiled, giddy with relief that Lily's blunder had been so slight and so accidental. He whispered, "How many children does His Majesty have at the palace now?"

Lord Willowvale surveyed his helpless prisoner. The thorns were now nearly three inches long, though the length could not be seen since so much was buried in the Wraith's all-too-human flesh. The barb at his throat was shorter; His Majesty Silverthorn would want to question him, and even the king could not revive him once he were truly dead.

"Twelve," said the fairy at last. "Does that irritate you?"

Had the magic been working long enough? Time seemed a fuzzy concept to Theo at the moment, but he felt that it was probably nearly time to act.

He opened his eyes to meet Lord Willowvale's icy gaze. "No. I am *furious*, my lord, not irritated." His voice shook, just a little, and he prayed the fairy thought it anger, not pain and dizziness. "But I do not hate you, nor the Fair Lands. There is much beauty here."

Lord Willowvale stepped closer to look into his eyes, bright pale blue to warm hazel. "I did not think there was anything on which we would agree." The fairy smiled coolly. "Yet you do speak truth now. I love the Fair Lands above all else. Why, then, would you seek to destroy it?"

"I do not." Theo smiled as warmly as he could, considering the haze that suffused his vision. "The soul of the Fair Lands is far too beautiful to save by sacrificing children, Lord Willowvale." He took a slow, agonized breath, feeling the thorns sliding between his ribs.

The magic must have had enough time by now. "Watch me save your land my way, and be ashamed."

His fingers had grown numb, but the thorns had left him just enough mobility to snap his thumb and finger. Theo and the vines surrounding him, thorns and all, fell into the tunnel that opened just beneath his feet. It closed with a snap just behind him.

Theo fell to the floor of the veil in a tangle of three-inch thorns that nearly put his eyes out. The sudden pain was so intense that he could not have screamed, even if he'd wanted to.

After a moment trying to steady his breathing, he used the whisper of magic he still carried to produce a bright yellow glow a few feet in front of his face. It was risky, to be sure; he could feel something big moving in the tunnel not too far away. But the thorns were near to eviscerating him, had already punctured several important organs, and it would be difficult enough to free himself with the aid of the light; in the dark, it would be impossible.

One thorn had cut a deep gash from his right eyebrow up to his hairline, and the blood kept dripping into his eye most frustratingly. He pulled a thorn from his left wrist, where it had slithered between the bones and out the other side. He brought the light to him and tried to heat it, but his magic was too weak to do much. He gathered himself and tried again, trading light and his dwindling strength for heat.

The vine hissed and protested, then began to unwind itself from him. Several of the thorns from the segments of vine wrapped around his back pulled back, and the piercing agony nearly brought Theo back to his knees.

He pressed the hot, fading flicker to his chest, and the warmth of it brought him clarity, if not relief from the pain.

Cedar would be waiting, if he were still free.

Theo pressed a hand to his chest and began to run.

CHAPTER THIRTY-SEVEN
A Courageous Foray Into the Veil

The grey light of dawn had just begun to make the trees distinguishable from the blackness around them. The shadowy mounds of bushes and hedges began to take shape.

Suddenly there was movement right at the edge of her vision, and Lily strained her eyes. Faint moonlight caught two figures hurrying toward the house.

Her breath of hope was quickly dashed, for there were only two figures, rather than three, and one of the two was unfamiliar to her.

Anselm must have been awake, for a splash of yellow lantern light from the manor door suddenly illuminated the figures, and Lily gasped. One was Araminta, still wearing the same dress she had been two days before, and apparently unharmed. The other was a dark-skinned, white-haired man, or fairy.

Lily ran to Theo's room and lifted the candle high to see the swords on his wall. She pulled the smallest sword off the rack and ran downstairs.

"Hello, Araminta!" she whispered. She held the sword up. "You know the Wraith, don't you?" she asked the fairy.

Anselm and the fairy stared at her.

"Yes," the fairy said. "Who are you?"

"His wife. Take me to him."

The fairy blinked and glanced at Anselm. Araminta gave a choked little laugh. "Lily, you have no idea how glad I am to see you!" She edged around the point of the sword and threw her arms around Lily's neck.

"I am glad to see you too, Araminta," Lily said sincerely. She focused on the fairy again. "He went to rescue my brother and Lady Araminta, and I did everything wrong, and I ought to be there with him."

"I don't think that's wise, Mrs. Overton," said the fairy. She was startled to see kindness in his turquoise eyes, bright as gems against his walnut-colored skin. "He will not be pleased with me if I bring you into danger."

Araminta nodded her acknowledgement of Lily's welcome and stepped back out of the conversation.

Lily brandished the sword at him, wondering if he could tell how ignorant she was of its use. He looked and spoke like a nobleman, so probably he had already ascertained she was hardly threatening. Nevertheless, she hoped it conveyed her seriousness.

"Take me to him. I'll obey whatever he says, I promise you. But I asked him to go into danger and I didn't even know who I was asking. Maybe I can help somehow."

The fairy bowed courteously. "I shouldn't, my lady." He turned away, apparently thinking the conversation was at an end.

She thrust the candle into Araminta's hand and grabbed at his sleeve with a ferocity that startled both of them. "Take me to him, fairy!"

He looked down at her small hand clenched on his sleeve and said mildly, "My name, my lady, is Lord Cedar Mosswing. Pray delay me no longer. I am required back in the Fair Lands for the next part of the Rose's plan." He began walking, and she clung to him, keeping pace.

"I will go with you."

He looked down at her but said nothing else for a moment as he continued quickly back toward the door to the veil, which he had left open.

When they reached it, Lily realized that Anselm had followed them. He now said, "Mrs. Overton, I really must insist that—"

Cedar stepped into the veil, brushing her hand off his sleeve with no apparent effort.

She jumped through after him, and the door snapped shut nearly on her heels.

"I really don't appreciate your effort to leave me behind," she said into the darkness of the veil.

Cedar sighed. "I do not want to quarrel with you, but it would be much safer if you would stay in the human world."

"I don't want to be safe!" she cried. "I want my husband!"

He sighed again, this time in resignation. "I should not do this," he murmured to himself. "Take my hand, and please have a care not to stick me with that sword you carry."

Lily gripped his hand with her left and kept the sword in her right, and thus she followed Cedar through the veil to the Fair Lands.

CHAPTER THIRTY-EIGHT
An Unexpected Meeting

Theo stepped out of the veil into the clearing just behind Cedar. "That was worse than anticipated," he said.

Cedar whirled, magic flaring, before his eyes widened.

Theo swayed as he looked around, noting Oliver's horrified expression. "Lady Araminta is safe?" Running had perhaps not been the wisest decision; something inside was bleeding more badly than before and there was an unpleasant burble in his chest.

But it couldn't be helped. The timing was critical.

"I took her back while you were freeing Mr. Hathaway." Cedar frowned and put a steadying hand on Theo's shoulder. The fairy lowered his voice in apology. "Your wife came back with me, though."

Theo twitched in surprise. "Where is she?" He spun about to see her step from behind Oliver. "You shouldn't be here. You're meant to be home safe."

Stricken, Lily covered her mouth and stared at him.

"Can you take her back?" Theo sagged against Cedar's steadying hand.

"Not if you want me back in time to meet His Majesty." Cedar's grave expression grew grimmer. "Stand still a moment."

Theo couldn't help looking back at Lily, though the haze in his vision made it hard to see her expression. He braced his feet a little wider so he wouldn't fall. Was she holding one of his swords?

Cedar stepped closer and murmured into his ear, "You're bleeding quite badly, Theo. Do you still want to do this?" As he spoke, he slipped his own magic through Theo's flesh.

Theo inhaled sharply, acknowledging the pain and then ignoring it. "Yes."

The fairy probed more deeply, finding the worst of the internal bleeding and slowing it. "It will take longer than we have to fix this. But I can keep you going a little longer."

"I'm all right." Theo focused on Lily's face. As Cedar's magic worked, the haze receded a little, and he saw how pale she was and how tears were silently sliding down her cheeks.

"What have you done?" she breathed. She was trembling.

He crossed to her and put his hands out to touch her shoulders, then hesitated. His hands were streaked with dark blood, and she was so spotless and pale. Instead, he took her hands lightly in his, barely touching the tips of her fingers.

"I told you I would bring your brother back to you," he said simply.

She gave a quiet sob.

"Forgive me, Lily," he said quietly. He knelt before her and looked up at her face. "I misjudged you in the worst way. I thought I had reason, and I meant only to protect my friends. But I was wrong about you."

"I'm sorry," she gasped through her sobs. "I'm so sorry. I thought…"

He gave a soft, low chuckle. "Oh, Lily. I loved you all the time. I couldn't help it."

She fell to her knees in front of him and buried her face in her hands. "I'm sorry."

Theo gently lifted her chin and met her gaze. "Please don't cry, my love. It grieves me that I have made you weep." Seeing her lips trembling, he leaned in to brush a kiss, light as a feather, against her cheek, then said, "May I kiss you again, Mrs. Overton?"

For a moment, he felt no pain at all.

Cedar said, "Theo, it's time." He helped Theo up with a strong hand and slid a little more magic cautiously into his friend as he did it. "Is that too much?"

The world narrowed to a tiny pinprick, and Theo's eyelids fluttered shut for a moment before he steadied himself. "No. It's helping." He took several slow breaths, feeling the magic working its way through his torn flesh. "I'll be all right. Your messages all reached their targets?"

The magic writhed within him, taut and golden, and he pressed his lips together to keep from crying out.

"Yes. The Elders will be there, and the most of the court."

Theo smiled. "Thank you, my friend." He indicated the wound on his forehead. "Would you mind?"

Cedar pressed his palm against the wound, then caught Theo's shoulder as the young man nearly fell. "Stand still," he muttered. "You're wobbly as a newborn fawn."

"I am not!" Theo protested. "It's just that the world is a little unsteady at the moment," he admitted. "Lily, why do you have my old sword?"

At her stifled sob, Cedar answered, "It is a testament to how determined she was to come aid you, Theo."

Theo smiled delightedly. "Did you threaten Cedar? Oh, I wish I had seen that! Are you all ready?"

Concern made a deep furrow between Cedar's dark eyebrows, but he nodded. "Mrs. Overton, Oliver, clasp hands."

Theo took Lily's other hand, his grip light but strong, and Cedar clasped Oliver's hand, putting himself at the rear of their procession. Theo opened a door and led them into the veil.

Cedar's magic slithered around Theo's veins, making the fog in his vision seem to glitter like gold in the darkness of the veil. It brought each torn muscle and pierced bit of skin to his attention, and it was all he could do to keep his footsteps reasonably steady.

"I don't know how you find your way in here, Theo," Cedar muttered. "The land loves you."

Lily's breath hitched, as if she wanted to weep, and Theo squeezed her hand gently.

"Because I love it," he said. The pain was receding, leaving a strange, hollow feeling in his arms and legs. His heart thudded raggedly, and he focused on the sensation; his head felt like it was floating away, but the unsteady rhythm of his pulse seemed to keep him grounded.

The farther he walked, the more it became clear that his lungs did not seem to be working correctly. Finally, he gasped, "A little more, if you don't mind, Cedar."

The Fair lord reached out and put a hand on Theo's shoulder. The magic slipped in gently, and Theo felt himself swaying against Cedar's hand like a sapling in a strong wind.

"I didn't know you could do that," he said thickly. The magic felt like a rush of golden light beneath his skin, and suddenly he could breathe again. The sparkles in his vision were so bright that he could not have seen his companions even if there had been light in the veil.

"I didn't want you to ever need it," Cedar growled.

"How tired are you? Will you be able to give me more, if necessary?"

The Fair lord hesitated. "I'd rather you not do whatever you're planning, but yes, I have more magic if you need it."

"Good." Theo blinked and shook his head, trying to remember which way was up and which was down.

At the doorway he paused. "I wish I could have taken you home, Lily and Oliver. But there is not enough time for that now, so it will be safest for you if you come with me. Do not speak, no matter what happens."

They murmured agreement.

"Promise me," he said, with more urgency in his voice. "No matter what happens, you will not speak."

"What if they hurt you?" said Lily in an agonized whisper.

"I am quite sure he will," said Theo. "Nevertheless, trust me, and promise me."

Lily murmured something like agreement.

"Oliver?" prompted Theo. "Please."

"Can you ever forgive me?" Oliver breathed. "This is all my fault."

Theo scoffed. "Don't be ridiculous! I was aggravating His Majesty Silverthorn before I even met you. How can it be your fault?" More urgently, he said again, "Promise me, Oliver."

"If I must." Oliver's voice cracked.

"Cedar?"

The dark lord blinked in surprise, then agreed. "If I must."

"Also, leave the sword in the veil, please, Lily. It's not part of my plan, and showing it will only make him angrier."

Lily shuddered. "Can't it be of some use?"

"It will only be a hindrance, though I do appreciate your faith in me, if you think I might make good use of it now." He waited while she laid it on the moss at their feet.

Without another word, Theo opened the door and led them out into the central garden of the Fair palace.

CHAPTER THIRTY-NINE
The Passion of the Wraith

His Majesty Oak Silverthorn had been walking directly toward the space they stepped out of, apparently in a thunderous mood. He stopped in shock.

Even Theo had only caught a few glimpses of him before, so in this moment of brittle silence, all four of them drank in the sight of him. His skin was a pale robin's egg blue and his eyes gleamed violet. His long hair was a blue so dark it was nearly black. He wore a circlet of silver upon his head, and it was so full of points that it might have been made of an elaborate arrangement of silver thorns. His shirt was a crisp white beneath his indigo jacket and trousers, and he wore a rich cloak of silver and indigo, with the bright, metallic silver fur of some fairy creature around the neck. He was beautiful and terrible, and Lily could not look away fast enough.

Theo swept a low, elaborate bow. "Your Majesty," he murmured. "Bow, everyone, please."

The others swept hurried bows and a curtsy, as appropriate.

"I have been wanting to meet you, Your Majesty," said Theo with another bow. "I believe I have something you might desire."

The Fair monarch's fierce eyes narrowed. "Lord Willowvale assured me that he had captured you. I was on my way to see you."

"He did capture me." Theo beamed at him cheerfully.

"Yet there you stand." The king straightened and gave a faint nod. The guards who had been following him fanned around the clearing to surround them, though Theo knew it was hardly necessary.

Vines crept up Theo's legs to his calves and held him firmly, though no thorns pierced his skin yet. Similar vines held Cedar, Lily, and Oliver in place. The garden shifted and a hush fell across the clearing as more Fair lords and ladies gathered around in a great audience.

"What do you have of mine?" the king asked. He sounded more curious than angry, but his eyes held a murderous glint.

"Your kingdom."

The air crackled with His Majesty Silverthorn's anger. "Explain." The word was sharp as a whip.

Any man but Theo might have quailed under the Fair king's regard. Theo smiled patiently and said, "First, Your Majesty, I would ask a boon of you, out of your generosity."

His Majesty Silverthorn burst into startled laughter. "What reason have I to offer you a boon? Are you mad?"

"Probably." Theo grinned at him. "Do I look utterly sane to you?" He gestured at himself, and the king took a long, thoughtful look at him. His clothes were pierced and torn in a hundred places, blood stains indicated numerous wounds, and he smiled with unfeigned delight at the king.

The Fair monarch tilted his head. "No, you don't. You may ask. I may deny it."

Theo swept another low bow without moving his immobilized feet. "Your Majesty, I would ask that whatever happens to me, whatever decisions you make, that you let my wife and her brother return safely to the human world, and that my friend Lord Cedar Mosswing suffer no repercussions."

His Majesty Silverthorn gave a slow, dangerous smile. "Why would you ask that? You ask nothing for yourself?"

"Because I love them, Your Majesty," Theo said simply.

The Fair king stepped slowly closer and examined Theo from arm's length away. His violet eyes swept over Theo's bloodied clothes and his face, then he turned to look at Oliver. He examined each of their company in turn, then turned back to Theo.

"You are the Rose," he said contemplatively.

"Honestly I preferred the name Wraith, because it implied that I wouldn't get caught, but yes, the name refers to me."

"How do you think you hold my kingdom?" The king's voice had lost a little of its murderous edge, but there was still crackling danger in it.

Theo smiled. "If you will indulge me for a moment, Your Majesty, and look at the mountains, do they seem more or less solid than they did this morning?"

The king looked up at the distant mountains, then stood transfixed by the horrifying sight. The peaks were drifting away like mist in a morning breeze, and the few shreds that were still visible were a dove gray that disappeared into the gray sky. Lord Willowvale arrived just then. He bowed to the king and glared at Theo, but he said nothing.

"Look at the indigo forests to the north," murmured Theo.

The king turned to see the forests turned a steely gray. The tops of the trees seemed as indistinct as a cloud.

"What have you done?" said the king.

Theo's quiet, triumphant smile did not flicker when the king snarled, "Fix it, human!"

"I will," Theo said softly. "When you promise on your life and your throne and all of the Fair Lands to never take or harm humans again, directly or indirectly."

His Majesty Silverthorn shifted and looked at him again, his eyes glittering. "How have you done this? You are human!"

He examined Theo again. "You have so little magic this cannot be only your doing."

"I have friends, though," Theo said gently. "Friends who love me, and I love them. I have borrowed a great deal of magic and threaded it through most of the Fair Lands over the last six months.

"The magic I borrowed knows me. The love I bear for my friends, and that they bear for me, has influenced the land itself and made it recognize, as much as it can, that I love it too.

"Every rose I left you was a promise to love and forgive the Fair Folk for the pain you caused those poor children. My heart cried out against you, and I wanted to avenge them, but I choose to save your land instead because I love my friends here more than the thought of your bloody end." Theo's voice sharpened and his eyes hardened before he sighed softly.

"The hills are dying because every rose I left was infused with binding magic, just a little, so you wouldn't see it and break it. I put it in the soil itself, and I bound the land to me, the hills and the palace and the forests, and the tiny points of binding reinforced each other and spread, so that every inch of the Fair Lands cries out to me.

"Lord Willowvale's vines caused the mountains pain. The vines must obey, but the land rejected his violence and recoiled."

His Majesty Silverthorn stared at Theo. "What will happen if you die?"

Theo raised an eyebrow. "I'd rather not have anyone find out. However, I did consider that possibility, and I have laced the promise of the land through several layers of potential heirs. They love the land too, and it will recognize them."

His Majesty Silverthorn drew a long breath in through his nose, his hand clenching spasmodically on the hilt of his long, narrow sword.

"If I die, the land will recognize one heir after another, as I have designated them. If you kill them all, the land will revolt against you entirely. I do not know what form that will take, but I believe it will be quite unprecedented."

The Fair king drew his sword and drove it through Theo's stomach.

Behind him, Lily and Oliver cried out together, and Cedar grabbed their shoulders in warning.

"Reverse it!" cried the king. "Unbind it!"

Theo, still bound at his feet by the vines, choked out a bloody laugh. "You. Can't. Make. Me."

"I can and I will," snarled the king, twisting the sword and driving Theo to his knees.

Theo looked up at him and gasped, "As long as I love the Fair Lands, the binding holds."

His Majesty Silverthorn's cold violet eyes flicked past Theo to Lily, Oliver, and Cedar. "What if I kill them one by one before your eyes?"

Theo's answer was low and cold, thick with blood and fury. "Then I will rip apart the Fair Lands at the seams, and all you have ever loved will be as dust."

"I don't love," said the king.

"I do." Theo stared back at him.

The king yanked the sword out of Theo's body, and the young man nearly fell on his face. The king put a foot against Theo's chest and shoved him back upright to sit on his heels. Theo pressed his right hand weakly to the wound, but it did nothing to staunch the bleeding.

The blood that poured from the wound in his stomach gleamed with golden sparkles. The golden gleam sank into the dirt beneath them with the blood, and the very ground seemed brighter as it began to tremble beneath them.

"What is that?" The king prodded at the golden stain on the ground. "Why is the earth shaking?"

Theo gave a soft, wet laugh. "Every drop of blood I shed on behalf of your land binds it more tightly to me." He gasped for breath and added, "It is readying itself to throw off your reign."

The ground beneath them trembled.

"Make it stop!"

"Will you accept my conditions, then? Never take or harm a human again, no repercussions for my friends, everything?" Theo swayed on his knees. He could see almost nothing but the golden glow.

"What of the fading of the land before we began to rely upon the human children? What will you do about that?" growled the king.

"That was you, Your Majesty," gasped Theo. "You need to love your land and your people." He groaned, coughed, and then whispered, "My love will keep them solid long enough for you to learn to care for them the way you should. They were solid in your father's day, you know."

His Majesty Silverthorn looked back at the mountains contemplatively, his feet braced as the ground's shuddering increased. Theo closed his eyes against the brilliance of the sparkles and the growing darkness that threatened to overpower even Cedar's magic.

"They were," the king said. "I do not know if I can love, but I will accept your conditions. You will love the land and keep it stable. I will try to love it, if I am capable of love." His Majesty Silverthorn looked down at Theo. "You will answer my questions, after your friend pours more golden magic into you."

The vines binding their legs retreated into the ground.

The ground ceased its trembling.

Lily darted to Theo's side, tears streaming down her cheeks. Oliver stood over them both, wordless and horrified.

Cedar kept his eyes on his king as he stepped close enough to put his hand on Theo's shoulder again.

The magic rushed in, bright and liquid, like a sparkling curtain over Theo's vision, a swell of strength that propelled him to his feet far too early.

He stood, swaying and more than half blind, and swept a low bow toward His Majesty Silverthorn.

"Your Majesty," he said in a voice as golden and bright as the magic writhing in him. "Believe it or not, I love you too, because I trusted you to see reason and serve your people more than your anger."

The king gave a shocked, offended bark of laughter. "Why would you do that?"

"You, too, are of the Fair Lands. What a weak love that would be, if I could only esteem the things that bowed to me easily or the things that did not cause pain! I had to love you as you are, and yet hope for you to be better, for your sake and for the Fair Lands I already loved." Theo sagged against Cedar's arm. "That's enough for the moment, Cedar," he gasped.

The magic twisted in his guts, and for a moment the rush and swirl was so strong he feared he would vomit golden sparkles all over the king's indigo boots. He felt buoyant and drunk on magic, his tongue loose and his mind full of shimmering light.

His Majesty Silverthorn regarded him steadily. "Can you speak, or is your mind entirely scrambled by Fair magic?"

"I can speak," enunciated Theo carefully. He blinked at the figures around the king. The audience had grown, though he had not been paying enough attention to them to realize how many Fair Folk watched until now. These were the witnesses Cedar had promised.

The king said, "Why did you let Lord Willowvale catch you, if you wanted to see me all the time?"

"I didn't let him catch me. He did that fair and square."

His Majesty Silverthorn looked at Theo in awe. "You put yourself where you knew he would catch you."

"One never knows what a fairy will do, Your Majesty," Theo said modestly. "One merely presumes to guess and hope that one is not too far wrong." He gave the king a brilliant smile.

"Yet everything seems to have conformed to your plan." The Fair king tilted his head and regarded Theo with something approaching horror. "You are mad as a March hare, and you were long before Lord Mosswing's magic filled your veins. I would much prefer that you stay in the human world, so your particular brand of insanity stays out of the Fair Lands."

"Your Majesty, I would venture to say, with all humility, I cannot stay away and do not want to." He blinked. "My headache's gone!" he said in surprise. "Thank you, Lord Mosswing."

His Majesty Silverthorn's brows lowered and he mouthed *your headache*, as if the words made so little sense he would not utter them aloud. Then he said, "If you leave the Fair Lands, will the mountains remain firm?" He raised the sword and examined Theo's blood along the edge, then looked back at the young man before him. Lily stood clasping his left hand, and Oliver had stepped forward to put himself between the king and his sister.

"Look." Theo gestured toward the mountains he could barely see through the golden haze.

The Fair king did not reply immediately. Theo waited, blinking sparkles from his eyes. The magic within him surged and rushed and receded, and he swayed with the force of it.

"They have color," the king said at last. "Will they remain firm?"

"Yes."

Lily's hand clenched Theo's more tightly, but she said nothing.

Theo said, "Look at the forests, Your Majesty."

His Majesty Silverthorn turned to see the forests a pale purple-blue in the distance.

"Your Majesty, I will take my wife and her brother home now. Lord Mosswing, you may come with us if you would like." Theo smiled warmly at the king, as if they were lifelong friends. "If Lord Mosswing elects to stay, he will be safe here, Your Majesty. You will keep your word."

"I will." The Fair monarch turned his violet gaze upon Theo again. "Why are you a friend of the Fair Lands, human?"

Theo, near drunk with pain and magic, said, "Your Majesty, with all due respect, I believe that is a story best told when I can think more clearly." He bowed, staggered, and caught himself. "It has been a pleasure, Your Majesty."

His Majesty Silverthorn swept his gaze up and down Theo's tattered, bloody figure, and bared his teeth. "A pleasure," he murmured. "Come tell me the story when you are a little less addled."

Theo bowed again, still holding Lily's hand.

He opened a door and ushered everyone into the veil, then turned to beam at the astonished king before he let it close.

CHAPTER FORTY
Returning Home

I n the darkness of the veil, Cedar rounded upon Theo with long-suppressed fury. "You should have told me your plan!"

"Would you have let me do it?" Theo asked mildly.

"No! That was madness! It shouldn't have worked at all. My magic isn't meant to heal wounds like that." Cedar's voice shook. "How do you feel? How are you even standing? Have you bled too much? How much do humans bleed before they die?"

Theo said philosophically, "It couldn't be helped. The king needed to see the land react to my blood, and the binding was only tenuous after Lord Willowvale's vines. It wasn't entirely secure until he stabbed me himself. You were the first in line to receive the land's allegiance, if he'd killed me, but I couldn't very well tell him that while you were standing there."

Lily's almost-silent sob caught Theo's attention, and he turned to her. "My love, I would pull you close, but I fear it would only grieve you. Certainly it would soil your dress. How may I comfort you?" He turned to her and bent to press a kiss to her tear-damp cheek, to her jaw, to the curve of her neck, then to her fingers one by one.

"I just want to know you're all right, Theo," she managed through her tears.

"Absolutely fine," said Theo through the haze of glittering gold. "Never better. Nicely ventilated and full of magic. My head might float away. Are you all right, Lily? Did he frighten you? His Majesty Silverthorn is actually not entirely a bad sort. I did research, you know." He swayed and nearly fell into Cedar, who slipped a little more magic into him. "Lord Willowvale, on the other hand, is really rather unpleasant, although I am loath to speak ill of someone who isn't present to defend himself. I shall try not to hold a grudge."

He took a deep, shuddering breath and turned.

"You're going the wrong way, Theo," said Cedar. "The human world is that way."

"The children," Theo enunciated carefully, "are this way."

He led them only a very short distance through the veil before putting his hand against the wall. "Cedar, I look a sight. Would you be so kind as to glamour me so I don't terrify the children?"

Cedar sighed. "You're mad," he muttered.

"I'm sure you're right. Please keep the doorway open." Theo twisted and pulled, and Fair light flooded into the veil. He thought absently that His Majesty's magic did not seem to fight him, even within the palace, as it had before, and wondered whether that was because the land adored him or whether the king the king had intentionally relaxed his magic to let him have the children.

Theo strode out into a bright room filled with alien plants and the buzz of a thousand wings. The floor was tiled in gorgeous cobalt glass with a shifting pattern in it that made it seem to Theo that he was walking on water; the effect accentuated his growing dizziness. The children were only a short distance away, and he focused on them.

The little group was in a circle, with three children of about seven years old sitting surrounded by nine older children, who were looking at Theo with open fear. He recognized two of the older girls as those he had already rescued, but he could not remember their names.

"Come with me now, children." His voice felt golden and bright, and he smiled radiantly at the group, unfazed by the oldest boy's defensive posture. "You will be safe with me."

"Who are you?" the boy said cautiously.

"I'm taking you back to the human world. Come now, before I lose all sense of direction. That will make things more difficult." He watched them rise, unable to decipher their expressions through the golden haze over his vision.

"Come now, human children!" Cedar said more emphatically from the doorway.

Theo counted them as they entered the veil, then leaned against the wall as the Fair lord let the door close behind him. In the darkness, Lily clasped Theo's hand even before Cedar stepped forward to slip a little more magic into his friend.

"Hold hands, everyone." Theo waited until the murmur of agreement subsided, then led them toward the children's home. "I'm taking you to a home where you will be cared for. Actually I'm taking you to the palace, because that's where the others have been for a few weeks, but soon you'll probably move back to the original home. If you have families to return to, you will be escorted safely to them straight away. Essie and John are kind-hearted and trustworthy. You'll have plenty of food and soon a lovely garden where you can play and rest, and you'll learn comportment and arithmetic and language and history and lots of other things, mostly enjoyable. You girls will learn flower arranging and how to make fruit pastries and I don't know what else, because I am not a young lady. Piano, I should think, and maybe voice lessons. I should ask Essie if they need more money for that."

One of the boys snickered, and Oliver murmured something that stopped the laughter before it spread.

"Thank you for rescuing us, sir," said one of the girls politely.

"You are very welcome." Theo's voice was warm and golden. "We're here already. Don't be frightened. You'll be safe and happy here." He opened the door with a twist and a pull of magic, then staggered out just in front of the garden in front of the 'cottage' that had been given to the children and their caretakers as a temporary refuge. The building was actually a spacious manor often used for hosting visiting foreign dignitaries, so Theo had been quite pleased when he learned the children would be so well-housed, even for a limited time.

Cedar's glamour on Theo had not faded, so the few onlookers saw a pale, green-clad fairy with golden hair fluffed up like thistledown stumble out of a strange gap in the world, leading twelve frightened children.

He opened the low white gate in front of the house, which served more to define the garden edges than as a barrier, and led the children through the garden to the door. He knocked on the door, then leaned against the door frame until Essie opened it, whereupon he nearly fell into the house.

"This is the last of the children, Essie," he said thickly. "Good day to you, and thank you."

Essie, with a shocked gasp, ushered the children in hurriedly and put a hand out to him, but he had turned away to stagger back through the garden toward the veil.

Theo turned resolutely toward home, and tugged Lily, Oliver, and Cedar along behind him.

"Cedar, do you know where we are? I believe my sense of direction has become rather muddled. The gold sparkles make it difficult to see. I do think you might have been a little overly generous with the magic. Do you see the golden sparkles or is that just me? I actually liked this jacket quite a lot; I should have worn an older one. I didn't plan this as well as I'd thought. It's lamentable to have destroyed such a coat when it was entirely predictable that it would be ruined." He had begun to slur, though his cheer was undimmed.

Oliver said quietly, "Theo, are you in pain?"

"You could call it that, but I prefer to think of it as the price of triumph. I have resolved not to complain about it though; it's bad form to malinger. Cedar, I am quite in awe of the strength of your magic. It's most commendable. Ah, here we are at last." He stopped and opened the door to the human world. The midmorning sun streamed through the opening into the veil, nearly blinding everyone. Theo stepped back to let the others out before he closed the door, though Lily clung to him.

"Cedar, I am honored and delighted to offer you the hospitality of the Overton estate for as long as you would like to stay. Juniper is in the east wing. You may stay in the east wing near him and my parents, or in one of the guest suites in the west wing nearer Lily and me." He swallowed and blinked, for the ground was wavering before him.

"Would you like a little more magic?" Cedar asked quietly. He removed Theo's glamour.

"I don't know." Theo took a few deep breaths, swaying and blinking like an owl. "Is it actually daylight or is that the magic?"

"You're still bleeding. Here." Cedar grabbed his shoulder and Theo gasped at the rush of magic.

"I feel drunk with it already, Cedar," he groaned. "I just want to sleep."

Cedar let him go, then nodded to Oliver. The two put Theo's arms around their shoulders and began to pull him toward the house.

"I'm fine!" Theo protested weakly, belying this with an agonized groan. By the time they reached the house, Anselm had seen them.

Within half an hour, they had changed Theo out of his ruined clothes, sponged the blood away, examined and bandaged his wounds, and hauled him upstairs to his bed.

"Thank you. I'm fine now. Just a little light-headed," he said in the general direction of Anselm.

"If you get out of bed, I'll have your mother come explain to you why it's a bad idea," said Anselm in a shaking voice.

Lily had felt rather pushed aside during this interlude, but she had very little idea of how to bandage a wound, and had not protested too much when Oliver assured her that they would take good care of her husband.

She had followed them upstairs to Theo's suite and was standing at the door, feeling unnecessary and dejected in the presence of so much bustling competence.

Theo said in a startled voice, "Lily! Why are you weeping?"

She stepped to the edge of the bed, where Anselm had propped Theo up against several pillows. "Because I was frightened for you, and because I couldn't bear to think how badly I treated you. I'm so sorry, Theo."

Anselm shooed Oliver and Cedar out, though he shot a stern look toward Theo over his shoulder.

Theo smiled radiantly at her, his hazel eyes glittering golden. "I forgave you long ago, my love. Please think no more of it. I am more grieved by your tears than anything else." He reached for her hand and brought it to his lips, holding her gaze with his own.

Lily couldn't breathe for a moment, then gave a laughing sob. "I was so frightened for you. Was that really your plan?"

Theo laughed and gasped and laughed again. "More or less. The land needed blood as proof of my love, and I wasn't able to give it on my own. Not that much, anyway! The very idea was too terrible to contemplate! Yet I knew Willowvale and Silverthorn would oblige me, if I gave them opportunity. So I did!"

He let his head fall back against the headboard. "I am glad that's done," he murmured, more to himself than to her. He focused on her again with no little effort. "Can you ever forgive me? I was abominable to you. I should have trusted you."

She wiped tears from her eyes. "There's nothing to forgive, Theo. Can you forgive me? I should never have said…."

His eyelids fluttered closed, and he murmured, "Please don't even think of it."

"Is there anything I can do for you now?" She hoped desperately that there was.

There was such a long silence that she thought he had fallen asleep, and then he slurred, "I think I should like it very much if you would keep holding my hand."

So she did.

He dreamed of his wife's smile, of dancing beneath cerulean trees and golden skies, of giving her a thousand roses of a thousand improbable shades just to see her laugh. While he dreamed, golden sparkles of magic ran through his veins, mending torn entrails and knitting muscle fibers back together.

While he slept, Oliver, Cedar, and Anselm explained the story to Sir Theodore and Lady Overton, who listened with white, horrified faces.

"Where is he now?"

"In bed, dead drunk on magic," said Cedar. "He'll be fine. I poured enough magic in him to kill a griffin." At Sir Theodore's flinch, Cedar added, "He needed it. He'll sleep it off and wake when he's ready."

"Lily is with him," added Oliver. "She's… we're all feeling rather shocked, I should think."

Sir Theodore regarded Oliver with sudden compassion, seeing that the young man was trembling head to toe. "Anselm, would you mind showing Lord Mosswing and Mr. Hathaway to the library and the garden and anywhere else they might wish to entertain themselves? I shall send a message to your parents, if you don't mind, Oliver, that you are visiting, and you may go to them when you wish. Refresh yourselves, rest, and we shall take luncheon together on the patio." He put a hand on Anselm's shoulder and spoke in a low voice to him. "You've done well, Anselm. Don't worry now."

The servant nodded jerkily.

Sir Theodore knocked on the doorframe so that he didn't startle Lily. "May we come in?"

"Of course." Lily looked up, then back down. They had been so kind to her, and she had underestimated both them and their son. What must they think of her now? She brushed tears from her eyes.

Sir Theodore stepped to her side and looked down at Theo, who was sleeping peacefully. He was so pale that his freckles stood out with unusual clarity, and it made him look boyish and young, aside from the shadows under his eyes. The scratches on his face and hands were already healing.

Lady Overton stood behind Lily and let out a soft, grieved sigh.

Lily's tears came in earnest then, but she said nothing, only looked down and let them fall. After a moment, Lady Overton put a gentle hand on her shoulder.

"I'm sorry," Lily whispered. Sorry for the distance that had so pained Theo, sorry for the way she had misjudged him, sorry for her own pain... there seemed no end to the regret that swelled within her.

Theo mumbled something unintelligible and lapsed into silence.

"Lord Mosswing told us what happened," said Sir Theodore quietly.

Lily trembled, and Lady Overton patted her gently.

"How long have you known he was the Wraith?" Lily whispered.

"Since nearly the beginning," Sir Theodore said. "I asked him a hundred times what he meant to do with the binding magic, and he never would tell us. I should have known it would be something like this." Unshed tears and pride thickened his voice, and he cleared his throat. "He would not want you to weep."

She nodded, unable to speak.

After several hours, Lily accepted a tray of tea, pastries, and fruit from Anselm. She ate one-handed at Theo's bedside.

Later in the evening, Anselm asked if she would allow Lady Overton to enjoy dinner with her at Theo's bedside, and she agreed. He brought a little table from near the window for the two trays. Lily noted belatedly that everything had been carefully prepared so that she could eat it with one hand.

"Thank you," she said, and he ducked his head solemnly.

The silence while they ate seemed at first painfully awkward, until Lady Overton said quietly, "I suppose we ought to have warned you that Theo loves with his whole heart. It is difficult to imagine what that means until you've seen it." She looked up to meet Lily's eyes with a soft, compassionate look. "Don't worry. He looks better already."

Lily looked at him, and it was true. The scratches on his face had already disappeared.

"Can you ever forgive me?" Lily whispered.

Lady Overton sighed. "It is difficult to see a beloved child suffer in body and soul. But it would be foolish indeed for me to hold anything against you when Theo would want unity; my own grievance would cause more grief to my son than what is already passed." She reached forward to put her hand on Lily's with motherly affection. "I have forgiven you, and my husband has as well. Do not fear any coldness from us. You are our daughter, you know, by marriage if not blood, and an injudicious misjudgment is not enough to break that bond."

Lily found the courage to meet Lady Overton's gaze. She found only warmth and sincerity in those kind hazel eyes, and she whispered, "Thank you."

"You're welcome, my dear." Lady Overton squeezed her hand, then rose. "I think Theo would be pleased if you slept here tonight. I do hope you will."

Lily's cheeks heated, and her mother-in-law smiled and swept out, saying, "I'll send Anselm in for the trays, and then we'll leave you alone. If you need anything, just ring the bell."

Several minutes later the servant came for the trays and bowed himself out.

Lily sat by Theo's bedside for another hour, listening to the night birds begin their songs. At last she gently extricated her hand from Theo's and began to rise.

He sucked in a long breath and his eyelids fluttered.

She bent toward him. "I'll be back in a moment," she murmured.

He turned his head and sighed.

In her suite, she changed into her nightgown, washed her face and hands, and brushed her hair. She slipped her dressing gown over her nightgown and walked back through to his suite.

Theo had not moved.

She slipped carefully beneath the covers and curled up beside him, moving slowly so as not to jostle or bump him. She took his hand between hers and closed her eyes.

CHAPTER FORTY-ONE
Beginning Again

L ily had not expected to sleep, although weariness tugged at every fiber of her being. So she was surprised to wake with the early light to the feel of being watched.

"You are the most beautiful thing I've ever seen," said Theo softly. He was smiling at her, his hazel eyes flecked with gold.

"You're still drunk," Lily said blearily. "I don't think you're supposed to be awake yet."

"You're still beautiful," he said. "I didn't mean to frighten you." His eyes fluttered closed again. "I think Lord Mosswing is displeased with me. I should apologize. Is your brother upset? Anselm was. I think I shall spend the next week apologizing." He shifted and hissed in pain. "How is Juniper?"

"Juniper?"

"I love you," he mumbled. Lily blinked the sleep from her eyes just in time to see him sigh as he fell asleep again.

She woke again in the late morning when he shifted. He sat up with a stifled groan and wrapped one arm across his stomach, then staggered to his feet.

"What are you doing?" she said.

He straightened and wobbled, then steadied himself with one hand on the back of a chair. "You can keep sleeping," he said. His eyes gleamed gold.

Lily slipped out of the bed and stepped closer to him, feeling strangely cautious. He sounded sober and unwontedly serious.

"How are you feeling?" she asked softly.

He gave a wan smile. "Like the Fair king ran me through with a sword only yesterday." He swallowed. "Alive, and glad of it. I owe about twelve people apologies. I also need to thank Lord Mosswing; he trusted me beyond what I had any right to expect."

"Why don't you sit down? I'll have them come to you," Lily said.

"I'm all right." He leaned against the wall, already more pale than before. "Although I think I will ask Anselm to help me dress."

Lily pulled the chain for the bell, but said, "I'd be glad to help you."

He smiled again, warm and almost shy, and said, "That is a kind offer, my love, but I fear I might make some ungentlemanly sounds of complaint, and I would rather have you think me unflinchingly brave."

At this moment Anselm opened the door.

"Theo, please sit down immediately," he said firmly.

"Good morning to you too, Anselm," said Theo. "Would you help me dress, please?"

Anselm shot a glance at Lily. "Tomorrow, perhaps. Lord Mosswing informed me you were to sleep all day."

"Lord Mosswing does not yet understand the depths of my hardheadedness. Pray do not fall into the same mistake," Theo said.

"Theo, *please*," Anselm said as he stepped forward to take Theo's arm. "Humor me just this once."

"I will take a nap later. I promise."

Anselm sighed.

"When I'm presentable," Theo continued, catching Lily's eye over Anselm's shoulder, "I would be honored to take lunch with you outside, my love." He flashed a sparkling smile at her, and his eyes lingered as she stepped out.

Lily went across the hall to her own suite and dressed herself, though it would have been entirely proper to call for a maidservant to help her. It still seemed a little frivolous to her to ask someone to help her do what she had always done herself.

When she finished and stepped back into the corridor, Theo's door was closed. A low murmur of voices told her that he was still within, so she wandered out to the little patio.

A short time later, Theo joined her. One arm was slung around Anselm's shoulders as if in easy friendship, but she didn't miss how frighteningly pale he was.

"Don't get up, please," Anselm said under his breath as he helped Theo sit carefully in the chair nearest Lily.

Theo beamed up at him. "Thank you, Anselm." Then he turned the full force of his hazel eyes upon Lily, and she couldn't help smiling.

Anselm bowed and left them alone.

"How do you feel?" Lily asked quietly.

Theo's smile wavered for a moment, then returned. "Let's not talk about that," he said quietly. "I'd rather tell you how grateful I am, Lily."

"For what?" She looked at him, bemused and slightly appalled.

He took her hand in his and looked down at it as he gently rubbed his thumb across her knuckles. He kissed her hand, then straightened with a wince. "For staying with me last night," he said at last. "I didn't deserve that, I think."

"Theo," she whispered. "You apologized already, and I have a thousand more reasons to apologize than you do. Please don't."

He met her gaze, hazel eyes warm and kind. "Did I apologize yet for being rather callous to you when we returned through the veil? I didn't properly think how terrifying it must have been for you. How brave you were for coming for me!"

"Now you're just being silly," she said softly. "You had good reason to be a little distracted, I think. But I will allow that I was terrified on your behalf." Her throat closed on a sob, and she pressed her hands to her face. "I don't want to lose you, Theo."

Then he was kneeling before her, looking up at her with his dear, sweet eyes as he caught her hands and kissed them. He murmured between kisses, "I'm far too stubborn to die from one little poke of a fairy sword, my love."

Her next half-sob turned into a laugh, and she looked at him with tears in her eyes. "Even now you joke about it! How can you, when I know you're in pain?"

His answering smile was as bright and warm as the sunlight on their shoulders. "Am I? I had forgotten in the delight of seeing you smile again." He sat back on his heels with a stifled groan, then chuckled at himself. "I'm too happy to mind any lingering discomforts. I have saved the Fair Lands for several of my dear friends, stopped the subjugation of children by the Fair throne, and more or less taken it for myself as collateral for the Fair king's cooperation. What's more, I," he said proudly, "am married to the kindest, bravest, most radiantly lovely woman in all of Valestria." He held her gaze. "And I have reason to believe she loves me back. Nothing can diminish my joy now."

When Anselm returned with lunch, Theo was sprawled bonelessly in the chair with his eyes closed, his long legs stretched out, and his left hand in Lily's right.

The servant quietly placed the trays upon the table and murmured to Lily, "I took Lady Araminta home this morning. Sir Theodore and Lady Overton asked if you wanted to dine privately, or if they might join you out here. Your brother and Lord Mosswing are here as well. But if he is asleep, I will let them know."

"I'm na'sleep," Theo mumbled.

"Yes, you are," said Anselm. "I can tell by the way your eyes are closed. Juniper asked about you, and I told him you would be happy to see him after you took a nap like you promised."

Theo slitted his eyes and looked up at him for a moment. "Tell him he's a hero." He took a deep breath and blinked, as if debating whether to sit up straighter, then sighed and slouched more deeply into the chair. "He saved the Fair Lands, you know." He smiled faintly.

Anselm blinked at him. "I think that was you, sir."

Theo's smile widened sleepily. "We did it together." He sighed. "Blast, I can't think straight. Did you say Juniper is well?"

"He's fine. I'll ask Lord Mosswing to come give you a little more magic, sir."

Theo winced. "Don't *sir* me, Anselm," he muttered.

A few moments later, Cedar strode out to the patio and directly to Theo. He put a hand on Theo's shoulder.

Theo took a deep, shuddering breath, and murmured, "Thank you, Cedar."

Several minutes later, Sir Theodore and Lady Overton joined them on the patio, followed by Juniper and Oliver, who had been introduced earlier that morning. Juniper was wearing his human glamour. By this time Theo was a little more alert.

"How are you feeling?" said Lady Overton gently.

"Brilliant, Mother." Theo smiled radiantly up at her from his sprawled position. "I am full of glittering golden magic, and I feel fizzy and bright and slightly drunk, but hopefully not so much that I embarrass myself further." He turned his gaze upon Lily and kissed her fingers one by one. "I adore you, Lily," he murmured into her hand.

Cedar's dark cheeks flushed. "Should I leave you?" he said quietly.

Theo's smile widened. "Am I embarrassing *you*, Cedar?" He gave a low, delighted chuckle. "I have never seen you blush before."

Juniper covered his smile with one hand.

Theo blinked, startled by a sudden thought, and shoved himself into a more upright position. "Lily, this is Juniper Morel, whom you saw in the garden. He has been in hiding here since His Majesty Silverthorn discovered his courageous support of the Rose's efforts on behalf of the children." He waited while the young fairy bowed courteously to Lily. "Juniper, this is my wife Lilybeth." He reluctantly let go of Lily's hand while she curtsied to his friend, then took it back again with a smile.

"I didn't mean to frighten you in the garden," said Lily gently. "I am sorry."

"I didn't mean to frighten you either," said Juniper. "Shall I maintain my glamour? I don't want to shock you."

Lily shook her head. "I don't mind your Fair appearance. I was only concerned for Theo, because the only fairy I knew was Lord Willowvale, and he was terrifying."

Juniper let his glamour drop, watching her reaction cautiously. She smiled to reassure him.

Theo said, "Father, did you let Lord Selby know that our effort on behalf of the children has been brought to a successful close?"

"We can send him a message now, if you would like." Sir Theodore nodded to Anselm, who strode off in search of a stable boy to carry the message.

The rest of the afternoon passed in quiet companionship. Lord Selby arrived an hour later and was told the entire story by Cedar and Oliver.

"How do you feel now?" Lord Selby looked toward Theo, who had been smiling sleepily at Lily.

"Triumph is a powerful analgesic, dear Fenton. If I had known how strong Cedar's magic was, I might have tried this three months ago." Theo's eyes glittered golden in the light.

"You didn't have enough binding magic for it to work three months ago," said Cedar seriously. "It scarcely worked now, even with Juniper's strength."

Theo smiled, as if to himself, and said, "Then it is fortunate that I am cautious by nature."

Juniper choked, and Cedar thumped him on the back. The young fairy blinked tears from his eyes and said, "His Majesty Silverthorn was right. You are mad, Theo."

Theo turned toward Oliver. "Oliver, might I speak with you privately for a moment?" He shoved himself to his feet, then swayed alarmingly until Cedar and Anselm grabbed at his shoulders. "I'm all right!" he protested. "I feel splendid, actually, and the golden sparkles are not bothering me in the slightest."

"You sit down," said Anselm firmly. "The rest of us will step away until Mr. Hathaway comes to fetch us." He put a gentle, steady pressure on Theo's shoulders until the young man sank back down into the chair, looking vaguely affronted.

"You're a tyrant," Theo muttered.

Lady Overton caught Anselm's eye and murmured her thanks. When she passed by Theo's chair, she leaned down to kiss him on the cheek. "I am proud of you, Theo, but please do not ever put us through this again."

He smiled up at her, his expression warm and sweet and remorseful. "I am sorry, Mother. I did not intend to cause you and Father to worry."

"I know." She cupped his cheek in her hand and held his gaze. Then she stepped away, leaving him alone with Oliver.

The two young men regarded each other in silence for a moment.

"Theo, I can't thank you enough for…"

"Please don't." Theo waved a hand dismissively. "I could not have lived with myself if I hadn't come for you. I wanted to tell you that you ought to visit Lady Araminta immediately and let her know how you feel. This is your moment!" His smile was dazzlingly bright, full of delighted excitement for Oliver's opportunity.

"What? I didn't do anything." Oliver swallowed. "Please don't mock me, Theo."

Theo blinked. "I'm not." He straightened and looked at Oliver more soberly. "I wouldn't do that, Oliver."

Oliver looked down. "I'm sorry. I know. But after what you just did, my little attempt at heroism seems so futile and foolish."

"That is your modesty speaking." Theo leaned forward to meet Oliver's gaze. "You braved a world utterly unfamiliar to you, and terrifying to any human, for the sake of the woman you loved. She is probably waiting right now for word of your return."

"But you're the one who saved us both." Oliver stared at him.

"That's utterly irrelevant!" Theo's passion surprised his brother-in-law. "Your heart and actions were heroic, and if she doesn't recognize that, she doesn't deserve you."

Oliver smiled shyly at the ground, no longer able to meet Theo's golden eyes. "I didn't know you were such a romantic," he said quietly.

Theo snorted. "It's not as if I've ever hidden that. Go on then, Oliver. Take Dandelion now and tell her you love her, if indeed you do. This is a perfect moment. Act with the courage of your conviction."

Oliver's ears turned pink. "What if she says she's not interested?"

Theo laughed aloud, then winced. "What if she says *yes*, though? Wouldn't it be better to love extravagantly, risking a little temporary embarrassment, than to hold back for fear of the unknown?"

Oliver smiled ruefully at him. "You would say that." He held Theo's gaze for another moment, then stood. "Thank you, Theo. It is a little silly, I suppose, that this feels more terrifying than going into the veil after her."

"Not at all." Theo stood, steadying himself against the table. "I await your happy news soon."

Oliver bowed to him and strode away.

Lady Araminta had, indeed, been waiting all morning and afternoon for word of Oliver's safe return, not to mention that of Lily and Theo. She had told her parents everything she knew, which, while far from the complete story, was enough to give Oliver's passionate declaration of undying love the additional weight of proven courage. Her father gave his consent for Oliver to speak with Araminta.

She smiled most charmingly at him and said, to his eternal surprise, "I have been waiting years for you, Oliver. Of course the answer is *yes*."

After Oliver departed for the Brickelwyte house in the city, Sir Theodore, Lady Overton, Fenton, Cedar, Juniper, and Lily enjoyed tea and orange pastries in the golden afternoon sunlight. Theo, eyes closed, grunted agreeably when asked if he wanted tea, but didn't drink it. He slouched further into his seat, still holding Lily's hand. Fenton departed not long after Oliver did, and Theo roused briefly to bid him farewell.

Fenton, unfortunately, had a much less peaceful evening than Theo or Oliver, being presented with the point of a fairy sword as he approached his own back door after leaving his horse in the care of a groom. But that is another story.

Finally, Anselm said, "You promised to take a nap, Theo. Let me take you upstairs."

"I did, didn't I?" Theo rubbed his free hand over his face; his other held Lily's hand. He spoke without opening his eyes. "Anselm, did I apologize to Cedar earlier? I meant to."

"I don't recall you doing so, but I wasn't out here all afternoon. He's right there, you know. You could ask him yourself."

Theo blinked blearily at Cedar. "I'm sorry. I've been terribly rude."

"I cannot think of anything you have to apologize for," said Cedar quietly. "If there ever was anything, I've forgiven you already. Go to bed, Theo."

Theo rubbed his hand over his face again, trying to look at least half conscious. "I also meant to thank you."

"For the magic?" Cedar smiled affectionately, and his white teeth stood out against his dark skin. "I owe you all my magic and more. Don't mention it."

"For trusting me that much. You really trusted me far more than I had any right to expect."

Cedar said with a little more heat, "Theo, for the last time, please stop. You had *every* right to expect it; you've always, without fail, been unsparing in your generosity and nobility." His voice shook ever so slightly, and he swallowed hard. "The only thing that angers me is that I did not know you needed my magic before you met Willowvale."

Theo smiled sleepily at him. "It would be foolish indeed to hold that against yourself, my friend. I could not be more pleased with the outcome, and the fact that this adventure was undertaken with my dearest friends made it all the sweeter."

Cedar blew out a breath and said, "Shall I give you a little more magic before we haul you upstairs to your bed?"

"I'm not in pain at the moment." Theo shoved to his feet and nearly toppled over, whereupon Cedar caught him by the shoulders.

"Hold still," the Fair lord murmured. "You're healing remarkably well, and more quickly than I'd expected."

Theo sagged against him, his knees beginning to buckle, and Cedar slipped more magic into him. The Fair lord added, addressing Sir Theodore, who had grabbed Theo's other shoulder, "That's why he's so wobbly. He's soaking up the magic like a sponge; he's healing so quickly the magic isn't lasting as long."

"Why?" Sir Theodore's voice had an edge of concern in it.

"I don't know. My estimate of his healing was based on what I knew of our Fair healing; I didn't really know how different human healing would be. I don't see any reason to be worried, though. It's probably because he has so little magic of his own. He's more open to it than a fairy would be, and it's both taking effect and wearing off more quickly."

Theo said, "I can hear you, you know." He smiled beatifically at them both. "There's nothing to worry about, Father. Cedar, I am thoroughly impressed with your magic, and I wish to express again my utter and complete appreciation for your skill and strength."

Cedar smiled reluctantly. "Go to bed, Theo."

"I think I will," Theo agreed with dignity. He still had not let go of Lily's hand, and now he looked down at her with a sparkling smile. "My love, would you mind walking with me? It is a beautiful afternoon and I feel guilty asking you to be shut up inside, but I would very much like for you to kiss me to sleep."

Lily's cheeks flushed pink. Cedar coughed delicately, pretending he had not heard, and Juniper covered his shocked smile with one hand.

"Yes, I will," she said softly.

He gave her a luminous, euphoric smile, then turned his brilliance upon the others. "Father, Mother, Juniper, and Cedar, I pray you have a wonderful afternoon."

Leaning on Anselm and holding Lily's hand, he made it all the way to his room without falling down. Anselm helped him undress again, and when Lily slipped back into his bedroom, he was already half-asleep beneath the covers.

"Ring the bell if you need anything," Anselm told them both.

They thanked him.

Once they were alone, Theo mumbled sleepily, "You don't have to stay, Lily. I'm boring now."

"I don't mind." Feeling rather bold, she leaned over and kissed him on the cheek, and he blinked up at her, startled.

"Have I mentioned that I love you, Lily?" he said, his voice filled with sincerity. "I feel I have not yet made it entirely clear how much I adore you."

"You have."

"Not enough." He kissed her hand, then rested his cheek against it. His eyes fluttered closed.

"I love you too, Theo," she said softly.

He caught his breath on a dry, quiet sob, and he pressed her hand tighter to his cheek.

"What's wrong?" Lily knelt beside the bed so she could see him face to face.

His hazel eyes didn't sparkle with gold; they were warm and sweet and apprehensive. He swallowed and said, "I was afraid you wouldn't."

Lily felt as though all the breath in her lungs had vanished, and the world spun around her. "I'm sorry, Theo. I do love you so very much. I haven't said it enough, but I do."

He sighed deeply, as if letting out long-held tension, and fell asleep.

Lily eventually called for Anselm and asked him to bring her a book from the library. He brought her a stack, noting that Theo, when young, had particularly enjoyed *At the Point of the Sword*. After an hour reading uncomfortably hunched at the edge of the bed, her back ached and her neck cramped. She carefully extracted her hand from Theo's, murmuring reassurances all the while, and rearranged the chair so she could hold his hand more easily.

Before she picked the book up again, she traced his auburn eyebrows with one finger. The shadows beneath his eyes were gone, but he was still so pale that his freckles stood out on his cheeks and nose. She traced the line of his jaw with her finger, the touch as light and gentle as a summer breeze. His skin was soft and smooth, but there was the faint rasp of a beard when she moved her finger backward. Perhaps Anselm had shaved him that morning; she could not imagine Theo could have done it, as unsteady as he'd been. She tried to imagine him with a red beard and could not picture that either. It had not been fashionable for young noblemen to have facial hair for twenty years.

She ate at his bedside again that evening. She told him quietly that she would return in a moment, changed in her own room, and then returned to slip into bed with him. He slept through it all.

Lily discovered early the next morning that she had forgotten to draw the curtains the previous night; the early sunlight streamed in and brightened the room with shades of gold. She opened her eyes to the brilliance and was startled to see Theo gazing at her with his warm hazel eyes. No glittering gold lit his expression, but his expression was, if anything, more dazzlingly bright than ever.

"You stayed," he breathed. "May I kiss you, Lily?"

"Please do."

So he did, with passion and dedication.

Theo and Lily spent that day almost entirely outside. After breakfast, he had a brief conversation with his father, which Lily did not hear, and dispatched a note to Lord Fenton Selby, apparently about the same matter. Then Theo took her on a delightful tour of the garden, showing her all the nooks she had not yet seen and kissing her in each one. They ate a delicious lunch in a white gazebo near a little stream Lily had not known existed.

Lily had realized that morning that Theo had eaten nearly nothing since… well, she couldn't remember the last time he'd had anything other than a sip or two of tea. Exhausted from kissing her so thoroughly, he'd slept through breakfast, although he was entirely unrepentant about the kissing. She guessed his last meal might have been that lunch on the patio before Lord Hastings' ball, when he'd looked so sad and dejected, and she'd been too lonely and frightened to go to him.

So she was relieved to see him eating well now. He enjoyed roast chicken, cucumber sandwiches, roasted squash and asparagus, melon balls and strawberries, and an enormous slice of blackberry pie covered in whipped cream.

After lunch they walked hand in hand through yet another part of the garden. He kissed her in a nook surrounded by gardenias which filled the air with their sweet scent, then led her to another sheltered enclave between viburnum and beautyberry bushes, where he kissed her again.

Then onward, where he kissed her beneath a jasmine-covered trellis. She laughed and pressed her head close to his chest, breathing in his masculine soap scent along with the sweet jasmine.

She did not dare to wrap her arms around him, for fear of hurting him, but he had no such qualms, and pressed his face into her hair, then leaned down to kiss her again on the sensitive skin just beside her ear, then her cheek, then her lips.

Then he said suddenly, "My love, I am apparently more tired than I realized. Might we sit down a moment?"

He stumbled to the white wicker sofa a few feet away and fell into it, suddenly pale and breathless. He put his elbows on his knees and leaned forward to let his head hang down.

"Is it hurting?" Lily said, trying not to panic.

"No," he murmured. "I'm just fatigued."

"Shall I go get you a drink?" She knelt in front of him.

"I'd rather you stay," he whispered shakily.

She sat beside him and slipped her hand into his.

A few minutes later, he had brightened a little, but his hand shook when he lifted her hand to his lips and kissed it. "I'm sorry, my love. I was only a little dizzy. I'm all right now."

She studied his face, and he gave her a sunny smile.

"Are you?" Lily bit her lip.

"I am. May I kiss you to prove it?" His warm hazel eyes danced when she nodded, and he leaned over to press a kiss to her lips.

After he had kissed her nearly senseless, she sighed happily and put her head against his shoulder. "Theo, there is one thing I don't understand."

"Then you're doing much better than I am. There are a great many things I don't understand." He closed his eyes and rested his cheek against the top of her head.

She took a tremulous breath and said carefully, "What upset you so much that first night?"

So he told her what Lord Selby had heard, and how Lord Willowvale's words had deepened and strengthened his fear and horror, and the terrible repercussions of her innocent blunder.

"How did you forgive me, then? How could you?" she whispered.

"Lord Willowvale himself assuaged my fears, though he didn't know it, when I asked him how he'd found the children while he had me wrapped in his vines." Theo chuckled softly, his voice thick with exhaustion. "I wanted to believe the best of you, Lily. But when I asked you, your answer sounded like a lie, and… I did not want to ask you more, because the thought of you lying to me was so painful."

"I wish you had, but I understand better now why you didn't." She squeezed his hand, noting his sigh of contentment as she did so.

"I am sorry, Lily."

"Please don't apologize any more, Theo. It makes me feel even guiltier for my part in the misunderstanding, and I don't want it to come between us anymore."

He sighed again, and wrapped his arm more tightly around her. "Will you dance with me on the patio tonight?" he said. "I believe we missed several weeks of wedded bliss, and I would like to begin to remedy that."

"Yes, if you will promise to kiss me until I cannot breathe." She twisted to look up at his surprised smile.

They walked back to the house in a haze of relief and joy, for the sad things between them had been washed away by honesty and a few remorseful tears.

"I think you should rest before dinner," Lily said as they reached the edge of the patio.

Theo hesitated, then said, with a sweet, shy smile, "I don't want to miss another moment with you."

She smiled up at him. "What about if you lie down and I read to you?"

He tilted his head. "May I put my head in your lap while you read?"

"If you would like." Her cheeks flushed. When she had slept with him, he'd been insensible nearly the whole night, drunk on pain and magic and half-dead besides. But they *were* married, and she could not, and did not want to, deny that every inch of her longed for him.

He waited wordlessly while she selected a book, and that silence told her he was even more tired than he'd admitted. She sat on the chaise lounge and looked up at him invitingly, and he sparkled at her with something of his first buoyant delight.

He put his head in her lap and curled his long, lean body into the remaining space.

Lily began to read, and then, in a moment of boldness, put her free hand on his head. His coppery waves were even softer than she'd imagined, and he smiled sleepily as she ran her fingers through his hair.

"Thank you, Lily," he murmured. "I love you."

"I love you, Theo."

At her quiet reply, he sighed in contentment and fell asleep, as happy and relaxed as a cat in the sun.

They ate dinner in quiet bliss and danced on the patio to the sound of the peacock's cry and the night birds singing. They danced as the stars came out and as the birds quieted. They kissed and murmured endearments to each other as the moon rose and the air cooled.

As the stars smiled overhead, Lily leaned close to Theo and whispered, "I'm a little chilly. Will you warm me up?"

Theo swept her up in his strong arms and kissed her again. "I am at your service, my love."

ABOUT THE AUTHOR

Thank you for purchasing this book. If you enjoyed it, please leave a review at your favorite online retailer!

C. J. Brightley lives in Northern Virginia with her husband and young children. She holds degrees from Clemson University and Texas A&M. You can find more of C. J. Brightley's books at www.CJBrightley.com, including the epic fantasy series Erdemen Honor, which begins with *The King's Sword*, and the Christian fantasy series A Long-Forgotten Song, which begins with *Things Unseen*.

THE KING'S SWORD
ERDEMEN HONOR, BOOK 1

I crossed his tracks not far outside of Stonehaven, and I followed them out of curiosity, nothing more. They were uneven, as if he were stumbling. It was bitterly cold, a stiff wind keeping the hilltops mostly free of the snow that formed deep drifts in every depression. By the irregularity of his trail, I imagined he was some foolish city boy caught out in the cold and that he might want some help.

It was the winter of 368, a few weeks before the new year. I was on my way to the garrison at Kesterlin just north of the capital, but I was in no hurry. I had a little money in my pack and I was happy enough alone.

In less than a league, I found him lying face down in the snow. I nudged him with my toe before I knelt to turn him over, but he didn't respond. He was young, and something about him seemed oddly familiar. He wasn't hurt, at least not in a way I could see, but he was nearly frozen. He wore a thin shirt, well-made breeches, and expensive boots, but nothing else. He had no sword, no tunic over his shirt, no cloak, no horse. I had no horse because I didn't have the gold for one, but judging by his boots he could have bought one easily. There was a bag of coins inside his shirt, but I didn't investigate that further. His breathing was slow, his hands icy. It was death to be out in such weather so unprepared.

He was either a fool or he was running from something, but in either case I couldn't let him freeze. I strode to the top of the hill to look for pursuit. A group of riders was moving away to the south, but I couldn't identify them. Anyway, they wouldn't cross his path going that direction.

I wrapped him in my cloak and hoisted him over my shoulder. The forest wasn't too far away and it would provide shelter and firewood. I wore a shirt and a thick winter tunic over it, but even so, I was shivering badly by the time we made it to the trees. The wind was bitter cold, and I sweated enough carrying him to chill myself thoroughly. I built a fire in front of a rock face that would reflect the heat back upon us. I let myself warm a little before opening my pack and pulling out some carrots and a little dried venison to make a late lunch.

I rubbed the boy's hands so he wouldn't lose his fingers. His boots were wet, so I pulled them off and set them close to the fire. There was a knife in his right boot, and I slipped it out to examine it.

You can tell a lot about a man by the weapons he carries. His had a good blade, though it was a bit small. The hilt was finished with a green gemstone, smoothly polished and beautiful. Around it was a thin gold band, and ribbons of gold were inlaid in the polished bone hilt. It was a fine piece that hadn't seen much use, obviously made for a nobleman. I kept the knife well out of his reach while I warmed my cold feet. If he panicked when he woke, I wanted him unarmed.

I felt his eyes on me not long before the soup was ready. He'd be frightened of me, no doubt, so for several minutes I pretended I hadn't noticed he was awake to give him time to study me. I'm a Dari, and there are so few of us in Erdem that most people fear me at first.

"I believe that's mine." His voice had a distinct tremor, and he must have realized it because he lifted his chin a little defiantly, eyes wide.

I handed the knife back to him hilt-first. "It is. It's nicely made."

He took it cautiously, as if he wasn't sure I was really going to give it back to him. He shivered and pulled my cloak closer around his shoulders, keeping the knife in hand.

"Here. Can you eat this?"

He reached for the bowl with one hand, and seemed to debate a moment before resting the knife on the ground by his knee. "Thank you." He kept his eyes on me as he dug in.

I chewed on a bit of dried meat as I watched him. He looked better with some warm food in him and the heat of the fire on his face. "Do you want another bowl?"

"If there's enough." He smiled cautiously.

We studied each other while the soup cooked. He was maybe seventeen or so, much younger than I. Slim, pretty, with a pink mouth like a girl's. Typical Tuyet coloring; blond hair, blue eyes, pale skin. Slender hands like an artist or scribe.

"Thank you." He smiled again, nervous but gaining confidence. He did look familiar, especially in his nose and the line of his cheekbones. I tried to place him among the young nobles I'd seen last time I'd visited Stonehaven.

"What's your name?"

"Hak-" he stopped and his eyes widened. "Mikar. My name is Mikar."

Hakan.

Hakan Ithel. The prince!

He looked a bit like his father the king. It wasn't hard to guess why he was fleeing out into the winter snow. Rumors of Nekane Vidar's intent to seize power had been making their way through the army and the mercenary groups for some months.

"You're Hakan Ithel, aren't you?"

His shoulders slumped a little. He looked at the ground and nodded slightly.

He had no real reason to trust me. Vidar's men would be on his trail soon enough. No wonder he was frightened.

"My name is Kemen Sendoa. Call me Kemen." I stood to bow formally to him. "I'm honored to make your acquaintance. Is anyone following you?"

His eyes widened even more. "I don't know. Probably."

"Then we'd best cover your tracks. Are you going anywhere in particular?"

"No."

I stamped out the fire and kicked a bit of snow over it. Of course, anyone could find it easily enough, but I'd cover our trail better once we were on our way. A quick wipe with some snow cleaned the bowl and it went back in my pack.

He stood wrapped in my cloak, looking very young, and I felt a little sorry for him.

"Right then. Follow me." I slung my pack over my shoulder and started off. I set a pace quick enough to keep myself from freezing and he followed, stumbling sometimes in the thick snow. The wind wasn't quite as strong in the trees, though the air was quite cold.

I took him west to the Purling River as if we were heading for the Ralksin Ferry. The walk took a few hours; the boy was slow, partly because he was weak and pampered and partly because I don't think he understood the danger. At any moment I expected to hear hounds singing on our trail, but we reached the bank of the Purling with no sign of pursuit.

"Give me your knife."

He gave it to me without protest. He was pale and shivering, holding my cloak close to his chest. I waded into the water up to my ankles and walked downstream, then threw the knife a bit further downstream where it clattered onto the rockslining the bank. Whoever pursued him would know or guess it was his, and though the dogs would lose his trail in the water, they might continue downstream west toward the Ferry.

"Walk in the water. Keep the cloak dry and don't touch dry ground."

"Why?" His voice wavered a bit, almost a whine.

I felt my jaw tighten in irritation. "In case they use dogs." I wondered whether I was being absurdly cautious, whether they would bother to use dogs at all.

He still looked confused, dazed, and I pushed him into the water ahead of me. I kept one hand firm on his shoulder and steered him up the river. Ankle-deep, the water was painfully cold as it seeped through the seams in my boots. The boy stumbled several times and would have stopped, but I pushed him on.

We'd gone perhaps half a league upriver when I heard the first faint bay of hounds. They were behind us, already approaching the riverbank, and the baying rapidly grew louder. I took my hand from the boy's shoulder to curl my fingers around the hilt of my sword. As if my sword would do much. If they wanted him dead, they'd have archers. I was turning our few options over in my mind and trying to determine whether the hounds had turned upriver or were merely spreading out along the bank, when the boy stopped abruptly.

"Dogs."

"Keep walking."

He shook his head. "They're my dogs. They won't hurt me."

I grabbed the collar of his shirt and shoved him forward, hissing into his ear, "Fear the hunters, not the dogs! You're the fox. Don't forget that."